I0611481

A Risky PLAY

A SUNCASTLE KNIGHTS STORY

MARISSA J. GRAMOLL

A Risky Play Copyright © 2022 by Marissa J Gramoll

All rights reserved.

No part of this book may be reproduced in any form or by any electronic or mechanical means, including information storage and retrieval systems, without written permission from the author, except for the use of brief quotations in a book review.

This is a work of fiction. Names, characters, businesses, places, events, locales, and incidents are either the products of the author's imagination or used in a fictitious manner. Any resemblance to actual persons, living or dead, or actual events is purely coincidental.

Cover Design: Sarah Sentz with Enchanting Romance Designs

Interior Formatting: Chelsea Timm

This one is for those who suffer in silence.

May you find your voice, and the peace to heal from your wounds.

Content Warning & Author's Note

This is an emotionally deep read with intense topics, some of which include:

Child Abuse (explicitly described).
Death of a Loved One.
Extreme Anxiety, including fear of dying from medical conditions.
LGBTQ+ Harassment, Bullying, Mistreatment.
Attempted Suicide Following Rape.

Intended for Mature Audiences.

Though all of the Suncastle College Series books stand alone, it is recommended to read A Game Like Ours prior to A Risky Play to avoid spoilers.

This is a work of fiction. Any reference to businesses, pop culture references, names of places, items, brands, and items is done so with respect and without endorsement.

The delicate topics written about in this book are written following research and experience. I did my best to represent this material in a respectful and meaningful way.

If you're the victim of bullying or abuse, please seek help.

PLAYLIST

"The Few Things" by JP Saxe, Charlotte Lawrenece

"Love Story" by Taylor Swift

"Need You Now" by Lady A

"Terrible Love" by The National

"Sometimes" by Britney Spears

"Love Like That" by Lauv

"Lucky" by Chelsea Cutler, Alexander 23

"If You Love Her" by Forest Blakk

"Down" by Jason Walker

"If the World Was Ending" by JP Saxe, Julia Michaels

"Kiss from a Rose" by Seal

"Bring Me To Life" by Evanescence

"Torn" by Natalie Imbruglia

"Open Your Eyes" by Snow Patrol

"Monsters" by Timeflies, Katie Sky

"She's Everything" by Brad Paisley

"Slow Me Down" by Sara Evans

"What You Want" by Mase, Total

"A Little Too Much" by Shawn Mendes

"I Will Wait" by Mumford & Sons

"Say Something" by A Great Big World, Christina Aguilera

"Scars To Your Beautiful" by Alessia Cara

"Tangled up in You" by Staind

"The Good Ones" by Gabby Barrett

"Cover Me Up" by Morgan Wallen

"I Melt with You" by Modern English

"All I Need" by Within Temptation

"Broken" by Seether, Amy Lee

"Piece by Piece" by Kelly Clarkson

"Break My Heart" by Dua Lipa

"No Judgement" by Niall Horan

"Beauty in the Struggle" by Bryan Martin

"Stay" by Miley Cyrus

"One Last Breath" by Creed

"Light of Love" by Florence + The Machine

"Fall For You" by Secondhand Serenade

"Hanging by A Moment" by Lifehouse

"Slow Dancing" by Aly & AJ

"Blue Jeans" by Lana Del Rey

"Love You Madly" by Cake

"Scars" by Papa Roach

"Teenage Dream" by Katy Perry

"Unlovable" by DIAMANTE

"Anyone" by Rain Paris

"Panic Attacks in Paradise" by Ashnikko

"Meant To Be" by Ber, Charlie Oriain

"Little Do You Know" by Alex & Sierra

"Alive" by Sia

"i love you" by Billie Eilish

"Where's My Love" by SYML

"Surrender" by Natalie Taylor

Part One

Prologue

Trish

Sometimes, in life, you're just wrong. No matter how much you want to be right, sometimes you're just wrong.

And my, oh my, was I very wrong.

April 2012

Trish

nly the good die young, they say.

Cody died so young and so full of everything that would've made for a long and happy life. One of my best friends. My chest aches. My eyes burn. My heart feels broken in an irreparable way. Overwhelmed with loss, I don't know what to do with all these feelings.

I remember watching Cody pitch, and it was like something sacred happened on that field. We'd all go silent as he wound up to throw, and observe him like he was an angel communing with God. Like his pitches were a beautiful kind of religion, and God spoke to every heart through the incredible power of his perfect form.

"I know, honey, I know." I squeeze Lexie tighter as her body shakes with tears. In all our years as BFFs, I've never seen her in this much pain. My heart burns, because I miss him, too.

Cody.

My body shivers as I smell the wet, misty air of Willardson, South Carolina. It rained the whole service. Like heaven's crying with us.

"He's g—" Lexie's voice cuts off. She can't say it.

He's gone.

Cody, our buddy since junior high—and her fiancé, is about to go six feet under ground.

"Shh," I cradle her close, eyeing the dwindling crowd. Raindrops patter against the awning. A cacophony of engines come to life in this land of the dead as vehicles pull away from the gravel cemetery road.

"You oughta go greet his guests." Lexie's mama pushes her shoulder. She's sitting behind us on these god-awful green velvet chairs.

"I'm not up for that." Lexie's stark whisper is followed by more tissue blotting on her running mascara that was supposed to be waterproof. So much for that.

"These people are here for you as much as they're here for him." Lexie's mama shakes her head, obviously disapproving.

"I can't talk to everyone." Lexie's eyes find the casket and linger. Cody's family is hovering around it, laying flowers across the top. His parents, sisters and little brother.

"Come on, let her be." Lexie's daddy stands from his chair. "We can greet anyone who needs greeting." He holds his wife's hand until she concedes.

Bobby walks toward us. He's trying to be strong. But he's broken... I see that too.

Bobby kneels in front of Lexie. "Hey," he chokes out the words. "I'm gonna go put some flowers on the casket. You wanna come with me?" He stands ever so cautiously, taking Lexie's hand in his.

"Yeah," Lexie wipes away more tears. I motion for Mickey and he comes over with us. The four of us. Supposed to be five.

One by one, we put our flowers on top of the polished oak. I set a hand against the cold, wet droplets. Lexie's hand goes on mine. Then Bobby's. Finally Mickey's. Like the cheers we'd do in junior high.

After several measured breaths, we return to our seats. Lexie doesn't wanna talk to anyone and I'm gonna stay by her so she doesn't have to. Her head rests on my shoulder as many others put flowers on the casket.

Preacher Davis shakes hands with a few older people that used to watch

Cody play baseball. A lot of the folks made this funeral the biggest event Willardson has ever seen. Surprised they didn't have to go and extend the city limits to fit all the people coming here. Not everyday a star baseball player gets buried. It's got as much pomp and circumstance as a celebrity event. I guess he is a celebrity around here. Well, I guess he *was* one.

My eyes burn from the many tears I've tried to cry but haven't been able to shed. It's like my body's holding them forever because it can't hold onto Cody.

I peer at Bobby and his teammates. Briar, Zac, Ethan, Dexter, Conrad, and the other members of the Suncastle College Baseball Team. Good for them to stay with him. He shouldn't be alone.

Where'd Mickey go? He shoulda come back to his seat like the rest of us. I glance at mourners, hovering by the grave. A mixture of people we went to church with growing up and kids from Willardson High. Vanessa Hodge sends me a wave and I wave back, trying to smile. My eye catches movement by the street. Mickey's lone figure heads to his old beat-up Honda Civic.

"There will be a luncheon at the fieldhouse tomorrow at noon." Coach Conners, Suncastle's head baseball coach, says to the boys. They nod.

"You all got rides back?" Coach Densen, Suncastle's assistant baseball coach, looks each of them over.

"Yep." Briar nods.

"Yeah, I have my truck," Zac says.

There's an unspoken exchange from Coach Densen and Briar that seems to say *look out for Bobby.*

Lord knows he needs someone more than Cody's angel looking out for him. Bobby usually looks like he has it all together, but right now–he's as wrecked as Cody's car.

I've known him long enough to know his tells. His tan fingers yank at his short brown hair, heavy eyes that say he hasn't slept in ages. He stares intensely at the flower covered casket, like he's trying to cast a spell on it. Maybe if he looks at it long enough he can turn back the clock and bring Cody back to life.

I imagine it working. Cody breaking out from the coffin, spilling flowers everywhere, in a triumphant wave of the hand telling all of us he got us roused up in the best April Fools style joke of all time.

Jesus, I wish my imagination could conjure reality. Bring Cody back for Lexie as she still sobs in my arms. And bring him back for Bobby, because, fuck, it looks like Bobby died right there with him.

Just a few weeks ago, we were celebrating. The Yankees were planning to draft Cody into the Majors. Lexie was gonna move up to New York with him.

Lexie stays frozen in her chair, gazing at nothing in front of us. She's in a daze. Has been on and off since I picked her up at the hospital the morning after he died.

"Come on, sweetheart. We gotta keep goin', keep movin', get through this." I stare at her for a long while, the silence making my heart ache even more. "Tell you what, I'm gonna go over and invite Bobby and the guys to Shakey's." Breath hanging in my lungs, I cross in front of the flowers.

The boys stare at me while I make my way over to them. All strapping young men in All-American Suits. I snap a picture. Lexie doesn't want to remember this day right now, but I have a feeling someday she will.

"Let's head over to Shakey's. I'm gonna see if I can get Lexie to go." I watch their faces, gauging for a reaction. They all look exhausted. Broken.

Bobby nods. I try to make them smile, like mentioning Shakey's usually does, but I'm not surprised all I get is somber nodding.

I return to Lexie. We sit back in the velvet chairs. She's not ready to leave and I'm not ready to rush her away.

When we are the only ones left, besides the men waiting to cover the grave, I nudge her. "It's time to go, sweetie. These people are waiting on us, I think."

She seems to notice them for the first time, an embarrassed expression covering her face as she stands. Cautiously, she goes to his casket and the picture I see is so sad I want to look away. She leans down to the fine polished wood and gives him a final kiss goodbye. For several moments, she looks at the casket and weeps. I reach out a hand and hold hers.

Fuck, Cody, why'd you have to go and die like this?

The rain hits our hair and shoulders as we walk to the car. Wish I'd brought an umbrella. I open up her door for her, noticing that distant look in her eyes as she slips back into that daze.

Turning the key in the ignition, my car stalls. Dammit. This battery is on its last leg. I rub my kitty keychain, almost as if for good luck. Daddy got it for me on our last trip to Kentucky before he died.

Now I've lost two loved ones suddenly. Two too many.

After a deep breath, I try to start my car again. There we go. I pat the dashboard lovingly. *You just gotta last a little while longer. I'll get you looked at, I promise.*

"How about you get in something comfy and dry." I toss her the bag of clothes she brought home from Suncastle. We tug off our dripping formal black dresses and change in the car like we did so many times in college when we had to rush from one function to the next.

She slips on Cody's AC/DC shirt and some sweatpants.

His favorite shirt he'll never wear again.

At Shakey's, the rain has slowed to a small sprinkle. Bobby's waiting at our booth in the corner with the guys. Looks like he's ordered for us, too. Lexie and my usual orders are among the feast.

Lexie's feet are planted. She turns around, facing the door instead of our booth. "I can't...I can't do this." She takes the keys out of my hand and pushes the door, ringing the entry bell.

Bobby rushes to me and puts a hand on my shoulder. "I'll talk to her." His eyes are bloodshot and his nose is all red and puffy.

"Okay." I nod, letting him go. Feels fitting, somehow, for him to offer her a bit of strength if he's got any left.

My gaze goes out the window, wondering if he'll take her somewhere quiet or what. Instead, they stand near his truck. I observe them talk for half a second before Bobby wraps her up in a long hug. My eyes burn.

I force a breath before I go and sit at the booth.

"Hey." Briar looks up from the menu as if he doesn't have a plate of food in front of him already. The guys had the same idea to change clothes because they're both in jeans and hoodies now instead of the suits they were wearing at the funeral.

"Hi there." I sigh, wondering again where the fuck Mickey hurried off to earlier. Would be nice to actually have him here.

"Welcome to the table." Zac smiles and deep dimples flash in his cheeks for a split second. "Did you grow up with Cody, too?" He's all tan from the first half of baseball season. Sun-kissed skin and dark wavy hair that sticks out a little behind his ears.

I've had a little crush on him since he showed up at Suncastle, even though he's a freshman. I know, I know, I shouldn't even be looking at him. We are in different stages in life. He's just started college playing baseball and I'm gearing up for my first photography job out in the real world.

But I am crushing on him. Maybe because I know we'll never be anything. He's safe. Like a call in baseball. Safe to flirt with. Safe to fill up daydreams. Safe to never have to worry about.

Safe to distract me from Cody's death and all the trauma I'm sick of carrying around.

In any other circumstance, I'd be happy as a bunny to be sitting at his table. Too bad this is the first time we've had a chance to hang out.

Man, if I could turn back time so this wasn't our first meeting, I would. Not too far though. Hell, he may not even be legal yet. Some kids graduate early and come play.

Fuck, he could be seventeen.

I realize he's been waiting for my answer while I'm lost in dream land. *Shit, pull it together, Trish.* "Yeah, Cody's one of my best friends. We were all really close since we went to school together here in Willardson." I swallow against my fiery throat.

"I'm sorry for your loss." Zac's eyes hold mine and they are the deepest hazel I've ever seen. A part of me wishes I hadn't left my camera bag in the car. I'd position my camera just so the color danced off the overhanging lights. The picture would be beautiful. Worthwhile to be hung at an art gallery or get lots of likes on social media.

I shouldn't be thinking about this. Not now.

His eyes hold mine and it's like he sees *me*. I'm not simply another mourner to him and I immediately wonder why.

"It's not just my loss." I raise my eyebrows, looking from Zac to Briar and back again. "I mean, y'all are like brothers. You actually played with him, spent time with him the last few years. I've just been catching the games here and there. Speaking of which, you've taken Suncastle by storm, Zac."

"Yeah, Zac. You've started more games as a freshman than anyone in Suncastle history." Briar bumps into his shoulder.

"Aww, shut up." Zac's cheeks rose over like he's insecure. Cute. "Not my fault Jerry threw out his shoulder the first week of the season."

"Yeah, but we all know Conners wouldn't let you play if you weren't good for something more than warming your pretty little ass on the bench." I shrug as if I haven't said anything suggestive. Hopefully he's at least legal.

"See, I told you the same thing." Briar shakes his head.

"I'm hopin' Jerry gets back before the championship. That's all I've got to say about this." Zac rubs his knuckles against his nose like he knows his face is all red and doesn't want us looking at him. Adorable.

"Yeah, well, Jerry's got some competition to come back to. You're gonna give him a run for his money as a starter, I can tell you that." Briar bumps his shoulder again. "You'd definitely be taking starting place if you'd focus just a tiny bit more on baseball instead of fucking around with your guitar and poetry every weekend."

"Who says I can't have both?" Zac raises his hands up in defense.

"You've got too many sides to you, Willey, that's for damn sure." Briar seems to be egging him on.

"Willey?" I ask.

"Yeah, his last name. Williams." Briar clues me in.

"Oh, gotcha." I say.

"Who says I can't have both?" Zac repeats with a shrug. "And it's not really poetry, it's song lyrics in coffee shops and bars."

"So playing guitar in coffee shops and bars huh?" I take a bite of my burger. "Baseball star by day, starving artist by night." I give him a teasing smile. "Sounds admirable."

"Oh, yeah, something like that." Briar snickers.

"Well, I once photographed a guitar player. Was one of the most beautiful shots I've done." I lick my teeth, feeling a gnawing sensation in my gut. I don't know that I've eaten much all week. Grief works better than any diet.

Condensation drips down the side of my glass. The milkshakes are half melted. The onion rings look like they're already cold. Glancing out the window, I see Bobby and Lexie still hugging. Or maybe hugging again. I'm not sure. Every time I look over, he's holding her real close.

I scratch at my fake nails. About time to get them redone. I should see if Lex will come along.

"Doesn't feel right to be here without Cody." I look at the table. Now that the conversation has died down, I can tell we're all thinking the same thing. His absence overwhelms this place. It's like a great picture with the wrong lighting. It could be perfect, but the most important element is missing and nothing can make up for that.

"Team will never be the same." Zac says.

"Bobby won't be the same." Briar looks worried.

"He won't take care of himself, so y'all are gonna have to carry him through this." I look at them with an intensity that surprises me. It's not my place to tell these boys what to do. Then again, when have I ever wondered about what is *my place* to be saying?

"Bobby lives in my building." Briar taps the tabletop. "I'll be there for him as much as he'll let me."

I let out a chuckle, rolling my eyes. "He won't let you." The chuckle frees a bit of the tension in my lungs. But it doesn't stay with any measure of relief. "We all know that B never lets anyone help him. Hell, he didn't even let Cody help with anything, ever."

"Ain't that the truth." Briar holds the back of his neck. Zac messes with a straw wrapper folding it in an accordion and back again.

"I just can't get over the shock." I say low into the napkin I'm using to needlessly blot at my lipstick.

"I wished it was a bad joke when I heard." Zac seems to convey what we all feel.

"Ain't right." Briar's gaze grows distant.

"If only it weren't real." I crumple the napkin in my fist.

There's a pain in my chest that gets bigger every time I glance out the window at Bobby and Lex.

Why, God? Cody had so much talent and was finally going to be able to show the world. His life was just starting.

Zac

"I'm gonna head home with Bobby." Lexie sets some keys down, standing by the table. She's talking to Trish, who I can't stop staring at. She's beautiful. There's three keys on the ring and a little kitty keychain that looks like it's seen a lot of love by the way the details are fading.

"Oh, okay." Trish nods, wide blue eyes focusing on me for the briefest moment. "I'll catch up with you a little later." Trish stands and hugs Lexie for a long time, and then gives Bobby a quick embrace.

"I'm gonna dip too." Briar stands, cleaning his jeans from the crumbs.

Trish plops back on the bench, drinking a melted milkshake while I finish my fries. She's wearing a white tanktop with lace at the top, a whisper of freckles peaking from below the lacey fabric. Over the top is an orange cardigan. She's got a simple silver pendant around her neck. I noticed it at the funeral, before she changed clothes.

"Guess it's just us then." She stirs her milkshake, mixing the whipped cream with the shake.

"Just us then." I offer a small smile, glad she stuck around.

"So baseball, guitar and poetry." She leans a little closer, her body language communicating clearly with mine. There's chemistry here. I'm surprised to feel it, but there's no mistake I like her and she likes that.

"You've got nice dimples." She smiles big and it makes me give her my full grin.

"Oh these? They're big enough to fit a dime inside." I burrow my knuckle into my dimple. With my other hand I grab a dime, and with some sleight of hand magic, I make it look like I pull the dime from my dimple. I hand the dime to Trish.

"A bit of a magician are you?" She chuckles, putting my dime into the jukebox and adding a song to the cue.

"Yeah, it was fun to learn a few tricks." I dip a fry in ketchup.

"Can't believe you fit a dime in your dimples. That's seriously impressive." Her thin eyebrows raise in surprise. "Don't know that I've ever seen dimples that deep." She lifts her hand and I wonder if she's going to reach out and touch my face. Her hand shakes as she sets it on the table, like she realized she didn't need to touch me.

"They used to call me Slater, like from *Saved by the Bell*." I shrug.

"I can see it. I mean that dark hair. Those brown eyes. Dimples for days. *Slater.*" The words leave her tongue. "I'm a bit of a connoisseur of nicknames myself. Trishy. Trishy Lou…well that's mostly just what Nana calls me. T-Sizzle." She shakes her head like she's being cool and I hold back a chuckle.

"T-Sizzle." I smile. "That's a good one."

"I mean, if they call Taylor Swift T-Swift, I can be T-Sizzle." She says it as matter of factly as possible.

"You're not wrong."

A little jingle plays on her phone. Ironically, it's a Taylor Swift song, "Love Story". She pulls out her phone and gasps. "One second."

She leaps out of the booth and stands by the back door. I observe her on a phone call she's extremely excited about. It makes me want to make her excited, about…other things.

A moment later she plops on the bench and sets her phone on the table. Every few seconds, she refreshes her screen until she grabs it and puts it up to her face.

"Oh, shit. Look at this!" Her shoulders shimmy while she angles her screen to show me an email. I hold it close enough to read the text.

"I've been applying for jobs and this is like my top pick. I got the interview and they sent me all the criteria for my portfolio!" She's grinning ear to ear.

"Oh wow, congratulations." I nod, handing her back the phone. "Is that who called?"

"Yes, oh, Zac…I've been waiting for this. I applied for several jobs, most of which weren't in Willardson because I hate this town. But then I found out my Nana is moving back here. She usually lives in Atlanta but she hasn't been feeling well as she gets older. Anyway, there's this assisted living type place she's gonna live in and so now I *need* to be in Willardson to stay near her. Jeez Louise, I can't believe they're offering me an interview." She reads over the email, scrolling up and down. "Sorry, that was a lot. I'm just super thrilled. I mean, I *wanted* this so bad!" She clicks her nails against the table top like she's nervous. "Oh damn, my portfolio needs a lot of attention. I'd better get."

The thought of her leaving spreads an ache through my chest. "But your song hasn't come on yet." I eye the jukebox, wanting to spend a little more time with her. I think to grab her number, but I'm not sure. Can I be the reason "Love Story" by Taylor Swift randomly plays on her phone?

Is she single?

"You'll have to enjoy it for me. They need to have my portfolio sent over before I go in for the interview in the morning." She gives me a nice smile.

"Oh, good luck," I gather up my tray and the trash the others left behind, trying to hide my disappointment. Grabbing a napkin, I wipe at the spills. Growing up at my Pa's restaurant means I know what a pain it is to clean up after guests when they leave the place a disaster.

"You clean up too?" Trish glances at the garbage I'm gathering from where she's been wiping up the other half of the table.

"Working at a restaurant will do that." I shrug.

"I know, right?"

I reach into my wallet and drop a ten on the table.

"Big tipper? I'm the same way." She points under the jukebox where I see she's set two fives. It's gonna make someone's day when they come to wipe down our table.

"I swear restaurant employees are some of the hardest working and most under paid individuals in our entire economy." I smile at the money. More than they make in almost three hours on a busser wage.

"Oh my god, I'm always bitching to Lexie about the same thing. People don't get it. They'll leave a mess, scrimp on the tip and never think twice about it. Drives me crazy." She's getting all fired up talking about it. Her passion is so incredibly hot.

"It's nice to talk to someone who understands." My cheeks burn from smiling so much.

"Thank you!" She holds her hands up in the air like she's shouting *Praise Jesus*.

"I'm always saying *everyone* should have to work at a restaurant so they understand what it's like. So many people have zero concern for others and it shows."

"You're speaking my language." She winks at me. "I feel exactly the same way." She picks up the tray.

"I got it." I adjust my hold on my tray to grab hers, too.

She walks with me to the garbage can and I take care of the trays. "It was nice to hang out with you a little bit." She leans over to give me half a hug. "Take care, Willey." She makes a kissy face and just like that, she's gone.

"Take care." I watch her go, hating that this could be it. A nice afternoon with an epic girl. And I didn't even ask for her number.

Trish

O h, come on.

I massage my forehead with one hand, and turn the key again with the other, trying to get the ignition to go. It's raining harder now and I don't wanna be stranded in the Shakey's parking lot for the rest of the afternoon when these puddles get big enough to make me a sitting duck.

The battery. It's good as gone. I lean against the steering wheel. Pull my keys out. Put them back in and turn. Nothing but a faint click or two. Not enough juice to start.

The photography studio at the mall needs my portfolio before my interview. It's nowhere near ready.

Every minute I'm here is another minute I could be working.

I think you can, I think you can....

Turn the key. Nothing. Not even a click now.

I could call Lexie, but this is the worst day in the history of ever to call in a favor.

I give it a minute and try again. To no avail.

The sound of puddle sloshing gets close and I look out the window to see Zac. I crank the window down.

"Need a jump?" He leans against my open window.

"You got cables?" I should really get a set to keep for moments like this.

"Yep. Gimme a sec." He jogs over to his truck and pulls it in the spot next to mine.

"Thanks for doing this." I get out of the car.

"Oh, please let me handle it. We don't both need to get wet." His deep voice offers.

"No, my hood is awful. I'll help you get it up." My cheeks blush realizing how that must've sounded.

"I'm sure you will." He smiles so big those dimples are killing me.

"I didn't mean that." I roll my eyes. Next thing I know, he'll be expecting *'That's what she said'* jokes coming out of my mouth. And I'm wearing a fucking white t-shirt. Might as well enter a wet t-shirt contest.

I wish Shakey's had a covered parking area. This is frigid. Shoulda worn my coat instead of this light cardigan that's getting more soaked by the second.

I pop the hood and mess with the dented corner until I get it to lift. Zac takes the burden off of me as I position the bar in place and go to help attach the cables.

"Careful now, it can be dangerous in the rain." He sounds like he knows what he's talking about, so I let him take control.

Rain falls over me like a sheet as a gust of wind blows hard. I shiver, hugging my arms tight to my body.

"Here," Zac pulls his hoodie off and offers it to me.

"Oh, no, I can't take that." I shake my head.

"Please, I'll be alright. You're freezing."

My teeth chatter as I stare him down with all my stubbornness.

"Put this on and go wait in the car. Last thing you need is to catch a cold when your car's not working." He drapes the hoodie onto my shoulder, holding it for me as I thread my arm through. Warmth spreads through me like a warm blanket fresh out of the dryer. It smells a million kinds of wonderful. Cologne? I can't quite tell what it smells like with the wind, but whatever it is, I love it so much I want to spray it on all my pillows and smell it forever.

"Hey, it looks better on you than it does on me." He smiles real bright. Sunshine on a rainy day. "Maybe you'll have to keep it."

I peer down at the embroidery that says *Williams, Charles W. Reed High School Baseball*. Must be his hoodie from back in the day.

"Don't think I look like a Williams."

"Oh, I don't know. I think the name suits you." He teases. "Now get in the car and let me get this working before you turn into an icicle and I have to find a way to thaw you out."

I chuckle at how silly he sounds telling me what to do. It's like he *could* be one of those Alpha Male types but he's more like a giant cinnamon roll.

After a few minutes, my engine is running.

"Praise Jesus. Thank you." I give him a hug. His body feels so warm against this cold wind. I pull back and see a peaceful expression on his face. The calm in a storm.

"It's just my damn battery. It's been on its last leg a while now. I shoulda gone to get it checked out sooner."

"Is there a good shop nearby?" He brushes some rain droplets away from his eyes.

"Yeah, about a mile away. Thanks again for the jump."

"I can follow you there, just to make sure you make it okay?" He offers.

"I'd appreciate that. Now, go get in your truck before you get any more wet." I back up and head down the road to the same mechanic I always go to, *Hendricks' Auto*.

Sure enough, Zac follows me the whole way.

"I'm all good now." I wave.

He nods as he drives out of the lot.

I park out front and head inside the office. Mr. Hendricks comes in from the garage after I ding the waiting bell. His kind smile finds me as he wipes some grease on a rag. "Well hey there, Trishy. To what do I owe the pleasure?"

"I think it's the battery." I lean against the front desk, remembering all the times I saw him over at Jimmy's house. "If you can work on it?"

"Oh of course. We'll take good care of you." He nods. "I'll have one of my guys squeeze you in, soon as I can." Mr. Hendricks pulls up all my info and I hand him the keys.

As I take a seat in the chair, I shiver, wrapping my arms around me like a hug. Oh, shit. I'm still wearing Zac's hoodie. I bet he's real cold. That truck of his didn't look all that new. Wonder if it even has heat.

I glance out the window knowing he's not still there, but wishing he was.

Zac

With Trish on my mind, I drive down the road until I find a coffee shop. That shiver made her shoulders shimmy. Her cheeks rosed over from needing help. I was just glad I got to keep hanging out with her. Now, I'm gonna get coffee to help warm her up. The only thing worse than having your car break down on the day of your friend's funeral is catching a cold from getting so covered in freezing rain.

Walking into the coffee shop, I grab two cups of coffee and have them put some creamer on the side since I don't know what she likes.

Circling back to the mechanic's place, I park and head in with the coffee. There's a dozen Jimi Hendrix posters on the wall. Whoever owns this place must be a big fan.

Trish is sitting there with an adorable resting bitch face as if asking the universe *why me*, scrolling through her phone. She's even cute when she looks frustrated. I can only imagine how she must feel after losing Cody, getting offered a job interview, and having car trouble. Maybe this coffee will make her day a little better.

When her eyes glance up and see me, a smile lights her face. It has all these butterflies swimming through my stomach.

"Don't think anyone's ever given me such a nice smile just for showing up." I sit next to her, handing over the cup.

"You brought me a coffee?"

"And sweetened creamer, in case you like that." I turn the cupholder to give her access to the to-go cup filled with that sugary goodness.

"Oh, I do. A delicious amount of creamer." Instead of pouring a little in her coffee cup, she pours a little bit of coffee in her creamer cup.

"A delicious amount?" I ask.

"Yes, a delicious amount."

"A copious amount. A generous amount. A considerable amount. A–"

"Oh stop." She elbows my ribs and I laugh, getting under her skin so easily.

"How 'bout some coffee with that creamer?" I take a sip of my scalding black coffee.

"Yeah, where's your cup of creamer?"

"I try to watch calories in season." I pat my stomach, remembering the small burger and fries I already ate today.

"You really are dedicated, aren't you?"

"I love the game. I'm just lucky I get to play for real. Lots of my teammates from highschool either don't play anymore or rarely get a chance to step outta the dugout. I'm wicked lucky." My eyes hold hers and I dare to hope she feels this bit of a crush blooming right along with me. "If your car's gonna be a while, I can drop you home. That way you can finish your portfolio." I rub my palms against my jeans. "I mean, if you want me to and it's okay with you for me to give you a lift."

"Oh, no, you don't have to do that." She sets her cup on the coffee table.

"I'd love to. Whatever you need."

"Are you for real? I mean we barely met."

"I know you don't know me that well, but I'm pretty sure Bobby and Lexie would vouch for me. I promise I'm not a creepy stalker. Like I wouldn't save your address and drive there again…." I shut my mouth before I dig this hole any deeper.

"I wouldn't peg you for a stalker, Willey. But I guess I should be careful." She winks and I melt into her warm-hearted smile.

"What if I'm the creepy stalker? I'm sure there's better things you have to do than help a random stranger."

"Can't think of anything." I hold those eyes of hers, wanting to get to know her.

Trish jumps up off the chair. "Jimmy?" She runs over to the counter.

A tall guy with an impressive fro comes around the counter. "Dad told me you were here." He wraps her in a hug that ends up twirling her in circles around the waiting room. Before he sets her down they kiss.

All those butterflies that were dancing in my stomach just got scorched.

Figures the most fascinating girl I've ever met is already taken.

So much for getting her number.

The Next Summer

July 2013

Zac

"**D**id you wanna go to the lake after this?" I turn toward my girlfriend Valerie in the front seat of my truck. She's got the mirror down while applying makeup.

"It's way too hot for the lake." She runs fresh lip gloss over her lips.

Too hot for the lake? When we're literally arriving at a barbecue? I'm even in a suit coat.

Arguing won't help.

I circle her parents' country club parking lot looking for a spot, biting my tongue so hard I'm tasting a drip of blood.

"Yeah, we'll go swimmin'. The lake will cool us right off." I wait a long time for her to look my way.

"No." She rolls her eyes like it's a horrible suggestion, but doesn't propose any other plans.

"You look beautiful." I smile, wishing for something to give me hope that this is just her stress about the barbecue and life and whatever else that makes giving me the cold shoulder reasonable in her mind. I think back to a year ago when we were inseparable. Now it's like she doesn't want to be near me emotionally or physically.

Once her mirror's up and all her makeup's back in her purse, I go in for a kiss.

She turns her head away, putting up a hand. "Don't you dare smudge this." Her tone is angry as I clench my teeth to keep from saying something mean.

As we walk up, my hand is empty while I wish I was holding hers. Things have been tense. A month has passed since we've even tried to have sex. Wouldn't say our relationship is *entirely* physical, but man do I miss her touch when she withdraws.

Sometimes, I love having her as my girlfriend. Sometimes, I wonder why the fuck we're together. With all this anxiety, it's hard to know how to feel.

Does every couple have moments like this? The ones when the relationship doesn't feel like something you really want, but at the same time you wonder what you'd do without the other person?

I guess I'm looking for more.

I mean, she missed half our baseball games last season. It's not like we live far from the field. She just got sick of watching.

I don't need her there. But she knows how much baseball means to me.

Once we're through the gate to the country club gardens, she full-on ditches me.

Okay, Valerie, so glad I came with you to this.

Until meeting these people, I hadn't realized barbecues were a suit and tie affair. I feel more out of place than a flamingo on a hot air balloon. Why that image pops into mind, I'll never know. Only, there *are* flamingos here because of a special Feed the Flamingos for Charity event happening. Figures.

These birds are so loud. They don't look happy. We're miserable at this country club, together. Maybe I can find a hot air balloon and take the flamingos out with me.

"Zac, how you looking for next season? That championship game really fell apart, didn't it?" Valerie's dad shakes my hand, standing among several of his golfing buddies.

"Oh, yes." I'm tired of hearing about how our team fell apart. It's all anyone says to me. We play a good, hard season. Lose two games that count and everyone forgets about the awesome season we had.

We live in a culture that cages flamingos for charity and can't forgive mistakes–they negate every single good thing you did.

"You gotta know when the team is one moment away from blowing it all and do something to stop it." Valerie's dad puts his hand on my shoulder like he's coaching me.

"Yes, sir." I sip from the glass of guava punch in my hand, wishing it was whiskey. It's almost my twenty-first birthday and then I can legally drink at these events.

"Oh, yes, his handle is Ballboy97."

My ears perk up at the sound of a woman mentioning my professional Sprinkle handle. Oh, shit.

The blood drains from my face. My heart beats strong in my chest. Air fills my lungs and holds there like it can't break free.

I need to run. Grab the flamingo, find a hot air balloon, and go.

Too bad I'm frozen. My feet won't move.

"Ballboy97?" Valerie's mother stands next to the lady who said the name of my handle. "Who's that?"

Hide me now. I reach for my cap to pull over my eyes. But there's no cap. Didn't go with the suit. Fuuccckkkk. I need to know how bad this is. Somehow convincing my body to obey me, I step around the ladies so my back is turned to them. I try to blend in with a group of people while I eavesdrop.

My professional Sprinkle is in that gray area for baseball. Technically, I can have an account where I post naughty content from the 'sin-industry', but it needs to be anonymous. My personal Sprinkle has tons of baseball stuff on there and my face all over it. But the pro one never shows my face.

Freshman year at Suncastle, my roommate sucked and I hated how noisy the dorms were. Spiked my anxiety levels sky-high. I needed to get out of there.

One night, I did some kinky baseball stuff and put it on Sprinkle without showing my face. Honestly didn't expect much of it. But there was a perfectly untapped market in baseball kinks. I started posting regularly, got a fan base, got paid well and moved out of the dorms.

I've never told Valerie about *how* I have enough money for us to pay for the apartment.

"What's Sprinkle?" Valerie's mother asks, clearly intrigued. I pray this woman doesn't actually say it out loud. She's gotta be too prudish to explain in public, right?

"It's an app. People exchange money for," her voice drops down low, "sexy things." She puts on a sly smile, like part of her likes the attention of mentioning something so scandalous at a country club. "They have options for things like videos or messages." She starts whispering. "It's just fun to see what you can buy."

Fuck. Fuck. Fuck.

Is this seriously one of my fans?

Please, God, let there be another Ballboy97.

Valerie walks to the ladies hovering over the phone.

This is not happening.

No, no, no, nooooo.

Flying fish sticks, my heart is surging.

"Wait." Valerie holds the phone.

I need to run.

Take it like a man. Pa's voice haunts me. *You knew better than to get involved in the devil's work.*

I swallow, pulling my neck tie loser, to the point I'm almost out of the knot.

Zac, it's not the devil's work. It's okay. It's gonna be okay. I need a clear head to put out this dumpster fire.

"He's some baseball player with the cutest little accent." The friend fangirls out. In any other situation, I'd be flattered.

She clicks one of my videos. My voice comes through.

Hide. Me. Now.

"I'd rather not watch anything like that." Valerie's mother smiles and nods, leaving the conversation. Thank fuck.

My heart starts to calm, but then I see a knowing look on Valerie's face.

Her eyes war with emotions, kinda like she's weighing in all the good and bad of our relationship and wondering what'll win. Real quick, it turns from contemplating expression to a hurtful glare.

I walk toward her. "Babe, let's get back to our place." I pull at her elbow hoping to get her attention long enough. "Come on, now." I pull a little harder, but she doesn't move.

"Zac?" She doesn't say another word, but she doesn't have to. Her mom may not have realized it's me, but Valerie did.

"Let's go." I try to gently pull her arm. She breaks free, but I keep walking to the truck.

I sit in the driver's seat and wait for her, clenching my nails into my palms. It feels like an eternity before she comes.

Her face is red, tears trailing down her cheeks.

Everything I think to say would come out wrong. The silence in the car adds to my anxiety levels, making my feet bounce against the floorboards.

I get sicker the longer we drive, worried I'm gonna vomit in my truck.

Don't vomit.

Don't vomit.

Zac, don't you dare vomit in this truck!

When she storms straight for the suitcases in the closet once we walk in the door, I know. It's over. Everything just disintegrated. I don't even bother trying to stop her.

I go to the sink and get a glass of water, trying to regulate my overloaded system. The room spins. Flashing lights flutter in and out of my vision.

Anxiety attack.

Just an anxiety attack.

It's been a while since I got a bad one. I go for my meds in the cupboard.

My hands are shaking so bad I can't open the child lock on the lid.

Have I taken this recently? Am I gonna overdose?

No, no, the bottle's full. Haven't taken it in a long time.

What if you forgot that you took it this morning? Anxiety says. *You can't take it twice in one day. That's too much, something bad will happen.*

A loud thump comes from our room.

I jump.

Val must've dropped something.

I rangle with the lid and pop a pill in my mouth. Sliding down the wall, I hang my head between my knees. Breath, two, three, four.

I take my phone out of my pocket and find my sister Sadie's number.

Me: Help

She knows what that means. We always text each other when we get really elevated like this. It's our little thing. I watch the phone screen until her reply comes through.

Sadie: You're safe. Heart beating?

I hold the phone tight to my chest. The thump, thump, thump hits my fingers. I'm safe. In a few minutes it'll shift.

Me: Still beating.

Sadie: See? Safe.

Exhaustion washes over me as I take several long breaths. I have to get back into this moment and try to explain things to Valerie. When I'm able to stand up, I go into our room.

Talk to Valerie, regulate later.

I try at some sort of an explanation, more for me than for her at this point. I need to be able to look back on this and know that I did my best, even with crazy high levels of anxiety racing through my system. "Look, it's not what you think."

"Not what I think?" Valerie slams the drawer shut, throwing her panties into her suitcase. Panties I ripped off of her dripping pussy two months ago, when we had incredible sex on this bed. She's taking them away. Taking herself away.

Why do I feel… relief?

"It's not." I hold my hands up in surrender.

"You've been selling porn to people for long enough that you have a huge follower count." She fills every word with more condescension than the last. "Now I know why you have a million baseball socks in the closet. You use them for your sexy baseball kinks."

"I haven't been selling porn for the sake of selling porn."

"You haven't?" Her eyebrows raise.

"No, I swear it is not like that." My hands are still up, hoping she'll believe me. "It's a job. I'm with you. When we're together, I'm with you. I promise."

She shakes her head. "Someone was showing your account to my mother, Zachary. At the annual country club barbecue, no less. Do you know how humiliating that was for me?"

"And why was your mother's friend on Sprinkle? In public? With us there?"

"Why are *you* on Sprinkle?" Valerie grinds her teeth.

"I have a following. It pays for *this* apartment. That's all it is." I yank off my necktie and unbutton the top of my dress shirt. "You know I don't come from money. You know my scholarship only covers tuition. This very popular account of mine has allowed me to go to school without a truck load of student loans and not have to live in the dorms. Doesn't that count for anythin'?"

"You're sex famous and never told me." She looks like she may burst into tears again.

"You never asked." I hold her eyes, wishing for some level of grace, some level of understanding. Is she capable of that?

"How would I know to ask you that?" she yells.

"I don't know." I sigh.

This is why I didn't tell her. I knew this would happen. She doesn't understand. Really, she's never understood me at all. The longer she looks at me, the more unnerved I feel. I hate it. Those eyes of hers are full of shame.

"Wow, just wow." She throws more shit into her bag. "We're over!"

I think about asking her to stay. I consider more lies. Maybe something like I have a twin brother. Or someone framed me.

There's a rock in my stomach that wondered how long this was gonna last. Maybe if she'd been my one and only, she'd know about my Sprinkle account.

Gosh, Zac. Don't blame her.

She struggles with the heaviness of her luggage, so I pick up her bag.

"Don't." Her eyes are aggressive.

"I wanna help." I focus on her, wishing I saw something I wanted to fight for.

"Okay, fine." She huffs down the stairs while I follow after her with the bag.

"I'm sorry you didn't know. And I wish you the best." It sounds funny coming out of my mouth. I don't even know why I'm saying it.

She rolls her eyes and gets in her car. "Don't call me." She slams the door shut.

"Wasn't gonna." I whisper into the trail of dust from her tires as she speeds away.

Trish

"Put the flowers on the list." Joni, a bride-to-be, says to Trent, her upcoming groom.

He pulls out a notebook and scribbles. "Is this the main bouquet or...?"

"How many times I gotta tell you this?" Joni grabs the pencil from him. Her hand flies over the notebook, scratching lead against paper. She huffs out a sigh, handing me the page where *"Stand-in flowers"* sits in sharp lettering.

"It won't be the real bouquet. Not for this." She gives an exasperated sigh while rolling her eyes.

"We'll be staging satin flowers to make sure the venue has everything you're looking for." I give Trent a sympathetic smile. Wedding stress can make the nicest brides lose their shit.

I finger through my portfolio. One of these days, I'm gonna say I'm a wedding planner and not just a photographer. I walk through every single detail with the couples, even the ones that go above and beyond a photographer's job description.

I have a good eye for these things, so I might as well help out while I'm here. The heavens and stars know someone needs to hold the bride and groom's hand through the process. Nana says I should charge more if I'm doing so much extra. She says I give too much of my time away for free. Maybe she's right.

"If you'd like me to come to the cake tasting, I can. Sometimes we can get some good pictures there." I open my spiral bound planner.

Joni's eyes light up. "Oh, we'd love that!"

"It's at what time?" I try to remember if she's told me.

"Nine on Saturday morning." Joni claps her hands like an excited little kid.

"I'll plan on it." I schedule the time slot. My phone buzzes. "I gotta take this. I'll see you Saturday."

"Thanks, Trish!" Joni yells.

Rushing to my car, I answer, "Hello?" I wedge the phone in my ear and turn on the air as fast as I can. It's a million and three degrees out here.

It's one of my clients needing to reschedule. I adjust the time in my planner. It'll be a long day, but I'll make it work. I always make it work. Because making it work is easier than telling someone no.

I can always do my best. Just like my Daddy always told me. That sting of pain settles in my chest. I miss him so much. Wish he could see me now. I think he'd be proud.

Hope you're watching, Daddy.

It'll be fun to take photos at the cake tasting. I did that with Lexie and Cody. It was the last photo I took of him before he died. I close my eyes tight, missing my friend. We sure had a lot of good times. He was there for me through some really tough shit.

I look at the clock on my console and realize I have just enough time to go grab Nana and me a frappe from Starbucks. Then I'm off to meet the Brooks family for their fall photo shoot at Elerish Mountains. It's not even close to fall, but she insists on taking the photos early and wants me to superimpose fall colors.

I open up texts, return messages, and go over call history. When everything's caught up for now, I start driving. My mind wanders, because I need that rush of caffeine to keep me focused. Instead of the normal shifting to my to do list, my thoughts stroll down memory lane.

I pull out my vibrating phone to see Cody's name light up. He hasn't called me in a while, so I answer. "Hey, dorkbutt."

"Hey, overachiever."

"I should change your nickname to stranger since it's been so long since you called. I barely recognize your voice." I chuckle into the phone. "What do you want this time?"

"Can't I just call and say hello?" he laughs.

"You never call to say hello."

"Well, how've you been anyway?" Cody asks.

"Besides this obnoxious Art History assignment due tomorrow, I'm good." I tap my pencil against the paper.

"I got a favor to ask you." He always does...

"Go for it."

"Lexie doesn't know, but can you print out a bunch of photos from that engagement shoot you did? We're gonna be on the road for the rivals game with the Wolves next weekend. I'll leave the key under the mat and maybe you can surprise her. Have the pictures up all over the wall? I'll pay you for them. Whatever it costs, just make it happen for her, will ya?"

"Wow, Cody. That's real sweet. I'll see what I can do."

"You're a gem, Trish. See ya." He clicks off the phone.

Eleven days later I got the call from Lexie, sobbing in the hospital after the car crash that took his life. I'll never forget the pain in her voice. The exact place I was standing in my apartment when the world flipped upside down.

Why did he have to go?

Nausea bubbles up my stomach. My nose burns like it wants to cry. Every part of my body feels icky. Still sick over this, almost a year and a half later.

I rest my head into the steering wheel, wishing this wave of grief didn't crash against me so hard. *God, why did you let him die like that? We weren't ready to let him go.*

I wasn't ready to let either one of them go.

Like every other time, the grief of Cody stirs up the grief of Daddy. The two people I wish I could just call up and talk to right now.

Rubbing my Kentucky kitty keychain, I swallow down these feelings and send a smile to Daddy and Cody in heaven.

I want to cry, but like so many other times, no tears are able to fall. It's a particular kind of torment to hold all of this inside.

I'm alone. An only child wishing for someone to comfort me like a brother or a sister.

No matter how hard I try, people never seem to understand me. See me. Hear me. I'm like a ghost, but instead of the afterlife where I can see Daddy and Cody, I'm doomed to earth.

I need to be seen. Heard. Listened to.

I send a text to Lexie. She's dealing with a lot right now, so I don't expect to hear back. Maybe I need more people I can talk to. Maybe even a therapist.

Strangely, the last time I really felt heard was after Cody's funeral. Sitting in Shakey's with his friends, genuinely enjoying each other's company. Zac took the sting out of the day with his quick smile and his ability to give everyone his full attention, like they were the most important person in the room. Or maybe it was just me he did that for? Then he helped with my car, brought me coffee and gave me a super soft hoodie I still wear all the time.

Zac. He's a happy thought. That baseball player with a heart of gold. In another life, we coulda been friends. Coulda been lovers, even. If I didn't have so much jumbled up inside, I'd love to be with someone like him.

My complicated life would dampen his sunshine and I'm not about to be guilty of doing that. He can be a happy fantasy. But nothing more.

Unless...

Wow, heat must be frying my brain or something for me to be thinking about him.

Time does a lot of things to all of us. And I have no idea why, but the only thing that brings comfort to my broken heart is to wonder what time has done to Zac.

August

Zac

Three weeks since the breakup and life won't slow down. I've got a million pots on the fire, all of them begging for my attention before they boil over and destroy every bit of my fleeting sanity.

Focus. Breathe. Be present.

I really want to grow my social media following. That's a big priority. It's a bit of a pipe dream, but if I can make a little more money each month I can save up for the future. Growing up, we never seemed to have enough. My folks both worked all the time. We didn't get to see them hardly at all and it was difficult to afford anything that wasn't an absolute necessity.

I never want to feel that way again. Because of this, I keep researching how to grow a following online. Sprinkle has been awesome. I'm ready to kick it up a notch… even if I'm battling all the shame I wish I didn't feel.

My phone goes off with a dozen pings before class is over. As soon as Professor Weyland finishes, I duck into the hallway and check over my shoulder before opening them up.

NotYourMom43: Can you send me some more of those Jizzed panties? The red ones again? Like last time. I'll pay you for rushed shipping.

A gift of four hundred dollars appears.

Me: I'll get that mailed tomorrow. Thank you.

Her reply comes almost instantly, like she's been sitting with the window open until I got back to her.

NotYourMom43: Send me a little surprise, too.

Another hundred dollar gift appears with a note that says *Keep me your favorite.*

I roll my eyes. They all think they're my favorite. It's just a job. Every one of these women make it too damn easy to say no to every other job out there, when five minutes of my time pulls in half the month's rent. I get a kick out of all these older women shamelessly flirting with a baseball player.

My phone rings and I close out my pro Sprinkle so I can talk to Sadie.

"Hey, how's it going?" I start walking to my truck.

"Zac?" Sadie sounds awful.

"What's wrong?"

She sighs into the phone. "Just a bad day."

"What happened?" My heart starts pounding harder. "Is it Pa?" I know he's had some heart trouble lately and I'm fucking scared that maybe *that* is why she's calling.

"No, no, it's not. He's doing good. They said his last checkup was better." Sadie talks real quick and I can tell by her tone she's feeling guilty for making me think the worse.

"But you had a bad day." I start up my truck and head to the apartment.

"I didn't make it as captain," her voice is choked up, "and now I don't know if I wanna even play anymore." Her words hit like a ton of bricks slamming into my chest. Volleyball is as much her life as baseball is mine.

"I know it's gonna be okay," I console her. "And you may not wanna play anymore *today,* but I bet you'll miss it if you quit."

"I really wanted this." She sighs with so much emotion in her words I feel it over the many miles that separate us.

"I know you did." I try to smile but it doesn't work, wishing I knew how to help.

"Being captain senior year has always been on my goal sheet."

Waiting at a stoplight, I close my eyes. The weight of my heavy eyelids mimics the weight of her words. Her goal sheet matters more to her than anything. She keeps her eyes on the future. She works hard. She's been through so much this last year with the other girls on the team, and this is just more bad news.

"I thought you had it. I really did." I massage the bridge of my nose, exhaustion weighing down my limbs. I was up 'til 3AM making videos last night. But this isn't just exhaustion from lack of sleep, exhaustion from the way they've been treating my sis.

Makes me want to go put dog shit in their brownies. Or lime green hair dye in their shampoo bottles. Okay, those are horrible examples of ways to get back at them. I can't think of anything better right now. I'm too tired. But something. Because they treat her horrible for no good reason.

But hey, Karma is a bitch.

Maybe Karma will be *my* bitch and stick it to these two-faced, stuck-up-barbie-doll-high-school-seniors.

Karma, let's make that sooner rather than later, hm?

"I'm so mad." Sadie's voice is low, like maybe she's crying and trying to cover it up. I noticed she didn't video call this time, like normal. Maybe she didn't want me to see her this upset.

"Hey, if it's not this, something else will work out, okay?" I have to stay positive.

"When you comin' home?" Her tone makes my heart ache. Like it's taking a leave of absence, jumping out of my chest and onto an ant hill. Each of those ants bite different areas of my heart. Poking, burning, stinging.

Maybe they are. Maybe I'm not really here. Maybe I've always been captive on an ant hill.

Okay, another example of how my brain is going haywire. *Get it together, Zac. Doc Rogers says to make sure you're getting enough sleep. After this, we're gonna take a nice long nap. Maybe a hot shower.*

"Zac?" Sadie needs me.

Stay in the moment. Right. Moment. Phone call with Sadie. Not on an ant hill. Okay, Anxiety, time to believe me instead of the psychosomatic itching of imaginary ant bites.

Why doesn't *Anxiety* believe *me*?

Why are we having *another* fit like this?

I tap my fingers against my thumb, working out the nervous energy. Come on, come on. I'm taking my meds. I'm eating well.

I'm not sleeping.

Gah!

It's the trifecta. Need every part to keep from these rushes.

Skip any of these things and it's back on the anxiety rollercoaster ride loop de loop de loop de loop. Time to get off. First stop, out of the rollercoaster. Next stop, land of sleep.

"When are you coming home?" Sadie asks again.

Stay. In. The. Moment.

"Soon, okay?" I swallow the lump in my throat, walking into my apartment. It needs to be now. Sadie needs me now. We can go to the movies and eat buttered popcorn until our insides bust. I can hop on a plane and take her away from her problems for a minute.

"Why does it have to be so hard?" She's crying. I can tell. Sadie's never been good at hiding how she feels from me. She puts on a mask for Ma and Pa and the entire student body of Elizabethtown High, but she's real with me. We're real with each other.

"What about youth group? You can still go out for a leadership role there can't ya?"

"Sadie Leigh?" Ma calls in the background.

"I'm talking to Zac," Sadie yells.

"Hey, Zac." Ma's voice comes over the line. "Sadie, go get your homework done. You've got volleyball practice tonight."

I hear rustling around and know that Ma has sent her away, and I'm alone to talk with her. "Hey, Ma."

Her voice goes quiet, "Sadie told you?"

"Yeah."

"It wasn't even a close vote." She keeps her tone hushed, "Nikki made sure to announce that in front of everyone while she was looking right at Sadie."

I rub my forehead, "Those girls–" *are a bunch of bitches* "–can be real mean."

"They're brutal. I don't even know how to support her. A year ago, she would've been the top pick. She's the same person."

"We know she is. And she knows it, too. I hate that it's happening. Can you call the coach?"

"I tried. He's not much better than Nikki."

Damn high school politics, why does everything seem to come down to popularity?

"That doesn't help." I squint my eyes closed tight. My hands flick at my neck and arms like I'm swatting away the imaginary ants. I'm itchy all over. Scary how real my mind can create sensations like this.

"Well, maybe you can come to her opener. I think it'd help her to have you here." Ma clears her throat. "You're not in season yet."

"Yeah, that is a good idea. When's it gonna be?" I rub my stomach, cramping something awful from all this stress. Why didn't I pick a local college? I got offered a full-ride at Western Kentucky University. But Suncastle promised me game time as a freshman which is almost unheard of.

"It's the third week of September. The Friday after your birthday. Probably your first week of exams. Not sure you can miss that."

"I'll look at flights." I have to be there for Sadie.

"And how are you doin'? I know I haven't asked much. I'm sorry. We've had so much on our plate." Ma's always piling guilt on herself real high. I wish she'd stop. Doesn't help.

"It's okay, Ma. I'm okay." I rub my forehead with my knuckles.

"I need to go make sure she's got something to eat before practice."

"Yeah, go take care of her. Give her big hugs for me."

"I always do." Ma clicks off the phone, and I look out the window.

The vote wasn't even close.

Enormous pressure builds on my chest as the imaginary ants continue to feast away at my beating heart. I want to go fuck up that coach that allows this kind of behavior from his team. Sadie's the star player and deserves to be captain. She earned it.

I rub my forming headache and flop back on my mattress. I've been praying for her every day. Giving her all the faith I can. Her life is so heavy. I'm so far away. What brother leaves his sister for college? Me. Dingbat brother who should be at home right now.

I took the scholarship seven hundred miles away. I didn't know she'd be going through this or I would've given it all up. I want to transfer back home and finish school at the local community college. But Ma wouldn't handle that.

I didn't pinch pennies to pay for all your baseball uniforms all those years for you not to keep playin' ball. Her words echo in my mind.

Maybe Sadie needs to figure this out on her own, anyway. I can't always be there to protect her, even though that's what I want.

I fall to my knees, closing my eyes and clasping my hands together. A shaky breath leaves my throat as I kneel humbly before the One who can truly help her right now.

Father in Heaven, can you please help Sadie? Be there for her when I can't be? I'll do anything to help from where I am. I just wish it was enough. But you're enough, Father. You can take care of her. Please. In Jesus name, Amen.

Trish

I'm amidst the whirlwind of wedding season. Last weekend I had two shoots. I'm finally getting a moment to recoup.

It's been a pretty good day. I'm sitting at my desk when my phone lights up with a call from Lexie.

"Hey, boo." I paint the top coat on my fingernails, cell phone burrowed between my shoulder and ear.

"Trish, I can't do this. I need you." Lexie sounds really upset. Then again, it's hard to remember a time when she wasn't.

"You have me, girlfriend. You know that." I blow on my nails.

"No, I need you to come visit. Like yesterday."

"I wish I could. I've got a million and three weddings to photograph since everyone and their Aunt Sally is getting hitched." My planner is triple booked. I've started writing little wishful notes to myself in the margins. Things like, *go grocery shopping if that gets done early.* My pantry is getting more bare because the hopefuls never happen. I'm barely getting my workouts in three times a week.

"I'll head down there soon as I can. But tonight's the only night I've had to even paint my nails in three weeks. Do I need to remind you how much it takes for me to *not* get my nails done?"

"No," she sighs. "Well if you can't come visit, can you at least tell me this wasn't just some huge and awful mistake."

My heart sinks a little bit. This has to be every kind of difficulty. She moved away when Cody died, but now she's back at the old stomping grounds trying to finish her degree.

I wave my fingers in the air, wishing it made them dry faster. "It's not a mistake. You're gonna finish school. One more year and you can leave South Carolina for good."

"Cody's not here." There's a choked sound in her voice.

"I know." I glance at the photo on my desk of the five of us. The five Williardsonights as we called ourselves. Cody's smile was always so big and bright even though he had one of the hardest lives of all of us. Wishing there was something I could do to take the pain away, I think through what may help. "Have you gotten your hair done yet?"

"I made the appointment."

"Good. Hair always helps."

"It does. I'm sorry. I'm just a mess right now." Lexie groans.

"We both knew it'd be a lot for you to go back to school." I lick my parched lips, hunting for some chapstick. "The last time you were on Suncastle College Campus was with Codester. We all miss him every day. Have you talked to Mickey? Or Bobby?"

"Not much." She sounds deflated.

"You know what you need? Get your hair done. Go eat lots of wings. And you'll get through this one day at a time." I try to reassure her.

"I guess so."

"You know what?" I look at my calendar and the thirteen weekends of weddings. "I'll come spend a couple nights with you in November. We'll go out and have fun and do whatever you wanna do."

"November?"

"It's the soonest I can."

"Okay." Lexie's voice holds a bit of hope, and I'm thankful.

"And Lexie?"

"Yeah?"

"It's gonna be okay. I promise."

September

Zac

My band plays at Garrison's, one of the local bars, and for once I'm feeling a break from all the stress I've been drowning in since Valerie left.

"You stole the stage tonight." Harvey puts his hand on my shoulder. I close up my guitar case so we can get out of here.

"You too." I nod as our band heads out the door.

"Afterparty?" Ethan asks.

"Nah, I've got some stuff I've gotta get done."

"Cool." He waves as he gets in his truck.

After I get settled at home, I pull up my Sprinkle accounts. Both my pro and personal accounts are dwindling since I haven't thought of anything clever to post lately. My tried and true fans are still there, but I'm definitely not growing like I need to in order to reach my financial goals.

I pull out my phone and text Ethan.

Me: We need to get more creative. Come film some content with me this weekend?

Ethan: Yah, I can do that.

Me: Are your views down from normal?

Ethan: Kinda…not much. But you haven't posted much in a few weeks.

Me: I know…

It sucks being alone in my apartment. There's a hollow feeling when I lay in bed. I went as far as putting a bunch of the socks in a pillowcase so I had something to hold while I slept. Is it wrong that it fills the void as well as Valerie would've?

Next time, I wanna be with someone who sees *me,* and not just an athlete. Someone who loves my music and thinks I'm funny. Someone who doesn't think it's weird I believe in God but don't buy into purity culture. Someone who likes having in-depth conversations. I want to find actual acceptance for who I am.

My phone buzzes on my nightstand and I click open a text. Sadie sends me a pic of her and a blonde girl, both of them doing kissy faces at the camera.

Sadie: My new BFF, Angela. She just moved here from Colorado.

Me: BFF? That was quick.

Sadie: She's awesome.

Me: 'Bout time someone moved in that isn't an asshole.

Sadie: ikr?

Seeing her happy lessens some of the worry I've carried ever since they told me she didn't make team captain.

As much as I wanna talk to Sades, Ethan's right and I have to get some work done. Keep putting it off. Can't do that. Need to be better. Have to be better. My parents don't have a penny to send my way. Wish the scholarships covered more.

I stare at my computer screen. Twenty seven unread messages that I can't bring myself to click. I need to. Rent's gonna be due. I've spent a lot on new baseball socks I need to mail.

Heaviness fills me, making me want to quit. Valerie couldn't handle that I did this. Maybe that means I need to stop. Maybe it means I never should've started.

I think back to when I met Valerie. The first few months were a lot of fun. We weren't always emotionally distant. Relationships are so much work.

I scroll through my profile. All my subscribers.

They wait for me to show up. I have to. People pay me for this content. Take more photos. Shoot more videos. Reply to their messages. Jizz all over socks. They're waiting for me.

I lean my head against the back of my office chair.

Why couldn't Valerie accept me? Why do I go out with people who don't?

But there's someone out there who will, right?

I hold a tight breath, staring at the cheap tile above me.

Is there anyone who could love me? All of me?

Maybe I'll just stay this way. With my screen and the people who pay to watch me. They accept me without question. I'm a sexy guy to fantasize with and fill needs they aren't getting met in other ways. Maybe some of them really do need me. The hope in a dark tunnel. A good part in a hard life.

They love me.

In some ways, it means more to me than Valerie ever did.

I press the record button and get to work.

Can't seem to sleep tonight. I know it's just this Valerie bullshit running through my head.

Valerie can take a hike. And I hope she does. I hope she goes on lots of hikes down our special trails and can't stop thinking about what a complete asshole she was for walking out like that.

Sick of cuddling my sock pillowcase, I toss it on the carpet. I pull up Ethan's number.

Me: You up bro?

Nothing.

Me: Sadie, you up?

Nothing
Again.
Just me and the ceiling.

My mind goes to an unusual memory. The cute girl from Cody's funeral. The way she talked was like honey rolling off her tongue. She could make me forget my worries, even for just a moment while I tasted some of that honey.

What the fuck, Zac? I must be tired and wanting a rebound.
Not like she'd want you anyway.
Sleep, Anxiety, sleep.
It won't listen.

Not gonna be able to settle until I put this haywire mind to rest. I pull up social media and get Bobby's friend list up. There she is.

Trish.

That's right. I'll make sure to remember her name.

A bunch of her posts are public. It's easy for me to get to know her online persona even while I'm logged into my professional account. Time passes as I read through the things she cares about. Passion shows from everything she says. A couple of her comments make me chuckle. There's something about this girl. I'm drawn to her, like maybe I'm supposed to be with her.

Holy crap, dude, get a grip. You've gone from a lifeless relationship with Val to dreaming about having an imaginary life with a complete stranger, like some eleven-year-old Jonas Brothers fan. You need some fucking sleep.

I massage my chest, this weird butterfly going all through my insides. Where I usually feel chest pain, I now feel excitement. She's Bobby's friend. Maybe he can help me ask her out.

Fuck, I'm half asleep, and this is *creepy. Stop.*

I set the phone down, but my thumb brushes the *follow* icon.

Uh, oh.

I stare in horror that I accidentally requested to follow her. I go to take it back when the notification bubbles that she followed me back.

No way.

The butterflies in my chest flutter bigger, overtaking my insides with a sense of wonder.

She followed me back? Instantly? Like she didn't even need to think about it?

It's the wee hours of the morning and she's online? Guess neither of us can sleep. What else do we have in common?

I'm shocked as hell.

Trish, the girl I've had unexplained feelings for since Cody's funeral followed me back. When I was with Valerie, I didn't think twice about her. But now? It's good timing.

Rolling onto my side, I feel peaceful. Before I know it, I fall asleep and get the best rest I've had in a really long time.

"Time to go, Bunny Butt!" Ethan's banging on my door startles me awake. Dang, I slept through my alarm.

"Five minutes!" I rub my eyes and throw on shorts and a tank top. Grabbing some juice from the fridge, I open the door. "Sorry, overslept."

"Yeah 'cause you were textin' me in the middle of the night." Ethan stretches his calves on my coffee table. "Bobby and Briar already left. I saw them when I was heading over here."

"We'll catch their second lap." I finish lacing up my shoes and grab my water bottle and backpack.

Ethan and I sprint to the lake, like we do every day for morning runs. Briar and Bobby have already run half a lap by the time we catch up. We all run another lap around the lake.

My chest burns. Fuck. I need to ask Mindy to give me a check up. I don't have time to keep worrying about this every time I workout. We're just getting in shape for pre-season.

"Hey guys." I bend, pressing my palms into my knees, exhausted from running so fast.

Anxiety, this is just exertion. My heart is fine. Don't you start making me go nuts.

"Zackeyyyy," Briar puts a sweaty arm around me. "Ethannnnn," he puts his other arm around Ethan, bringing us into a hug. "Didn't know if you'd make it."

"Someone needs a new alarm clock." Ethan rolls his eyes at me.

"If I coulda fallen asleep before 4 AM, my alarm woulda woke me up fine." I try to get more air. The adrenaline rush isn't good on this little sleep. Even after a lap, I'm not fully awake. Need to sprint to Starbucks and get a double latte. Or maybe that wouldn't be good to push my heart like that. I don't need it beating out of control again. I'll wait to get some coffee until I've settled down from the run. Maybe. Maybe I'm overthinking things…again. They all drink coffee after our morning runs and they're fine. I'm fine.

"You're not sleepin' well either?" Bobby pulls the top off his water bottle and chugs. He's not even winded. Goals, right there. I need to get to his level.

"Wish I could say I had a good reason." I sip some water.

"That kind of insomnia is the worst." Bobby looks annoyed, and I wonder why he can't sleep.

"Get closer you guys. Zac needs better content and we're gonna help out." Ethan pulls his phone out of his pocket. "Can't let our fan base miss out on a run vid." He does a video of all of us sweaty and making supid faces. This will go on my personal account, so it's fine to show my face.

"How many followers you up to now?" Bobby asks.

"Um, forty three thousand last I checked." I tend to get a hundred or two new followers a day. It's slowly becoming a significant account.

"Forty three thousand last he checked." Briar echos. "Which was what? Five minutes ago?"

"Last night." I chuckle.

"You mean all night." Bobby's face is smiley, and it occurs to me that I really haven't seen him happy all that often as of late.

"It's sooooo much better not to check first thing in the morning," Briar gives us shit. "He's only halfway addicted," he looks from Bobby to me. "If you try really hard, I think you can aspire to Ethan's dedication. I mean, clearly he's checking every two seconds."

"You're so full of it," Ethan knocks Briar's shoulder. "You just wish you had as many fans fawning over you."

"You think I don't? Here's the difference…mine are real." Briar winks, putting on a smile like he's posing for the cover of a magazine.

"Forty thousand *real* friends. Yeah, right." Ethan elbows his ribs. "I doubt you know more than ten people who aren't on the team or letting you cheat off their exams."

"Shit! Speaking of, I've got an exam in half an hour. Let's go." Bobby pulls Briar toward their apartment.

"You're gonna pay me ten bucks tonight when you find out that my pretty face got you an extra thousand views." Briar walks backward, yelling at us.

"It's on!" Ethan shouts.

"Don't feed his ego any more." I scoff.

"I don't know why he doesn't do more collabs with us. Ride our fame." Ethan lives in a delusional world where he thinks our videos are already viral.

"We aren't famous." I stretch my neck.

"We're more famous than anyone else I know." Ethan puts his phone in his pocket.

I wanna run to catch up with the guys so I can ask Bobby about Trish.

No, that's a bad idea. I don't wanna be weird. That was a year and a half ago. She did follow me back, though.

I rub my eyes, wondering if I imagined that. My phone is back at the apartment, and I can't check to make sure it's real. Damn.

I shoulda got her number when I had the chance. God, was I stupid. Flying fish sticks.

Before I get in the shower, I check my phone. There's a few dozen new followers from last night. I scroll through. Must've dreamed the bit about Trish following me.

No. Her pic appears.

It wasn't a dream.

But man, oh man, she is.

Trish

I need a release and a good fuck. Take my mind off work and family stress. Mostly because today I had to deal with my mother. I go to lunch with her and Nana every other Thursday. I only do it for Nana…and I guess to pretend I have a mom instead of whatever version of herself is left after years of being married to Dipshit, aka my evil stepdad.

It's every kind of exhausting to watch her living in a fantasy like she's in a good enough relationship to stay. What he did to me should be reason enough to make her walk away. But she lost her strength years ago.

It's sad, really. Watching the shell of a person she once was dwindling deeper and deeper into delusions just so she can live with herself. Meanwhile, I work myself to death because I've never had anyone to depend on. Not really.

Except Nana. Hence why I appease her every other Thursday and pretend we have a happy family for an hour over cobb salads and raspberry lemonade.

My eyes blur from looking too long at my laptop screen. I glance away, blinking and rubbing until my vision normalizes. This brain of mine is on overload after working on this edit for hours. I'm so frustrated with it. No time for myself. Zero Trishcare.

Fuck it. Work can wait.

I brew my favorite coffee and pour a delicious amount of creamer, remembering

Zac teasing me for my adjective. That was a nice thing…helping with my car, bringing me coffee, leaving me with his hoodie. Hope he's doing well.

Sipping on the porch, I go through my laptop. One-by-one, I save all my open projects and close out of them.

Freedom.

Time for me.

The stars look beautiful tonight. *Hey, Daddy.* I touch my fingertips and blow a kiss to the stars, where he is. I cannot wait for the trip I have planned next month to go up the canyon and take pictures. He's the one who put a camera in my hands when we camped in the mountains of Kentucky. The stars always remind me of Daddy, too. I feel close to him when I gaze at the night sky.

You're taking someone with you, aren't you? Mama's voice crowds my thoughts. I am so over her control antics. I can go camping by myself if I decide to. Or I'll just take the flavor of the week.

Speak of the devil, that boy is messaging me. I unlock my phone.

Click.

Dickpic.

Lovely.

I roll my eyes. Why do guys think that's hot? Don't get me wrong, I love when it's inside of me, but I don't want a glam shot. Or rather, I want a glam shot worth looking at.

Can you take a *good* glam shot of that body part, though? Hm.

I've done several boudoirs with male models. Does the dick look good then? No, we usually keep the actual appendage covered. It's that sweet part of skin just under their waistband that's so sexy and lush in a photograph.

I text him back.

Me: Put your trousers down low and send me a sexy ab pic.

It'll probably scare him off, but I don't really care. I have more fun on my own, frankly.

That's just what I need.

I pull up Sprinkle. There's this cute baseball player who followed me in the wee hours of the morning when I couldn't sleep. Stupid nightmare got me up and it took forever to settle.

I pull up his account: Ballboy97.

Something about him is familiar, but I can't place it. I do love his content. Some of it is real sexy, like panty-melting-sexy. A lot of it is super sweet, too. I don't know which I like more. The pussy clenching videos where you can tell he likes to take charge. Or that sensitive side that asks how you're doing and if you've had a good day. There's a totally different appeal to both sides of him. I wonder if it's all staged or if this is really how he is.

He's pretty private, from the way he holds the camera. I find it ridiculously clever how he positions himself so you can see just enough to want more. Compared to most accounts, that's genius. I have a feeling it's because he doesn't want the world recognizing him. Maybe that means he does play ball for real.

He hasn't posted any new content. Dammit.

Oh, wait. One new upload.

Oh man, is he yummy. Yeah, see, that's how you take a sexy video. Flavor of the Week needs to learn from this guy. Ballboy97 could teach the college level course in sexy. Give this guy a PhD in hot and bothered. I'll stay after class.

Sipping my coffee, I watch him until my panties are drenched, and I go in my shower to finish what he started. Hot water pulses against my skin as I wiggle and flick. Thinking about his silky voice. His gorgeous lower abs leading into the perfect V shape of his Adonis belt.

Riding the wave of orgasmic bliss, I brace myself against the shower wall.

Thank you Ballboy97 for giving me all the release I need tonight.

I wanna know this guy in real life.

The message button tempts me. I'm half curious if he's one of those asshole types or the kind that engages with his fans. I click onto his stories and casually reply to one of them. Guess we'll see what happens.

Don't disappoint me, Big D.

If he's not too far away, maybe we can hookup.

Zac

I've been sitting at the airport waiting for my flight home, staring at Trish's message to me. She messaged me.

Me.

Okay, so she has no clue it's me. But still.

I'm the kind of guy that reads every direct message. All the story replies. All the comments on my posts. I read them and if it's not some troll I tend to reply. A lot of my clients are really great. We chat about life. Sometimes they tell me when they're having a shit day and I do what I can to cheer them up. It feels good to be there for people, even random strangers on the internet.

But I've never been nervous before. I'm not sure how to play this.

Baseball is simple. Rules. Calls. Even our workouts are predictable and controlled.

This is coming out of left field.

I type out a response. Delete. Type out a different response. Delete. This goes on until my thumbs get tired.

If I message her from this account, she won't know it's me and if I end up asking her out on the miracle she's currently single, that'd be starting things off on a weird foot.

I log out of my professional account and pull up my personal one.

Please remember me…

I send a friend request. A few seconds later she accepts.

Pulling up messenger, I type out something. Here goes nothing. I won't have service to send it when I'm on airplane mode, so it's now or never.

Me: Hey, how've you been?

Trish: Oh, hey Zac. I've been good. How about you? Drinking delicious amounts of creamer until season?

I stare at the message. Holy fuck. She remembers me and the stupid way I teased her about creamer. I do a little happy dance in the airport. A few people look at me and I feel my cheeks getting hot. With a chuckle, I go back to messaging.

Me: You know it. Been drinking about this much:

I walk around the airport terminal until I get to one of the little cafes and take a pic of the biggest bottle of creamer I can find.

Trish: LOL

Me: I mean, gotta make that sugar last. It's like hibernation.

Trish: Gotta have enough.

Trish: Well catch me up. How you been?

Me: I've been doing well. What's new with you?

Trish: Still living in Willardson. Oh, I quit working at the studio at the

mall and now I'm a full-time freelance photographer.

Me: Glad to hear it. How's your Nana?

Trish: She's doing real good. I go see her every week. Thanks for asking.

Me: I gotta go catch a plane…ttyl.

Trish: Have a good flight.

Boarding starts up and so I close out the messages, in awe of our conversation. I sure would like to get to know her more. Wonder if that one guy is still her boyfriend?

Once I'm in my seat, I scroll through her posts one more time. If she is with that guy, she doesn't post about him. I'm gonna hope that means she's not and assume so until I have reason to believe otherwise.

Flying always makes me nervous. I hate that even though it's only an hour and a half nonstop I still deal with all the anxiety. We fly sometimes for baseball, so I try to drive whenever I go home. But it didn't make sense to drive ten hours when I'm only gonna be there a couple days.

I somehow survive the flight and grab my carry-on as I wait forever to exit the plane and head to the pickup area. Mom's old Honda Accord pulls up and she puts the car in park. She and Sadie rush to meet me.

"Hey, Ma." I bring her in for a big hug. Her gray hair is pulled back in a ponytail.

"Hey you," Sadie says right before she jumps up to hug me, and I squeeze her real tight.

"Let's get goin' so you have time for supper." Ma opens the trunk and I pop my carry-on into it. We drive across town to Pa's restaurant.

The smell of pasta and garlic bread hits me as soon as we walk inside. The hint of spices tickling my nose brings back so many memories of helping out in the summer and coming here after practice, doing my homework in the corner while I waited for Pa to drive me home after he closed shop. For as long as I can remember, this place has been my second home.

"Oh, my little Zachy, you're growing up too fast." Rosa stands at the hostess station and shakes her pencil spoon at me. "Get over here."

I go around to give her a big hug. "Good to see ya. How's Luca doing?"

"Luca is doing great. He's about to finish middle school and I can't believe it." She looks up at me. "You've grown two feet since I saw you last. Who said you could leave us all to go to college, hm?"

"Rosa, I'm the same height I was when I left." I chuckle.

"Well you still look taller." She gestures to the dining room. "Pick any table you like. I'll tell Marco to get your order started."

"Thanks, Rosa." Ma smiles and we go to one of the tables by the window.

The dining room is almost empty. That's odd for this time of night on a Friday. Usually it's so crowded we wait for a table. Pa's restaurant has always struggled to make ends meet, but even this is less than normal. The popular dinner rushes are the only thing that keep this place alive.

"Oh, hey there." Marco sets coasters on the table. "The usual tonight?"

"Yes please." Ma hands him the menu.

Marco brings out some food without any delay.

"Is Mitch gonna come to the game?" Sadie eats a bite of her salad while I shovel some pasta into my mouth, famished from the stress of flying making me lose my appetite all day. Mitch is my best friend, but he's always been like another brother to Sadie.

"Yeah, I texted him to meet us there." I check my phone again and see a notification from Sprinkle. Trish posted. It's an auto click from seeing her name and opening the app. It's a gorgeous photo of her in the mountains. Her long light hair is in perfect waves on either side of her chest. That smile is insanely captivating, red lipstick and all. Her eyes hold all the confidence in the world.

"Who's that?" Sadie sounds impressed as she grabs my phone out of my hand. "Goodness gracious this girl is on fire."

"Hey," I grab my phone back. "You open your eyes any wider and those eyeballs of yours are gonna fall right out. Gonna be hard to play tonight without being able to see a damn thing."

"Language." Ma says.

"Oh my gosh, you *like* her." Sadie elbows my ribs. "Have you asked her out yet?"

"I just broke up with Valerie like three weeks ago. Gimme a second, would ya?" I turn my phone away.

"I'm glad you broke up with Valerie. That girl was a bitch."

"Language, the both of you." Ma shakes her finger with an extra serving of sass to go with these bowls of pasta.

"She was, though. A nasty woman." Sadie shakes her head. "I'm still amazed you managed to spend as long with her as you did."

"Hey now, Valerie was cool." I wrinkle my brows.

"Yeah, until she wasn't." Sadie looks at me, and I let out a deep sigh.

I was company and someone to keep her warm at night. I hate to say it, but that's all I ever was. Oh, and that pressure that one day I'd be a real MLB hotshot. To her, I was a potential celebrity with a wealthy future.

"So who's that on your profile?" Sadie leans over to see my screen.

"It's Trish. We just started following each other." I unlock my screen and show Sadie her account.

"Wait. You won't follow *me* on Sprinkle, but you follow her? She's one of the five people you actually follow back?" Sadie holds the phone close and scrolls through Trish's posts.

"Technically, I followed her first on my professional account. Then later I friended her with my personal account." I watch Sadie, smiling at some of my favorite posts of Trish's that I've already spent way too long looking at. "Besides, I told you not to get a Sprinkle account until college. No way can you see what's on my pro page." I keep my voice down so only she can hear.

"You're just as bad as they are." Sadie tilts her head to Ma, wrapped up in a kiss hello from Pa.

"Hey, Sport." Pa reaches around to give me a side hug before he takes a seat next to Ma. He's sitting with us? Why does he have time? Even if the place is all but empty, I'm sure he has a million things to do in the back. I remember him always running about and never getting much of a break. An uneasiness sits in the pit of my stomach as I watch Ma and Sadie to see if they give me any explanation.

Something's up. The only meals I've ever eaten with my father are Thanksgiving and Christmas. Even then, sometimes he'd get called into work and have to leave early.

"How's the sauce tonight?" He looks at my plate. None of them tell me what's going on, and it's grating on my last nerve. But I'm not here for me, I'm here for Sadie, and I've got a feeling that whatever they shoulda already told me can't be good. It can wait until after the game.

"Good." I nod.

"Zac's got a new girl." Sadie teases.

"I do not." I shove my phone into my pocket.

For the next few minutes, we eat dinner as a family. It's like living something I always wanted but never got to have.

"You got a minute, boss?" Marco comes over to the table. "We've got a problem with the delivery."

Knew it was too good to be true.

"I'll try to make it to the end of the game." Pa kisses Sadie on the forehead and waves goodbye before rushing into the kitchen. I take a breath. Maybe this is just anxiety. I swear the worst part is not knowing when something is *really* wrong and when it just seems like it.

I look around for some clues. The restaurant isn't as busy as it needs to be, that is factual evidence. My folks were barely making ends meet when I lived at home. This can't be good for their pocketbooks. Wish I could do more to help.

Why is it that life is *always* hard?

We finish our meal and head over to the school gym.

"Dude, good to see ya." Mitch sits next to us on the bleachers just as Miranda spikes the ball to the ground and the crowd erupts in cheers. Miranda used to be Sadie's best friend. I wonder if they're still close or if she turned on her too. I should ask.

"Hey!" I give him a fist bump. "How's it going?"

"They're looking good out there." Mitch glances at the volleyball team. Sadie's on the bench. Alone. Several feet between her and the other girls. It's like she's contagious and none of them wanna get close.

"Why aren't they putting her in?" I lean next to Ma and keep my voice at a whisper.

"I told you." Ma's eyebrows raise. It takes me a second, but I realize that no one's sitting near us, either. Miranda's family always sits by us. So do several of the other girls' parents.

But they aren't here. I hoped they were running late or something. But as I look around the room, it's clear as day. They've formed their own circle away from us. My folks used to be pretty popular. Even though the stands are crowded, it's like no one wants to get too close.

I hope that's not why Pa's restaurant had a lot of empty tables. Come to think of it, I always used to see Miranda's family there before a game. Guess I don't need to ask anymore. Everyone's turned on Sadie. Even her best friend.

A knot forms in my stomach and my worst fears start circling. What if Sadie's not safe? I mean, it's one thing not to like a person. But what if some of the people here actually hate her? What if this costs Pa's business more than they can afford.

Would they tell me?

"You mean Coach Dixon won't even let her play? That's ridiculous. She's a star player. He's asking to lose the game." My molars grate on one another, so much anger riddling my system as I put two-and-two together.

"This town is small and full of well meaning people, Zac. People who think they're doing us a favor. Like it'll bring us closer to God if they show us how unholy it is for her to be attracted to women." Ma's voice is quiet, but the message is so loud it makes my ears ring.

My eyes start spazzing out like I can't focus on the room around us. My hands tremble. My heart rattles against my chest like it's trying to break free.

"They can't do this." My throat burns, and I wanna go down on the court and give that coach a piece of my mind. But it won't help.

"They can, and they are." Ma looks at her shoes.

"It ain't right." I mutter under my breath.

"No, it ain't." Mitch shakes his head.

I've never felt so utterly helpless in my life. I'll have to think of something I can do.

Please, Father in Heaven, help me know what to do.

November

Zac

The semester is flying by. Trish and I have been messaging almost nonstop. It's so easy to talk to her. Doesn't even matter what it's about. We've got a running joke of who can find the most unique bottles of creamer to send pics of. She went to Whole Foods and sent pics of almond creamer. I went to Quickies Grocery and took pics of the cookies and cream flavor. She sent me a pic of her pouring a bottle of Gustafson Farm Chocolate Milk into her coffee. I convinced Bobby to take a pic of the giant bottles of creamer when he went to Costco.

Every time a new creamer related photo comes through my phone, I end up smiling or even laughing out loud. Who knows, maybe this *could* be something.

While we're waiting for team photos, I make plans with Bobby and Mickey tomorrow. Ethan and I were supposed to shoot content for our personal accounts tonight but he's not feeling good. We don't do anything above PG-13 level together–some of our fans like topless baseball guys talking shit on videos. Ethan's also good at holding the camera when I wanna get a bigger picture than is easy to get from propping my phone up.

I'll have to find time to make the content myself so I don't wait too long between posts and have my views tank again. Test tomorrow, paper due Monday…there's so much going on.

I wait behind Dennis as we shuffle toward the gym. Out of the corner of my eye, I see Bobby almost fall over and Briar steadying him. What the fuck? Something's wrong. My heart beats hard in my chest. What's messing him up?

"You alright, man?" Briar holds Bobby's elbow.

Bobby hesitates to answer, and I watch closer. The training room isn't far. I can go get Mindy.

"Just stood up too fast." Bobby shrugs. "Thanks."

"You sure you're okay?" Briar says to him, and I look away so they don't see me staring. Bobby wouldn't want that.

I take a breath, suddenly realizing that I haven't since Bobby stumbled.

Fuck, Bobby, you need someone to help you if you're falling over just from standing up.

Since we have that test, I offered to host my study group.

"Ready?" Harvey waits outside my apartment with Samantha and Krystal.

"Yep." I welcome them inside.

"Did you get the notes from yesterday?" Harvey plops down on my couch while I bring over two chairs from the kitchen table.

"Yep." I grab my backpack and pull out my notebook. "Y'all want drinks? There's soda in the fridge, water. Make yourselves at home."

"I brought the study guide so let's just review what's gonna be on the test?" Samantha's the type of person who's always running the show. Leader and overachiever all the way.

Valerie's face pops in my head abruptly, like one of those jack-in-the-box toys. Disruptive and disturbing.

Maybe I shoulda just told you a long time ago. Maybe you just shoulda been the type of person I could be honest with.

Not that I want to victim shame her. It's just her family is all high class and such. They frown upon porn. Well, and mine isn't even up-standing porn–if there's a such thing. I do kinky shit and that makes it somehow seem worse.

Her family would never approve. I know so because Valerie always condemned it when I did try to tell her. One time, when I thought it'd be good to talk to her about this, I pulled up some sexy videos. Told her it could help spice things up for us. She shot it down pretty quick, preaching to me about how trashy it was. Guess that's when I decided it was better not to push the subject. How it was okay I was cock deep in her center every day, but watching porn isn't, I'll never understand.

"Earth to Zac." Samantha snaps her fingers in front of my face, and I catch a whiff of her fruity perfume.

"Sorry, it's been a long day." I shake out of this haze. I've always been bad about zoning out unless I'm on the field. That's a big part of why I love playing. It's important for me to have some focused time in my cleats.

"Well, should we go over the study guide?" Samantha pulls her pencil out and starts doodling in the corner of her notebook.

Wait. It's Thursday. I try to remember if Valerie was coming by today or tomorrow for the rest of her stuff. It's been so busy my days are all running together. It'd be better if I didn't have everyone here when she comes by.

I finally texted her when I kept finding things of hers. Maybe once all that's gone, I'll stop thinking about her and can get a real fresh start.

"You have a nice place." Samantha notices.

"Thanks."

We're halfway through the notes and everyone's talking about all kinds of random shit.

"I gotta get ready for work." Harvey stands, offering a hand up for Krystal. "Thanks for the study sesh."

"Do you mind if I stay?" Samantaha's really worried about this test.

"Please." I give her a smile. It'd help me to keep reviewing a little bit more.

I walk Harvey and Krystal out. After he helps Krystal into his truck, he hangs back to talk to me. "Well, Samantha is definitely crushing on you." He elbows me in the ribs. "Lemme know if she stays over."

"Would everyone stop trying to tell me to move on?" I shake my head. "When you broke up with Mary you wallowed for a whole seven months before you asked out Krystal. That means I've still got six more months before I need to think about it."

"Dude. Mary was my forever. I never heard you say that about Valerie. Ever." He's got a point.

"Mary clearly *wasn't* your forever. Besides, you say that about everyone. Has there ever been a girl you didn't say *I love you* to after your second date?"

"I didn't with Jess." He protests.

"Okay, well that's still like four girls you told that to right away. I move slower than you and so that really means I've got a year to think about moving on."

"You won't make it a year. Just sayin' Samantha is really loving your attention. Do something about it." He opens his truck door. "I gotta go. See you on the lake Saturday?"

"It's supposed to warm up by then?" I pull my hoodie tighter around my chest.

"Yep. Cold front will pass by Friday night." Harvey climbs in his truck.

"I'll be there." I walk back into my apartment and take a seat next to Samantha on the couch.

"Thanks for letting me stay." She smiles.

"Totally. I need all the help I can get. It's been so busy lately I've barely been able to focus in class." I lean back on the cushions.

"Aren't you in the off season right now?" She asks.

"Yeah, but I stay busy all the time. Guess it keeps my mind from having too much time to think." I shrug.

The door opens, and I think it's the wind. But then I see her.

Valerie.

My heart pounds as I swallow down how hard it is to see her again. Like the key to everything I locked inside, seeing her brings every feeling to the surface.

"Hey, um one sec." I jump up and get Valerie's boxes from my room and follow her to her car. It hurts everywhere. Seeing her represents all the rejection.

"You've already moved on, huh?" Her tone is ice cold.

"Oh, no, that's just study group." I readjust my hold on her boxes.

"You don't have to keep lying to me."

"I'm not. She's a study buddy. And I never meant to lie before." I set the boxes in her trunk. Perhaps my only regret is keeping it from her. "I'm sorry you found out the way you did and that I wasn't transparent when we were together." I give her the smile she used to love so much.

Her face softens a little bit. "You're a good guy, Zac. You're just not my guy." She hesitantly puts her arms around me. I grasp a bit of relief. We weren't it for each other, and that's okay.

"I think we both knew for a while this wasn't what we needed. I'm sorry I stormed out on you. And I do hope you can move on." She kisses my cheek and I'm thankful.

"You too. Really, I do." And I'm surprised to realize it's true. I want her to be happy. She has a lot of good things about her. We wouldn't have been together so long if I didn't care about her. There was plenty to justify us splitting up, but it wasn't all bad.

"You deserve to be happy, Val." I hesitate, then add, "...we both do." I know this isn't the kind of break that ends in friendship. We already did a good enough job fucking it up.

"Yeah, take care." She closes the door to the driver's seat.

I watch her go, glad that I can feel a touch of closure. When I go back to Samantha in my apartment, I'm lighter. This heavy weight of Valerie hating me is melting away.

I didn't know I needed this, but I did.

Now, it's like my heart can heal.

Maybe I won't need those twelve months after all.

Trish

I'm in Suncastle, visiting Lexie. We spent the afternoon decorating her beach house and are now at the best pizza place in town, The Splat.

"Well, look what the cat dragged in." I gape at the front door. Lexie's just told me she and Bobby are doing an awkward dance at flirting. He literally just showed up here, of all places, with his friends.

"It may just be your lucky night, my love." I raise one eyebrow toward the front door. "Must be fate or somethin'." I get all dramatic and shit. "It's my lucky night, too. Zac is with him." Goodness gracious. My eyes go wide, focusing from his shoes to his hair. Once over. Twice over. Thrice over. It oughta be illegal to be this good looking. He's been messaging me tons. I'm pretty shocked to see him. "Good thing I brought my big purse with all my hair stuff and a change of clothes." I wink.

Lexie all but loses consciousness with how hard it hits her that her man is standing at the door. Wow, the look in his eyes sends a shiver down my spine. Damn, I don't think a boy has ever looked at me like that. No wonder she's as confused as a badger in pajamas.

Has he always looked at her this way? Maybe he's wanted to be with her longer than any of us noticed.

Mickey's here, but man does he look like he's been dealing with life very well. I better make sure he's okay.

My gaze holds Zac's. His mouth curves in a smile. He remembers me. It's been a year and a half since I've seen him, and wow has that year changed *a lot*.

Please be single, please be single, please, Sweet Baby Jesus, let this boy be single.

One look at him has me tingly in all the right places. He's got this broad form of perfectly sculpted muscles. His hair is lush dark brown, getting long enough I'd call it shaggy. He's turned his attention back to Mickey now, those deep brown eyes focus intently on whatever he's yapping about.

He's wearing jeans and a button up that hugs every curve and every ridge. It's those nice kind of jeans. The kind that I don't see on guys very much because it means he actually knows his way around the mall. Dark eyebrows sit above deep set eyes with so much hope and life in them. A god among us.

Imagining what it'd be like to get him in a hotel tonight sends a zing from the tip of my panties to my nipples, getting hard beneath my bra.

There's electricity in my chest, hoping this will be one of the best fucks I've ever had.

I'm gonna go doll up.

Just in case.

Dreams don't come true on their own. You gotta make them happen.

I slip my purse on my shoulder and head into the grungy bathroom. Gotta love this college town with people who let the paper towels overflow in the garbage can. Disgusting. Have some respect for the people who work here. Jesus.

I take a minute to pick up the floor, mostly because I worked at a restaurant in high school and hated more than anything how many people just let their garbage fall all over the place. How hard is it to clean up after yourself?

Zac cleaned up the table at Shakey's. That conversation was so easy. So memorable. I've thought about it several times since. He was so good to me that day. Taking care of me when he didn't need to.

If Bobby walking in here to be with Lex is the stars aligning, maybe they're aligning for me and Zac to get reacquainted.

Done scrubbing my hands, I plug in my curling iron and get to work. I dig to the bottom of my purse and pull out my good makeup compact. Thank goodness I don't leave the house without it.

Zac looks so good tonight. That image of him standing by the menu board is etched forever in my mind. He looked good before. He looks amazing now. Damn, how did he get more chiseled than he was a few years ago? Looks like I'm not the only one chasing after my dreams. Call the MLB now. He's ready.

And well, I think I'm ready for tonight.

Hopefully Zac is too.

An angel just sat in front of me.

"Oh my gosh, you're here." I smile.

"Oh my gosh, *you're* here." She echos, a bewildered expression on her face.

"Look at you. You look amazing. Good to see ya." I grin so big my cheeks burn. "What's your name again?" I tease her as she gets settled in her chair.

"Trish." She plays along, offering me her hand for a handshake. A sweet vanilla scent fills my nose as I grasp her soft hand. We both chuckle, and I finally let go of her hand realizing I'm still holding it.

"This place has quite a lack of creamer." She laments.

"It really does. I mean, how're we supposed to enjoy pizza without a delicious amount?"

"I may have to run over to the 7-Eleven." Her pictures are stunning, but nothing compared to how breathtaking she is in real life. Wow, she looks incredible tonight. Her hair's a big grouping of light brown curls pinned up by some kind of hair clip that's a huge flower. Bright red lipstick.

All the confidence in the world.

So fucking hot.

"I may just have to come with you." My dick strains against my jeans.

Welp, that was quick. I'm usually one to take a bit before a girl really turns me on. Not Trish, apparently. The longer I sit here with this beauty, the less control I have over my cock.

Flying fish sticks, I wasn't expecting this. She's been occupying my thoughts for weeks while we've been messaging back and forth. It's so easy to talk to her. I've loved the back and forth. But I didn't know fate would bring us together like this.

She looked my way when we got to The Splat. Now she's sitting with me. I came with the right group of friends tonight.

I catch her spare glances. All flirt. All fun. All that I want.

My phone buzzes in my pocket.

Sadie: Gosh, can they just find something better to do? I'm not that interesting.

Me: Those girls being bitches again?

Sadie: They don't know how to be anything else. I'm not sure how much more school drama I can take.

Me: Jeez, I wish they'd stop.

An emotional rock lodges in my chest. She doesn't deserve any of this. Sadie is the nicest person in the world. Makes me furious at the thought of how much she's dealing with. The fact she's talking about it means it's more than something random.

I take a deep breath. It's eating me up that I'm not there. Sometimes I wish I could take a break from it all.

While we're in the middle of eating, Bobby leaves. Lexie follows.

Wait? Is something going on there? I think it's cute if they're gonna go out. I mean, they both were super close to Cody. I'm sure that helps to have a foundation to build upon.

I sip from my Sprite thinking about how I'll pull back on sugar soon while we double up on preseason training. Coach Conners is pretty strict, and I'm not quite ready to give up sweets, but committed to doing as I'm told. Each slow sip lingers on my tongue, remembering the taste for when I have to give it up.

Trish looks at Mickey for a while but he zones out again. She slurps from her glass until it's empty, then stands to get a refill.

"May I?" I stand just as quick, reaching for her glass. "Orange soda, right?"

"Observant, aren't you?"

"I try to notice what I can." I smile.

"Thanks." She brushes down her top, making it hug tighter around her boobs. Every curve of her body makes my mouth water. There's a guilty smile on her face, like she knows, and wants to make my body hot.

I want her to make me hotter.

Oh, shit.

What is happening to me?

She's gorgeous. Funny. Her Sprinkle profile is filled with fire. Our messages put a permanent smile on my face. She's not just some random person. She's someone I'd hate myself for *not* trying things with.

But I need to slow the fuck down. I'm so turned on, I could take her to the bathroom and fuck her to heaven on the countertop.

Get to know her, Zac.

There's two people ahead of me at the drink station. The ice machine hums as they fill up their cups.

My hands shake as I fill a quarter of the glass with ice and the rest with soda, watching the bubbles foam until I can fill it the rest of the way.

As I walk back to the table, she's licking her lips, pupils dark and dilated like she's ready to follow me into the bathroom and send us both to nirvana.

Drink in hand, I return to her.

"Thanks, Willey." She remembers my nickname.

Bobby and Lexie come back...together.

"We are studyin' for Myers' mid-term after this." Mickey waits until Lexie looks from Bobby to him. "You took his class, didn't you, Lexie?"

"Oh, yes, junior year." Before it's out of her mouth, she's already turning all her attention to Bobby. Something's definitely happening between the two of them.

"What do we need to know?" Mickey's basically seething.

"Myers mostly takes the exams from the slides. At least he did. I'm assuming that hasn't changed." Lexie reaches for Bobby's hands.

"Do you have your old tests?" Mickey taps the table, like he's trying to get her attention.

"Yeah." She startles from the tapping and nods at Mickey.

"Can we come grab them?" Mickey's looking like a kettle about to blow from all the steam.

"Sure." Lexie makes it sound like he asked her for a kidney.

"Those two." Trish shakes her head, and I try to get a read on what she's ticked about. "Here I go, dropping everything in my schedule to come down for the weekend. Welp. Guess I better just go."

Lexie puts her finger to her lip to shush her. "I thought you were happy for me." She frustratedly whispers.

"Of course I'm happy for you. I just don't know what to do if Bobby's taking you home." Trish whispers back.

Bobby's cheeks turn real red. "I'm not getting in the way of you two." He holds his hands up like he's surrendering.

"No, you're not." Lexie's tone is sweet as she reaches across the table to hold Bobby's hand. "Trish understands, don't you Trish?" She barely turns her eyes away, locked on Bobby, like there's something magical going on there.

"I'm just giving y'all shit." Trish picks up the table, wiping away the crumbs and gathering up all the trash. Reminds me of when we went to Shakey's after

Cody's funeral. She drops a ten under her orange soda glass. I put two fives next to it and wink.

"I still have your hoodie." She chuckles.

"No way." I remembered giving it to her but wasn't holding my breath to ever see it again. Part of me loves that she's kept it all this time.

"You know, I think about that day sometimes. Was so kind of you to take care of me." Her smile is genuine and it makes me feel warm despite the cold air blowing through the open restaurant door.

She's a fucking siren.

"I do too." A similar feeling spreads through my stomach, like when I got the call from Coach Conners and he promised me game time as a freshman if I took the risk of playing for Suncastle. Despite how much I wish I was home for Sadie's sake, I know this was the right move for me. It was a golden opportunity that I'll never regret taking.

"Those dimples of yours." She pops a piece of gum in her mouth and offers one to me.

"Thanks." I chew the Bubble Yum. Been a while since I've had this kind. "You know, we never did get to hear your jukebox song."

"Eh, it was just *Bohemian Rhapsody* by Queen."

"You like that song?"

"I just figured maybe I'd get to talk to you more. It's pretty long." She shakes her head. "It didn't even matter that I rushed outta there. You coulda given me shit for that. Instead you were kinda like my knight in shining armor."

"Well, I am a Suncastle Knight, so that's the same thing right?" My comment earns a sincere smile and I get a little dizzy in her gaze.

"You definitely take pride in that. Good thing I had you that day."

"It might've been more than one day. Too bad you were taken." I hold her eyes, wondering how she'll respond. She's been acting like she's available, but I've been wrong before.

"Taken?" She wrinkles her brow. "Oh, I wasn't...." She does an actual facepalm. "Jimmy? You thought Jimmy was my boyfriend?"

"He…wasn't?" I swallow back my shock.

"No, I mean we were high school sweethearts, I guess. But that's been over for a long time."

I can't help but feel a sourness in my gut, regretting eating all that pizza as I ruminate on how I could've asked her out.

Is now our second chance?

"Ready?" Trish reaches her hand out to me. The feel of her skin on mine is soft and tingles work through me as she pulls me toward the door. "It's not hard to get to Lexie's place, just follow me."

"I'd love to." I hold her eyes and I feel like we're having one of those little movie moments where you have a really good connection with someone. Like you've known them forever.

"I'll tell him how to get there." Bobby teases Trish for pointing out the obvious.

"Ride with us?" Lexie raises up on her toes, gripping Bobby's collar.

"Alright, baby." He kisses her nose. *Baby?* Yeah, something's definitely changed. I don't think I've ever heard Bobby say *baby* to anyone.

"I'm gonna throw up." Mickey shakes his head. "Get a room," he mumbles as he sulks toward my truck, shoulders hunched, kicking the curb as he steps onto the asphalt.

"Like I said, just follow me and you won't get too lost." Trish blows a bubble with her bubble gum. The image is like one I'd expect to see in a magazine. Cold dark concrete. Girl in a tight black shirt and matching miniskirt with a long pink cardigan. Bright pink bubble gum bubble framed by her vibrant lip color.

I want to take a picture for my social media accounts. Streetlights. Red lipstick. Pink bubblegum bubble. Perfection.

Will you share any bit of this perfection with me, Trish?

Cheesy rice and chicken. Did Mickey drop some mystery pills in my Sprite? I'm not thinking like I normally do.

"Were you even listening?" Trish chuckles and I swear she *is* an angel from

Heaven. Soft blonde curls. Rosy cheeks. Streetlights giving her gentle glow. "Follow me and you won't get lost, Willey." She winks and I feel my jeans get tight again.

I will not survive tonight. I will not. I'm already dead and buried inside of whatever hypnotics this woman's exuding onto me.

"Don't. Get. Lost." She wiggles her adorable little nose. "I'll not lead you anywhere you don't wanna go." Another perfect bubble forms from her mouth like she's the holder of the Guinness Book of World Records for the best bubblegum bubble ever blown.

"Is that wishful thinking or–" I imagine what it would be like to pop her bubble with my teeth, take it onto my tongue and make her fight me to get it back in her mouth.

If I was half-stiff before, I now have a raging hard-on like my cock is trying his best to get closer to her.

"It's a promise." She smacks the bubblegum back into her mouth, and I know I want her to do that same motion to my cock.

Luckily Mickey is glued to his phone and Bobby and Lexie seem to be in their own blissful world so no one's noticing me and Trish all but eye-fucking in this parking lot.

I'm standing here praying my boner down, thankful it's dark out, wondering if it's a good idea or not for her to know *exactly* how entranced I am.

Fuck, too deep. Too fucking deep.

Take me deep, baby.

I watch those eyes of hers as they keep on mesmerizing me. She's magical. Desirable. A fucking goddess. "Oh, a promise, huh?"

"And I don't make those very often, so you better feel special." She bites her lip and my heart races, ready and wanting every promise she can make.

"Oh, I do." *...feel very special getting so much of your attention, little miss.*

Mouth as hot as astroturf in the summer, I watch her go to her car. My thoughts are conjuring up all kinds of daydreams as my truck follows her car the whole way to the beach house.

"So you guys have been going to the same school since junior high?" I ask Mickey as I put the truck in park, but he's ignoring me. Or he's in a daze.

It's been a long time since I've been here, but it looks different.

"Nice place." I kick the dirt off my shoes on the entry rug.

"I've been helpin' Lexie redecorate. Seems you like my taste." Trish stands beside me, and I take in the cute decorations.

"Oh, I do." I lean in a little closer and say against her ear.

"Let's not crowd the kitchen." Trish takes my hand and pulls me into the living room. Her fingers are warm and soft and fit in my hand like a ball in my mitt. She flops on the fluffy white couch. "I was gonna stay the weekend, but it looks like Lexie has plans." She glances at Bobby standing in the hallway.

"Does that bug you?" My heartrate's gotta be high. I slip two fingers into the gap of my wrist, feeling for a pulse to calm my nerves before they take over. I find the steady beat of my heart in a good rhythm *instead* of the chaotic pounding.

"Not really. I'll make my own arrangements." She winks.

My cheeks scrunch up with how big I'm smiling. "I doubt you'll have any trouble finding a place to stay." It's just short of an invitation and she clues into it with all the hope reflecting in my eyes.

I know I wasn't this smooth with other girls. With Trish, I'm calm–so calm it shocks me.

The beat hitting my fingertips is slow and steady. Comfortable.

"Oh, can you help me bring some stuff in from my car?" Trish asks. "Lex and I went shopping earlier."

"I'd love to." I smile and we walk to her car. The bags aren't too heavy, but I'm glad she invited me to help.

When we get back inside, she gives the room a whole makeover in a matter of minutes. I'm quite impressed. If she wasn't already cute enough, watching her take such pride in a task like this makes her even more irresistible.

"You like decoratin'?" I stand next to her, amazed that she's able to make it look so much better with just a few adjustments. "Because this looks like it's been done by a pro."

"I like to make things fit just right." She shifts some more stuff around.

Just when I'm about to ask why, footsteps head into the living room to join us.

"Let's go to Garrison's. Claudia's gonna meet us there." Mickey says.

"Then why'd we come here?" I ask.

"Because we need the notes. Now I need to go see Claudia." Mickey zips up his hoodie.

"I'll go see if Lex and Bobby wanna come." Trish heads for the hallway. The moment she leaves the room, I feel it. I'm already starved for her presence.

Lord help me, this is the biggest crush I've ever had.

Trish

Trying to keep my worries in check, I go to find Lexie. I'm so worried about her jumping into something with Bobby when he's always been such a player and he's clearly not over Cody's death. Her tender heart won't handle it well.

Mom and Dipshit got together when they were both going through tons of shit. Most of the time people are too selfish to do anything besides drain each other dry.

At the doorway to the spare room, I see Lexie with Bobby.

"Oh." I gasp, pretty sure Bobby's tongue is down her throat. Guess they figured something out. He's gripping her body tight to his, like it'd smush anything that tried to get between them. Her breathing is fast and almost moaning, like she's having the best kiss of her life. I blink over and over, wishing I could wash out my eyeballs. I don't want to watch a porno starring my best friend. Ever.

"Didn't mean to interrupt." I clear my throat.

Bobby steps back from Lex and shoves his hands deep in his pockets, his cheeks turning red.

"Mickey says a bunch of us are going over to Garrison's." I try to act cool, but my heart's pounding.

"What happened to studyin'?" Lexie turns to me.

"Some girl texted him, and he's gonna meet her there." I shrug. "It'll be fun. You deserve a night out. Wanna come?"

"Oh, um no." Lexie rocks from her heels to her toes, glancing up at Bobby.

"You can go," Bobby stutters over his words. "We can go." He corrects in a hurry. "Whatever you wanna do."

"Maybe next time." Lexie smiles and her cheeks are the bright red color of her hair. I leave the room rubbing my forehead. What did I just see? My God. They couldn't even wait until we weren't here.

I lean against the hallway wall until they come out.

"Give us a sec?" I nod toward Lexie and give a stern look to B.

"Sure," he heads toward the living room.

I pull Lexie into the hall bathroom to have a chat without everyone listening. "You sure you're gonna be okay?"

"It's just Bobby." She gives me an incredulous look. "Why wouldn't I be?"

"It is just Bobby...who's a player. Who, I cannot tell if he wants to sleep with you and never speak to you again *or* actually wants something more based on his actions tonight." I huff.

"Look, he's grieving." Lexie pulls Bobby's hoodie tighter around her as she shivers. Reminds me of when Zac gave me his hoodie.

"I can see why Bobby's acting weird. Give him some time, okay?" Lexie pleads.

"It's been almost two years." My words come out colder than they should.

"You don't have to remind me of that." Her eyes gloss over.

"I'm sorry." I lean against the marble countered vanity. "I'm worried, okay? If you're both in a really dark place, I'm not sure it's a good idea to be turning to one another."

"I'll be okay." Lexie brings me in for a hug. "Let us figure this out. Plus, if I stay here you can focus on Zac. He looks like he's ready to hit a home run with that bat he's been carrying around all night." She opens the bathroom door, and we walk into the hallway.

"Oh, it's a grand slam waiting to happen. Did I tell you we've been messaging?"

"You and Zac?"

"Yeah. It's been this random obsession with creamer." I pull out my phone and show her the message history.

"That's too cute. See. Y'all will have a great time." Lexie smiles as we head toward the guys.

"Ready?" I glance at Mickey eating spoonfuls of hot brownies, fresh out of the oven.

"Yep." Zac shoves his hands in his pocket for his keys.

"How about you ride with us? It's easier that way." I offer.

"I'll go anywhere you wanna go," he smiles.

Zac is the one good thing about this night. I swear I wanna murder my friends. They're all acting batshit crazy. Mickey making spontaneous brownies and ditching. Bobby and Lexie making out in the back room.

I want to climb all over Zac right now too, but I'm not. I can wait for a few hours until we're alone. They could at least wait a few minutes. Jesus. Are they just sex-starved teenagers or what?

Everyone climbs in my car, and before too long we're at the best underage college bar in town.

Garrison's is on the corner of town, in an alley between two old strip malls and in a place that doesn't have good paving. I park in the lot, surprised there's a space available on the far side of the building. Posters announcing Country Night shine in the displays while we wait to get in.

We lived here freshman year, so much I should've paid Garrison's rent instead of the dorms. All of us hanging out here every night of the week, even when we had finals to study for. My throat burns as I remember how much Mama and Dipshit were let down by my choices. Coming to Garrison's was everything Mama taught me not to do and Dipshit said made me a stupid disappointment.

I loved every second of it.

We climb out of the car and, before I know it, Mickey's ditching us for whoever this *Claudia* character is.

"You wanna get a table?" Zac's looking around after we pay the entry fee.

"How about over there?" I tilt my head to the dozens of tall tables with bar stools.

"Sounds great." He flashes that smile, and wow, is he beautiful in this light. In every light?

What about in the shadow of my darkness? Can he handle that?

"Oh, hey, Zac." A waitress comes over, obviously recognizing him. "Y'all need a minute to order?"

"I'm ready." I start unzipping my wallet. "Strawberry margarita, please."

"Jack and Coke. I've got hers," Zac hands his credit card to the waitress.

"I'll get those started." She nods.

"Thank you." I linger in Zac's smile before I look around the familiar room. College days dance through my memory like the couples country swing dancing on the floor. Getting drunk and nursing the hangovers through class. This was our sanctuary.

"You graduated from Suncastle?" Zac asks. "Right after Cody's funeral?"

"Yep. Well I didn't actually walk for graduation. I just had them mail me the diploma since Nana was moving around that time. It was all pretty hectic. Finish exams, get a job, help Nana get settled."

"That sounds hella busy."

"Yeah. I think I saw you a couple times around campus before then though. Or at the games." I scratch my head, wondering if I would've seen him outside of baseball.

"So are you Bobby's age then?"

Oh. The age question. I'll play it off easy.

"He's the oldest out of our group." I lick my lips, glancing in the mirror hanging on the wall, making my red lipstick shine in the lowlights of the bar. "I'm the youngest." I raise my eyebrows, watching for his reaction. "Age is just a mindset, anyway." I lean toward him, "right?"

"Here I was thinking it was how many days we've been alive." He gives me a smug smile.

"You knew what I meant." I shake my head.

"Yeah." He gives me a smug smile. "I'm the oldest in my group of friends."

"So how old are you?"

"I thought it was just a mindset." He teases.

"My mindset and actual age is twenty-two."

He smiles. "My mindset and actual age is twenty-one."

"So we're like a year apart?"

"Guess so."

I think for a moment about what we haven't messaged about yet.

"What are you studyin'? You and Mickey have the same class. Same major?" I glance at the menu, then set it down under my crisscrossed hands because I know the menu by heart. It never changes. Full bar with lots of cheap drinks and appetizers that aren't half bad.

"Computer Science." He nods.

"Computer Science? Why you taking Myers' class then? Doesn't he only teach phys ed type stuff?"

"I had a spot in my schedule, and it was close to the athletic building." Zac makes an adorable face while he looks up at the ceiling.

"Fair enough." I chuckle.

"And what about you, Trish?" He raises those thick brows.

"Got an Art History degree. After working at the mall, I started building my client base. Now I work full-time freelance as a photographer." Mentioning work sets off reminders of all the unfinished things on my to do list. I've got twelve open editing projects that need to go in for orders or the prints won't arrive on time. It's a lot to keep up with.

The entire reason I came to Suncastle was to help Lexie. And who knows? Maybe redecorating helped her let go so she can move on. I just hope she's moving on in the right way.

"No way," he gasps. "You seriously built a whole business in a year?"

"Guilty." I shrug. "I mean Willardson is a small town and there's not a lot of photographers there. I got lucky with a lot of business."

"Can I see your work?" His eyes light up in genuine interest.

"Oh, it's nothin' much." I'm a master at deflecting.

The waitress brings our drinks and I spit my gum into a napkin, offering it to him to do the same.

"Thanks. And I wanna see," he takes a sip of his Jack and Coke. "Please?" He says the word slow, and it tickles the parts beneath my skirt, imagining how much I'd love to see him beg me for pleasure.

Our eyes hold tight while I debate how much to give. Guess I might care about this one's feelings a bit. Uh oh. My heart beats a little faster in my chest. Maybe I'm just over sensitive because of the Lexie and Bobby crap with Mickey as the cherry on top. Too much emotion rolling through the rooms tonight. Zac's fun and cute and I'm all about casual.

"Alright, I guess." I pull up my phone and scroll through the recent shoot previews.

"Oh, wow," he meanders through them, taking his time with each one. "These are really good."

"Eh, they still need editing." I lean a little closer to see where he's at. He's only gone through a handful, like he needs to go slow so he won't miss anything.

"Well, even without edits these are really good. Do you have a website?"

"Not yet. I've been busy just with word of mouth." I gently take my phone, stopping his scrolling, and stuff it back in my purse before he finds my latest nudes. Not that I'd mind. Maybe I should pull them up for him. I always photo edit the shit out of them anyway.

"I need to get a website, but the thought is overwhelming. It's one of those things where it's gonna be a lot of work to set up but would probably make my life easier. If my clients could just schedule appointments online, it'd save me so much time trying to coordinate everybody's schedule. And if I had a billing system that would just be so much easier. You know, like a client portal website." That drowning feeling that always comes when I can't get my mind off my work deadlines flows through me like I'm underwater.

Dammit. I'm sitting across the table from a guy that I'm really into, and all I can think about are the projects piled up back home. So freaking frustrating. Wish I was better at leaving work at work.

"I could hire someone to do my website, but the thought of giving so much money to someone when I *could* learn it myself is hard." I get this insane level of self sufficiency from Mama and Dipshit. They've always been forcing me to overachieve and yet I'm somehow still not good enough.

Most people, especially with how much I bring in, would hire a developer without a second thought. Maybe one day I'll give myself permission.

"I'm pretty good at websites if you ever want me to take a look." Zac saves me from my tunnel of self loathing, a welcome distraction from the place I hate going mentally. It's really kind of him to offer. I should let someone help me. Why not him?

"I may just take you up on that." I sip my margarita, the sweet strawberry offsetting the burn in my throat with how nice it was for him to offer. He genuinely seems like he wants to help.

"Yeah, I'd love to. It's good experience for me, anyway." He's implying he isn't planning to charge me. Seriously? Now that he's offered, I'm feeling a lot better. My to-do list is so piled high, having the website taken care of will be a huge relief. Like he threw me a raft, and I'm not drowning underwater anymore.

"But I think it'd be something good for me to learn how to do on my own." The deflection comes naturally, before I mean to say it.

"Can I teach you?" He runs his hand down the condensation of his glass. "I mean, I'd be happy to show you some stuff. I can tell you're brilliant and I swear it's not hard to learn."

"I'm brilliant?" I raise my eyebrows.

"You'd have to be in order to start an entire freelance photography business on your own and get it off the ground in a year."

"I told you I was lucky."

"That's not just luck, Trish. I do my own kind of freelance work and it's all uphill to build and maintain clients. I'm in awe. You're doing so well. There may be some luck involved, but it's mostly brilliance."

Warmth spreads through me, not from the alcohol. This is something else. It's like he knows what I need.

No, that's silly. He's good at talking. Time will tell if he means any bit of this.

Lots of men lie and use words to get what they want.

My back burns as I absently rub scars under my top that I wish weren't there. Breath lingers in my lungs, as the faint smell of someone smoking weed at a table nearby drifts in my nostrils. It reminds me of all the drugs Dipshit smoked while pretending I was his ashtray.

I won't think about Dipshit right now. He doesn't deserve any more of my thoughts.

Grasping for something to change the subject, I exhale.

"So tell me about your program. Is it good? Just kinda a get through school until the draft sort of thing, or?" Focus on him. I'm here, in the moment. And I want to be. This moment is quite fabulous.

The past me into its vortex.

Zac's folding a straw wrapper like an accordion, thinking about my question.

Focus on the now, Trish. Keep going. Keep moving. Get through this.

I'm stronger than what happened to me. Control is mine.

I love that Zac *wants* to sit with me. That he offered for us to get a table together. That he's buying my drink. We just got pizza, but I could eat tons. With all the running around I do from one photo shoot to another, I feel like I constantly need to refuel.

There we go. Don't be pulled into the past. Stay in the present.

"It's definitely something I can do after baseball." He sets the wrapper down now that it's formed into a rose. "I mean if baseball happens."

"Oh? Holding out for the draft then?" I shimmy my shoulders, adding enough excited inflection to my voice to earn a smile.

"Potentially, if all goes well this season. No guarantees though. I mean, I'm not Bobby." There's an insecurity in his tone that's adorably sweet.

That's a first. I usually go for more of the drunk asshole type. Why? Because I was mostly raised by one. I'm barely getting to know him, but Zac already feels so different. It's like he's treating me like *I'm* worthwhile.

"No one's Bobby." I chuckle. "Funny thing is he doesn't think much of himself, either."

"He's takin' like twenty credit hours this semester or some shit." Zac's expression reminds me of someone giving a good scolding to a child.

My jaw drops. No wonder he hasn't made time for Lexie.

"I'm spread thin, and I'm only taking sixteen credit hours." He shakes his head.

Our waitress returns, and I order a tray of wings and another round for both of us.

"You wanna keep this on your tab?" She asks Zac.

"I got it–" I pull my card out of my wallet and go to hand it to her.

"Keep it on mine," he nods at the waitress.

"Oh, you don't have to. My round." I object.

"I'd like to. If that's alright?" His smile tells me he's not *really* going to back down even if I fight him on it. Apparently he *wants* to take care of me.

This is so goddamn refreshing. Most flavor-of-the-weeks make a huge ass deal about who's paying for what. I'm fine with splitting checks, but when they're obsessed with it nothing turns me off more.

"You're a little old fashioned then?" I fold my arms on the wooden table.

"I wanna make sure you have everythin' you want." He winks.

Fire runs between my legs all the way up to my heart. I swear I just lost all ability to see straight.

That.

Wink.

Will.

Kill.

Me.

Indulging in the fluttering feeling building in my chest, I clench up all my places riding into a mini orgasm. Fuck. He's so damn hot. And nice? Usually *the twain shall never meet.* Just like Nana says.

"Lots of your friends still live in Willardson?" He leans toward me, to hear over the music.

"Oh yeah. Lots of people live and die in Willardson without setting foot out for long." Our knees brush as I match his body language. More sizzles light up my insides as I ride the wave of desire.

He smiles like he knows exactly what he's doing to me. "A lot of my friends stayed back home, too."

I sip my strawberry margarita, thankful for the heavy pourer tonight. "I could tell your accent wasn't from here."

"Nah, I'm from out of state. But Ma seems to think I've been here too long and am losin' my drawl."

"Well you just need to hang out with us Willardson folk more, we'll bring it right out."

"I'd like that." His line has a lot of intention. The heat rising through my core intensifies. Eye contact lingers for several beats, his body leaning toward me until our faces almost touch. I scan over his features. Almond eyes, a beautiful shade of brown beneath thick brows. A smile with dimples on both sides. Kissable lips in the most full shape. Tingles flicker against my panties. I welcome them, arousal blooming in my chest the longer I stare into that gorgeous gaze of his.

Clenching muscles make my vision blur. Another mini orgasm leaves an ache so painful I long to be indulged. The way he's flirting with me is swarming my insides with anticipation.

I want him, as soon as possible. Could go out to the car right now.

No, I want something classier.

He's not just a back of the car hookup.

More. I want more with him. Something memorable. Something to relive over and over on my more lonely nights.

Or do I want even more than that?

I shiver, suddenly cold. I *want* something with the guy sitting in front of me? An electric bolt goes down my spine, like a bucket of water dousing the sexy flames I was enjoying.

Damn it, Trish. Don't do this to yourself again. You always get burned when you go down this path. You don't know this kid and Lord knows guys are always smooth when there's something they want. You know better than to even hope you'd be lucky enough to meet someone who wants to bring you home to their mama. Just have fun and walk away. You know the drill.

Our waitress sets wings on the table, and I dive in. Zac grabs one, waiting on me to lather mine up with ranch before he does the same.

"I definitely don't want a relationship." I want to make this clear as day.

"Me neither, just got out of one." Zac's shoulders relax, like he's feeling the Jack and Coke.

"I don't have time for anything. Casual is a must."

"What is it with relationships taking so much time?" Zac shakes his head, that defined jaw showcasing a bit of scruff. Damn, he's nice looking close up.

"A lot of relationships are just controlling." I take a drink.

"My last girlfriend, in a word." He downs half his drink, and I sense he's far from over whatever happened. His broken heart is written on his face.

"You wanna talk about it?" I bite my tongue.

"No, I honestly wanna stop thinking about her." He shakes his head.

I raise my glass and he lifts his to touch mine with a clink. "Good riddance."

"Good riddance." He takes a long drink. "So you take a lot of pictures. What else you do?"

"Like I was saying before, I've got more clients than I can really handle. Honestly, I like it that way. I enjoy being busy. Really, I'm a workaholic."

"Workaholic? Like a total workaholic or like a moderate one?"

"Total. Definitely."

"We'll get along then. I feel like I never slow down."

"I know this feeling so well." I stir my drink. "But yeah I take photos and edit and advertise. I've gotten some of my prints into local art shows a time or two. The combination seems to be working out." I bite into another wing.

"The combination *definitely* seems to be workin' out." His mischievous grin makes my body clench down under, all that fire returning. I need to feel him. There's an urgent rush flowing through me.

"You wanna get lost?" I give him a coy smile.

"I think I already am." He does that lean-in-closer thing that he keeps doing and my breath catches in my lungs.

Already lost?

Sweet Baby Jesus, this man is smoother than a bowl of Nana's banana pudding. No doubt he's on board for a quick fuck at the hotel down the road.

"You wanna dance first?" He offers his hand, shocking me that he's not in as much of a rush to fuck into eternity as I am. It's something that would normally annoy me. But something about it feels respectful, almost. Like this isn't just about where we end up at the end of the night, but about all the steps in between, for once.

"Dance?" I look down at my platform heels. They're one of my more comfortable pairs.

"We're at a dance club, aren't we?" He looks at the couples covering the floor with a sparkle in his eye.

"We are, and I'd like that." I mimic the way he said that earlier, and he smiles, catching what I'm sending. If we're this in sync after a few moments together, I can't imagine how explosive we're gonna be under the sheets.

"I'm up on stage a lot, but I like to be on the floor." His hand takes mine. Warm and safe, like a million things I didn't know I needed. I pull my purse onto my shoulder, not willing to leave it.

"You're on stage a lot? Last time I checked, baseball is played on a field." But then I remember Briar teasing him about playing guitar in coffee shops when we went to Shakey's after Cody's funeral. "That's right, I'll have to hear you play one of these days." My hand enjoys the feel of his, holding it just right.

"I'd like that."

We get to the crowded floor where he woos me with all sorts of country swing moves I wasn't expecting. I keep putting my purse strap back on my shoulder in between songs.

"Can I hold it?" He looks at my bag.

"Oh, yeah, thanks." I hand it to him and he secures it on his shoulder like he doesn't mind holding it for me.

What a gentleman.

He's spinning me, twirling me, sliding me under his legs. People make a small circle around us. And man, can we move. I've never felt this synchronized with a guy before.

At the end of the song, we pause to catch our breath.

"So you're a hell of a baseball player, a crazy good dancer, and yet somehow still passing junior year of college? How do you have time to perform?"

"It's a little band. Nothing much. But yeah we play here sometimes. My last girlfriend wasn't into the atmosphere, so we never came to dance." His cheeks flush. "Sorry, I keep bringing her up." He looks down at the floor.

I take my hand and tilt his chin up. "I get it, I promise." And I do. I'm not sure how, but it doesn't bother me that he's bringing her up.

"Thanks." Zac draws me near, the music melting into the song "She's Everything" by Brad Paisley. We go into a two-step.

The world stands still and silent, yet there's some part of me still moving closer to him. My soul is stretching out to mix with his. We're paint running together, never to be separated again.

What an idiot that other girl was to let him go. I want to go find her and slap her for the pain she caused him.

An ache rises in my chest at the thought of her still with him and this moment not being possible. Maybe I'll hug her if I ever see her, instead. The ache turns into a deep heaviness, like falling into bed and anticipating a much needed refreshing night's sleep. He's luring me into him and I want to let myself go. Let go of the past. Embrace the future unknowns.

Trish

"Let's go over there, alright?" He tilts his head to the far edge of the dance floor where it isn't so crowded.

"Yeah, sounds good." I inhale his scent, his arms so warm and strong. I usually don't like to be held tight, but he's holding me with just the right amount of strength.

"There's a little more room to spin around. If you want to?" He leads me to the other side. "I got somethin' cool I wanna teach you."

"Oh, I'm good with anythin'. You'll just have to show me how."

"I'd love to." Bringing me close to his chest, we hold and sway, in perfect step. His body against me stirs up a million butterflies. He's confident, gripping me, leading me, letting me know how to follow.

He pulls away just a touch, "You're gonna step out and follow my spin, alright?"

"I can do that."

"Oh, I know you can. Ready?" There's something about his voice. Even though this room is fucking loud, he's all I hear.

"Ready."

"Okay, great." Lifting his arm, he spins me, twirling several times in quick succession, the world a blur as I return to his embrace. I grip his shoulders hard, extra dizzy from my drinks. I'm met with solid muscle. Hot damn, this is eleven kinds of wonderful.

"Steady there, princess." He holds me up until I nod. "You good?"

"So good." I smile and he repeats that fancy dance move.

"Perfect, baby. Just like that." He lifts his arm. "Yeah, baby," he talks into my ear, swaying us in time with the beat.

Baby?

I swallow, because fuck that sounded so sexy.

The song "American Saturday Night" by Brad Paisley comes through the speakers.

"You like Brad Paisley?" I need something to say, something to distract me from all I'm experiencing. It's like feelings overload over here.

"He's alright. This song used to play on the radio all the time."

Next thing I know, Zac's singing into my ear. It's deeper than the Mississippi River.

"Are you the lead singer and guitar player of that band of yours?"

"Something like that." Modest, too.

As the chorus ends, he spins me–keeping it going in a triple rotation and dipping me low as the song concludes. His hold is sturdy, like he'd never let me fall.

Before he brings me up, his head leans toward mine. There's a flash of insecurity in his eyes. My slow intake of breath invites him to do whatever it was he was wondering about.

He covers my lips with a seductive kiss.

About time.

Fucking bold.

It's soft and warm and my head melts into some place out of this universe. The lingering flavor of whiskey prickles against my tastebuds. I kiss him back, brushing my lips around his, savoring, tingling, lost in the rapture of his caress.

And I love it.

"Thank you, little lady, for dancin' with me." He brings me close, and I'm seven kinds of dizzy. The feel of his lips linger on mine, like I couldn't forget his kiss if I had amnesia.

Holy wow.

"Thank you," I manage to say.

"Was...was that alright?" His cheeks turn red.

"It was more than alright." I grab the back of his head and let my lips find his. It's never felt so right when I've kissed someone. His mouth opens as I dip my tongue between his lips. The roof of his mouth sucks me deeper, and I moan against the warmth.

When I pull back the look in his eyes is like he's had his first drink after years of being lost in a desert. Like he might have died of thirst if we didn't kiss right then.

Why do I feel the same way?

"You're gettin' really good at this new move." He escorts me off the floor.

"I've always been a quick learner."

"I believe it." He leans his arm against our tall table, propping against the wood, sleeves rolled up above his elbows.

"Had I known it was Country Night, I woulda worn my boots." I look down to my heels, feeling the blisters already like the day I was shooting a wedding from dusk 'til dawn.

"Kick 'em off." He looks at my heels, too.

"You want me to dance barefoot?"

"That or you can borrow my sneakers, though you may trip on 'em. Looks to me like your foot is about half the size of mine."

"Nuh, uh." I scoff at his insinuation.

"Nuh, uh? Yes, huh." He sticks his tongue out playfully and all I want is for him to shove it down my throat.

"What are you? Seven?"

"No, not even close, I'm an eleven." He teases, pointing to his shoes.

"Yeah, I guess eleven is about right." I playfully stick my tongue out at him.

"I wasn't kiddin', though. You've already lasted way longer in those heels than I woulda been able to. Let's get you some relief." He takes a knee like he's some prince, and I'm his Cinderella, and delicately pulls off my heels.

"Now what are we gonna do with them?" I give him a skeptical look, worrying my very expensive heels would be snatched if left unattended.

"Take them back to the car. Lock 'em up in your trunk."

"I think not. No way am I walking back to the car without shoes. Did you see all that gravel?"

"Then I'll carry you."

"Carry me?"

He leans in close. "Carry. You." His voice is so silky smooth I may come. A million and three sizzles work through my system as I stare into those gorgeous brown eyes.

Before I know it, he scoops me up, carrying me and my heels out to the car. I pop the back and tuck my heels and purse inside, all while he's still holding me.

"Last thing you need tomorrow is sore feet. Bet you've got a photo shoot and all that. Isn't Saturday the busiest day for most photographers?"

"Normally. But tomorrow, actually I don't. I came here to spend the weekend with Lexie." I wrap my arms around his neck, enjoying the way he's holding me, "but it looks like she and Bobby have plans with each other." I try to hide the disappointment in my tone, but it's too late. Zac has caught on to it.

"That's pretty shitty of her to ditch you." He kicks the door to Garrison's so we can walk back inside, setting me on the ground free of gravel.

I tuck my keys and phone into my skirt pocket.

We walk back to the table. He orders us a couple waters so that it's not just alcohol while we're dancing hard.

"You've got the grace for dancin'." He's all smug as he gives me the compliment, bringing me to the dance floor.

As the songs keep playing, he twirls me around and around, my heart racing faster as I go through the steps he's teaching. As tired as I am, something about dancing with him energizes me.

"God, you're gorgeous when you're outta breath." He whispers against my ear. His breathing sounds a lot more even than mine. He's barely working his body. I'll hand it to him, he's in better shape than I am.

Zac will be amazing in bed. The longer I dance with him, the more I know it.

"Need You Now" by Lady A starts up. It's one of my favorites.

"Oh, I love this song." Zac leads me in an intimate two-step with some fun spins here and there.

"Where'd you learn to dance like this?"

"Our youth group had country swing classes growin' up. I ended up drivin' my sister Sadie and found out I was into it, too."

"I've always wondered what it would be like to have a sibling. I was really close with my cousin Rick. He's the closest I have to a brother. Think that's half of why our friend group got along so well. Most of us don't have siblings we're close to. How old's your sister? "

"Seventeen."

"Oh, is she gonna come out to Suncastle next year?"

He grimaces. "I wish she'd come out here right now. She's dealing with a lot of shit back home. Needs to go somewhere new."

"That's too bad." I frown.

"It really is." His body tenses under my grasp. "So she was dating a girl secretly for a while. They ended up making out in the school hallway at the Spring Formal. Well, turns out it was a set up. They recorded it and sent it out to basically the whole school. The one who set it up claimed Sadie was harassing her. Everyone took that girl's side without even asking Sadie. Next thing you know, Sadie's not making team captain like she thought she would. These "friends" keep giving her all kinds of shit." He shakes his head. "Sorry. That was too much. I don't need to pile this on you. Let me dial back." A conscious look reaches his eyes.

"No, it's okay. Talk as much as you need to." I rest my head on his chest as we sway. "High school is hard enough. I'm sorry your sister's dealing with this."

"Me too." There's so much weight in his tone; he really worries about her. It's sweet how much he cares.

"I would'a loved to have a protective big brother. Sadie's a lucky girl."

"Thanks." He grips me tighter, like that comment meant a lot. For the rest of the song, I hold him, our bodies creating a sort of comfort between us like a kindling flame.

He kisses the top of my head and he whispers, "I'm having a really nice night with you."

"Me too." I snuggle into his shoulder. Hums and sizzles compete for my attention. Every curve and line of his muscles with only a little fabric between us. I relax into him, each breath in perfect rhythm. His body is firm in all the right places. I relax into that, too.

My hands run up and down the muscles of his back, rubbing away tension. He holds my hips on his as I press against his cock. I'm warming from head to toe. He smells so fucking good. I want to drench my pillows in whatever he's wearing so I can smell it all the time. A wave of desire flows through me as I step my feet between his so I'm as close as possible. Every available inch of our bodies connects.

I swear we're fucking on this dance floor. But it's not just physical. It's emotional. I should fight against it, but part of me doesn't want to.

His touch drives me wild, and we aren't even naked in the dark yet.

I hope he'll be okay with the dark.

I don't fuck in the light. Then he'd see the scars. No one gets to see my scars. Not since that fuck gone wrong with my high school bully. I wouldn't let Jimmy see and he was closer to me than any other guy. If I send nudes, I photo edit them out. The skin feels different, but in the throes of passion no one notices. Seeing them in light though? I'm so mutilated.

I shouldn't have to bear the mark forever when my abusive stepdad has gotten off scot-free. I won't be used again. I won't be in a situation that ruins me again. No one can hurt me. Not one little bit.

"You still here? Seems like you're somewhere else all of a sudden." Zac's eyes hold concern and I'm surprised he notices. All the blood in my body rushes to my face. I can't show him vulnerability. Gotta shift this momentum from dancing into fucking, and then kiss his sweet face goodbye in the morning.

"What hotels are your favorite around here?" I ask, not because I don't know–I went to every hotel within a twenty mile radius when I was in college– but to change the subject.

Zac gives me a look like he recognized my blatant dodge of his question. Is he gonna press the issue? Looks like he doesn't know if he should or not. "I'm not really sure if I have a favorite."

My walls are fully in place again. No more hints of that crack from a moment ago. Alcohol or not, I refuse to open the walls of my heart.

"Or we can go back to my place? Come to think of it, I don't know which hotels are nearby."

"You don't know?" I wrinkle my brow.

"I mean kinda." He breaks the hold on my hand and grips the back of his neck for a few heartbeats. "I don't know how to say this."

"Say what?"

"I um…" he stammers.

"You um…?" I tilt my head toward him.

"I…like you too much to just fuck around with you." As if he's absorbed all the vulnerability I'm hiding, his face looks relieved to admit this.

"You *like* me?" My heart beats faster in my chest. Dammit. This was going so well. "In all of the one evening we've spent together you already know that?" I tsk, looking him up and down. "You don't like me, you like my boobs."

I turn around, looking at the door.

"Psh, I know more about you than your boobs. We've been chatting for weeks and dancing for hours. And that day at Shakey's." He steps closer to me.

"Besides, *you* were just askin' if I wanted to get a hotel. Pretty sure it's okay if I'm a superficial asshole if that's all you want."

"Superficial asshole is right." I start tucking the mints from the table into my pocket for later. Eight mints. One to eat now. Seven in my pocket. I unwrap the eighth mint and start crunching hard on the candy. The chewing relaxes me enough to not *totally* freak the fuck out at Zac.

"Hold up." He lifts his hands beside his head in mock surrender. "Okay, I admit it, I don't know you very well. Not yet. We could go get a hotel. You just want a quick fuck? Sure. You just wanna tangle in the sheets the rest of the night and leave in the morning? Fine. But if you think I don't know you, at least a little bit, in the time we've shared while I've been observing every little thing I can possibly notice, then you're wrong."

"Oh? And what do you know?"

"You think I didn't see whatever it was that flashed so heavy in your eyes a minute ago? Whatever you had to bury inside of you right away? I know you're fuckin' scared of anythin' more than a one night stand."

"Then maybe I am." I grab my keys from my pocket. Mints scatter on the floor. I bend down to pick them up and he's down here on the ground with me. I pick up three mints. He hands me the four he's gathered.

My heart pounds so hard I don't know what I want anymore. This tension whooshes around in my chest. When I find his eyes again, they're pleading...wanting.

"I just need some air." I look at him, debating if this is blowing any shot we may have had. "I'm gonna go sit in my car for a minute." My bare feet dig into the gravel of the unpaved parking lot of Garrison's, wondering if he's gonna come after me or not.

Wondering–even harder–if I want him to.

Trish

Heart pattering against my ribs, my mind wanders into memories I wish I didn't have. Zac's being too sweet. Too kind. I can't have it. He's too good. All that's wrong about me will just rub off on him, corrupting that big heart in that thoughtful soul. We can't have that. Can't have any fucking bit of it.

Making it to my car, I flop into the front seat and brush the bits of gravel off my feet. I rub my kitty cat keychain, the one I got in a Kentucky gas station on one of the last good family trips we took when I was a kid.

Daddy would stop for gas and take my picture at the 7-Eleven, etching them both as my two favorite numbers. We'd go inside and get a strawberry soda and a keychain. I've got a whole collection of key chains and soda caps at my apartment. The kitty's my favorite. Kinda like the last piece I have of Daddy, always with me.

I've always wanted to live in Kentucky. The beautiful grassy hills, where I was born. Mama met Daddy in college but she wanted to move to South Carolina. We road tripped to Kentucky every year until Daddy died. One day, I'd like to visit his grave. It feels weird to think about going alone, though. Mama refused the many times I've asked her to take me.

One day, I'll go.

I've carried my kitty ever since I got it. It's my safety. My special thing that makes me remember that, once upon a time, I was loved by a good man. The velvet covering has all but worn away on the little animal no bigger than a big square of Bubble Yum Bubble Gum. But it's mine. Never getting rid of it.

Part of my heart wants to share this with someone. To find someone who can handle every bit of my story. But I don't think that's possible.

I like you...too much to just fuck around with you.

Zac's gesture and all it means for the potential ethereal *us* makes me all kinds of messed up. The adorable first baseman in his junior year of Suncastle College refuses to just hook up with me because *he likes me.*

Fuck.

I let out a sound that's like a little kitten getting stuck under a barn door.

I like you.

Yeah. Well. You can't. Hear me, Zachy boy? You. Can't.

No way in heaven or hell or the moon or the sun or the stars or eleven different solar systems is this gonna work.

I'd love to fuck you tonight in a hotel. But that's it. That's all I'm up for... ever since Dipshit broke me a long time ago.

It's not fair.

I take several breaths looking up at the car interior. At what part of life did I become this way? When did I refuse to let things get serious? I worry more about *not* making a mistake than giving someone a chance.

The sound of shoes crunching against the gravel registers in my ear. Risking a glance out the window, I see Zac standing there. Sexy as hell, with hands tucked in his pockets. There's a distance between him and the car, like he's respecting my boundaries.

He says something, but it's so muffled by the glass window, I can't make it out.

I roll down the window just a crack. "Hey."

"Hey. Can we talk?" He comes closer, walking real slow, like he's not sure if it's okay. *Damn straight. It ain't okay. You can't go and make me feel things when I've only come for a quick fuck.*

"Look, Zac, you seem like a great guy. But I'm not ready for anythin'.""

"I'm not either."

"You're not? Even though you just said you like me?"

"No. I mean I do like you, and we can just hookup if that's what you want. I'm sorry if I confused you a minute ago. Let's take this one step at a time."

I roll the window down, contemplating. He leans down so his forearms are resting on the window frame. Solid muscle with definition highlighted in the parking lot lights. "I know this is cliché as fuck, but can we start over?"

"Are you cliché as fuck?" I look at the way his dark hair frames his face. A little sweaty from all the dancing.

"A little bit, yeah." There's that smile again, his out of this world gorgeous dimples on full display.

I'm gonna see where this night can go.

"Okay, well, get in. Let's start over."

He walks around the side of the car and sits in the passenger seat. I click down the sunroof and let the cool November air fill my lungs as I hold my kitty keychain tight.

For several seconds, we stay still and quiet.

I lean my seat back and see those incredible bits of heaven's glitter.

Hey, Daddy, I miss you somethin' fierce. I swallow, hating this conversation being one sided, apart from what I pretend he's saying back. *Yeah, I think Zac's a nice guy. Oh, you do too? Wish you were here. It'd be a lot easier to make sense of things.*

I close my eyes and remember his hugs goodnight. The way he'd listen to Oldies Hits Radio and laugh at the stupid jokes the disc jockey told.

I turn toward Zac, hoping I can stop acting *off*. It's not that I want to be so…I don't even know what to call it. Guess it's just new. "I like taking photos of the stars."

"They're beautiful tonight." His voice is calming and tender almost.

"Sometimes I go up into the mountains and take a whole album's worth."

"Maybe one day you can make it into one of those photo books." He suggests.

"I really should."

"You still have the same keychain you had at Shakey's." He notices.

I unhook it from the chain and show it to him. "It's my favorite one. Take it everywhere."

There's a nudge, almost like Daddy wants me to open my heart. I can imagine his voice saying to me *Trish, it's okay to let people in sometimes. Do your best and see what happens.*

Zac's been nothing but kind to me tonight. There's an ache in my heart wanting him to know.

"This kitty has received a lot of love." He holds it carefully.

"My daddy got it for me, before he died." I take a deep breath, knowing this isn't the sort of conversation I have often. "You say I'm guarded and scared, and you're fuckin' right."

If I want to have a different outcome, I have to try a different approach. Knowing full well this may bite me in the butt, I listen to that voice in my head telling me it's okay to share even just a tiny bit of myself. "And if you wanna hear something cliché..."

Zac sits in somber silence, like he wants to listen.

"My daddy passed away when I was nine. The heavens took his soul. I like to pretend he's up in the stars, looking down on me." I look out the sunroof. "It's probably because I was obsessed with *The Lion King* when I was nine, but yeah."

"You were just nine when your dad passed?" He sounds choked up, and when I look over, his eyes are somber.

"Yeah." I look away and sigh into my chair.

"God, that's rough." His voice is compassionate.

"Have you ever lost a parent?"

"No, I haven't."

"Y'all close? You and your parents, I mean."

"I'm close with my sister." He plays with his finger nails.

"And what are your folks like? I take a lot of family photos. It's always interesting to see the family dynamic."

"What're they like? Hm…." He scrunches up his nose to think. "Ma's the hovering type, tellin' me all the time I don't come home enough." He stretches out his neck. "Pa's that emotionally distant kind of guy that doesn't show any kind of affection, even when I was a little kid. He's pretty old fashioned."

"Old fashioned? You mean like toxic masculinity?" I realize at once, I've overstepped. That wasn't kind. I don't know his parents. "I'm sorry. That's what my mind jumps to when I hear people say that a man is 'old fashioned' it's like they're sugar coating something. But that doesn't mean that's what you meant at all."

"No, you're right. I was sugar coating it." He lets out an awkward laugh. "I haven't thought about it too much, but there was definitely some toxic masculinity going on there." His eyes are thoughtful.

"Wow, I wasn't expecting any bit of that."

"What were you expecting?"

"A shallow asshole that can't see the truth if it slapped him in the face." I snicker.

"That's superficial asshole, to you, little miss." His eyes glimmer under the stars and I soak him in. *Little miss* leaving his tongue gets me all kinds of hot and bothered.

I love nicknames. Always have. And tonight, he's already given me several. But man, none of them is as hot as this one.

Little miss.

Oh, yes, please.

He reaches across the armrest, caution in his eyes, a touch of insecurity behind those gorgeous browns. That nice head of thick locks, so tempting to grab and yank on.

I give him a little smile, letting him know I'd like him to hold me. Fuck, do I want him to hold me.

This feeling terrifies everything in my being.

Just a quick lay. He's smart. He'll figure out what's best once I explain it to him. Have a really fun night, memorable even. Then kiss goodbye before morning.

His lips take mine, giving comfort and fondness. Kisses turn faster, his hands cradling the back of my scalp.

"I like you, Trish. And if all I get with you is one night, I'll take it." He whispers against my lips.

"You'll take it?"

"And never look back." His kiss sends me into another universe. It's tender and devoted, showing that bit of lust as his hands slip lower down my back. I untuck my shirt, and he slides his hands against the skin of my hips.

My clit spasms with need.

How's he doing that? It reminds me of the first time I got kissed, when I was ten and Jimmy Hendricks was pretending we were Leonardo DiCaprio and Kate Winslet from *Titanic*. I let him sink off the side of our pool floatie, too.

How's Zac bringing up all those same butterflies in my stomach? I never get this way with guys...ever. Time to make this happen so I can stop trying to make sense of it.

"Okay, *superficial asshole*. I know you *likkkeeeee* me and all. But I promise, I know this better than you do."

"You do now?" He raises his eyebrows, all kinds of skepticism working through his face.

"Yes, I'm gonna drive this car. We're gonna go to the Holiday Inn down on Fourth Avenue. I'm gonna fuck the living shit out of you all night long. I'll bring you back to your apartment where we kiss goodbye."

"And then?"

"Then we're gonna pretend like this never happened. Or you can go back in there and I'll just drive myself home."

"So those are the options?" He leans a little closer, like he knows exactly what he's doing to me. I'm so twitterpated. Me. I don't get twitterpated. Little ol' Jimmy Hendricks cured me of that when I gave him my V card at thirteen. But man, is my heart pounding at the sight of Zac's eyes and the sound of his voice ringing in my ears.

I'm pretty sure I'm about to come harder than I ever have before.

"Those are your options. Although, I suggest the first one. The Holiday Inn sometimes has those little cookies in the lobby and all."

"Cookies? Well, you can never go wrong with cookies," he winks. Winks. Sweet Baby Jesus, who is this boy? Nicknames and winks?

"You never can. So I'll give you one good night. Deal?"

"You, little miss," he arches his eyebrows like he realized I liked when he called me that earlier, "have yourself a deal." He shakes my hand as if we're in some skyscraper agreeing to a business contract, and I'm already drenched.

Zac

*D*on't fuck it up, Zac, don't fuck it up.

Trish, the most gorgeous, ambitious woman I've ever met wants to fuck the living shit out of me. Stat. My cock is so tight against my pants. Imagining being inside of her? I'm holding back not to jizz just thinking about it.

Trish speeds in her car all the way to the Holiday Inn, like if she doesn't get us there ASAP then one of us won't go through with it.

"One room." She pulls out a silver glittery wallet and gets her credit card.

"No way, little miss." I noticed her perk up when I called her that before, so from now on it's her nickname. Intercepting her card with mine, I give the desk clerk my card.

"Oh, no, no, no," she pushes hers at the clerk in one of those ridiculously awkward fights of who's gonna pay. "You paid for all the drinks tonight. Plus, my idea to get a hotel, my card we're charging'."

The clerk finds my eyes.

"Run it." I say.

"No." Trish throws her card over the desk. "I'm paying." She nods to the clerk.

"What do you want me to do?" The clerk holds out both cards.

"Split it." We say in unison. I bite my lip to keep from chuckling at Trish's horrified expression.

"Jinx, you owe me a soda." I make a silly face at her.

"What are you, seven years old?" She shakes her head but I catch that little smile like she's loving my playful side.

"No, we've established I'm eleven." I chuckle at how she's getting all hot and bothered while I'm egging her on. With one step closer, I feel this energy rising. She can tease me all she wants, but it's clear as day I'm making her body do all kinds of things.

"Room 208." The clerk gives us the keys and our cards, an annoyed expression on her face.

I take Trish's hand as we head to the elevator.

"You think you can just take charge like that?" She lets out a sound that makes me get even harder. This level of eye contact rivals every other level. I've never had anyone hold my eyes this tight. Ever.

"Oh, I know I can." The elevator door opens and we step inside. She grabs my collar and yanks me into her sudden kiss. Every bit of her scent washes over me. The feel of her hair as I grasp her head closer to mine. Our lips colliding, kissing, tasting, melting into each other.

My heart's pounding so hard I don't remember to push the button. The next several emotions taking over my body are an unexpected mix: Lost in her kiss. Shocked that *she* took charge like this. Surprised that I fucking love it. We're still in the elevator.

Without letting go of her kiss, I reach out to the buttons, blindly hoping for the right digit.

"What?" She pulls back and looks at the number keys. "You don't want to be stuck in an elevator with me?"

"I'd rather have you on some sheets." I use all the depth my voice can muster.

"Oh yeah?" She searches my eyes.

"Yeah." We get out of the elevator and down the hall until we find the right room.

My arms wrap her back, bringing her in for another kiss. "I'm glad we're here." I say against the smooth warmth of those ruby red lips. I wanna be covered from head-to-toe in that lipstick.

"You'll be even more glad in a few minutes." Trish puts the room key in the reader.

"Um, I already know that. But why only a few minutes? Don't we have all night?" I say with lots of snark.

"Fair point. But, Zachy boy, you're gonna be the type that keeps coming back for more. I can feel it." We walk through the hotel threshold and she flicks the lightswitch off, making the hotel room dark. "So do me a favor and don't get too attached. I know you want to."

"You don't know a damn thing, little miss." I tease her.

"Shut it."

"Make me." I flick my tongue, and it's like I can feel her tingling from several feet away.

Holy hell, I want to remember everything about this night. She's making it so memorable already. I don't think I've ever been this into someone.

She stands against the wall, the lowlights of the hotel showing me a *come and get it* sort of smile on her face. I press my body against hers, binding her to the wallpaper and slip my lips onto hers.

"You like that?" I whisper, pressing hard with my tongue until she parts for me. "You like rough?"

"Mmm hmm," she purrs.

I'm hungry for everything that sassy tongue of hers can give me. Lustful in a way that presses me deeper. She wars with my tongue, ragged as we gasp for more.

My hips come to hers, like they're meant to be together.

"Ohhhh," she moans, pressing into my hard cock, coming in for another kiss. Every part of my body responds to hers, like we're in some kind of cosmic dance.

I pull away, breathless.

"Not so fast." She draws me back.

"What're you waiting for? We only have right now." I literally just made that up. It's my mantra. Officially. As of two seconds ago.

I'm not ready for *any* of this.

She says it's just gonna be tonight. But man, I hope not. If she's half the person I think she is, then I'm already falling fast.

"May I?" I pull up her black skin-tight shirt between kisses, gliding my hands across her luscious skin.

"Please." She unbuttons my shirt, pulling my arms out of my sleeves.

"You want this?" I unhook her bra, taking her boobs in my hands. They fill me with a warm weight as I tenderly massage them. It's too dark to see, but I feel enough to imagine perfectly.

"So much." She hums into my touch. The rougher I get, the more she moans.

"You like that?"

"I want more." She's begging.

"You get it all," I lick circles around her nipple. She lets out a whimper, relaxing into my touch. That's my signal. She wants me to be fierce with her and really stimulate the heck out of these celestial tits.

"Now, you let me know if I go too hard."

She nods in a promise that she will.

"This is all about you." I straighten my back to give her a sweet, promising kiss. I search her craving eyes in the low lights, before I bend into her chest. My mouth forms a latch over her nipple, and I suck with gentle pressure, warming her up to my touch.

A satisfied coo echoes through my ears as I brush my tongue against her ridges. They're hard against my tongue as I take a turn with each, alternating sucks and flicks.

She clutches my hair, tugging me tighter into her. I'm surprised she likes it this rigorous, but man, I do too.

Her hands move around my waist, unbuttoning my belt. "Get out of these."

I kick off my shoes and stumble out of my jeans.

"Your turn." She slams me against the wall. Deadly kisses sucking my mouth. There's so much intensity. So much need. Coming at me.

I am losing all control to this pleasure. I unzip her miniskirt and wiggle it off her soft hips. She clings to me. We tumble into the bed, not bothering to turn down the sheets.

"Now." She grabs a handful of condoms from her purse and puts all but one on the nightstand.

"Let me get you ready first."

"Believe me, I'm ready." She bites open the wrapper and slides the condom over my cock, wiggling my boxer briefs off my ankles. She slips her panties to the side, not even taking them off. Fucking hot. I let her line me up at her entrance, then arc my hips to insert deep on the first try. Holy heck, she's wide open.

"Fuck me long and hard. I want you rough. Don't hold back."

"You got it, little miss." I position her on the edge of the bed, rocking my hips into hers.

"Harder." She begs. I slam into her, giving her everything she pleads for. "Yep, oh, yep." She moves us faster. Fuck, I barely have a chance to feel her before she tightens all around me. So fast.

"Flip me over."

"You got it." I slip out and grasp her shoulders, rolling her onto her belly. She's bent over the edge of the bed, her feet coming near mine, beautiful ass popped out and ready. I slip into her from behind, pushing hard until she whimpers. I take my fingers, get them wet and stimulate her asshole. "Good with that?"

"Oh yes, don't you dare stop." Her body vibrates at my fingers. I put more pressure on her asshole, wrapping my other hand around her front and rubbing her clit while I keep a constant speed of thrusts. She starts screaming.

I freeze. "Too much?"

"Fuck no! You're incredible, keep going." She catches her breath as I start us up again. She's shaking to my rhythm. She's relaxing and pulsating with each wave of repeating orgasms. Heaving for breath, mixed with blissful hollars, fill my ears.

I thrust harder and faster, coming close to my climax.

"Give it to me," she yells and it's all I need to come completely unglued. My abs go tight. Despite the dark room, my vision goes white like I'm staring into the sun. I ride the wave of pleasure, lasting longer than it ever has.

"Mmmm," She grabs the sheets. I hurry my pace, filling the condom as she trembles in after waves. It's like we were made for each other and this incredible pleasure is our bodies thanking us.

I slide out and help her turn around, my skin pressed to hers. I lather kisses on her mouth, holding her like we can't be close enough.

"You're pretty good at that." She pulls back, going for a tissue. "Get ready for round two."

Oh, little miss, I already am.

Trish

Damn, he is sexy. I could tell he really wanted to do what made me feel good. The sex wasn't about him, like it is with a lot of guys. He was rough enough. Tender enough. How he balanced that so well our first time together is astounding, really.

Knew I needed to experience his home run. And oh, did I experience it.

He tapped me so deep. His cock is pure magic. Filled me so full.

After a few minutes of freshening up, I click the light off in the hotel bathroom. He switches places with me, and I relax on the bed, covering up in the sheets, my body cold since withdrawing from his heat.

He leaves the light on in the bathroom when he returns, wearing nothing. Beautiful muscles cover his form. He's an athletic deity. A baseball playing sex god. I shift under the sheets making sure I stay covered now that the light's on.

For a moment, the past calls to me.

"Don't you wanna take your top off? It's so hot." Jimmy lays with me on the blanket, sweat beading down my face in the hot summer sun. It's a million and three degrees in our secluded section of Elerish Mountains.

"I'm good." I wish I didn't care if he saw. These scars are mine. Always a one piece swimsuit. Always a tanktop during sex. Never naked all the way.

They can't see. I don't care how much of my body they embrace. These scars are mine.

"How'd I do?" Zac brings me back to the present. He climbs in bed with me, a confident smile on his lips, making me wonder why he's even asking.

"Ya know, it wasn't so bad. What'd you think?" I play coy, swirling one of his curls in my fingers.

"Yeah, it was alright." He slides his lips up in a smile, those dimples flashing for a quick second.

"You left the light on." I tilt my head to the bathroom.

"Yeah, I wanna see you." He looks at me awhile, and I melt into this moment. Swoon. He's all swoon.

"What?" He crinkles his nose.

"You're not gonna make this easy, are you?"

"I'm all about easy."

"Okay, well, I'm all about dark."

He goes and clicks the light off. Good. Glad that wasn't a problem. He pounces on top of me, skin on skin. Warm and connected. I grab the covers and put them around his shoulders. He kisses me in slow motion, like I'm in a time warp. It's like those still frames I take of a couple in love. The ones where the camera captures everything before they move an inch.

He slides his tongue, slipping it over my lips, as I make him work to get inside.

"You told me to get ready for round two," he brings his mouth to my ear, "and I have a secret for you."

"Oh, do you now?"

"I'm ready." His whisper clenches me so tight that my thighs are contracting to relieve the torturous ache between them. He reaches for a condom on the side table, and I'm glad I had a handful.

Already primed, this time is about exploring. Under the blanket, he brings his tongue to my clit.

"Heavens above, Zac." I gasp. "How're you so good in bed?"

"Me?" He pokes his head up. "How're you so good? I've never gotten hard this fast."

That makes two of us. My clit is as excited as an erect cock, I swear. Every sweep of his tongue, every hook of his finger as he drives pressure into my g-spot. Sweet Baby Jesus, I've *never* been with someone who can multitask so well.

"Pinch your tits." His gruff voice vibrates against my body, and I do exactly as he suggests. An orgasm ripples from my head to my toes, the insane pleasure making me drench his mouth.

"Oh, yeah, gimme that." He jiggles his tongue, triggering another wave of sweet release.

"Get back inside me." I open my legs, and he descends perfectly in place. We rock the headboard. I grip the sheets. He presses a delicate kiss on my forehead.

"You're a fuckin' treasure, Trish." He fucks me to heaven and back again. His elbows hold his body up so he's all the way out of me. Then he plunges in deep. Pulses reverberate from my very being. Woah. I've never been loved on this hard.

My orgasm lasts a very long time.

But as we fall asleep in the afterglow, all I can think is: *Oh, no...*

Zac

I open my eyes. A shaft of light bounces off my face from the split in the thick curtains. Wait. This isn't my room.

Hotel, with Trish.

Oh, yeah.

Did she go? I rub away the crusties from my eyelashes, turning my head. Like Sleeping Beauty, she's snuggled into a pillow beside me. Her eyes flutter open.

"Hey," I kiss the skin under her ear. "Good mornin' beautiful."

"You're still here." She blinks back surprise.

"Where else would I be?"

"You coulda got a ride or something. They're not usually here when I wake up." She yawns.

"Oh, I'm here." I move the blanket and lay on top of her. She gasps and brings the blanket tighter around her side.

"You cold? Let me warm you up." I start rubbing her shoulder with one of my hands, holding her closer to keep her warm.

"No, I'm not cold. Where's my top?"

"Probably somewhere on the carpet." I smile, but it falls when I realize she's upset.

"Can you close your eyes?" Her tone is almost frantic.

"Yeah?" I give her a weird look, having no clue what she's getting at. Does it have to do with the dark? Is she really conscious about being naked?

Next thing I know, she's pushing me off and taking the blanket with her while she searches the room for her shirt. Then she goes into the bathroom and comes out dressed.

"What was that about?" I'm still naked in the sheets.

"Oh, don't worry about it." She goes around with the garbage can, cleaning up the hotel room.

"Is this it, then?" I lift up on my elbows, watching her act all awkward.

"Yeah, I gotta get going."

"Weren't you taking the weekend off to be with Lexie?" I feel like I'm grasping at nothing, but I don't understand why we woke up together for her to hurry out.

Last night blew me away. I glance at the clock saying it's 10 AM. Damn, I slept better than I have in ages. "We don't have to check out for another hour." I rub the sheet beside me, inviting her to return. "I mean, if you wanna go now, that's fine. I know this was just a one night thing."

She drops her bag and walks over to me, straddling me with her legs out wide beneath her miniskirt.

"No, you're right. I don't have to go." She leans in and kisses me. "Last night was probably the best sex I've ever had."

I grip her hips, bringing her tighter against my growing cock. "That makes two of us."

"And I know what I said about just the one night…"

"Don't tell me *you're* gonna be the one that keeps beggin' me for more?" I tease her.

"You're really somethin' else, aren't you?" She holds my eyes, and there's something new in them, a sense of desire that neither of us can ignore.

I'm shocked to see it. Shocked even more to feel it. So soon? Maybe I'm just high on really good sex. "I mean, I guess since we're incredibly physically compatible, I could make an exception this time. You know, take the one night thing and turn it into a weekend long thing. Yeah, I could do that."

"Oh," she brings her fingers to her lips in mock surprise, "You'd do that for me? How noble." She bats her eyelashes, and I feel a bit of precum oozing out because hot damn how does she tease me in a way that's so insanely hot?

Flying fish sticks, she drives me w-i-l-d, wild.

"You know, I think maybe I'd be indebted to you forever." She looks at the ceiling like she wouldn't be bothered by the prospect.

"Well, we need to go get you a swimsuit. I've got plans with my buddies out on the boat this afternoon. Unless you've got one in that big 'ol Marry Poppins bag of yours, I'm just gonna have to take you to the mall."

"I don't usually bring a swimsuit with me in November." She smiles. "I guess we'll have to shop for a nice one-piece." She sighs in mock exasperation. "But I'm not going as your date. We aren't dating."

"Not dating." I nod. "Just extending a really nice night into a weekend. Because, for you, I guess I can make an exception." I tease again and she elbows my ribs.

"I'm just so glad you'd do that for me." She bats her eyelashes and then rolls her eyes.

"There's all kinds of other things I'm gonna *do* for you, little miss." I flip her over so I'm on top of her, the sound of her giggles as I dip my head under her mini skirt, heaven to my ears.

Unlike a lot of people I know, I think clothes shopping is really fun. Going there specifically for Trish made it even better. She tried on a bunch of adorable swimsuits, and I insisted she let me buy her two favorite one-pieces. She didn't consider bikinis. I'm not sure why, because she'd seriously rock one. Every inch of her body is perfect and I'd feel that way no matter what size she was.

We bought a bunch of lingerie, too. She promised me a fashion show, since she insisted on keeping them a surprise until then.

"Harvey's had a boat since freshman year. It's really his dad's boat. But we use it a lot. We met Tyler in one of our elective classes. We all got along great and decided to play music together in the JBB. Pretty soon word got out and we were asked to do little gigs here and there."

"Oh, cool. Wait, did you say Harvey?" Trish looks up from her makeup mirror thingy...compact? Is that what they're called? I'm sure Sadie's told me ten times.

"Yeah, he's one of my best friends. Plays drums in the band." I smile. "Excited for you to hang with us. Ethan's sick or he'd be here too. He's on bass guitar."

"Harvey was my daddy's name." Trish's smile drops, then the corners of her mouth dip up like she can't decide if she wants to smile or cry. Her expression sends a crushing sensation through my chest. Again, I think about nine year old Trish sitting at a funeral, saying goodbye to her dad. It's heartbreaking.

"Oh, that's cool. It's a good name." I wait for her to say more. Silence instead. "What do you miss most about your dad?"

She gives me a look I don't understand. Confusion? Agitation? Maybe a sort of melancholy.

"Oh, um, we don't have to talk about it." I backpedal. I'm sure it's a hard subject even though she kinda brought it up.

I turn into Harvey's neighborhood that borders the lake. As cold as it was last night, today is all sunshine. Gotta love flip flop weather in South Carolina in November.

Harvey's gated community has lots of big, beautiful homes. Many of them have private docks in their backyard. The mature trees hang overhead as we round the corner into his driveway.

"You been out on Lake Cleary before?" I glance at Trish.

She turns her head my way, "Pretty sure I haven't. Your friends aren't gonna mind me tagging along, right?"

"Nah, they won't care. The guys are real nice. I won't let them harass you too much."

She shuts her compact makeup thingy. "It's not just gonna be *the guys* is it? I don't wanna crash your party. 'Bros before hoes' and all that."

"No, no, of course not." I snicker. "Delilah would be here but Ethan's sick. I'm sure Krystal's coming. Tyler's with a guy, Tommy."

"And Harvey?"

"Yeah, Harvey's dating Krystal. And Krystal usually brings her friend Britney." I add quickly to make sure it's not just sounding like a big group date.

Trish's face softens and she nods. "We always hung out with the guys in high school, but I had Lexie with me. It's not the same when you're the only girl."

"You won't be the only girl. Promise." I give her a serious look. Damn, those eyes. If I look at them for hours, I still won't see all they hold.

After she finishes her makeup, I rush around to open her door.

"May I?" I look at her backpack with sunscreen and such.

"May you what?" She wrinkles her brow.

"May I carry it?" I risk a hand on the strap.

"Oh, yeah, thanks." She pulls it off her shoulder, and we go out toward Harvey's backyard, leading to their private dock.

The bowrider looks ready to go.

"That's Harvey." I show Trish to the blond surf god in our group. For a millisecond, I worry she's gonna think he's hotter than I am.

Harvey shakes Trish's hand. "Nice to meet you."

"Wait." Trish puts her finger on her lip. "Did you take pottery with Doctor Smith?"

"I did." Harvey looks at Trish for a long time. "Shit, that's right. You always sat in the back."

"Didn't really wanna be there." Trish bites her nail. "And I avoided Doctor Smith's spittal when he talked."

"He was always spittin' everywhere." Harvey shakes his head. "Tyler!"

Harvey waves him over. "This is Trish. She was in our pottery class a couple years ago. Remember?"

"I remember that pottery class. Didn't you have different hair then?" Tyler comes over and shakes her hand.

"Yeah, I change it a lot." She brushes her hair out of her face like the comment is making her self-conscious. I slip a hand around her waist to try and put her at ease. When she squirms a bit, I move it away. Whoops. She doesn't want that.

"Tommy here yet?" I fistbump Tyler.

"Yeah, I'm gonna go help him with the cooler." Tyler hikes up the path to Harvey's parents' house passing Krystal as she comes down to the dock.

"Hey, I'm Krystal." Harvey's girlfriend extends her hand to Trish.

"We're ready to head out, I think." Harvey motions us toward the boat.

"And they think we're–" Trish starts to ask.

"Friends." I shove my hands into my swim trunk pockets, giving her a reassuring smile. "I texted them before we headed over."

"Friends," she nods.

"And I won't put my arm around you."

"Yeah, I mean, that seems like more than friends. Even if it's hard for you to stay away." Her eyes hold teasing and I'm glad she's not upset about it. To go from hooking up all night long, staying close at the mall and now *not* touching her is a bit of a change. But she's totally right.

Butterflies flutter through my insides. I'm feeling good about her being with me all weekend. Maybe at some point she'll be open to more.

"So do you go to Suncastle?" Krystal sits next to Trish, wearing a long, yellow summer dress. "I don't think I've seen you? What's your major?"

"I graduated in Art History." She shrugs.

Harvey drives us out on the lake and we take turns tubing. Can't seem to take my eyes off of Trish, even when Tyler's talking to me.

"I've always loved lakes. That's the first thing I ever took a photo of.

There's this gorgeous lake that has a really weird pink cabin on the side of it. I was basically obsessed. That's when I knew my eye belonged behind a camera." Trish gestures to the water. "Zac, honey, can I have the bag? I'm gonna grab my phone and take some pictures."

I give her the backpack, thinking about how I've been to a lake with a pink cabin on the side. Wonder if it's owned by the same folks. Maybe there's a whole association of people who own pink cabins by a lake.

She takes several photos of the lake and the surrounding docks. It's fun to watch her concentration. When she's done, she hands me her phone to see.

"Dang, how can you get those angles just right?" I marvel at the pics.

"I didn't get a job doing this from having nice finger nails." She snarks and I check out her manicure. That attitude is driving me wild.

"How long have you been doing this?" Krystal asks.

"Since I was nine, but using one of those old school disposable cameras that came in a three pack from Walmart."

"I remember those." Krystal says. "I've got a huge photo box with all my One Hour Photo envelopes in it."

"Me too." I recall all those days waiting for the film to develop.

"Did y'all ever do those scrapbooks?" Trish asks.

"Oh yeah. My friends would have sleepovers and we'd paste a bunch of papers around the edges of the prints." Krystal says and I can't help but appreciate the way Trish is with our group. It was always hard to get Valerie to come on the lake, much less engage in conversation. There's nothing wrong with being introverted, but Valerie was standoffish because she felt too cool to be around my buddies.

"We'd get a million of those Lisa Frank stickers and put them in as embellishments." Trish says.

"Sadie has like every Lisa Frank *embellishment* put carefully into a sticker book. Pretty sure she had crazy anxiety with the placement of each sticker. How'd y'all handle that stress?" I chuckle at the memory of Sadie losing her cool over how they fit on the pages.

Trish gasps and pulls her hand to her chest. "How dare you call me out on a Saturday like that?"

We all laugh and it feels good to have fun with her and my friends.

"I'd get so stressed out trying to figure out where to put my stickers that I'd give up and put them on the shelf half finished." Krystal's confession gets a big smile out of Trish.

"I know, right?" Trish chuckles.

"Alright, y'all." Harvey docks the boat on the little island in the middle of the lake. "Let's get this party started. Gotta inaugurate Trish properly."

Trish

Zac's friends are cool and I'm having a great time already. I'm glad he invited me out here today. Krystal and I have been chatting a lot since we got off on the islet. It's like Harvey's little hideaway. There's a gazebo and metal polls to set up a beach volleyball net.

Tyler and Tommy set out a few blankets. Zac and Harvey carry a cooler with lots of drinks and snacks while Krystal, Britney and I set up the net.

"How often do y'all come out here?" I ask Krystal.

"As often as we can." Krystal tosses me a volleyball and I back up far enough to serve it over the net to Britney.

"I haven't played beach volleyball in forever." I send the ball over and Britney dives into the sand, missing.

"You guys better get over here before Trish slaughters us! Looks like she can play some mean volleyball." Krystal tosses the ball to me for another serve. I catch Zac grinning out of the corner of my eye. Those dimples are dang precious.

After several rounds of ball, we take a break for a light picnic.

"Now, Harvey's parents make tons of food so make sure you save room for that." Zac hands me a sandwich from the cooler.

"Let's just share a sandwich, then." I walk over to the corner of one of the blankets with the sandwich, while Zac brings a gatorade and some bottled water.

I open up the sandwich to find a bunch of pickles. Eww. I carefully remove them, leaving only the cold cuts, mayo, and bread.

"You don't like pickles?" Zac asks.

"Oh, sorry, I can leave them on your half." I tear the sandwich. "Which one?"

Zac picks the smaller of the two. "I don't care if you leave them off." He chuckles. "And definitely not worth stressing about."

I look down to where I'm frantically reassembling the pickles onto the bread.

When I find Zac's face, he's grinning so big those dimples of his glisten against the water reflection.

"Something about a hot day and a cold sandwich is an amazing combo." Zac says.

"I completely agree." I wipe some mayonnaise off the corner of my mouth.

"Oh, you missed some." He uses his thumb to get a little bit off my face, his touch delicate and warm.

"Thanks," I hold my hand up to my nose, a little embarrassed.

"Do I have anything in my teeth?" Zac smiles real big.

"No, you look good." I pull my phone out. "See?" I take a quick picture and show him.

"Thanks." He smiles.

"I could take some pics of everybody if you want?" I offer. Sometimes it's nice to have a friend who takes pictures so the day can be remembered.

"Awwww. That'd be awesome." He says.

I get up and take a bunch of pictures. Some of each of the couples and even a group photo of everyone.

"You'll have to send them to us." Krystal says, putting her number into my phone.

"I'd love that." I'm surprised how happy I am with this group of people. Most of all, I'm surprised at what a great time I'm having with Zac. He's been nothing but sweet and thoughtful this whole day.

Maybe I do want more than just a hookup with him. I mean, after today I'd consider us at least friends with benefits.

Zac

By the end of the afternoon, I've got it worse than when we started.

The sun shines bright on her face, and I lean into her to block the direct sunlight.

"Thanks, Willey." Trish snuggles onto my shoulder as the sun sets over the beachy part of the lake.

"I've always loved photography." Krystal's doting over all the pics Trish took today. "You're seriously so talented. No wonder you're booked out so far with your clients."

"Well thank you." Trish smiles. "Y'all really come out here all the time?" Trish leans against her elbows, popping a grape in her mouth. "It's like living in a dream right now."

"Oh yeah, every weekend if the weather's good." Harvey puts his arm around Krystal.

"It feels like home away from home." I think about McNeely Lake, where I spent every summer since I was a kid. The water is my home.

"It's probably time to head back." Harvey starts packing up the cooler. Trish and I get up and fold the blankets. Krystal and Britney take down the beach volleyball net. Tommy and Tyler start loading up the boat and we all climb in. Water shimmers against the late afternoon sun as we head back to

Harvey's place.

His dad has ribs on the grill and his mom's mixing a big old pot of mashed potatoes in their kitchen bigger and nicer than the one at my Pa's restaurant back home.

"Y'all remember to drink plenty?" Harvey's Mom gives us hugs as we come in from the lake. Even though we're in college, she treats us like we're still kids, but I don't mind.

All kinds of fruit and veggie trays line the counter, inside. Homemade root beer brews in a five gallon cooler and the ice cream churns with fresh vanilla ice cream for floats.

"This is Trish." Harvey introduces her.

"Hey honey, you make yourself at home, alright?" Harvey's mom says. "We've got Gatorade in the cooler, beers, sparkling water. Whatever you want. As much as you want. Supper'll be ready in a few minutes."

"I will, thank you." Trish smiles. "Can we help?"

"You've got a sweetheart here dontcha, Zac?" Harvey's mom squeezes my elbow. I feel the heat rise to the front of my cheeks while I look to Trish to see how she took it. Maybe I should correct Harvey's mom.

"I think he needs someone sweet with how sweet he is." Trish plays it off, and I take a breath. She winks over Harvey's mom's shoulder as they walk into the kitchen.

"So, um, I think I need a new calendar or something because I'm pretty sure I heard you say it was gonna be twelve months before you moved on." Harvey whispers as we hang back. "That's the shortest year I've ever lived."

"Shut up." I elbow him lightly in the ribs.

"Just friends, huh? How long's that gonna last?" He asks.

"Don't know." I shrug.

"I wouldn't waste any time if I were you." He chuckles, going toward the sliding glass door. "She's a catch."

"Where can I put the plates, Momma D?" Tommy's carrying a stack from his chin to his waist of fine china.

"Just here." She pats an empty spot on the counter. "We'll serve it up, buffet style."

After everyone's got their plates, we sit around Harvey's dining room table. The food is great and the company is even better. When we've all eaten and chatted for a long time, I catch Trish with a big smile on her face.

"I'm so glad you brought me." She reaches under the table and squeezes my thigh.

"I'm so glad you came." I smile.

"Now, save room for dessert, ya hear?" Harvey's mom gets up from the table and starts gathering dishes. We help clean up the meal.

"Everything was fabulous." Trish says. "Thank you so much for having me."

"You're welcome here anytime." Harvey's dad has that loud and welcoming sort of voice that makes you feel super comfortable the moment he starts talking to you.

We head into their backyard while Harvey sets up the projector.

"What are we watching?" I pull over some bean bags with Tyler and Tommy.

"Batman Forever." Harvey holds up a special edition case.

"You get that at the Comic Convention?" Tommy skips around his bean bag and takes a look at the epic artwork.

"That I did. Best reason to go to Columbia." Harvey's eyes light up like an eight year old at their birthday party. "Check out the artbook." He hands Tommy his new prized possession.

"When you gonna take me there, babe?" Tyler puts his arm around Tommy.

"When's the next one?" Tommy says.

"Not 'til next year." Tyler pouts.

"Well, then maybe we'll travel somewhere and find one happening sooner." Tommy says.

"Y'all ready?" Harvey starts up the movie.

"Yep!" Krystal pats the beanbag for Harvey to come sit. "Get over here, big guy. You've been working too hard." After he plops beside her, she rubs his shoulders.

"Careful, I'm already feeling that sunburn." He stretches his neck and then scoops her up to cuddle.

"It's been a while since I've seen this one." Trish snuggles next to me on our own beanbag.

"Well, Harvey's basically obsessed. We've dressed up like the characters for Halloween every year." I grab my phone and show her the photos. "Since Garrison's has us at the big Halloween bash, we get requests to keep performing as the *Batman Forever* Knights."

"Oh, wow, y'all go all out." Trish looks through the pics. Harvey as Two-Face, Tyler as Riddler, Ethan as Batman, me as Robin.

"Looks like you're missing Dr. Chase Meridian." Trish observes.

"Maybe next time you can play her."

"You think I'd pass for Nicole Kidman?"

"You've got the red lipstick." I reach beside me for a throw blanket and tuck it around her so we have a buffer against the evening wind off the lake.

"Ha. You're not wrong." She leans against me as the opening credits play. "This is really nice. Great night for an outdoor movie."

"I swear November in South Carolina is the prettiest. Look at all those stars."

"They're amazing." Her body feels perfect. Holding her through a movie is the best. We laugh at the same parts. She grabs me tight when it's intense. It's comfortable, the way we fit together.

Zac, don't get too attached.

"Oh my god. That part when Robin does laundry." Trish laughs. "I forgot that was in the movie but man," She shakes her head. "Iconic."

"It really is." My eyes linger on hers, thoughts shifting in memories of last night and how much fun we've had today. I want to be the Batman to her Dr. Chase Meridian. The longer I hold her gaze, the more I wonder. Does she feel this too? The incredible connection?

As the credits play, the song "Kissed By A Rose" by Seal fills the air. Trish's face comes close to mine. Our lips almost touch, taking every bit of breath out of my lungs. We hover, less than an inch apart. No one else has taken my breath like that. Her nose rubs against mine. I shiver from my head to my toes.

She licks her lips and I lean a little closer. I still can't breathe. Like she's holding my life captive. And I want her to.

Her bottom lip finds mine, the top one sucking gently as her tongue pleads for entry.

We've kissed before, but this feels like our first time. It's different, this moment. Something is different. All the other kisses were just casual compared to this. But this kiss? This kiss feels committed. Needed. Like she'll always hold my life captive, and I couldn't wish for anything better.

My hands find her neck, her hair, pulling her closer, kissing her deeper. She moans hot air into my mouth, and I'm holding her life captive, too. There isn't a divide between us. We're intertwined. Can't get any closer. It's not possible. She's holding my heart. I'm holding hers. She's stealing my breath. I'm offering it willingly.

Take me anywhere, Trish. Take me anywhere, and I will follow.

I'm giving it to her. I want her to have it. My breath. My life. My heart.

Her kisses come faster, a rush as the rhythm of the music matches our pace.

This connection is insane. It's like my pulse is a drum beating in my ear to the notes of the music.

The rhythm of our beginning.

I didn't know I would ever *want* to give myself to someone.

"Just friends, huh?" Tyler scoffs. "And yeah, I'm just here with my roommate." He kisses Tommy.

"Best roommate you ever had." Tommy snickers.

"Damn straight." Tyler smiles.

"Whooooo!" Harvey, very much drunk on beer and kettle corn, hollers.

"Told you it wouldn't stay just friends for long," he shouts to our friends.

I startle back enough to see her eyes, worried this will push her away. She doesn't want commitment. Though her kiss made me sure I can never commit more to another human being, I don't know if it's what *she* wants yet. I worry she may not want it at all.

"Your cheeks are rosy." She licks her chapped lips, looking as raw as mine. But her face is happy.

Thank you, Jesus.

Cat calls come from Harvey. I roll my eyes.

"Harvey's an asshole when he's drunk. I don't know why he's doin' this." I look down. "I'm sorry."

"Alright, let's get you inside." Krystal takes Harvey's beer out of his hands and leads him in through the back door.

"He's so wasted." Trish plants another light kiss on my mouth, and it's like I'm in another sphere of existence. Harvey's gone. Everything's gone. Just me and her.

"He's an ass." I chuckle.

"I don't care." She rubs her nose on mine. "Let your friends think whatever they want."

My heart relaxes. Something must've changed for her, too. She brings her lips to mine again. We may not be talking, but I swear our bodies are speaking the same language.

"Let's get outta here." I whisper against the shell of her ear, letting my hand drift down her back and onto her hips.

"That's a great idea."

After helping clean up and saying our 'thank yous' and 'goodbyes,' I walk with her to the driveway.

"Everyone was so nice." Trish steps into the truck. "Until Harvey got drunk." She snickers, the truck lights shimmering off her face. Remnants of sunscreen mix with her delectable scent. All the makeup is washed away.

"I consider them my college family." I run around to my side, putting the key in the ignition. "It's been nice to have them here since I don't go back home much."

"Oh, that's right. You're from out of state, aren't you?"

"Yeah, I'm from Kentucky." There's a long silence. I watch her face, but I can't quite read it. Everything was so happy but now it feels somber. She messes with her kitty keychain for a while, dangling from the side of the backpack.

"Where did you get that?" I feel there has to be some reason for the way this moment has suddenly shifted.

"Kentucky." She looks like she's about to cry. "It's the last thing Daddy ever gave me," she pinches the bridge of her nose as if she feels pressure building. "I'm sorry." She forces a breath and her walls are right back up. I saw them come down, that touch of vulnerability. She wants to be close.

Beneath her usual foundation, there's a hint of freckles. I take a moment to let my lips envelope each one. Her freckles are a constellation leading the way to my heart.

"Come here," I offer, pulling her small frame into a hug around the center console. She relaxes into my embrace, holding me for a good long while. That oneness returns. It's just like when we kissed on the beanbag.

"I had a really nice time with you tonight. And this is gonna sound stupid and crazy and maybe I had too much beer in there—"

"No, nothing you say could sound stupid or crazy." My thumb caresses the smooth skin of her cheek. "Promise." I look into her eyes. Eyes full of pain. Eyes that want to have someone to lean on but don't know how to let themselves. Eyes that can't decide if I'm worth that trust.

I know you're scared, Trish. I am too.

"I just always thought maybe there would be a sign." She squeezes her eyes. My throat tightens with a rush of emotion thinking about how hard it must've been for her to lose her dad so young. I've never lost anyone, until Cody. And even then, it wasn't close to losing a parent as a little kid.

"A sign?" I raise my lips in an empathetic smile, wanting her to know that I don't think it's stupid at all. I believe in God. She believes in signs.

"A sign that Daddy would give me when I was heading to the right place." She squeezes her eyes tighter, and I wrap my arms around her, wanting to take away what is causing her so much anguish.

"I'm here, baby, I'm here."

"That's just it. You're here." She takes a shaking breath. "Like my sign." She holds up the keychain. "I've carried this with me everywhere since I was nine years old. And now I find out that you're from the same place as this keychain." She shakes her head. "I'm being stupid." She leans against the seat, pulling away from our hug. No physical connection. "Whoo, too much beer for me."

And it's shifted. Walls up again. Pushing me to the other side. Protecting herself.

There's no contact between us and it's like I'm dying.

I'm shattered.

"It's not stupid. Not even a little bit." I put my hand on the armrest, not touching hers, but making it available if she needs it. "I want you to know that I'm here. I don't know if I'm the sign or not. But I love being with you. I can tell you've been through so much. I just want to be here for you, if that's okay?"

"But you don't even know me."

I can tell she doesn't value herself half as much as she wants the world to think. That brings such an ache to my chest. In the little bit of time we've spent together, I just keep thinking she's more and more incredible. And it's not just the surface stuff. She backs it up with hard work and dedication.

"I don't know you very well, no. But I'd like to get to know you more."

"How can I be worth the trouble to you?" She looks out the window, like she can't face my eyes. Whatever happened to make her this guarded must've been awful.

"You are." My heartbeat slows into a determined rhythm, like I'm at a game and the last batter up in the inning. I know the next few minutes matter and I need to choose my words with care. "You may not see it. You may not understand. But think about this." I grasp for anything that can help. My eyes catch the rearview mirror. Yes. That's it.

"We can't see ourselves clearly." I swallow, hoping to speak clearly. "We're too close. Living in our own heads twenty-four seven. Like a blurry lens. But let me hold up a mirror for you, baby. Because you're incredible. And this," I gesture between us. "There's something here. I feel it. I've never felt this way with anyone else, and I get the feeling that you haven't either."

"I haven't." It's a hoarse whisper.

"So I want to be here. And if you'll let me, I'd love to be your sign that someone loves and cares about you just as you are. That I accept every bit of who you were and who you are and who you're gonna be." I lean closer. "Because Trish, I feel that."

She eases closer, her lips coming to mine, as if her soul is asking me to be what she needs.

I have a lot to thank God for tonight. Because tonight is the first time that I'm letting myself hope that maybe we can be together.

Maybe she is that something more I've been hoping for.

"Oh, woah. What time is it?" Groggy eyed, I sit up a little bit and reach for my phone. It's almost five p.m. "Fuck, I'm late. I was supposed to meet Bobby at the field an hour ago."

Trish lays atop me, wearing silky purple lingerie. "That was a really good nap." She yawns.

"This one is my favorite of the lingerie we bought." I run my finger on the soft lace. Man, I don't wanna leave. After Harvey's we came back to my place. She stayed the night and we spent all of Sunday eating fun food, playing card games and fucking like there's no tomorrow.

"I love it too. Suncastle purple." She shimmies her shoulders.

"I gotta go." I whisper a kiss onto her forehead.

"Oh," she moves off of me.

"I mean, do you wanna come?"

"Oh, don't worry, I *came*." She winks. "Come with you to the field? That's what you meant?"

"Yeah, you don't have to go back yet, do you?" I grab one of my jerseys and slip it over my head.

"I don't want Bobby to think we're dating." She pulls her leggings on.

"Oh, right." I swallow.

"I do wanna go to the field sometime, though." She grabs her cardigan. "Maybe when you invite me back." She brings her body close to me, the most passionate kiss I've ever had overtaking my lips. I don't know how each kiss gets better.

"I like the sound of you comin' back." I smile.

"Figure this weekend was good enough I'd do it again."

"I figure you're absolutely correct." I grin.

"This is my favorite one of your jerseys that I've seen so far." She traces my number with her finger. "Hugs you just right." She gives me another kiss. "You'll have to wear it again for me sometime."

"You got it." I grin even bigger.

With that, she's gone. The click of my apartment door closing makes me sure of one thing: I'll be having her back as soon as I can.

Fuck, I'm already in too deep.

Trish

"I'll have some preview photos to your email by tonight. Next weekend, I should be finished with the edits and then if you want any custom work, just let me know." I click off my camera. It's been a week since I was in Suncastle.

"Thanks, Trish. You're the best!" Miss Abigail hands me a check for two hundred dollars and gathers up her youngins that I've spent the last hour and a half capturing. It was a pain in my butt to get them to hold still, but I think we managed.

"I'll send you a text when they are heading to your inbox." I wave goodbye.

"Sounds great." She hurries off, chasing one of the kiddos who's throwing his clip-on necktie into the bushes.

I'm not sure I ever want any little monsters like that. Miss Abigail has her hands full and then some.

Pulling up my planner, I have a break for dinner, then my family shoot for the Thompsons, a Sweet Sixteen shoot for Cassidy Turner right before the last Bikram Yoga class at the gym on Main Street. I still need a handful of models for a new project I'm gonna pitch to the local museum.

Zac video called the other day and walked me through setting up a website. It's been a dream come true. All my clients can go in and schedule appointments without even talking to me. That alone is freeing up so much time in my schedule.

I double check my bag for everything I brought, taking a much needed drink of water. My phone's got eleven notifications. Naturally, I open Zac's text first.

Zac: Hope you're having a good day!

My stomach flutters and I grin. A warmth spreads through my body as I type out a response.

Me: As long as I can make it to dinner before my stomach eats a hole right through me.

Zac: If you were here, I'd make you some dinner.

Me: If I were there, I'd be even hungrier from all the calories I tend to burn when you're around.

Zac: That's why I'd make you dinner and then give you all the dessert you want.

He sends a wink emoji and I close out the text window before I drop everything, get in my car, drive to Suncastle and lose all the clients I stand up. Not sure what I was thinking letting him get my number. I swore this wasn't gonna go anywhere.

Guys rarely distract me, but numerous times I've remembered all those ways he made my body feel good. It was easy to be around him. So comfortable. Like we've known each other for years. I've never felt *this much*. Makes me curious to see if it *could* last.

Doubt it.

As I'm walking out, I see Anna Mae Jones–Cody's little sister–at the park with her kid siblings. She may as well be their mom with how much she's got them. We run into each other on the regular and I love our chats.

"Hey, Trish." She smiles, bouncing one of the little ones on her knee.

"How you been, Mae Mae?" I pull out my bag of Twizzlers to share.

"Already wishin' school was out for the summer." She chews on one of the Twizzlers and breaks off a bite sized piece for the youngin on her lap.

"Oh, man. Who you got for homeroom?" I ask.

"Sigman." Anna Mae groans in disgust. The little one wiggles a bunch until she lets her down on the ground to go play.

"Ugh, she's the worst. I can still taste the gross bubblegum she made me chew when she caught me putting mine under the desk." I rub my tongue along the roof of my mouth, trying to get the memory of the taste away. "She had me scrape three pieces of old gum off the wood and chew it in front of the class. Wicked witch."

"You're not kiddin'." She's wearing the same shirt she normally wears.

"Cody was always wearin' this, wasn't he?" Heat scalds my throat as I swallow. I'm surprised how much it hurts to bring him up. It's nice to sit by his sister on this park bench. But I know how much she lost. The newspaper headline pops in my head: *Local Star Pitcher Dies in Fatal Car Accident*. They'd used a picture I'd taken for the Willardson High yearbook in the article. It had Mae Mae in the background, though no one would notice her on the benches. She'd come watch him practice that day and I didn't edit her out. Now, I'm glad I kept it.

It's the picture that comes to mind now. Her smiling at her brother. So proud. Her dreams died along with his, I think. She stopped playing softball the year he died.

"It's weird, but I feel close to him when I wear it." She pulls at the fabric.

"That's not weird." My fingers find my kitty keychain and rub the soft texture.

"I miss him." There's a hollowness to her expression. "Like just the other day, Toby was watching The Sound of Music and it made me think of how Cody'd wake us up for school singing *Climb Ev'ry Mountain* off key."

I chuckle at the idea of him waltzing through the trailer singing to his brother and sisters to wake them. "Every day he did that?"

"Yeah, he swore it'd help us all feel better."

"He couldn't sing worth shit." I chuckle.

"He really couldn't." She lets out a sound that seems to mix laughing with crying.

"I miss him, too." I put my arm around her and we hug until she pulls away and wipes at the corners of her eyes.

"How'd your shoot go?" She looks at my bag.

"Here, you can look." I show her the previews.

"Wow, these look incredible," she clicks through the pictures on the view screen. "Man, I wish I knew how to work magic in a camera like this." She hands it back, and I place it carefully in my bag.

"So school sucks. But how's it at home with your old man in jail?"

"Better than it was."

"That's good to hear."

"Yeah. Shithole deserved it. Mama qualifies for aid now. It's been real good everybody gets lunch at school with the free and reduced program." She gasps, fingers to her lips like she just figured out what the fuck she said. "You won't tell Mama I called him *Shithole*, will you?"

"Of course I won't." My lungs get tight as bad memories come to mind. I spent hours on my knees praying for Dipshit to leave us alone. Praying for Mama to realize she didn't need to stay with him. After years of silence, I stopped praying. But that longing never left. If someone were to put him in prison, I'd feel relieved. I'm glad Mr. Jones is reaping the reward of his criminal activity.

I've always known Anna Mae's a smart girl. Her old man is in the same category of human refuse as Dipshit. I look at her and see so much of myself.

"You know you can trust me, girl." I remind her. "Judgment free zone."

"That's why I talk to you." She puts her arm around me in a side hug.

"You been thinkin' about what I asked you last time?" For ages, I've been trying to get Anna Mae to work for me. She loves photography. It'd help her to have some experience. It'd give her an escape from her endless hours of school and babysitting and picking up grocery shifts.

"You think you still need me?" There's a funny sound to her tone that reminds me how self-conscious I was. It happens when caretakers don't take care. The kid is left with all sorts of insecurities.

"Yeah, if your mama agrees."

"How about you talk to her?" Anna Mae looks hopeful, and I remember the times I tried to talk to my mom about things and she didn't listen well.

"Yeah, for sure. Is she over at Shakey's tonight or at Publix?"

"It's Thursday?"

"Yeah."

"She's at Shakey's."

"Okay, well I also need you and your siblings to do some posing for me. Think you have time Sunday after church?"

"Yeah. It's not like we go anywhere."

"Well, if I'm gonna catch Mama at Shakey's, I'd better scoot. Good to see you, boo." I pull my camera bag onto my shoulder and head to my car. "Bye!"

"Bye, Trish!"

The smell of onion rings and burgers fills my nose the moment I walk through the door. I order at the counter and take my number to *our* booth. It's been so long since I came inside the restaurant. I always just drive up for curbside to-go.

It's crowded in here, the buzz of a bunch of high school kids hanging out. Man, I miss those days. I see us here, in the faces of these youngins, yesteryear yanking me tight. The days that got bad and I'd text everyone to meet for shakes. No matter how bad things got at home, I could come here.

Shakey's was my sanctuary.

I run my finger over the skin under my tank top. The delicate layer that didn't heal right after Dipshit burned me. Forever a part of my skin. Always a reminder of what he did, branded deeply on my soul.

Those who abuse often have a way about them. They try to get you to think it's all your fault. That what comes from their hand is because of something you did.

And I believed him.

Every time, I fight against that fear deep inside of me wondering if he's right. That maybe if I woulda been different, then I coulda been okay. That if I woulda just known how to make him happy, then I woulda been able to live a happy and peaceful life.

Mama Jones brings out my order. Her graying blonde hair is in a messy bun on top of her head. Dark circles under her eyes remind me of how hard she works. As long as I've known her, she's had two jobs.

"Haven't seen you in a while, Trish." She sits on the edge of the booth across from me for a minute, repinning up her messy bun. "How've you been? How's your mom?"

"I've been good. Yeah, I see Mama about once a week. How you been?"

"Oh, just hanging in there."

"You know, Anna Mae wants to come work for me a few times a month. I wanna show her some technique before she gets ready for college. Is that alright with you?" I dip my onion rings into the ranch.

"I doubt she has the time." Mama Jones rubs her eyelids.

"She's told me she wants to get more comfortable with a camera. Doesn't have to be much. Just when she gets an extra minute." I explain.

"There are no extra minutes." Mama Jones stands abruptly. "I wish there were, but that's not our life." Her sad eyes look at her shoes.

"I didn't mean to upset you." I reach for her shoulder. "I'm sorry."

She purses her lips, folding her arms. "We're a little short handed at the moment." It sounds like she's talking about the restaurant, but I know she's talking about how she doesn't have her husband or Cody or anybody to help. But that doesn't mean it should fall on Anna Mae. I can't let it. Not when she really wants to learn how to take pictures.

"How about I go over to your place? I can help with the kids and when we have a few minutes, show Anna Mae what she wants to learn." I plead with her to reconsider.

"Well, if she can still keep an eye on the babies, then sure, I guess." Mama Jones gives me a sad smile and a nod before getting back to work.

Zac

Sadie and I like to chat after my last class every week. I'm standing outside the athletic building, with her on video chat.

"It does happen." Sadie brushes some of her long brown hair out of her face. "Not that I really know how to read people." She's still hurt from the fiasco over being volleyball captain. I know most of the people in our small town are super homophobic. Would've been one thing for her to come out publicly. But for them to expose her that way? A sick feeling stirs in my stomach every time I think about it. Falsely accuse her of harassment. Not even investigate to find the truth. It's like they never knew Sadie at all. She values consent and usually doesn't pressure anyone to do anything–especially not anything physical.

What so many people don't understand is that love is love. Sexuality isn't something chosen or sinful or dirty. Sadie doesn't deserve to be surrounded by people who treat her that way. I want her to move here so I can show her not everyone is as narrow minded. Sure, Suncastle is a small town. But we have the Suncastle Pride Club and more open minded people.

"Hey, now, those kids were awful. I wouldn't have seen it coming." I've told her over and over it wasn't her fault, but she still blames herself. "Look, maybe if you woulda picked up on their vibes earlier it woulda helped. But who knows? People who are that cruel are really good at looking innocent."

"I wish it didn't work so well. Zac, no one even asked me."

"I know they didn't and it's really fucked up. Guess we both need to learn how to stop taking on all the guilt when things go south, huh?" I stretch my shoulder, wishing this dang knot would break up.

"For real though." She shakes her head. "Oh, hey, how are things with that girl from Sprinkle?"

"Trish?"

"Yeah, Trish."

"Um, really good actually." I nod my head yes. "I like her a lot. Hopefully I get to see her again soon. School's been really busy. I'm super stressed." I've been thinking about Trish constantly and messaging her non-stop. I don't even care if things stay casual. Having her in my life is rewarding in any form and I want to do whatever she's cool with.

"That's great." Sadie smiles.

"How're things with Angela?" I ask.

"I look up to her a lot. Not sure why, but she's convinced I'm awesome and wants to take me under her wing." Sadie's expression is all shock and awe. Even though she's living it, she can't seem to believe it. "The other day Angela came over and ran drills with me for hours. It was incredible. She knows so much. We can just help each other grow. Be queens together when I start up at Western Kentucky University. She's a freshman there and she promised to be there for me when I go. I mean, you should see how she plays. And she's so dedicated too. Like even down to her training schedule. It just inspires me so much." Sadie's eyes go dreamy like she's thinking about Angela as more than a friend.

"Wait, are you into her?"

Her face blushes and she covers a gasp with her fingers.

"You are, aren't you?" My big-brother-protective-instincts are on high alert. Part of me wants to treat Sadie like glass. I know she's being extra careful.

Most people are good. But some are real assholes. A lot of times it's hard to tell which is which.

But these alerts are founded. Angela is in college. And Sadie is in high school.

"A little bit…yeah."

"And she's in college?" My eyes go wide and I work to calm my surging heart. It's basically the worst time to over react, or Sadie won't trust me anymore. With a measured breath, I do my best to be supportive. I *am* on her side and how I respond is gonna matter a hell of a lot. "How much is a little bit?"

"We've maybe…." Sadie trails off and I wait.

"You've maybe hooked up?" I fill in the blank.

"Zac!"

"You're the one who's not telling me." I shrug.

"We haven't hooked up. All we've done is make out a few times. Yeesh."

I try to digest the information. "So you're making out with a college girl?"

"We aren't like *together* yet. But Zac, she means so much to me. I'm done trusting people who aren't worth my time."

"And Angela is?" I raise my eyebrows.

"Ugh, Zac. Yes. I really like her, okay?"

"Okay." I let out a sad sigh, trying to ignore what doesn't quite sit right with me about her making out with a college girl. "Is Angela a lot older than you?"

"Oh, no, just a few months. She graduated early. Her birthday is in March, and she'll be nineteen." Sadie reassures me.

"Be careful, alright?" I try to feel okay with them being almost the same age. I'm sure it's hard for both of them to find someone to care for in our hometown.

"I just want us to be happy. Whatever that looks like." Sadie says.

I raise the corner of my lips. "Me too." I rub my sternum. It's hurting something awful. Always seems to get worse when anxiety amps up. Reminds me of when people get an aura before a migraine. Part of me is really worried it isn't anxiety. What if having anxiety wears so much on my heart that it's degenerating?

"Zac, your heart's fine." Sadie says, like she's reading my mind. "You keep rubbing your shoulder. Have you talked to the athletic trainers about it pulling on your chest? That's probably half of it."

"Oh," I move my hand down. "It's been givin' me a fit lately."

"You're stressed out." Sadie shrugs, and I know she's calling it. For whatever reason, this fear of a heart attack has taken root and even though there's no logical reason for me to believe I'm having one I can't seem to stop the panic.

"True." I lean against the brick wall.

"It's just anxiety and some strained muscles." Sadie gives me a look that's a mix of compassion and *move the hell on with your life and quit worrying already, Zac.* How she manages to convey both those messages simultaneously I'll never know.

As I walk to my truck, Sadie's phone call replays in my head. I can't fault her for liking Angela. I understand what it feels like to fall for someone you admire and look up to in lots of ways.

But this feels wrong. My chest is so tight when I walk into my apartment I spend ten minutes stretching my shoulders and neck. Sadie made a good point. I'm stressed and my shoulders are tight. Those things can cause chest pain that's totally normal and not at all a medical emergency.

Hear me Anxiety? I'm talking to you!

After finishing up my assignments, I call Trish. She doesn't answer, but I love hearing the sound of her voice on the machine.

"Hey, hope you're having a great day. I know it's out of the blue but I was wondering if you wanted to meet up? I have to see you again. Please? K, thanks, bye." I click off the voicemail wondering if anyone even listens to those anymore.

A few minutes later a text lights up my phone and hope spreads through my chest when I see it's her name.

Trish: fuck off, you stalker.

I bust up laughing because I know she doesn't mean it.

A second later, a picture comes through of her in a red dress making a winky face followed by her blowing up my phone with a bunch of texts.

Trish: Stalk me…in a non creepy way.

Trish: Or better yet….

Trish: Meet me at the Marriott in Harbrooke at eleven pm?

Me: Done.

Trish: We're gonna go all night.

Me: We better.

I get all my stuff together, texting Ethan that I'm gonna ditch tonight. Nothing else matters.

I drive to Harbrooke.

She's outside the hotel, popping a bubble gum bubble. "Bout time." She shoves a roomkey in my pocket, takes my hand and pulls me through the fancy lobby.

A funny thing about me I've yet to mention to Trish comes to mind: I hate elevators.

Like yeah, most people probably don't love them. It's a means to get somewhere without too many stairs. But I hate them. They make me so fucking anxious. Ever since I was a kid and got stuck in one.

Alone in our ascent, she pins me against the elevator wall, tongue diving deep into my mouth. "Missed you."

"Missed you." I kiss her back, relishing how she's good at distracting me from my fears. Thank fuck.

Ding. The elevator opens on the third floor. She pushes back as I step away from her. We get a funny look from the old man that enters. I feel my cheeks heating up, but I feel my cock burning harder. I need to fulfill her every wish. Her every desire.

We hear the ding for our floor and I wait for her to go first.

Even though I managed to not be scared in that elevator, anxiety levels are high. It must just be from the drive over and Sadie's phone call. I don't know.

My hands shake as I press the key into the key reader. It blinks red.

Not now. I don't want to be anxious right now. I want to be with her. Leave all of that behind. I'm so afraid of doing something stupid and ruining everything. Since I like her so much, I really wanna make a good impression. Make sure she wants to see me again. If I screw up even something like this room key thing, it's gonna be a point against *us*.

I try the key again and it reads wrong.

"You alright? Here, lemme help." She puts her hand on mine to steady it. This is a simple task. I should be fine. But no. Anxiety monster comes along with me everywhere I go. And all these feelings are definitely making it hard to keep my levels regulated.

I can do this. I want to do this. We want to do this.

Anxiety, calm the fuck down.

I look at her eyes, shocked. Because she looks so understanding. Like she doesn't care if my hands are shaking. Like she's happy to help.

"Sorry. I get shaky sometimes." I take a deep breath.

"It's all good." She sounds like she means it, and I dare to hope she does. That she isn't the person who'll mock my little nervous tics and use them against me.

I wait for her to give me shit, but she doesn't. We just go into the hotel room and get settled. Trish puts the key on the long desk.

"I'm really glad you called." She brings her lips to mine, that pleasure working away remnants of anxiety. Fuck, she provides me the most immersive escape. Our tongues tangle, bodies grabbing each other harder, tighter.

Exploring every inch of her, I run my tongue along the ridges of the roof of her mouth and find the permanent retainer she has on the back of her bottom teeth. I need her in every position. Need her in every room. On every surface of this hotel room. There's even a big jetted bathtub. We could relax, in there, and work some of the tension out of my shoulder.

She clicks the lights off.

Her hands unzip my jeans. I slip her out of her sleeveless red dress.

"I'm really glad you invited me." I pin her body to the wall.

"Oh, you're definitely invited. Suck my tits, Zac. Pretty please?" She's hungry, I hear it in each word. Every letter. Every vowel. Every consonant.

"Oh, you want me to suck your tits?" I tease. My hand cups between her legs as her body vibrates in want. "Is that what you want?"

"Right about yesterday." She arches her back so her boobs are in my face.

I flick my tongue around her. Fuck, this is the most perfect body I've ever touched. I want every bit of her. Can never get this craving satisfied. I'm gonna die if she doesn't give me endless hours of this.

I suck her hard and she relaxes into me.

"Zac, oh my god."

"I am your god." I lick my lips, moving from one nipple to the other.

"Hell yes, you are. My baseball playing sex god." She gets so wet. I stimulate her clit while I suck in a faster rhythm. She grips my hair, driving me harder into her chest. My finger slips into her center, while my thumb keeps rubbing her clit.

She's moaning, screaming, heaving for breath.

"Yeah, baby." I relish the orgasm forming. Her body tightens as she screams in delight. This is even better than the last time. I leave her swelling nipple with a gentle kiss, bringing my lips to hers.

"How do you do that?" She's breathless. "Really. How? I don't understand."

Because I'm already falling for you. The thought comes to mind and thank fuck I don't say it out loud. I'm sure it would scare her. Send her straight outta my life.

She presses her body against my hard cock.

"You have condoms, right?" I just realized I didn't grab any.

"Don't you have some in your wallet?"

"Don't you have some in your purse? Or glove box?"

"Dagnabbit," she messes around in her purse. "Let's go to the drug store." Fast as ever, we stumble into our clothes. She heads down to the elevator, and we stand there in silence. I wanna pin her up against the wall again. But I can't. Not now. There are people here. We'll get kicked out of the Marriott.

She runs to her car, and I follow behind. My hands shake. Not now. Please, not now.

We get to the old drug store on the corner of Ninth and Fifth.

Trish is looking at the sexy aisle, picking out a bunch of stuff. It's no sex store, but she gets some of the flavored lube and fancy condoms I'm surprised to see at a place like this. She holds the six pack and then puts it back for the mega box. I chuckle.

"You weren't kidding about going all night, were you little miss?" My mouth is on her earlobe, whispering every word, slow and steady.

Trish walks around the back of the aisle.

"Ain't that all we came for?" I look around.

"And ice cream and chocolate." Trish acts like that's as normal to buy on a night like this as the condoms and lube.

"Because?"

"When I come, that's what I crave. If we're gonna keep going with whatever this is, it's about time you learn my preferences."

"Absolutely." I nod.

She has come cravings? That's fucking hot. I'm never gonna think about ice cream without remembering her cravings.

Trish's phone goes off with a loud song filling up the quiet drug store atmosphere. Two people on the painkiller aisle look over. Heat rises to my cheeks as I give a sheepish smile to the few patrons looking at us. With sexy adventure-time supplies, I feel a rush of embarrassment.

Trish pushes the button to silence it. The call goes off a second time. She lifts it out of her purse to look at who's calling.

"I better take this. I'll be right back." She lets out an exasperated huff while I hold the hand basket and look over the options. I pick out some stuff and check out, happy to avoid another one of those who's gonna pay scenes.

Back at the car, Trish is talking about edits. Photo edits. Because she runs her own photography studio, and once again I'm in awe of her. She's smart, hard working and driven. Yet she's kind, beautiful and adorable in a way that makes me want to wrap her up in my arms and keep her there as long as I can.

I motion for her to pop the trunk and set the bags inside.

She puts her hand over the phone mic as she whispers to me, "You didn't need to buy the whole store."

"Sure, I did," I wink. "You said you need it when you come, and I figure you're about to come a thousand times." I keep my voice quiet while she blocks the mic with her thumb.

She rolls her eyes, taking the car down to the Marriott while talking through things with her client. The way she's professional and repeats back everything they wanted reminds me of how detail oriented I am. It's cute she keeps such good track of what they need. I know it's her job, but just like my job, she takes it to the next level.

With the engine running in the parking lot, she hangs up with her client.

"Give me two minutes." Searching through her purse, that may as well be a duffel bag for how big and full it is, she emerges with her planner and jots down some quick notes. This schedule is full. She wasn't kidding when she said she's a workaholic. Every line has words written neatly and cramped in close together, and even some of the margins have more notes. Her handwriting is big and bubbly with tiny hearts dotting all the 'I's.

For several minutes, she recaps the phone call in the notes section. I can tell she's not doing this to show off or blow me off either. It's because she cares about her clients enough that she'll take a call this late at night and make notes to keep track of what the call was about.

"Oh, shoot. What was that other thing?" She chews on the edge of her pen while I glance over her notes. "Oh, it was rhetorical. I don't expect you to keep track of it."

"I know, but I overheard. May as well help." I squint, reading out the list. "They wanted the long dress pics darkened in the back." I recall.

"Yes! Thank you." She pulls the pen out of her mouth and scribbles that down. "Okay, I'm ready."

"So ready." I lean toward her, watching her eyes soften as my lips meet hers in a tender kiss. "I've just gotta say that I definitely got the most amazing girl from all of South Carolina in the car. And I wanna know why the fuck she's spending all this time with me?"

"I don't know, but your dick sure helps." She pulls back with a smile on her face. Her playful wink sends shivers down my spine.

"Just my dick?" Those low burning nerves crank up a notch. She doesn't actually mean that does she? I know, this is new. But I feel so connected to her in more than just a physical way.

Please don't tell me this is still all you want.

My lips grasp hers, begging her to understand how much she *already* means to me. She breathes into my mouth and I feel so close. This is what I want it to feel like when I kiss someone. My tongue goes around hers, tasting, tangling, exploring.

The longer we kiss, the more I wonder if this may be the only time in my life when I feel this connected to someone. Lightning doesn't strike in the same place twice, they say. How I'm lucky enough to have it once is beyond me. But I already don't want to let this go. What if this is the only chance I'll ever have to feel this enraptured with another person?

"Trish?" I'm ready to tell her I want this to be more. She may not go for it. It's against what we agreed, but there's this need working through me. She needs to know how I feel. I need to tell her.

Or maybe we need another hot night to prove it.

No, I wanna tell her now.

Nausea bubbles in my stomach, because I'm worried she'll lose her shit. I get the feeling every time we're together, she has no intention of tearing down these walls. But I hope she can. I don't know how she's managed to keep herself so locked up, but I want to find the key. She's worth whatever it takes to help her be in a place where she can see that this is real. Every bit of my soul wants to be with her. It's not about the past. I don't care about her past. Or mine. Or anything.

I care about being with her.

Maybe I need to find another time. Maybe I need to find a better way to show her. That thought makes me sicker. The last thing I want is to keep this to myself. I need her to know. I can't keep pretending this is just a fling. For me, it's not. The conversation will loom over me all night and keep me from staying in the moment if I don't share at least some of it now.

Please, baby, let me show you what we can have together.

"I've been thinking a lot about us." I keep my face close to hers, watching that beautiful ring of brown that encircles her slate blue eyes, lit from the parking lot lamp. "And I need you to know–"

Her head jerks back, making me stop mid sentence.

"We should get going." She nods, emphatically. "Ice cream's gonna melt." Her door is open and she's sprinting to the back.

Just like that, she's gone again. I sigh into my hands. Maybe it was stupid to try and talk.

God, I have no clue how to do this. There's faith blooming in my chest. Everything will be alright. Maybe she needs more time. I can wait. I'll do whatever I can to be here for her. It's all I want.

Maybe waiting to talk about this is a good thing.

Working through my disappointment, I take one of the bags from her hands. We get up to the hotel room.

"Where's the room key?" Trish shuffles through her purse. "Goddamnit."

"Think we left them when we rushed out to the drug store."

She lets out a noise–half grunt and half scream–making me a little scared she's gonna freak the fuck out. I rattled her and she's unraveling. I shouldn't have said anything.

Anxiety levels skyrocket. Simmers of nervous energy turn into the crackle and popping sensation. The hairs on my arms stand up straight. My heart pounds in my chest. I feel woozy.

Alert! Alert! Something's wrong!

It's just anxiety.

"They'll get us a new one." I stuff my hands into my pocket double checking that I don't have the key.

When I look up, Trish's gone. I race to the elevator to catch up with her, leaving the sack outside the hotel room door. What's she in such a hurry for? We've got all night. We've got much longer than that, if she feels even a little bit of what I'm feeling. But she's off like the wind.

Breathing heavy, I reach the elevator.

"I win." she smirks.

"You're something else, aren't ya?" A wave of relief washes through me. She didn't do this for physical distance. She's staying emotionally close.

I chuckle, shocked at how each moment with her is unexpected. She's keeping me on my toes. But it's worth it. So worth it with how much I love being with her.

"Maybe I am." She shrugs her shoulders with a playful expression. When the elevator opens I rush in, pushing the button before she has the chance to.

"I feel like a little kid right now, and I kinda love it," she giggles, pinning me to the wall of the elevator. "That's my button."

"Didn't have much of a childhood, so I'm making up for lost time." I let out a laugh as she keeps trying to swat my hand away from the call button menu. "The button is already pressed, little miss." I see her eyes glimmer as I use her nickname.

"No! It was only pushed by you and not me, so it doesn't count." She shoves my hand hard and pushes the button a dozen times.

"Of course it fucking counts, and you just negated it." I spin her around, both her hands entangled in my grip.

She brings her lips to mine, and it's heaven. I wipe at her red lipstick that she's gone and smudged all over my cheeks as we emerge to the lobby. From the look on the clerk's face, she's quite amused by us. I wonder how many awkward couples she gets.

Probably a lot.

"Can we have a replacement key?" I lean against the counter.

"Of course."

"Thanks." I take the card from her, hot out of the key encoder.

Trish rips the key from my hand and runs to the elevator. She pushes the door shut before I can get in.

What the fuck?

I click the button to get the next elevator called. A wave of panic rips through me. I can't do it. I can't get in this elevator. It's not safe. I'm gonna get trapped all alone in the dark. No. No. No.

I wring my hands into tight fists at my side. Giving into anxiety, I take the stairs.

I'm not sure what to make of what Trish just did, but I head to the hotel room, anyway. Since she took the key, I knock.

Please don't be an asshole, Trish.

I knock again, harder this time. "Helps if we're both on the same side of the lock, little miss."

"One second." She calls in a sing-songy voice. "I've got a little surprise for you."

Another funny thing about me: I hate surprises.

Keep an open mind, Zac. Keep an open mind.

I hear water running. She's drawing a bath? I wrinkle my brows, leaning against the hotel room door.

Adrenaline rushing, thoughts spinning, I start pacing. Because what else am I gonna do? Miss *I only do one night stands* just locked me out of our shared hotel room.

She opens the door just enough to dip her head out and takes my hand. "Oh good, you're still here."

"Not like I can be anywhere else."

She stops me from stepping into the room. "Close your eyes."

"Excuse me?"

"Close your eyes."

I play along, anxiety boiling over.

Her cold fingers cover my eyes while we stumble over each other into what I'm guessing is the bathroom.

"Strip." She keeps her hands pressed tight on my eyes. "No peeking."

Okay, Trish... Okay.

Don't come unhinged.

Don't come unhinged.

Do not come unhinged.

I want this, right? It's consensual, right?

If I wasn't having a panic attack, I'd be all for it. Just have to get through the next few minutes. I can talk to her after. Yeah, I'll tell her I don't like surprises. It'll be okay.

Pain in my chest gets intense, making it harder to breathe. Suddenly, I'm eight years old and trapped in a dark elevator where I couldn't see anything. My body shakes as I try to ground myself.

I want Trish and I to have a good night together.

I force a deep breath as I wiggle out of my jeans, unbutton my shirt. I put my fingers to my wrist, catching the thumps of a rapid pulse.

"When do I get to open my eyes?" I try to sound confident, but there's a squeak in my voice.

"Later."

My clothes on a heap on the floor, I kneel on the frigid tile. Surprises are okay. Surprises are fun. *Surprises are fun, Anxiety, fuck off. Please just leave me be.*

"Can you tell me what all this is?" I'm begging Trish to take the anxiety away. Give me some calm in this storm. But I'm out in the ocean and she's on the shore.

Several seconds pass in excruciating silence. "Just a sec."

I hear her messing around with something and it makes me jump. I'm trigger happy right now. She could put a piece of chocolate in my mouth and I'd spit it out. She could kiss my lips and I'd turn away. She could leave me alone...

Just like the elevator.

No! I'm safe.

"Okay, you can look."

I cautiously open my eyes, wiping sweat off my brow. She smiles, wearing the towel wrapped around her. "Just thought it'd be fun to try something different and exciting." Her face falls as she looks at mine. "You didn't think so." She seems irritated.

I open my mouth, trying to talk, but I can't. My lungs are really tight. I rub my chest, burning like it's on fire. I hang my head between my knees, trying to get a breath.

"What is it?" She kneels next to me. "You're breathing weird. What's going on?"

I'm safe, Anxiety. I'm safe. I try to self-soothe, reaching for any measure of calm.

"You okay?" Her face turns pale.

"I am…not okay." I stare at the floor until it blurs over and refocuses. She puts her hand on my shoulder. When I reach to hold her hand, mine is trembling.

Leaning my head against the wall, I finally get my first full breath as the anxiety plateaus. In a few more minutes, it'll taper off. Always does. It'll shift. I'll calm down.

She's the calm to my storm. The lighthouse leading me from this hazy panic into reality. She got in a boat and found me lost at sea.

I'm not alone.

"Sorry." I clear my throat, trying to find my normal voice instead of this frog croak.

"Was that a panic attack?" Shock plays on her features and I wish I wasn't so conscious.

I nod and press my palms into my eyes, holding them shut tight.

"I just didn't know." She squeezes my fingers.

"It's okay…I'll be…okay." I let out a shaking breath.

We sit for a long time. I lean my head against the wall, that pop and sizzle of leftover nerve response slowly circulating. The adrenaline rush leaves me shaky and exhausted.

When my eyes find hers, I offer a sad smile. Guess it's better she finds out about all this sooner than later.

She turns off the bath and pulls the drain, then walks me over to the bed where we sit.

"Maybe this was a bad idea." She looks at the TV in front of us.

"Please don't say that." I keep my eyes on hers, leaning toward her. "I like you. A lot." I lick my dry lips. "Here's what you need to know about me. I suck at surprises. I've had bad anxiety ever since I was a little kid. Things can really set me off unless I know what's happening. So when you ran off to the elevator, it triggered me."

"What? I'm so sorry. I didn't mean to." She gasps, "I never want to trigger you."

"That same thing may be fine with someone else. But with me, I need a little more clue to what you're thinking." I brush some hair out of her face.

"So what about tonight triggered you? I seriously just meant it as a fun surprise. I don't get it."

"It doesn't make sense. Anxiety rarely does." I sigh. "When I was eight, I got stuck in an old elevator. It was one of the scariest moments of my whole life. I felt totally trapped and it was dark and I was stuck and surprised and…"

"You couldn't see." Trish fills in.

"Yeah. So something about being in an elevator coming up to the room and then not being able to see, and I don't know. I'm probably just sabotaging myself by wanting to be the perfect hookup–"

"Hey, if you have anxiety, that's not your fault." She runs her hand on my cheek.

"It sure feels like it." I sink into her calming touch. "And now you know about the anxiety thing." I take a deep breath. "That's why my hands were shaking." I look down to my quaking fingers. "Are shaking."

"Dammit." She flops back and stares at the ceiling. I lay beside her. When I can gather a breath, I start to connect the dots. I had to keep my eyes closed because she was undressed.

"Wait. Why won't you let me see you naked?" I look down at my body, wearing nothing but socks.

When I find her eyes there's something there. My heart beats faster, realizing that as hard as it is for me not to have control, she *needs* it.

"You need this, don't you?" I put my hands over my eyes. "You need to feel safe and in charge."

"You didn't phrase that as a question." She pulls my hands down and looks at me.

"Baby, I told you. I wanna know. I'm naked. You're not." I don't know why, but it's like I need to push this. I'm missing something and maybe that's what's underneath a lot of the anxiety.

There's a reason she's covered in a towel. A reason I haven't seen her topless. Since I don't know what that is, everything feels unsettled.

That morning after our first night, she took the whole fucking blanket with her before she got dressed. I can touch every inch of her but I can't see it? There's gotta be an explanation. Maybe she's got a big birthmark or some kind of weird skin thing.

"What happened to you, baby?" There's a catch in my voice I didn't expect. It's like I know this runs deeper than flirting or games or anything. This is trauma. Something must've happened.

My heart beats faster as the weight of this moment presses me harder into the mattress, like I'm melting into the bed. "I want to know." My hand goes to her face, cradling her pain, wishing I knew how to make it all go away.

"I don't know how to be close to someone. And well, until you, I never really wanted to." She turns her head, and I look into those gorgeous eyes.

Did she really just say that?

"I wanna be close to you, too." I say.

"But Zac, I seriously don't know how." She looks at the ceiling again. "All I can do is live in this moment. The one where we fuck sometimes. The one where after we fuck I go home and don't have to wonder about our relationship status, or worry about you with someone else..." She looks at me, hopeful. "One day, I may let you see me. Maybe. Maybe not. Can you live with that?" Her eyes find mine.

"Yeah, yeah, of course I can." I nod. "Can you keep me in the loop of where you're at?" I just need to know what to expect.

"I think so." She brings her head onto my chest. "And yes, a lot has happened to me. I have a past." I understand if that's not what you want. If I'm not what you want–"

I hover over her, connecting my lips to hers. "You're what I want. Moment to moment. Whatever you need."

We hold in bed for a long time. It relaxes my system. I grab a drink of water and splash my face at the sink.

I'm better now. Over most of that spiral. It always shifts.

Coming back to the bed, I hold her lips with mine.

"You're what I want, too. Right now." She gazes at me with so much hunger.

My cock is hard against the towel wrapping around her. "And if this is all we are, it's still what I want." I lick my lips, then suck her into another kiss.

"Me too."

Holding for several heartbeats, I connect with her, soul to soul. "I don't know all the answers. But I don't have to." I slide off of her and help her up to the pillows. I dash over to find the shopping bags.

Looks like she's unloaded everything, put the ice cream in the hotel mini-fridge and set the sexy stuff on the long desk. Biting the box of condoms open, I slip one over my cock. Wetting my hand, I reach under her towel. "Do you want me to hit the lights?"

"No, just let me keep the towel?"

"Of course." I lean against her, pressing another kiss on her lips. "And if you change your mind, tell me. We can pause at any time."

"I will." She moves her legs, giving me room. With a thrust of her hips, she pulls me inside of her. Everything melts away. Every bit of tension and worries dissolves.

She looks amazing. I stare at her face, trying to remember every detail of how she looks when I fuck her in the light. I get to love her, here, while I can see her expression for the first time. Her eyes are closed while I take her lips in mine, kissing in rhythm with our hips.

She's everything I've needed. Everything I want.

I watch her content expression as we lay on the bed, caught up in the afterglow. "Can we try that thing again?"

"The thing? Missionary style is hardly a thing." She chuckles.

"No, no, the one where you surprise me with the bathtub. Now I have a heads up, I think I'll be fine."

"You sure?" She angles her eyebrows upward.

"I'm sure."

"I don't ever wanna trigger you again."

"It's different now that I know what's happening."

"Okay, yeah let's try it.." She jumps off the bed and turns on the water to refill the tub.

"I'm closing my eyes."

"Keep 'em closed."

"Okay." It's fun now.

She wiggles down my body, her touch making my cock rock hard. Her hands take mine and she brings me to sit on the toilet lid. Then my socks come off slowly. Her touch teases and coaxes me while she secures a new condom over my cock.

"Eyes still closed?"

"Don't *you* have your eyes open? Can't you tell?" I snark.

"Fair point." She laughs. "I'm gonna take you over here. Step in, yep, there."

My feet land in the warm bath, hand holding the condom to make sure it doesn't slip off.

"Okay, sit." She lowers down with me, straddling my cock with her warm cunt. Her body envelops me, relaxing in the heated water.

"Wow, Trish."

"Keep your eyes closed."

"Can't I see you?"

"Not yet." Her mouth takes mine, wrapping it in the most tender kiss. "Can you trust me?"

"I'm learning how."

"Okay, hold on." She climbs out of the bath and turns the light off. "Okay, now you can look." Always in the dark.

"Hey, beautiful." I smile as she comes back into the bathtub, only able to see the shadows of her face.

"I like the dark." She brings her lips to mine.

"I like what you like." I kiss her harder, my hands wrapping her butt and bringing her closer to me.

"That's part of why you're so sweet." She rubs her cheek against mine.

"Wow," I whisper against her ear.

"Told you to trust me. Bathtubs are quite magical."

"You're right about that." The warm water, her tender skin, the motion of her body. It's so sensual. So perfect.

"I'm ready to come." I exhale her ecstasy.

"So am I." Her body opens around mine, inserting my cock deep within. "Fuck, do you feel good." She arcs her hips, and I mirror her moves with thrusts of my own. "Oh, yes. Deep as you can. Mmhmm."

I thrust harder.

"That spot. Oh, yes." She moves us faster, harder, water splashing outside of the tub and making a huge puddly mess. I use my thumb to get her clit as she rides the wave of her first climax. Close to filling her, I hold back. We clutch each other, breathless for several seconds, before going again. Faster this time. Harder this time. Bigger orgasmic pleasure plays from her body to mine.

"More," she begs, and the sound makes me crazy coming from her lips. Even though we're in the water, I feel warm liquid moving from her body to mine. Man, do I love making her squirt. I want to absorb it. Want to absorb her. Want to feel every bit of her wonder. Again. I drive her into pleasure. Again, I thrust, I tease, I coax.

"Oooooo," she moans against my ear. "Come with me, this time."

"You got it." Bracing my arms on the side, I arch upward to create enough leverage to give her all she needs.

"I don't know how you're strong enough to hold us up this way." She marvels.

"It's all the workouts." I wink.

"Well, they're working me just right."

"It's what I'm here for. We're gonna keep going until you've had all you can take." I pound her harder and longer than we have other times. I've lost count of the number of orgasms she's had. My mouth wraps hers, kissing her until my lips burn.

We come together.

Wow.

She slips out from around me. I carefully find my way around the dark bathroom, to dispose of the condom and wipe off before I get back in the tub. But I'm not worried. I want to be at a point where we don't need condoms. I want to feel her, with all of me.

I lay on the back of the tub, and she snuggles on top of me, her heart pounding with mine.

"That's the best one I've ever had." I play with her hair.

"It was really awesome."

"You're so good." I kiss her head. The relaxing afterglow within this warm water is all that I need. She covers me with the warmest comfort. All that tension in my shoulders melts away. My chest feels good. Doesn't hurt.

"And now that you told me about the anxiety, I can help you."

"Awwwww, baby. You don't have to." I swallow back emotion at her offer.

"No, it's good you told me. I'm sure it's not something you broadcast."

"A lot of people just think I'm a wimp." I sigh, feeling the insecurities I've had forever. The times Pa told me to just get over it.

"You're not a wimp." She runs her fingers over my pecs.

I'm not anxious anymore.

She's eased a level of the fear I live with constantly.

I hold her tighter, hoping my body can thank her for giving me a break. I'm not going to tell her in words. Not after what happened in the car. But I'll tell her with my touch.

All night long.

Trish

I stand at the mirror, door locked in the Marriott bathroom. I let the towel fall. My scars, every one of them, are still there. All twenty two. The cigarette butts making constellations on my skin above the worst disfigured part of me.

I can't stop thinking about that moment in the car. The moment I didn't let Zac talk. He wants to get close. But he can't. It's eleven million kinds of a bad idea.

He's more perceptive than most guys. The fact he realized I won't let him see me topless and isn't being an asshole about it shocks me.

Will I ever be able to show Zac my scars? What will he think? Will it scare him away?

Zac doesn't know what's underneath. Would it be so bad if he saw?

A memory I hate comes to the forefront of my mind.

I'm fifteen and hooking up with Dez. He's been pushing me to go farther. Says if I just give him what he wants, he'll move on to another girl. I finally agreed so he'd leave me alone about it. Whatever. It's not like I'm a virgin. Jimmy and I have had lots of sex when his dad's at work.

But Dez is rough and not in a good way. "Take your clothes off." He fiddles with his jeans while I strip down to my tank top.

He throws me against his bed and pins me down. I may be into it if he wasn't such a jerk all the time. Why did I agree to this? Ugh. I'm stupid. That's why.

He puts his dick in my mouth and makes me suck. It smells gross. Does he even wash it?

"Come on. Suck me like you mean business." His tone is angry. This is ridiculous. I spit his dick out of my mouth.

"I'm going home." I shove him away.

With a possessive grunt, he grabs my arms and slams me back where I was. My heart jumps into my throat, worried he'll do more than push me around.

"No. Let me finish. You agreed to this." He forces his dick in my face again. I swallow my disgust and give him what he wants. One time and it's done. I can go back to Jimmy.

Dez moves away from my face and tries to grab my tits. "Why are you still wearing this?" He pinches the fabric of my tank top. "What the hell? Bitch, take that shirt off."

I wiggle out from under it, trying to keep my scars to the bed.

He pauses, his eyebrows scrunching tight while his eyes travel to my side instead of my exposed breasts. "Wait. What is that?"

He grabs my shoulder and turns me to get a full view of my back.

I squirm out from under him, and roll away, snatching my shirt.

He doesn't grab for me, it's like he's stunned. Then his nose wrinkles up and his lips curl down in obvious disgust. "What the fuck is wrong with you? You're just a branded cow."

Dez called me *branded cow* every time I saw him after that. Or he'd *moo*. Hushed whispers as I passed him in the hallway, followed by laughing from whoever was nearby. He didn't say it loud enough to draw attention, intentionally. That made it all worse. Like a dirty secret.

He and his small group of friends kept the joke going, taunting me on the rare occasions I had to see them.

Kinda wish I woulda told my friends. I'm sure Bobby and Cody woulda stuck up for me. Hell, Jimmy would've, even though Jimmy didn't care when I kept my tank top on during sex and didn't have any clue about my scars.

I know Zac's not at all like Dez. But what if he looked at me like Dez did that day? I don't think I could handle seeing his face disgusted by me. I hope he wouldn't respond that way, but I don't know.

I'm not ready to risk it. Don't know if I ever will be. He can't know why I can't have him…because that would be the end of this.

I want to hold on to these hot nights for a little bit longer.

So no, he doesn't know.

Doesn't know why I make him fuck me in the dark and always wear something if the lights are on. That I'm scared of the moment when he sees. That I'm not ready to tell him why I can't have him. He's the first guy I've considered showing.

These scars are much deeper than ugly marks on the skin. They've scarred my soul.

Memories plague my mind. The times Dipshit hit me. Used me as a fucking ash tray. Made me do things for him. Favors. Told me nothing happened, and I imagined it.

I believed him.

The body remembers all of the things that happen to it. So even when he'd convinced my mind nothing happened, I could touch each scar and know it was a lie. Everything out of his filthy lips has always been a lie.

Zac needs someone better than me.

No one deserves my damaged goods. No one deserves someone who battles these demons so much that they can't see around them. No one deserves someone who is so hard to love.

I wake up with night terrors. I'm a workaholic. I'm constantly pushing people away because I'm afraid if they see the real me it's too much. It gets lonely. I've never been able to fix any of it despite how hard I try.

Zac hasn't been around me on the days when I get angry for no reason. I'm not the girl of his dreams. I mean, his dad's old fashioned. Maybe he's wanting some kind of perfect housewife in the future. That's not me.

I'm the girl who got broken by an evil man.

My heart breaks for me. And it breaks for the many others.

It breaks for Cody. We bore the same kind of scars.

Sobs loosen from my chest, rattling my ribs while I gasp for breath.

"Trish?" Zac's knocking on the bathroom door. A few seconds later he says, "You okay?"

I run the sink water. "I'm fine." I work to make my voice sound strong. I'm done thinking about this. Never seems to help. My beautiful escape is waiting for me. I hope it's okay I'm using him this way.

It probably isn't. But I can't carry any more guilt. I have too much already.

Keep going. Keep moving. Get through this.

I taught that to Lexie. I learned it because it's all I could say to myself when Dipshit lost his temper.

I pull on a tank top and the boxer shorts I like to sleep in. Making sure the mess from the tub is cleaned up so we don't slip, I fix my hair in pigtail braids. Maybe it's time for a change. That always helps Lexie. New hair, new you. I'll call next week and make a hair appointment.

When I get back to Zac, he's naked in bed with the ice cream and two spoons. "Hey." He smiles. My body warms instantly. The cold, dead heart, all broken inside, puts a bandage on for now. Temporary fix.

He holds up a pint of ice cream. "You're gonna have to tell me your favorite flavor for next time."

"Oh it's Ben and Jerry's Phish Food."

He busts up laughing. "No way!"

"I saw you picked the right one."

He unwraps the napkin around the pint to reveal the exact flavor. "I was prayin' to Jesus you didn't have an allergy to soybeans since there's an allergy warning on the label."

"No, no, I'm good with anything."

"And I'm good with what you're good with." He winks. "Now get over here, it's fixin' to melt."

"What if I say no?" I bite my bottom lip, heat flowing straight down my legs as I watch his eyes glow.

"Then I'll eat every bite?" He plays off a stern expression, and I'm so tight down below I'm gonna orgasm if he keeps being this cute.

"You're too adorable." I throw my hands in the air.

"Too adorable? Me?" He feigns surprise, and I pounce on him.

"Yes, you." I take a spoon full of ice cream. "Because if anyone's eating all of it, it's me." I hold the spoon on the tip of my tongue. He pushes the spoon away and takes my lips, eating half my bite of ice cream out of my mouth. I dive my tongue into his and fight for it.

"I win." I swallow the bite.

"You did not just go there." He flips us over so he's on top.

"It's *my* ice cream." I stick my tongue out at him. No clue why he brings out this playful side of me.

"It's *our* ice cream." He reaches to the side and gets a big spoonful. He licks the spoon and paints ice cream on my face with his tongue. Shivers work through me at the cold sensation. It's so erotic and sexy.

"Do you like this?"

I close my eyes, relinquishing my need for control in an attempt to follow his lead. Breathing deeply into my lungs, I relax against the sheets. His tongue moves onto my neck. He starts to pull my shirt up.

"Nope, not there cowboy." I stop his hands. My heart rate goes from zero to a thousand.

"You don't want it on your chest?" His face is surprised.

"Lights off?" I hear fear in my tone, feel in my bones this worry that he'll get mad, that he'll lose his shit.

I've gone too far.

First the bathtub, now not letting him do what he wants.

A knot forms in my throat. This is it, I can feel it. He's gonna lose it. I'm gonna be a punching bag.

That's what I deserve.

Zac raises his arm up and I brace myself, gripping the sheets tightly. My body stiffens. The times Dipshit hit me rush back in full force. His words haunt me:

You're a good for nothing idiot! A stupid pig that leeches off of me. You'll never be worth a damn thing!

The lights go out.

My eyes crack open from the death pinch I had them in.

Zac didn't hit me?

He reached for the lightswitch and turned the lamp off.

My teeth chatter against each other.

"Sorry, I forgot. Just thought the ice cream would be fun to lick off your chest. It's totally cool. I'll remember for next time." Zac's messing with the ice cream, like he's gonna keep being cute with it. There's no anger in his tone.

I snap out of the fear, realizing the past has pulled me to a place that doesn't exist. My body isn't hurt. Zac's a good guy. He didn't hit me. It was a flashback.

"You okay?" All his playfulness is gone, replaced with concern. "Is this not alright with you?"

No one's ever asked me that. The knot in my throat increases to the point I can't talk. My eyes burn. My body quakes. I'm trying to be here, but I'm just a little girl doing her best with a monster taking advantage of me.

The ice cream clunks as Zac sets it on the end table. "Hey, now, come here." He scoops me into the biggest hug. For several seconds I just hold him.

"I'm sorry." I choke out. "I'm not usually like this. I swear I'm not usually like this. I'm so fuckin' sorry."

"For what?" He strokes my hair.

"I've got some past shit that's comin' up. I don't want it to. Believe me, I wanna melt into your ice cream flavored kisses. But this is what's goin' on inside me." I snuggle into his embrace, hoping my fear can soften.

I'm safe now. This is different. I'm with Zac. Zac's never hurt me. I can get through this.

"I'm here, okay?" He holds me tighter. "And I'm glad you told me."

"You're glad?" I tear away from his arms. "How can you be glad about that?"

"I have bad anxiety. I get it."

"But it's anything but sexy."

"This isn't about sexy. Not to me." He holds me closer. "I just want to be here for you. Through whatever you're dealing with." His tone sounds sincere. I dare to hope this *is* different.

Can there be someone who doesn't judge me for being broken? Someone who cares enough that a badly timed mental breakdown doesn't ruin their night? Someone who is chill enough to hit pause on a fun evening and talk? Or comfort me? Or watch reruns of Grey's Anatomy until I'm feeling more like myself?

Is that someone Zac?

"Trish, what I was gonna tell you in the car..." He pauses and I feel my heart pick up a little bit. Maybe it is him. These flutters. These feelings. These moments of raw vulnerability.

"I'm honestly terrified to tell you this." Breath comes out of his lungs in a hard sigh. "Trish, I care about you. You haven't told me much about your past. And you haven't told me why it is you're so guarded, but I can see that you are. I can see that you need to be. That whatever's happened in your life is so much that you're not able to really trust someone. And that's okay. We all have our scars–"

He keeps talking while my mind lingers on his last word. Scars. The scars I bear. The ones I won't let him see.

"Did you mentally check out? I noticed, because I do that same thing all the time. Where'd you go?" His hands hold mine in the pitch black room.

"Can you just hold me?" I swallow against the pain in my chest.

"Of course." His tone is soothing as he wraps me with his muscled arms.

For several heartbeats we're still.

I startle as he hops up from the bed.

Oh, okay. Yeah. He's gonna go.

Must not be him.

I feel a little heartbroken that he's leaving. My fingers find the scars on my back, running back and forth against the damaged skin.

Then I realize he hasn't left. He's wandering through the dark room until the light of the mini fridge illuminates as he puts the ice cream away.

He grabs his phone and shines the flashlight far away from me as he goes to the bathroom. Coming back to the bed, he has a wet washcloth. His flashlight goes off and he sets his phone on the nightstand. Slowly, he cleans the sticky ice cream residue off of my face.

The water on the washcloth is warm and his touch is tender. Is this what it feels like to be cared about?

Tossing the washcloth onto the floor, he snuggles beside me in the bed, not caring this is supposed to just be a hot night, but I'm falling apart in the Marriott.

"I mean it, ya know?" He says softly.

"Mean what?" I cuddle into his chest.

"That I care about you. Not just the sex. Not just how cute you are, even though you're freakin' precious. Not just because you have so much mystery it drives me wild with wanting to know what is behind these walls. But you. Trish Montgomery. The sweet angel I'm holding in this bed. The girl you are. The one that's trying so hard."

"I don't feel like I'm tryin' hard enough."

"I know you don't." He kisses my head. "But I see it. Remember the mirror? You're too close to see it." His arms tighten securely around me. "You don't have to tell me what all you've endured. But please know I'm here. Please know I want to support you. Even if this is all we ever are for each other."

"Isn't there a song about that?"

"Yeah, hold on." He reaches for his phone and finds the song "I'll Be Your

Mirror" by The Velvet Underground.

I listen to the beat of his heart mixing with the music until mine calms to his rhythm.

"Maybe we can try the ice cream thing again later?" My voice is timid, like I'm a scared child.

"But you didn't like it. Why would we?" His tone is caring.

"It wasn't the ice cream." I swallow hard, debating how much to share. He's perceptive. It's okay to share with him. I take a deep breath. "It's taking off my shirt. I actually loved the ice cream. And you can put it on my legs if you want. It's really just my back and side I keep covered."

"Oh, you can always have a shirt." His chest relaxes, like he understands. "Whatever you need. Seriously."

All the times I've been wrong in the past make it hard to put any bit of trust in his words. But his actions are backing it up. Though we planned on a hot and heavy night, he's comforting me in bed.

"It's just a hard moment." I lean into him, sad we've both dealt with more than our fair share of trauma.

"I know how those go." He runs his fingers sweetly through my hair. I feel safe in his arms.

Please, Zac...be real.

December

Trish

I'd like to do something nice for Zac to repay him for helping with my website so much. He's got it working almost as much as a personal assistant would. Best of all, he video called me and showed me how to maintain it all myself. It's helped a lot.

I wonder what I could do for him.

You're growing too attached. I shake away the thought. I'd love to help him because this has been a huge favor.

When my brain is fried from editing for so long, I take a break to clear my head. Scrolling through my phone, I catch a post from Jimmy Hendrick's buddy, tagging him. I loved going out with him, but neither of us want more than the late-night lonely calls we've been to each other for years.

I'm not sure I want that anymore…if I have Zac.

The thought sends pure terror up my spine like a jolt of lightning. Zac's been texting me every morning and off and on throughout the day. Sweet messages asking how I'm doing.

My phone digs with a text from Zac.

Zac: Plans this friday?

Me: I can maybe be available. Why?

Zac: Pencil me in on that planner of yours?

Me: My planner, huh?

Zac: You know, so it actually happens.

Me: As opposed to it not happening?

Zac: Yeah, see you're that kind of person who lives by their planner. So if I'm in there, I figure it's gonna happen.

I jot down his name in fancy block letters on my planner for Friday. Snapping a pic on my phone, I text it to him. He replies with a big grinning emoji. I shove all my stuff in my bag and drive to Anna Mae's house.

"Knock, knock." I announce as I wave through the open screen door.

"Oh, hey." Anna Mae greets me. "You're early."

"I'm usually running late. Sorry."

"Just gimme a minute. Come on in." She goes to the cluttered tiny table in their kitchenette where she's got a bunch of books out.

"You applying for any colleges?" I plop down in a dining chair.

"Yeah, I'd love to. But I can't get a sports scholarship since I stopped playing ball." She frowns. "I'm sure I can't afford it now. Wish I could."

"Well, what if you get a photography scholarship?"

She looks at me like I've just turned into a cat or something. Those wide eyes seem to have no room for the thought of her going to college.

"It's what you want, ain't it?" I step over to her AP calculus book. There's an old test tucked in the corner with a big 98 written in red ink on the top.

"Well it looks like you've got the grades for an academic scholarship and

I bet I could pull some strings in the Art History department if you wanted to go to Suncastle?"

"You really think I could go to college?" The doubt in her tone makes me wanna scoop her up and take her out of this situation. I see so much of my pain in those eyes. She deserves better.

"I really think you can go." I give her a reassuring smile.

"It'd be like a dream come true." She looks happier than I've ever seen her. "You'd really do that?"

"Of course I would, Mae Mae. Whatever you need."

She gives me a huge hug. I make a note in my planner to email some of my old connections at Suncastle.

For the next couple hours, I give her some lessons. She's a quick study and I'm really impressed.

I order some pizzas for everybody. I'm starving and from the looks of things, they are too.

I bring the cheese pizza to the small table and the kids rush over, pushing each other out of the way.

"Kids, take turns. Jeez." Anna Mae moves the pizza until they form a nice line. When everyone's eating on a blanket in the backyard, I come back in the house with Mae Mae.

"Tell me again, when's your dad getting outta prison?" I look at the house. It needs so much TLC. I oughta do to their place what I did to Lexie's. It needs some serious help in the decor department.

"When's dad getting out of prison? Not sure." She's looking out the window, chewing her pizza.

"Do you want him back home?"

"Fuck no." She puts her hand over her mouth. "Whoops, don't tell Mama I swore."

"She still washin' your mouth out with soap?" I take a bite.

"Bleh, no, thank heavens." She shakes her head. "Might as well though, with the scorn in her eyes when she looks at me." Anna Mae lets out a heavy sigh.

"Anything you wanna get off your mind? It's been awhile since we had a good chat. My stepdad was a real piece of crap. I understand what it's like to be the only one who sees through their bullshit."

"Thanks." Her face is timid, but I think it'll help to know someone's on her side. Even if we never talk about it, she can have a safe space. I would've given anything to have someone there for me when I was her age. Several times I tried to talk to Jimmy, but he wasn't one to care. Too much going on in his own head to give any worry about the hell I was dealing with.

"It does get better, just so you know." I nudge her shoulder. "I mean, I've got all the freedom I want now. Besides taking care of Nana, I can go anywhere, do anything."

"How's your nana doing?" She asks.

"Real good." I smile. "But yeah. You've got a great life ahead of you. I mean look at these pictures you took today." I gesture to the camera. "You're going places and I'm just thrilled I get to watch."

The smile on her face is worth every bit of my time and the effort it took to convince Mama Jones. Our neighborhood is full of folks who aren't kind. People who are rude and not accepting of anyone, no matter what you do. Everyone is so stuck in their ways.

But I can be there for this girl. I can show her that no matter what situation she grows up in, she can have the life she wants. I'm living proof. Mostly.

Zac wants me to see the good in myself the same way I see the good in Anna Mae.

As I head for the front door, she stops me.

"I can't thank you enough for this." She wraps her arms around me and a lump forms in my throat. "I don't know anyone else that ever gives a shit." She puts her hand on her mouth again. "Whoops. My dirty cussing mouth."

"I don't care if you swear, honey." I smile. "I'm just glad I get to show you some things." I pull out my planner. "I've asked before, but do you think you can help me with some of the local photo shoots? I'll pay you for it."

"You have one a week from Saturday?" She looks at the date.

"Yep." I show her the time slots.

"I'll ask Mama."

"Okay. I'll see you on Thursday for lessons."

"Bye Trish!"

"See ya!" I head to my car.

My phone dings and instead of dreading a potential cancellation, my heart sings when I see Zac's name light up.

Zac: Okay, it's 90's night at Garrison's on Friday. Come prepared to dance.

Me: All penciled in and ready to go.

Me: Is it cool if I invite Bobby, Lex and Mickey?

Zac: Awww, that's a great idea. Please do!!!

He's such a goofball. It's adorable how excited he gets over little things. I pull out my phone and text Lexie.

Me: Dress up like Lisa Frank characters with me for 90's night this weekend?

Lexie: That'd be way fun. Text me when you have your costume together.

I click to our group chat and make sure everyone can make it. I add Zac to the group.

Over the next several days, I spend every spare minute looking for cute stuff for the costume. Lexie and I coordinate all our ensemble. This is gonna be amazing.

90's night is by far their best themed night. All week I've been on pins and needles waiting for this day.

I walk up to Zac's apartment, and he opens the door.

"OMG Lisa Frank!" He runs his hands down my pale blue spaghetti strap dress. I bedazzled a rainbow heart over my chest.

"Made it myself." I do a little twirl so my skirt flares out. "Took a few trips to the craft store, but I like how it turned out." My hair is frosted rainbow colored under a white baseball cap. I'm holding a rainbow colored paintbrush.

"Inspired by the Panda Painter, right? We had so many of those stickers. Sadie loved them." His face lights up so much when he talks about her.

"I'm glad you got it." I was half worried it wouldn't be clear.

"Heck yes, you nailed it!" His sexy smile warms me up. He's wearing a long sleeve flannel shirt over a Star Wars graphic T, long straight light blue faded jeans, combat boots. On his neck, he's got several stacked puka shell necklaces. "You think I look nineties enough?"

"These bring me back." I run my finger under one of the puka shell necklaces. "You're like a Backstreet Boy."

"Brian or Nick? Maybe Howie? Whatever you do, do not say AJ." He doesn't miss a beat and I chuckle that he's listing off the Backstreet Boys.

"Um, you'd never pull off blond so not Nick. Besides, you're the sweet one. Brian all the way."

"I'll take that as a compliment." He smiles so big his dimples show. "Ready?"

"Yep." I take his hand after he locks up, and we head to my car.

"I'll drive." He pulls so we walk to his truck, opens my door and helps me in.

"I got you a little somethin' for when it's Country Night again." He reaches behind me and grabs a cowgirl hat that's white, lacy and eleven kinds of adorable.

"Aww, you didn't have to get me anything." I take off my baseball cap and switch it out for the cowgirl hat.

"No, you gotta wait 'til it's Country Night." He scolds me and fire rises through my middle in a sexy thrill. It's cute because I know it's playful. "It'll ruin your costume. Don't you dare wear that tonight."

"Watch me." I blow a big pink bubble gum bubble, and he pops it with his teeth, fighting me for the gum.

It's so fucking hot.

"If you don't get me in there now, I'm not gonna be able to wait to pound you 'til we're done dancing." I kiss him deep, still not letting him have the gum.

He runs his tongue slowly along his bottom lip. "I wasn't counting on waiting too long."

"Start this truck or we'll stand up all our friends." I look at his keys sitting idly in the ignition.

"I might be okay with that." He chews the bubblegum he stole out of my mouth and brings it into an impressively large bubble. I kiss around it and take my gum back.

"Now move it, Backstreet Boy."

"Okay, but only if we get to come home early."

"I don't believe it Mr. Dance All Night." I shake my head. "You hear the music and you won't stop until they kick us out."

"I won't even stop after." He winks again and I feel that surge of heat. Next time I meet him in Suncastle for a dance, I'm coming early for a quickie in his room before we have to go.

He turns on his truck. "So, um, is it okay if Bobby and Lexie know we're dating?"

"Are we dating?" I ask.

"I thought we weren't...?" His cheeks turn red. "I guess we aren't?"

"You're cute when you're worried." I rub his nose with mine. "Technically we aren't dating. But yeah, sure. Why not?"

"Sure, why not?" He wrinkles his brow.

"I just mean I don't care what they think anymore. I like you." I give him a smile and immediately worry I've said too much to get his hopes up. "Not exclusive, though. If you wanna date other people then…"

"I don't." He looks at me for a while. "But I don't want to scare you either."

"That's really kind. I appreciate you not wanting to scare or pressure me." I turn up the corners of my lips. "Let's take this one step at a time." I suggest.

"Aww, well that sounds perfect."

We go into Garrison's and sure enough, Bobby and Lexie are at a table waiting for us.

"Um, this is fabulous." Lexie hops up and gives me a big hug.

"I love how yours turned out, too!" I eye her gorgeous outfit inspired by the Lisa Frank unicorn. Bobby isn't dressed up.

"He didn't wanna match?" I eye Bobby as he and Zac start talking about baseball.

"Didn't even ask." She snickers.

"You look real happy." I say.

"I am. Trish, this is seriously the best. I'm basically living at his apartment. We're settling into this unexpected and wonderful relationship. I had no idea he wanted so much. I want it too. Like, I really want it."

"I'm genuinely happy for you, boo." I'm surprised to feel my heart warm as I say this. I wasn't sure about them getting together, but it looks like it's been really good. It's like the life is back in Bobby's eyes when he seemed down-hearted the last few times I've seen him.

We spend the evening catching up and having a great time.

She pulls out her phone and snaps a bunch of photos of all of us.

Photos with me and Zac. I don't take pics with guys.

Mickey and Claudia join us at the table. All of us order drinks and some food to share. I ordered a double. After the week I've had, I shoulda just asked for the entire bottle of tequila.

"Sometimes" by Britney Spears comes through the speakers bringing me back to junior high.

"Oh, I love this song!" My face lights up, that alcohol doing its trick.

"Awwwww, of course you love it." Zac chuckles, that bright dimple shining smile of his tugging at my insides like he does. We set down our drinks and head to the dance floor.

"You do?" I wrinkle my brow, looking into those gorgeous brown eyes for a joke I think he's gonna make. They glimmer off the lights, but don't hold a bit of teasing.

"Um, it's Britney." He gives me a look that says it's obvious he would love her even though I'm completely surprised.

"Seriously?" I try not to chuckle, but I find this eleven kinds of funny.

"Uh, yeah." He smiles so big I can tell he's being real.

I bite my lip, bounce my head to the music. I start singing along to the first verse, mixing up some of the lyrics. Zac bobs his head in time, correcting my words and joining when the chorus starts.

"Oh, so you're a fan enough to know the chorus, but not enough to know the verses." I snark.

"Who says I don't know the verses?" He spins me, my skirt flowing up. When he brings me back, my cheek presses into the strong muscles of his shoulders and I melt into his embrace. Fuck, his body is doing it's thing, getting me revved up way before it should.

He leans his head down to my ear, whispering the second verse, knowing all the words. They echo in my ear, the same way they have a thousand times. The song reforms in my mind. It's not the song to soothe the broken heart of a preteen anymore. It's mending it, instead. No, Zac's mending it. He's changing the meaning of the song, because with him everything means so much more.

Resistance pulls at me. But I know that's not what I want to feel. I want to feel him. *Please, Trish, just let yourself pretend he's different. It can just be for a little while. Just let yourself have a good night.*

Let him mend that broken heart of yours. You don't need to avoid this. I promise.

A knot forms in my throat. I want to trust. I want to love.

I don't know how.

"Will you play this for me when we get back to your place?" I look up into those gorgeous brown eyes. "I've always loved music. And if it's anything like your random dance singing, I'm sure a personal concert would be a really good time."

"I'd *love* to give you a personal concert in my living room."

And he does. After a night of fun, we get ready for bed and he plays me several songs on his guitar. I fall asleep to the sound of his voice. It's heaven to my ears.

Please, always sing for me.

We spend the weekend at his apartment. I'm so pleasured and satisfied. Can't seem to stop smiling.

"I've been thinking." He props up on his elbow to face me after we've both caught our breath.

"Yeah?" I match his position.

"Now, this isn't a pressure thing," he pauses and I nod. "I'm getting tested."

"And you're wondering if I want to so we don't have to bother with condoms?"

"Yeah." He's got this adorable shy smile on his face. "No pressure."

"Are you playin' around with other people?" I think about the past few months and the handful of guys I've hooked up with. Since Zac, I haven't felt a need to be on my dating apps or go to the bar.

That doesn't mean we're together. I still don't need anyone.

"I'm not, at this moment in time, playing around with anyone besides you. In a very much casual, no strings attached kind of way." He gives me a funny look, and then bops me playfully on the nose. "But really, I hate condoms.

They're annoying and that one time we didn't have them was super annoying and yeah, I'm cliché as fuck, remember? I wanna *feel* you."

I roll my eyes but part of this is really sweet. He's giving me space. Pretty sure he'd propose to me tomorrow if I was on board. But I'm not. Relying on someone else isn't something I'm capable of.

I like being with him, and I'm not ready to throw that away. But I don't *need* him. Since Daddy died, I've never needed anyone. I've relied on *myself*. And I like it like that. Less disappointment that way.

But Zac is fun. I'm allowed to have fun. That doesn't mean I'm tied down.

It would be nice not to fuss with those rubbers, though. "Um, yeah, I think I'm okay with that."

"And while we're talking about it…what about birth control?"

"Oh, yeah, I'm on the pill." I shrug.

"Okay, cool." He smiles.

"Okay, cool." I echo.

Zac

Taco Tuesday is my religion. If it's Tuesday, there better be a taco in my mouth. End of story.

Ethan, Briar and I walk into the little Mexican restaurant on fifth street. They have the best tacos in all of Suncastle.

"Hey, boys." Megan takes us to our usual table in the back corner. "Samantha will get your order in a jiffy." She returns to the hostess station.

"What're we drinking tonight?" Samantha hands us the menus. "The usual?"

"Yep." I nod.

"It'll be out in a minute." She saunters to the kitchen.

My phone buzzes in my pocket. Sprinkle notifications. Even with the recent likes and comments, I'm down from where I want to be engagement wise. Damn, I wish these videos got a few more views. I keep trying new things. I guess I'll take what I can get.

A few of my regulars messaged me requests so I jot those down in my notes app.

"So then what happened?" Ethan leans his elbows on the table.

"Well, all the cows got loose."

"No way!" Ethan bangs his fist on the table like a caveman.

I clearly missed something.

"Yeah, so it'll be a while before I go back." Briar shakes his head.

Samantha brings our drinks and bowls of chips and salsa.

"Thanks," I smile at her. "What'd you get on the test?"

"An eighty-four. You?" She grabs some straws out of her apron and tosses them in the middle of the table.

"Ninety-six." I didn't find the test that hard, honestly.

"Damn, I need to study with you more." She lets out a frustrated sigh. "Taco's will be out soon."

"Thank you!" Ethan yells. "You and Samantha gonna *study* each other one of these days?" Ethan eyes her from the bar.

"Nah." I drink more of my beer.

"Oh hey, there's Carter." Briar looks at the table where our new catcher sits alone.

"Let's invite him over." I stand and walk to his table. "It's a sin to sit alone on Taco Tuesday, brother."

"Oh, hey man." Carter lifts his soda to me as I approach. "A sin, huh?"

"You can't eat here by yourself. You're welcome to come to our table." I tilt my head toward the booth.

"Sure. Thanks." He follows me and we move so there's room for him.

"You guys come here a lot?" Carter takes a chip.

"Every Tuesday." Briar tips his beer.

"It's Zac's religion." Ethan says. "Speak of the devil." He looks at the table next to us where a couple guys in suits and nametags sit on the bench. Mormon missionaries? They've knocked on my door a few times.

"Hey, Briar. Random question. Didn't you grow up super religious? Aren't those like your people?" Ethan sips on his beer.

"Yep." Briar nods at the missionaries, but then looks at our table. There's a hint of something in his eyes. Regret maybe? "But I think I'd burn if I walked through the chapel doors now." He tips his beer. "They don't take too kindly to this. No alcohol or coffee."

"I'd die." Ethan scoffs.

"You still believe in it at all?" I sip from my bottle.

"Between how awful they are to women and that there's no support for the LGBT community, I've got a lot of reservations." Briar lifts his coaster up, flips it over and puts it back on the table.

"What about God, though?" Ethan prompts.

"The God I believe in wouldn't care about all that stuff. All He'd care is if I'm a good person." Briar points his finger.

"Yeah," I think about my faith. "Organized religion goes a little too far. They get really caught up in things that don't matter." I sigh. "I don't understand the lack of acceptance." I let the alcohol take the edge off my day.

I'd been going to church every week until all the drama with Sadie came up. It was too hard to go to a place where people thought my sister was going to hell and loved to give me an earful about. It hasn't damaged my relationship with God to step away from attending. In fact, I really appreciate campus ministries. That's enough for me to feel a spiritual recharge.

Ethan pulls out his phone and starts filming. "Smile for the mama's."

"Suncastle MILFS, how you ladies doin' tonight?" I raise my beer into the camera. We do some glam poses and Ethan ends the video.

"Suncastle MILFS, huh?" Briar shakes his head.

"I see a T-Shirt coming on." Ethan pulls up his notes app and adds it to the list of more than a dozen shirt ideas.

"You gonna convince Coach to let you have a little stand outside the games? Pay for your dorm room when you spend all your scholarship money on Taco Tuesday?" Briar says between bites of chips and salsa.

"Dude, would you slow down?" I chuckle. "Remember when Cody swiped chips from the kitchen when we walked to the table? Then he'd scarf down all the chips before Samantha even got the drink order?" I pull the chips away from Briar so the rest of us can have some.

"I'm still wondering how that guy ate so many frickin' chips and never gained a pound." Ethan says. "I can eat like this before baseball season starts, but not during."

"Cody?" Carter asks.

We all go quiet.

"What'd I miss?" Carter looks at each of us.

"Yeah man, you didn't hear?" Ethan clears his throat. "Cody Jones played for Suncastle, before the accident."

"And where is he now?" Carter says the words. I glance at Briar and see the pain in his eyes. For the first time in a long time, that pang of missing Cody hits hard. It occurs to me that Ethan and I are the last ones who'll remember playing with Cody. Once Bobby and Briar and the other seniors graduate this year and Ethan and I and the other juniors do next year, it'll be a whole team that never played a game with him.

The realization makes me so hauntingly sad. It ain't right. None of it's right.

"He got in a car accident a year and a half ago." Briar chokes out the words like they're still hard to say. The table goes silent. Somber.

"Oh shit. Was it bad?" Carter asks.

"Didn't make it to the hospital, it happened so quick. Look." Ethan gestures to the framed picture of Cody they've got hanging up on the wall. Like a handful of places in Suncastle, there's a tribute on the wall for him.

Life can be so fleeting. Someone's here one minute and the next they're gone.

Samantha brings out all our plates of tacos.

"Where's Bobby? Is he coming tonight?" Briar wrinkles his lips, pulling out his phone.

"He's been ditching all our plans lately." Ethan says.

"Drooling over that redhead." Carter observes.

"Oh, Lexie?" I ask.

"Yeah, that's the one. I think she's fine as hell." Carter whistles.

"Don't let Bobby hear you talk that way." Briar warns. "She's his goddess, soul mate, alter ego, true love, companion, partner, best friend, the peanut butter to his jelly, the rice to his meal prep, the very reason for which his soul exists." Briar does a chef's kiss into the air. "…need I go on or do you get the picture?"

"Seriously?" Carter raises a brow.

"You arrived a year too late." I poke him with my elbow. "Bobby's never so much as gone out with a girl twice in a row, until Lexie. But now she's off limits, and apparently so is he."

"Sounds like a challenge." Carter nudges my shoulder.

"I wouldn't risk it if I was you." Briar shakes his head real slowly.

"Y'all all seem to worship Bobby even more than this Cody fella." Carter scoffs.

I swear Carter must've been a hotshot where he was last playing ball. It's like he wants us to worship him when we've barely met. What is he? Some baseball god? Prove it, man.

"Hey now, you watch your mouth." Briar folds his arms, sitting taller, all the unspoken threats he's making crystal clear.

"My mistake." Carter holds his hands up in surrender. "Still catching all the dynamics around here."

"See, that's the funny thing." Bobby's voice comes from behind us and I hold back a chuckle, wondering how long he's been standing there. He reaches between me and Carter and lifts a taco off of Carter's plate. "You thought this was *your* taco. But I saw it and it looked really good."

Carter's expression is horrified until he puts on a front of cocky arrogance.

"I could say it's a challenge." Bobby takes a big bite off the taco. "Or I could just remember that taco isn't on my plate." He returns the taco to its little stand next to the pile of rice. He pats Carter on the shoulder and we all know the message came across.

"Hey, man." Briar scoots over and Bobby sits by him. He sets the tray of tacos between them to share.

Carter stares at the bite taken out of his taco.

"I'm good. Ate with Lex. But I couldn't miss Taco Tuesday." Bobby slides the tray back to Briar. "Thanks, though."

My phone buzzes in my pocket. As my fingers fumble to unlock my screen, my heart races. Trish's name.

Trish: You busy?

I look up at the guys. With half my beer still in the bottle, I'm totally still safe to be driving. *Hear that Anxiety? Safe.*

Me: Just tell me when and where. I'll be there.

Trish: Do you think you could drive to my place? Is that too far?

Me: Not at all, little miss.

Trish: Bring your guitar?

Me: Awwwww.

Trish: You and your Awwwww.

Trish: Really though, bring it.

Me: You got it.

Next thing I know, she's sending me the address.

"I gotta run." I look up from my phone to a bunch of gloomy faces. "Y'all look like I just told you we lost the playoffs."

"It's Taco Tuesday, man. Don't tell me you're losing the faith." Briar wrinkles his brow.

"Yeah, we just got here," Ethan bitches.

"I have a date with destiny." I pop another quick chip in my mouth for the road. "Don't count on me for the run in the morning." I scoot out of my chair, tossing fifteen bucks on the table to pay for my share. "Carter, have my tacos."

"Remember your condoms." Briar calls as I give him a half assed wave while I rush out of the restaurant.

Ever since Trish and I started this ring-around-the-rosy bedroom edition, I've been keeping a box of condoms in my glovebox, just in case.

I'd love to feel her for real, without anything between us. I'd never dream of sneaking off a condom or fighting her on wearing one, but man it'd be nice to just go with our spontaneous moments without that little interruption every time.

I got tested so I know I'm clean. Last time Ethan got chlamydia he was super uncomfortable. That's enough to make me extra careful. Wouldn't wanna pass anything along to my customers, or Trish. She told me she hasn't been exposed lately but she'd get tested too. I'm not sure if her results came back or not but that'd be nice.

Racing down the sidewalk, I get to my place as fast as I can. Wearing her favorite of my Suncastle Jerseys and dark-wash jeans, I fix my hair real quick. I'll leave the jersey with her so she can wear it and think about me until our next time. Even though it's barely been a week and a half since she drove here for the 90's night at Garrison's, it feels like it's been a lifetime without her.

There were supposed to be no strings. But, no. I go and lace up those strings good and tight. Now I'm like her little puppet, just waiting for her to pull on those strings.

What are you doing to yourself? It's just gonna hurt more when she cuts you loose.

This sounds crazy, but it may be worth whatever pain may come.

Her texting for me to come as soon as possible is proof she's as hungry for me as I am for her. Fuck, I'm thrilled she texted me to come over. Don't even care if I have to drive the whole way to her.

Wait, it's Tuesday. I have a midterm tomorrow. Last test before the final.

I'm standing on third base, ready to steal home and the batter strikes out sending us to the dugout before I score. Goddammit. It's not a weekend, and I have responsibilities.

I'll miss my morning classes.

I'm gonna miss class for a girl? Really? This hasn't ever been tempting.

Trish isn't just some girl, even if she's still thinking of me as just some guy. I'm hoping one day she'll be open to changing that.

I grab a couple things and toss them into my backpack. Books? No. Won't have time. Pills? Yeah, better keep anxiety levels as low as I can. Wallet. Keys. Backpack. Guitar. Ready.

I turn the radio up loud, tapping the steering wheel over and over to keep me from speeding. The hour and a half drive flies by. Giving me her address is a big deal. Since we went to a hotel that first time, I can tell she's not one to just invite anybody over to her place.

On the way, I stop at Publix and buy a bunch of stuff to make her for breakfast in the morning. Oh, and the ice cream and chocolate she loves when she comes. If I didn't have a test, I'd stay with her all day and forget about the consequences.

The drive felt so familiar. Like coming home.

It's a little cold for December in South Carolina, but I'm all warm inside. Before checking the apartment number, I have a feeling I've found hers. This looks like where she'd live. When I glance at the number, I chuckle because I'm absolutely right. It's got her signature design elements I recognize from when she was decorating Lexie's house.

A large teal rug sits under a gray outdoor sofa with adorable black and white striped accent pillows. Lots of hanging plants dangle from the ceiling. It's so cozy. Most of all, it's hers. I want to stand on this porch forever, with my girl.

Slow down....

Kicking the dirt off my shoes, I notice the welcome mat that says *Come on in, but only if you brought the good stuff!* It brings a smile to my face.

Since my hands are full, I knock on her door with the toe of my sneakers. I've got my backpack, a few sacks of groceries in one hand and my guitar case in the other.

Trish isn't just a hookup–although every time is fucking fantastic–she's more.

"Hey, doll baby." She opens the door a peak, teasing mystery in her eyes. "I'm wearing something special." When she does an adorable shoulder shimmy, I catch the purple lace of her lingerie.

Happiness swells in my chest. Something washes over me. A feeling kin to hope, maybe?

Can she feel it?

The look in her eyes tells me she loves that I'm here. I may not be super experienced with casual, but I'm pretty sure that's not just lust in her eyes.

"That's my favorite outfit." I lean against the door, pressing a hot kiss on her delicate red lips. Can't wait to have those stamps all over my skin, the marks of her claiming me.

Gripping my collar, she yanks me inside her apartment and shuts the door. Needy kisses plaster my lips. She tastes like Juicy Fruit gum. Her tongue runs against the roof of my mouth, and I let out a sensual moan, needing her. My hands burn from the grocery sack straps and my guitar handle, but I don't even care. I glide my tongue under hers, sucking her breath. The air that filled her lungs is now in mine, a rush of sensations making my pecs tight.

"Make yourself my home." She draws back, leaving me wanting. "Make yourself *at* home, I mean."

"Freudian slip?" I take in the adorable apartment she has. It smells like vanilla with candles flickering all over her dimly lit space. She wasn't kidding about preferring the dark. I set down my stuff on her freshly vacuumed carpet.

"Something like that." She runs her hand down my chest. "I love this jersey."

"I love everything you're wearing." I whisper low against her ear. "And I know you love this. You wanna wear it?"

She looks incredible. I'd hate to cover that up, but I noticed our first weekend she loves wearing my clothes.

Her smile makes me so happy. "Mmmhmm." She bats her eyelashes, covered in mascara.

I take it off and slip it over her head. She giggles, then does an adorable pose, bringing her knee up and one arm in the air like she's a cheerleader.

Please, little miss, cheer me on at every game.

She puckers up her lips. "Give me a Z," she waves imaginary pom poms and spins around. That tight muscled ass of hers is barely covered by her purple lacy thong, "Give me an A," she does another adorable shoulder shimmy. "Give me a C! Gooooo Zacky, myyyyy Zacky!"

"Gosh, you're so damn cute." I run my hands down her hips. "I think I've already won the game."

"Well good thing you still wanna play. But my lingerie surprise is all covered up now. Is that really what you wanted, Willey?" She brings her mouth into a playful pout, and I'm so fucking ready to play.

"No, no, you're right. Definitely better without." I pull it over her head and she bursts out laughing.

"Much better." I draw out the words, licking her lipstick off my lips as I indulge myself on every bit of her body.

"Talk dirty. Play dirty. Make me covered in a disastrous mess."

"I love *your* mess."

"Work me baby, work me like you do those machines at the gym."

"Oh, I'm gonna work you." I taunt her earlobe with a nibble. "And then I'm gonna play your body like it's the best game of baseball ever."

"You better play my body like it's your winning game. Then you better make it a double header."

"Double header?" I free my dick out of my pants and grip the length, stroking. "This head? Giving you a double?" I run my thumb around the tip, "or a triple?" Precum drips from my seam and Trish shivers.

"Just you wait, baby doll," I flick my tongue, deliberately teasing her with this nickname. "I'm gonna make you my MVP."

"I'm counting on it." She heaves a breathless sigh. "Give me your All American special? Make me *your* team captain? Play for my team?"

"They don't exist." My arms cradle hers. "They've never existed since you walked into my life." My pace shifts from hot and quick to slow and tender. "Only you."

She licks her upper lip. "Really?"

"Yeah, really."

Stepping into her warmth, my bare chest rests against her lacy framed cleavage. The hum of our skin connecting takes me to another universe. "I've missed you." I unbuckle my jeans and kick off my shoes.

"My test results came back." She whispers against my ear. "Clean as a whistle."

My cock gets so stiff, it's hard to get him free of my boxer briefs.

"You know what that means." She bites her lip, "Willey."

"I know exactly what that means, little miss." I growl against her neck, bringing kiss after kiss on her soft skin. I *want* to have her all the way. My body's starving for her skin against mine in the places we feel most connected.

Out of my clothes, I grab her until she's pressed against my hips. Going to her kitchen, I set her perfect ass against the counter. Slipping my fingers under her lacy thong and into her beautiful folds, I take in her smooth skin. Taking my sweet time, I rub and stimulate every bit of her skin. Her juices drizzle onto my hand, the sweet satisfaction of knowing I'm turning her on. The lingerie lands in a heap on the floor.

"I'm ready." She grabs my cock in her hand and positions me at her opening. I slide in real slow, letting every second of this last as long as it possibly can. She feels different than anyone else.

I'm sure now. No matter what, I *need* her.

"Oh, Zac." She holds me closer, and it almost feels like she's telling me it's special for her too.

"Fuck, Trish." I slide in and out, repeating the motion in a slow and wonderful rhythm. Her skin against mine. She's what I've always wanted. What I've always needed.

"You're so good." I whisper into her ear, bringing our chests closer, hugging her with every bit of my body. She adjusts our position until I fill her deeper. We bounce and thrust, holding onto this moment for dear life.

Time slows. I bring my lips around hers, taking control of our motions. She tenses around me and I feel *everything.*

"Ohhhh." She clutches my shoulders as I drive in hard and fast until we simultaneously explode.

"Dang boy, you've been holding out on me." She's catching her breath. Those heavy breaths speak to my soul. I'll always love getting her hot and bothered.

"Oh, shit! The groceries." I step away from the mess of sweaty goodness sticking us together and wash my hands at the sink. Stumbling into the dark entryway, I grab the food from the bags.

"What'd you bring?" She eyes me with curious interest.

"Breakfast." I smile, the light of her fridge blinding me for a second as I get to rearranging some things to make a spot in her fridge.

"You brought breakfast?" She sounds skeptical.

"I did." Move the leftovers over here. Make some space on the shelf. Yep, there we go. "Well, the stuff to make it."

"That's really sweet of you." She looks genuinely touched.

"No one's ever made you breakfast when they stayed over before?" I set a bottle of Gustafson Farm chocolate milk on the shelf and close the fridge.

"No, no one's ever stayed over to make breakfast. They usually rush out pretty quick. Sometimes before I wake up." She's acting tough, but I catch the hint of sadness in her tone. I'm not sure if that's the kind of guy she normally wants or just the ones she's normally with, but she seems unhappy about it.

"Well, they were rude." I step close to her. "They obviously didn't know the rewards of banging after breakfast. And rushing out the door? That's just ridiculous. Even for hookups. I've never understood that. Like you can be casual without being callused, right?"

"I know, right?" She gives me a look like she can't hardly believe me but she's still hanging on my words, wanting to see what I'll say next. I want to say so much more than I dare, like how much I'll show her the love she deserves and be the man she needs but hasn't ever had. But I don't want to scare her away.

"So long as you and I are still doing this thing, Trish," I say her name slowly, pointedly, making sure to inflect my tone and hoping she knows I'm so much different than those dicks who orgasm and run. "You'll be treated like you deserve. With respect, and tenderness and breakfast in bed." I rub her nose with my finger. "That I'll be here when you wake. That I'll help you sleep." I wink.

"You do help me sleep. I used to have so many nightmares."

I think about the nights we've slept and the times we've woken up. I haven't noticed anything but peaceful sleep when I've held her in my arms.

"You make the demons in my head a lot quieter." I bring my lips to hers. She jumps into my arms and I carry her to her bathroom for us to clean up.

"Have those demons always been in your head?" She looks over from the sink.

"Um, yeah. Ma always swears I was a really anxious kid. Pa seemed to think I just needed to spend more time in the sunshine or something. They often quarreled about if I should get some actual mental health support or not." I tsk. "Ultimately we couldn't really afford it anyway. We rarely had any kind of medical insurance. Pa's restaurant has never done as well as we'd hoped and Ma's job doesn't offer any sort of benefits. I get insurance with my athletic scholarship now, but yeah I didn't have it most of the time." I think about all those anxiety attacks when I was too young to have any clue what to do with them. "My first year at Suncastle, my athletic trainer found me in the middle of a bad wave of panic. I've been seeing the team psychologist ever since. Taking meds. Regular therapy appointments. It helps, but certain things still rev it up into hyperdrive." I dry my hands on her super soft teal towels. She must like this color since it's all over the apartment.

"That must've been a lot to deal with as a kid." Trish runs her hand up and down my shoulder. "I'm sorry you had to go through all that." Her tone is caring, like she understands what it's like to go without. "A lot of kids need resources they don't get. I've been helping Cody's sister, Anna Mae, learn photography. I just want her to have that support we didn't have as teens, ya know?"

"That's really cool."

"Yeah, I know Cody was doing a lot for their family. But he's not here. Anna Mae is actually really good at taking pictures. I think it'll help her get her feet off the ground. She's about Sadie's age, I think."

"That's awesome."

She goes into her closet and comes back in nothing but my jersey. "I'm keeping this, by the way."

"I was planning on leaving it. Pretty soon you'll need a Zac section in your closet. What with the hoodie already there. Now the jersey." I pick her up and carry her to the living room couch. Our kisses get deeper, tongues tangling, reaching for the back of our throats, trying to get as close to each other as we possibly can.

I wonder why no one's been there for her. It makes me sad that she's been as alone in this world as I have. That we've had warm bodies beside us so long as they get a sexual pleasurable reward, but then we go back to being by ourselves.

Alone.

But we aren't alone anymore. Doesn't matter what she calls it–this thing we're doing–it's not alone.

"Play for me?" She eyes my guitar, and I feel my cock getting stiff. I love how much she loves my music. That she *wants* to hear me play.

"Requests?" I grab my guitar and get it out of the case. Difficult to see in this lighting, but I'll manage.

"You know what I like." She settles in beside me while I start tuning my strings.

"I've never played naked with someone." At my first exclusive Trish concert in my apartment, we were wearing pajamas.

Her smile comes in and out of the shadows of the flickering candle light and makes me warm all over. "Well I'm honored I get to pop your play-guitar-naked-with-a-date cherry." Her eyes glisten like even if I couldn't see any other part of her I would still know she was irrevocably happy.

I clear my throat and start up the note pattern to "Sometimes" by Britney Spears listening for the strings that need more tuning.

"Seeing as you need to be more cultured and learn all the correct words to the first verse–" I tease.

"You're never gonna let me live that night down, are you?" She chuckles.

"Uh uh." I sing the rest of the first verse. "Besides, it's our song now."

"It's our song?" She laughs. "I can think of a lot better songs for us."

"Oh no you didn't." I groan as if she reached out and punched me, "You've mortally wounded me talking about Britney that way. There's no one better than her." I poke her nose gently, "except you, little miss."

"Oh, no need to lie to me. I know you like her better." She snuggles into my shoulder.

"Not true." I state the fact.

"Yes, true." She contests.

"If both of you were here, I'd pick you. So there." I stick my tongue out.

"There you go being seven years old again."

I put on my best obnoxious little kid voice. "I don't know how many times we have to go over this, Trish. I'm eleven."

"You're just proving my point. I don't believe you'd pick me. Especially if you're eleven years old, you're choosing Britney Spears over me because of playground bragging rights alone."

"Well I can't very well prove it, so we're gonna have to go off of faith." I give her a challenging expression. "Bet you can't come up with any reason to distrust this adorable eleven-year-old, now can you?

"You're a mess."

"No, I'm not. We literally just cleaned up in your teal accented bathroom."

"It's talent, really that you can *still* be a mess right after cleaning up." She shakes her head.

"You love my mess." I wink. "Now, let's get this concert goin' little miss." With a couple more strings tuned, I clear my throat and sing. The song becomes more sensual and seductive. It's fitting, like these lyrics are the picture of all we aren't yet but could be. I'm carrying notes to her heart, to her soul.

When I finish the final chorus, she helps set my guitar carefully on the table.

"Is there a reason you decided to start playing guitar?"

"Pa wasn't around much. Not that he didn't wanna be. But work took all his energy. I got really close to my music teacher in junior high. When he put a guitar in my hand that was the end of it. I'd spend hours playing after school when I wasn't at the field for practice."

Her warm body melts into mine. "I love that."

"I love sharing it with you." My hands glide across the skin along her spine, touching every ridge. Under my fingers, I feel some breaks in her silky skin, changing a little different in texture. Maybe it is a birthmark? Or a scar of some sort? I've noticed the spots before. Maybe one day she'll be comfortable telling me.

"Thanks for playing." She bounces her body up and down against my crotch. "Are you ready to play another way?" Her words enter my ear as she licks around my earlobe. She grinds against my growing cock.

"I'm absolutely ready to play any way you want." My heart races, hungering to taste her from the inside out. I'm scrambling for a condom before I remember the test results.

"What?" She asks.

"Just glad we don't have to worry about condoms anymore." I bring my lips to hers, sucking and tasting the last remnants of her Juicy Fruit gum.

"Mmmm," She moans as I grind harder onto her, wanting every bit of my cock inside. Juices seap from her body onto mine, warm and wet and everything I want. I take my thumb and massage her exquisite clit, earning more moans and sighs of pleasure. The way her skin feels under mine while I watch the look of pure delight on her face is incredible.

We make love all night. Think we may have slept a couple hours. Mostly it was waking up to go another round, falling asleep for a power nap fueled by afterglow and then going again. Dozing off before one of us wakes the other up with sweet and seductive touches. Her sheets are destroyed. I'll make sure to help switch them out before I go.

When morning's here, I'm totally spent. It was so worth it.

We stumble into her kitchen.

"That last one. Jesus Christ, Zac. How're you so perfect?" She starts up some coffee, and I go for the food I tucked into her fridge last night.

"How am I so perfect? You're the one that's perfect." I bring a kiss to her forehead, tasting that sweet skin. She's wearing nothing but my jersey. Looks fucking amazing on her. She can have my entire closet if she wants. It's a little too big and covers the top half of her booty. I cup her ass cheeks where the fabric ends, giving them a sweet little squeeze.

"It's never been this good for this long. I keep waiting for you to get sick of me." She teases.

"Don't think that's possible." Somehow I manage to let go of her perfect butt, wondering how anyone ever got sick of her. Those other guys must've been total idiots. What did they see in her they didn't like?

Opening cabinets, I hunt for a bowl and a whisk, mixing together some pancake mix. She tries to help.

"No, no, no, you're gonna sit that pretty little ass down. I forbid you from lifting a finger." I guide her out of the kitchen and help her plop down on the couch.

As I walk to the kitchen, I see a really awesome hardbound photo book on the table. "Did you take these?" I plop next to her and open the book.

"Yeah, they're photos of my cousin's band." She scoots closer to share the book.

"Wait what?" I know this band. I've been following them.

"Yeah, that's my cousin Rick." She points to the main guy.

"Oh my gosh. Trish," I gasp, bringing my hands to my cheeks. "That's so crazy you've not only met him, but you're related to Rick Norton *and* you got to take pictures of his band."

"I didn't know you were such a fan." She smiles. "I can introduce the two of you sometime. Hey, he'd probably love to jam. Let you be the guitar to his piano."

"Holy fuck, I'd die Trish. Like literally die. Rick Norton is the next Elton John. I'd die." My eyes go so wide.

"You're adorable when you get all fanboy on me." She grins.

"It'd be almost as cool as meeting Lou Gehrig. Like he's in the same league of epicness as my idol." I run my fingers through my hair and pull tight. "Goodness gracious. That's seriously so cool. I can't believe he's your cousin. Please introduce me." It takes all my willpower but I get off the couch to start breakfast, knowing our minutes are numbered.

After a bit, I get everything set in motion in the kitchen. Start the bacon in the oven. Get some eggs ready to scramble. When I've got some pancakes going, I put a bunch of chocolate chips in them.

Just like I learned working all those years in Pa's kitchen, I make sure all the food gets done at the same time.

"I have to be out of here by noon." I look up from the pan to Trish, who's absolutely horrible at relaxing.

"That soon?" She leans against the counter, and I feel so weak that one little plea from her would make me stay and miss my midterm.

Forget passing my classes. I'll drop out today if that means I get to have her.

"I told you to sit your pretty ass down and forbade you from lifting a finger. Now, shoo." I grab the whisk out of her hand, not letting her mix the batter in effort to help.

"I don't know how to *not* help." She gives me an exasperated sigh and swipes the whisk out of my hand. "You sure you have to go though? I mean, there could be an unexpected blizzard or something. It has been cold for South Carolina this time of year." Her face is an adorable little pout and my, oh, my, it's hard to say no to this expression.

"We slept pretty late. Got just enough time for breakfast. If I didn't have a test, and baseball this evening, I'd stay baby. I promise, I'd stay." I bring my chest to hers. Every part of my body gets close to her, reaching out to be one. My cock gets harder than the handle of this frying pan while her hands glide up and down my spine.

"I want you to stay." She whispers against my lips. "But I know you can't." She runs her thumb up and down my cheek and warm comfort transfers from her fingertips.

"I want to spend the day with you." I press hot lips against hers as she hikes up my jersey and grinds my cock against her lower abs. So firm. I love her body.

"I want to spend the week with you." Her kiss lingers on my lips, neither of us willing to let go. It's breaking me, knowing this rendezvous is about to end.

"How about you come with me when I have to shoot a wedding far away?" She offers. "Oh, it's a destination wedding in Hawaii over Christmas." She hikes up one eyebrow. "If you'd like to come?"

"Is it the week before or after?"

"It's during. Like they actually booked it on Christmas." She explains.

"Oh, dang it, I can't. I promised Sadie I'd be home for a Kentucky Christmas–which you're totally invited to but sounds like you also can't make it. I know how you like Kentucky."

"Yeah, it's been years since I went back. I oughta go see some of my relatives up there. It's been too long. I can't go for Christmas though. Dammit." She bites her nail. "Maybe the next destination wedding? You can come and we'll stay an extra day or two. Make a little trip out of it."

"If I can. But baseball season's about to start. As much as I hate it, I'm not gonna be able to drop everything once we have games."

"Fine, that's fine. I have a career too, I get it. No big deal." She rests her head on my shoulder, wrapping her arms around my waist. We hold each other like this for so long I almost burn the chocolate chip pancakes.

"Here." She gets a couple plates, and I serve up the food.

"Let's eat on the porch." She grabs her plate, and I follow her with mine. "It's my happy place."

"I can see why. It's beautiful." The weather's nice as we enjoy breakfast on her adorably decorated porch. I hurry to help with the sheets and the dishes so she's not burdened by my visit. She works so hard all the time, I'd hate to leave her with a mess.

"I wish you could stay." Her eyes are so sad as we kiss goodbye.

"Awwww, I've loved it too."

"When can we do this again?" She puts her hand on my cheek.

"Pencil me in this weekend?"

"I love it when you reference my planner." She smiles real big.

"Just make sure I stay on your schedule." I wink.

Trish

It's after midnight and I'm exhausted.

Zac's taken over my world. I'm becoming a little obsessed. All day I text him random shit that reminds me of him. I'm looking for reasons to talk. Keeping him on the line after every phone call because I can't handle the thought of going to bed without the sound of his voice in my ear.

Being with Jimmy kinda did this to me but it wore off over time. Maybe it's the newness of Zac being in my life. I won't say *relationship* because it's not quite there. But honestly? Would I hate it if it were?

I guess I'm wondering what part of me isn't able to just try it. He can be my boyfriend for a hot minute. Worst case, we break up, right?

I can't tell if it's healthy or not for me to keep resisting what we both feel. Zac's invested. He's made that clear as day.

Would it kill me to see where this goes?

I get to see him play guitar this weekend at Garrison's, and I cannot wait.

I look at the photos on my computer. Touchup here. Enhance brightness there. Make their photos into masterpieces. Every moment taking what we started with and turning it into more than it was.

Can that happen with my heart? Can Zac take the pieces that are here and edit them into something else?

Is that what I want?

The photos are fake. They aren't real. I've altered them. I've made them counterfeit like a dollar bill produced in someone's basement.

Once a heart is broken, it's broken. You can't fix it. No amount of love can change what happened. If I'm with someone, it'll be just like Dipshit was with me. I won't be able to be with someone for real.

I'm at a constant war with myself over getting close to Zac and keeping him at arm's length.

Zac's too good. He's too pure. Even I can't take my corruption. How can I expect him to handle what I barely cope with?

If he's a photo editing program, I'm a damaged photo that's too old and ruined to stand a chance of being repaired. I'm the photo put in a muddy puddle and torn to shreds. Even if he had the best tools, he couldn't fix what's broken inside me.

Taking my camera in my hand, I think about the way it's all about focus, all about light, all about position.

I see the love stories every day. Some of my clients started as a wedding and transitioned into family photo shoots. Having a babe in arms and another on the way. They look happy through my lens.

Gazing at the LCD screen, I wonder what Zac would look like if I posed him. Those brown eyes shine with that dimpled smile. That dark hair that always seems to look just right, even when he's all sweaty from playing ball or country dancing.

Sweaty after sex.

That night when we first hooked up plays on repeat in my mind like my favorite movie. No matter how much I try to think about work, it always loops back to him. Or when he asked about my keychain. The way I could tell him about Daddy even though it's something I rarely mention. Or when I was sure Daddy was telling me to share that part of myself only to hear Zac is from the place Daddy loved most. The one location that ties me to Daddy is where Zac calls home.

Kentucky.

My sign.

I go to my desk drawer and pull out the first photo I ever remember taking. Back before the days of cell phones, when we had to go to the Eckerd Drug Store to get One Hour Photos developed. It's Daddy standing in front of McNeely Lake in Louisville, the same day I got my kitty keychain. I keep it in my drawer because it hurts too much to look at it.

Every time I see these happy families, I just keep thinking about mine before he died. We were so happy. So perfect. He was that daydream of a dad. The kind that really likes being with his kid. We went out for ice creams and on all kinds of daddy daughter dates.

I miss you so much, Daddy.

My throat is a tight cylinder of throbbing pain. I curl up into a ball on my carpet and hold the old photo to my chest like I'm giving Daddy a hug.

I wish you were still here. You'd know what to say.

I've always believed in his sign coming to me from heaven. I just don't know what to do now that it's in front of me.

Maybe you got this sign wrong, Daddy. Zac's too good for me. Maybe I got it wrong, and it wasn't even meant to be a sign?

I pick myself off the floor and wipe away my makeup. My phone vibrating on the desk across the room pulls me out of my wallowing. I glance at my clock. Even though my clients sometimes call late, they never call *this late*.

It can be one of two people: Lexie or Zac.

No one else would try me at this hour. Nana would sooner drive herself to the ER in the middle of the night than call and wake me up. When it keeps ringing, I know it must be Zac, because Lexie only calls once and then texts me a bunch until I return her call. But this is the second time Zac's called. Holding back a squeal–because who am I to be squealing over a boy?–I answer his call.

"What're you doin' right now?" Zac's voice comes through the line.

"Talking to a hot guy on Snapchat," I say.

"You're what?" That twinge of jealousy colors his tone.

"Um, yeah, have you checked your notifications lately?" I chuckle to myself as I hear him click out of the call.

"Hot damn, Trish." His tone is deep and breathless.

"Thought you'd like that." I smile into the phone. "And what're you up to?" I snuggle into my pillows.

"Missin' you." His voice is a sexy whisper that makes me clench in my satin jammies.

"Thought maybe I could sing you to sleep?"

"Don't you need to save your voice for Saturday?"

"No, I need to sing you to sleep." He hangs up and before too long I get a video call coming through. And there he is. In a baggy Suncastle t-shirt and flannel pajamas that don't match, sitting criss cross applesauce–like a kindergartener–on his bed. His Yamaha acoustic guitar is stretched across his legs.

"I guess you get to see my *Wicked Witch of the West look* since I already took all my makeup off." I roll my eyes. "You didn't tell me to expect a video call at one am on a Tuesday."

"Hey, Trish?" He leans closer to the phone so it's up near his gorgeous face. "What?"

"I need to tell you something." He holds my gaze while I wait for him to go on.

"Well, what? I'm on pins and needles, now." I wait for an eternity while he draws out the suspense.

"Expect a video call at one am on a Tuesday, every week from now until, ya know, we one day, potentially…" He stammers, "…move in together."

"Oh, and are we moving in together?" I raise my brows.

"I'm hoping so." He's serious. Oh fuck, he's serious. I mean, I know he likes me. He won't shut up about that. But he wants to sing me to sleep every night and at some point move in together?

"You're hoping so?" My jaw drops a little. I clamp my lips shut.

"Think you heard me, little miss."

Then I see the twinkle in his eye. Oh, damn, he *was* kidding. Once he can tell he got a rise outta me, that little dimple peaks out from his grin.

"Fuck, Zac. I thought you were being serious." I kinda wish I could punch him with how hard my heart's pounding.

"Serious?" He laughs. "Oh, you know, like all people move in together suddenly when they're in a casual, non-committal, not-quite-relationship sorta thing. Especially when they can't seem to go more than a day or two without texting constantly and so far haven't spent a weekend apart." His eye contact makes me so wet. Well, these panties are wrecked now. Every part of my body is responding to him over the phone.

An ache spreads between my thighs, begging to have him penetrate me deep, like he does. Parts of me I didn't even know a cock could ever reach. His can. And I need it. Right about yesterday.

If we moved in together, he'd make me breakfast and hold me all night long. I wouldn't have as many nightmares.

Somehow the thought of us living together and partaking in every kind of horizontal tango possible each night has me *hopeful*.

Me?

Hopeful?

It's like I've had an icepick lobotomy. Like someone is slipping a little something in my water bottle, because I swear to fuck that I don't ever feel *hopeful* about a guy who I play disco-stick tug-of-war with.

Looking into his eyes, it's like he feels it. What he's constantly trying to explain to me. That we *need* to be together.

Kentucky.

"I was teasing you, Trish. But I mean, the offer is there if you wanna entertain it. No pressure." He waits until I nod before he continues. "But yeah, if you wanna spend a little more time here I wouldn't be opposed." He clears his throat and takes a sip out of his water bottle. "I have to stay put in Suncastle for now, and I know you have your clients. But if you wanna get set up here for editing and stay at my place on the days or weeks when you're in between photo shoots, I'd love to have you."

A small smile comes to the corner of my lips. This apartment gets lonely. His company always seems to make me feel better, even when I'm having a rough day.

"What do you wanna hear?" He changes the subject like he knows I'm gonna need time to think about it.

"You like Country. Sing me some."

He nods, playing out the first few chords or rifts or whatever they're called, leading into "She's Everything" by Brad Paisley.

By the end of watching him play and sing over the phone I feel peaceful. Like he's taken me out of my current destroyed photo and we've landed on a new one with the stars and solar system at our fingertips.

Before I know it, he's singing all of Country Music's popular hits. For me. My personal concert with a guy who's good enough to have concerts on the weekend at local bars. The guy who not only sounds amazing on guitar, but plays a mean game of baseball. And as if all that wasn't enough, the guy who is casually in love with me and not bothered by the many times I've pushed him away.

"I'm gonna sing you one more and then we both need to hit the hay."

"Deal." I cover my yawn, nestling under my soft blankets.

"Sometimes" by Britney Spears comes through the phone speakers.

Our song.

Why do we have a song? We're not together. I'm too tired to fight it. I only feel.

Trish

It shouldn't take this long to get from Willardson to Suncastle. Did I drop everything to come see my not-quite-boyfriend on a Thursday? Yes. Will I pay for it later? For sure. Do I care right now? Not nearly as much as I probably should.

The other day, I gave him my address and he drove the whole way. As much as the distance is a headache, it means a lot he wanted to come over. I'm starting to open my heart to really dating him.

It kinda doesn't scare me like it used to. And *that* scares me the most. But I feel good when I'm with him. He's one of the kindest, funniest, sexiest men I've ever met.

I've been on the freeway for an hour and a half longer than normal. He's gotta be worried sick. I've had really spotty signal so I can't get in touch with him. Every few minutes I check my phone, looking for service. Finally enough bars to send a text.

Me: Sorry sexy… coming as fast as I can.

Zac: Just glad you're okay.

He tends to worry if I'm even a few minutes late. When he told me he gets bad anxiety, I looked up as much as I could about how to support him. After a bit of research, I wrote a list of all the tips in the notes section of my planner:

Validate his feelings.
Ask about his symptoms so I know when they're coming on.
Remind him I'm here.
Know his triggers and try to avoid them if possible.
Offer soothing distractions like music or going for a walk.
Listen to what's on his mind.
Create and maintain a low stress environment.

It's not hard to text if I'm gonna be late, and it saves him a lot of anxiety.

I get close enough to see the reason traffic's been at a standstill. On the side of the road is a huge wreck, reducing the four lanes down to one. The whole front end is missing from a maroon SUV and the car on the other side of it is so mangled I can't tell if it was a two-door or a four. I try not to rubberneck, but I'm stuck.

Both emotionally and physically.

Every time I see a car accident, I think about the one that occurred on April twenty-eighth, on a rainy night, on Oak Street.

Cody never made it out of that crash.

I don't wanna feel this right now.

But it's here with me.

Grief: The name of jumbled feelings coming up when I see a car torn to shreds. When I imagine Cody's corpse so mutilated, even the mortuary couldn't make him look quite right. I picked up Lexie from the hospital the night he died and they'd covered him with a sheet because the wreck was so gruesome. Crushed chest. Lacerated face. The crash was bad enough to do that even though he was wearing a seatbelt.

Miss you, Cody.

A shaky breath comes out of my lungs as I offer my positive thoughts to those involved in this crash.

Back in the flow of traffic, I dial Zac on the phone.

"Hey," He sounds wrecked and I wish I coulda texted him sooner.

"I didn't have signal until now. I'm sure you've been worried."

"Think I wore a hole in the carpet from pacing." He lets out a sigh

"It's so good to hear your voice." My heart's stirring and I think some of that snuck out in my voice.

"Are you okay?"

"Hardly." I take a slow exhale. "It's a car accident. A bad one. We were totally stopped."

"Oh, shit." Understanding fills his poignant tone and moves right into my chest, lifting the heaviness.

"Always brings up all sorts of memories for me."

"You're not hurt though, right?" Concern riddles every word of his coming through the line.

"No, baby. I'm gonna hang up and drive safely. I'm still twenty miles away."

"I'll be here waiting." He waits for me to hang up. I set my phone in the cup holder and turn my music up louder. Since we're both driving so much, I burned a CD of a long distance playlist I made on my computer. It's a bunch of music we both like. I burned a copy of the CD for him, too.

I'm finally off the Suncastle exit. I take a moment to gather myself. It's so stressful when plans change and everything runs behind. It's even more stressful when it's because of shit like this.

I pull down the visor and look at my makeup. Fresh red lipstick glides across my lips as I pop my gum into a tissue and suck bubbles out of my all but empty cup of Dr. Pepper.

Running to his apartment door, I give an urgent knock.

He pulls me inside and locks his door. "I'm so glad you're okay." His kisses lather my lips, desperation building kiss upon kiss. When we pause to take a breath I see his hair a disheveled heap on his head like he's been yanking at the strands.

I take his hand and bring him into his room, knowing we don't have much time before class.

"I need you." I kick out of my leggings and reach into his top drawer. Squirting lube onto my hand I stroke, making sure I'm open and wet for this wild ride we're about to have. "It's been too long."

"It's been two days," he chuckles, that adorable goofy grin on his face as he unzips his jeans.

"That's too long."

"You're right." He plays with my pussy, rubbing his cock against me. His scent fills my senses. I close my eyes, relaxing into his touch.

He slips inside me, slowly easing his whole length as far as he can.

The tender sting makes me moan, my body heaving with need. I arch my back, bringing him deeper. He thrusts with power and care all at once.

"God, I missed you." I hold my breath, a million sensations blooming through my body as he thrusts in and out.

"Cream my jeans, little miss. Let me smell you all the way through class, until I can devour you again. Come right now."

When I open my eyes, his lock on mine, a smile wide on his face.

"You're incredible." He goes faster. "Come for me, baby."

He takes my ankles and hooks them over his shoulders.

"Valedictorian." I sigh out the name of our current sex position. "Mmmmm." The way he taps me has me going wild. "You're the top of my class, baby. The top of my class." I bounce with each of his motions, my g-spot happy to have her playmate back in town.

"I told you to come for me," his face is teasing me and it makes me giggle.

"That laugh." He smiles, shaking his head. "I'm always gonna be high on your laugh."

"Then you better keep making me laugh." I raise my eyebrows.

"Then you better come for me, like I've told you to several times now." He slows the last word, riveting me into the level that gets me there. "Come. Right. Now."

And I do, my body, heeding his commands like I couldn't hold back if I wanted to.

When I return to this universe after an earth-shaking orgasm, I feel him still incredibly hard inside of me. I don't know how this boy can hold back when I come so vigorously around him, but he has. Thank you, Jesus. The sweat on his brow suggests it was incredibly difficult. I'm glad he put in the effort.

"Flip over." Something about his commands make me weak in the knees, my whole body filled with *need* to do whatever he says. He's only like this in bed and I find it fiercely attractive.

"You got it." I bite my lip, pulling my body to his in a sweaty hug.

I turn around. He leans his chest against my back, inserting me from behind while my feet are on the ground and I brace my elbows on his mattress.

"Ahhhh," I purr. He holds still as we embrace the connection. Ever so slowly, he moves in and out. In rhythm with his touch, I edge closer to my climax.

"I need more cream on my jeans, little miss." His words tip me over my threshold, another orgasm breaking free. I shake, gripping the sheets so tight as he thrusts.

His abs tighten against my buttcheeks, proving he's about to come. I ride my orgasm with his until we're both trembling in aftershocks. He wraps me in the sweetest hug from behind, catching his breath. Delicately, he turns my body to face his.

"Give yourself more." He smiles, reaching to take off his shirt. I scoot so I'm laying on his pillows. He puts his shirt under my butt, kneels on the bed, and gives my clit a nice, sucking kiss.

"Lemme watch you go again." It's not a question, and something about that sends vibrations from my head to my toes. He knows I wanna come more, and I fucking love that. It's so hot, how he tells me to touch myself where he can watch.

I alternate between rubbing my clit and fucking myself with two fingers, feeling Zac's cum inside of me. He watches, willing to be late to class. In mere seconds, I'm soaking his shirt. Squirting my sweet release, knowing he loves every drop. He brings me to a new level. A new wave of passion that has been missing with everyone else.

When I'm fully satisfied, I take his shirt and rub it all over my mess. He grips it to his face and breathes me in, then tucks it safely under his pillow. "For later," he winks.

"You gotta go." I hop off the bed and peck his lips while I go to his dresser to get him a new shirt. "I'll stick around and we can grab dinner after practice."

"Was hoping you'd say that."

"Was hoping you'd want that." I bring him in for a long hug, my finger gripping his hair, pulling back only to entangle my tongue with his.

"Of course, I want it." His eyes are a sea of longing, hoping that I'll just let him have every piece of me. Every bit of myself that I keep so locked up and guarded. Maybe he can have it. I can learn to let my walls down just a little bit.

This fortress keeps me safe. But maybe, one day I can know if Zac is safe. I feel good when I'm with him. That's a start.

"I'll text you when I get done."

"I'm waiting, already." I grab a tissue from my purse and wipe off some of the red lipstick. "You look like a circus clown." I laugh.

"I'll manage," he winks, and I'm still aching where he's more than filled me.

"Thanks for getting me through the day." I kiss him, clinging for dear life, wondering how anyone can make me miss them when it's only gonna be a few hours 'til I see them again.

His tongue runs against the roof of my mouth, shivers working through me as he sucks against my lips. At this moment, I know. He can't let me go, and I don't want him to.

"I'll skip class." His whisper is more of a whine, like a child who needs to get his way.

"No." I put my finger under his nose, rubbing away more smudging lipstick. "You go to class. Keep your grades up. So you can graduate, and we don't have to be long distance anymore."

"Oh, here. So you can come and go as you please." He hands me a key to his apartment.

I look into his eyes and time stands still. That connection we have gets stronger. The look on his face says that he's all mine. That he always has been. That the moment I'm really ready to dive in, he'll be waiting.

He doesn't know it yet, but I'm staying all weekend. My next in-person commitment is on Monday night. Like he mentioned on our video call, I can spend more time here between the photo shoots.

While he's at class, I head to the mall with Lexie.

"I need to pick out something nice for Bobby. I have a feeling he's gonna go wild with stuff for me. But I don't know what..." Lexie sips her iced vanilla latte as we walk through Suncastle Mall.

"He's kinda hard to buy for." I lead her toward the sports store. "Can't go wrong with White Sox." I gesture to some of the caps.

"Nah, he's wearing Yankees now." Lex's face goes somber and I know it's because Cody was supposed to play for the Yankees.

"Let's start there, then." I move across the hat display to the navy and white snapbacks.

After Lexie's bought just about the whole store, I head over to get something for Zac.

For a while now, I've noticed Zac compulsively checks his pulse. Like even sometimes right after sex, he'll slip his fingers into the notch on his wrist to count his heartbeats to make sure he's alive or something.

My cousin Rick has one of those fitness watch/band things and he loves it. After a while of shopping, I pick out one for Zac. It's kinda pricey, but I don't care.

Maybe this means I'm ready for something more. I guess I'll see how the watch goes.

When I get back to my car, I hold my kitty keychain. It's like Daddy's right here looking out for me.

Sometimes when I had a really bad night with Dipshit, I'd fall asleep holding my keychain. I felt Daddy there with me then, even though he couldn't do anything to help. He's here with me now. More and more I'm seeing Zac as a man Daddy woulda been proud to welcome into my life.

One step at a time, Trish. You can learn to let someone in your heart if you keep trying. You don't have to be alone anymore.

Zac

After I got home from class, I picked up Trish and took her to my favorite local burger dive.

"So, I know you've got your concert tomorrow night." Trish stirs her strawberry milkshake. "And I technically don't have anything until Monday, so can I stay over?"

My eyes go wide, thrilled at the concept.

"You're phrasing this like a question, but little miss you don't need to ask." I scoot the fries over so they're in between us and she doesn't have to reach far to dip them in the ketchup.

"Okay, good. Because I penciled you in."

"I swear you could turn this into some kind of organizational dirty talk."

"Oh, you mean like this?" She takes a pencil from her purse and runs her fingers up and down, like she's stroking a dick. "Use this *eraser* to make my *answer* correct."

"Is this our next role play scenario?" I run my finger down her knuckles. "Because I'm pretty sure you could say anything and it'd be hot."

"Anything?" She bites her lip.

"Anything at all."

After we get home from dinner, I text the guys I'm gonna miss the run in the morning.

"You mind if I come to class with you?" Trish goes into my dresser and picks out some of my pajamas for her and for me.

"I only have two classes on Fridays so that'd be great."

"Yeah, I'll just bring my laptop and work on edits." She slides her arms through the sleeves of my long sleeve gray shirt. Her nipples stick out from the thin fabric. Gosh, she's gorgeous.

"Oh, and I got this." She goes to her purse and pulls out a CD case.

"What's it for?"

"Oh, shit. Does your truck have a CD player?" She wrinkles her nose.

"Yeah." I say, thinking about how I had one put in last year.

"Okay good. It's for when you're driving to come see me."

"I'm gonna put it on now." I take the CD out of the case and put it in my stereo. The first song is "Sometimes" by Britney Spears.

"You're so freakin' cute." I go to her and tickle her under her ribs until her laugh fills my senses.

"And don't worry. I own all the songs. It's not pirated. Just loaning them to you for the purpose of thinking about me all the time." She does an adorable shoulder shimmy.

"I wasn't worried and I don't need any help remembering you. But this is super sweet and thoughtful. Thank you." I bring my lips to hers in a long and appreciative kiss.

"Good luck tonight." Trish stands with me backstage. We finished the sound check. Everything's good to go.

"Can't wait to hold you after." I move my guitar out of the way hold her for a second.

"It's time." Harvey says.

Trish gives me a kiss and heads out to the dance floor. Our fans congregate near the stage. She sits with Lexie and Bobby at one of the nearby tables. When she's not sitting there, she's dancing front and center, watching me sing and play.

It's the most fun I've ever had at a concert, and that's saying something since I love performing as much as I love playing ball.

I watch her body sway, singing all the words with a glass of beer in her hand. It's fucking precious. I've never wanted to play more for someone in my entire life.

"You looked awesome out there," she comes backstage to give me a huge hug.

"Loved playing for you." I kiss her, sweetly.

As we walk to my truck, I'm thinking about how much I've loved having her in Suncastle. Every minute with her has been smooth. Where I normally stress and fret over every little thing, it's been okay. I've been okay.

This morning I burnt the toast and it was okay. Last night I ran out of shampoo, and it was okay. After class yesterday, I needed to study for a few hours and it was okay. All these things that would normally set off anxiety I've been able to navigate with her here.

I drive her back to my place, and we start making out the moment we get inside the door.

Everything's different. There's been a shift. She's ready. We're here. We're gonna actually dive in the way I've craved.

For real.

She doesn't have to say a word. I can sense it.

"You seriously blew me away." She brings her lips to mine, a soft warmth filling my soul on the moment of contact. I melt into her mouth, licking each line on her lips, feeling the shape of her gums, the permanent retainer she has on the back of her bottom teeth. Her sweet tongue collides with mine, begging it deeper, the roof of her mouth sending needs through my body the longer we kiss. I'm panting for breath, gripping her head and bringing it closer. Deeper. Harder. Kisses and bites. Sucking and relaxed. A symphony of sensations. A chorus of chaos. A wondrous world of wild.

My Trish.

I pull at the buttons on her top, and she sheds the sleeves off her arms. I stumble toward the lightswitch.

"No," she stops me.

"The lights."

"No, it's okay." Her words seep deep into my ears, making time stand still. We've never fucked in the light. She's never let me see all of her. Always dark.

"You sure?"

"Zac," she kisses me with so much desire, "I've been thinking about this. As hard as it is for me to get close to people, I'd like to get close to you. You've been so patient while I've tried to work through my shit. It's hard for me to rely on anyone. But when I'm with you, I still feel independent. You let me be who I need to be. It's changing everything."

It warms my soul, hearing her talk about *this*. My throat gets tight with emotion. As I inhale, it's a comfortable breath, loving she's trusting me.

"Really?" I search her eyes. They're so sincere it melts my heart.

"Really." She brings her lips to mine in the most tender kiss we've ever shared. "I want you to fuck me with the lights on."

"You're sure?"

"I'm sure." She sits on my lap. "This started as just sex. You want more. Maybe I do too? I mean, I keep coming back. I think about you all the time. I don't want to see anyone else." She gives me a timid smile as I absorb her words.

"So does this mean we're maybe, almost, like, potentially, together?" I swallow back worry that I'm misreading all this. "You wanna be my girlfriend?"

She laughs. "Let's not go *that* far just yet. Sleep on it at least. I think maybe I'll be ready for that soon, though. If it's still something you're wanting?"

I let out a surprised chuckle. "Hell yes, I still want that. Honestly, I'm pretty shocked right now. I'd love to make this as committed as you're comfortable with. Whatever your terms are, I'm here for it. As much as I like you and love spending time together, I don't want you to feel any pressure from me. Ever."

I sometimes worry I'm coming off too strong. I need her to know I'm not a creepy guy who won't leave her alone if she asks him to. But if there's *any* part of her that wants *us* to be *committed* then I'm about ready to run a victory lap. It's as good as winning a close game.

"I guess that's why I'm ready to show you. You've been really good about meeting me where I am. I appreciate that and it helps me feel safe and comfortable with you." She lets out a shaky breath. My hands rub her shoulders, whispering to her skin beneath the collar. Her fingers tremble as she unbuttons the top of her sweater dress. She closes her eyes and takes a cleansing breath. Next, she bites her lips and shakes her head, almost like she can't believe she's actually doing this.

Trish

I hope I'm ready.

Here goes…everything.

My heart pounds in my chest. Part of me always wanted *someone* to see. Zac's seeing all of *me*.

I hold my breath for three long seconds.

"I'm nervous about this." I take Zac's hand in mine, finding that concerned expression on his face I've come to appreciate so much.

"You want gum?" He asks.

"Maybe after." I give him a contented smile. If he can handle this, I'll know we can be together. If this doesn't go well, I'd rather know now.

There's a little bit of faith blooming in my chest, hoping I'm right.

What if I'm wrong?

The darkest parts of my past come rushing toward me like I'm being sucked into the vortex of my past.

No. I'm in control. This is for me and Zac. Telling him will help.

I lift away the fabric, getting ready to pull it off. "I've never shown this to anyone besides Lexie."

He holds my eyes. "There's no pressure. Only show me if you want to."

"I do." I lift the corner of my lip. A man loved me once. He loved me so perfectly and I lost that love. It's taken a lot for me to try to find it again. But I want it. Daddy would want it for me.

Zac loves me. I have a feeling he's going to be kind. Flutters go through my stomach and chest. My hands start shaking. The look in his eyes brings me comfort. He's the one I can share this with.

I slip my arms out of my dress sleeves and set it next to me on the bed.

Maybe Zac can help me feel a little less broken. Maybe he can be what's been missing. As much as I wish I was over the past, I'm not.

I have to focus on the here and now. Zac's shown me many times in this short while how much he cares. If there's anyone who can see this, it's him.

"Zac, I want to do this. With you." I glide his hands to my bra strap. "I think in some ways, I need to tell you about what happened. Like it's all stuck inside me and if I can just get it out, it'll help. Can I tell you? Is that okay?"

Zac

"**O**f course." I reach my arms around her chest to help her unhook her bra. She takes a deep breath and holds it. Slowly, her arms come out of her straps, and she turns, showing me her back and side.

All that silky skin interrupted by raised ridges I've felt a hundred times makes more sense, now that I can see it. My eyes get wet realizing how big of a deal it is that she *wants* to show me. I've never seen this part of her body. She's never shown it to anyone she's been with.

Her back is covered in…scars?

"Baby…what happened?" I keep my tone careful, everything pounding in my heart. She's guarded. She's been hurt. Fuck, she's been so hurt.

On her side, a little above her hips is a large ring of scars that makes a target.

"My step dad…" She closes her eyes for a long blink. "I'd been cooking dinner and he was drunk as fuck. He got mad about how hungry he was and told me I couldn't do anything right. The eggs stuck to the pan was the last straw. He took a hot pad and removed the heat element from our electric stove. He pinned me to the counter and seared the hot stove element into my skin. Branded me like a cow. I tried to fight him off me but he just pushed me harder into the countertop." Her words are matter-of-fact, like she's had to become numb to what happened.

I gasp, but my throat swells up. "How old were you?"

"Thirteen."

I swallow hard. That age is horrible enough for most kids. I can't imagine wanting to fight back but not being able to. Wanting to be safe with your caretaker and instead being abused.

"I tried burn creams and all sorts of stuff. But some things don't heal, not even with time." She forces a smile, but it's far more sad than happy. "All those little ones are cigarette burns from when he yanked up my shirt and used me like an ashtray."

The words register in my ears like a loud hum. My lips start trembling. All I can do is wrap her up and hold her.

"Baby," I bring her closer, against my chest. "I'm so sorry." Thinking about how so often it's more than the physical assault. That my baby was battered and burned by someone she should've felt safe with. Someone who should've protected her from harm. Someone she should've been able to trust. She endured so much more than what I can see here. She's had to be so strong going through things that no one should ever face.

"He had a lot of bad nights." Trish sighs. "Nights when it was easier to beat me than to stop. Most of the wounds he inflicted just turned to bruises. But this one stayed. And this one." She rubs a spot with her thumb, where there's a long slash. "His belt buckle, that time."

Looking at Trish's back and imagining the bruises she mentioned makes my stomach drop. I've seen something like this before. The memory churns my insides. It looks a lot like what I saw when Cody would change in the locker room. Hate to think they both went through something like this.

"I didn't want you to be scared of me." As much as she sounded numb before, her tone conveys that this part stirs up feelings. "I keep worrying that because of what I've been through, you can't be with me. That you'll be too careful. Treat me different. Or you'll think I've gotta be too damaged to be worth putting up with. That something will snap and I'll be that monster that hurt me all those years. I don't know. And hell, maybe I am too damaged. I've worked so hard to leave that in the past. I'm still broken." Her voice shakes, and she cries into my arms.

"Is that why you keep pushing me away?"

She nods, and I feel us both breaking. Scooping her up, I grip her tight. She starts to sob, and I hold her closer.

"You're safe now." My throat is closing in on itself, tears coming out of my eyes. We've never cried together. Something about this is beautiful and tragic all at the same time.

"I don't want to be broken." Her chest shakes as she tries to get a deep breath. I stroke her hair, keeping her face to my body.

"You're not broken."

"I am." She pulls back and her eyes are unusually dry for someone who's been crying. Hot air blows from her pursed lips. "But I don't want to be anymore."

"You're never broken when you're here." I take her hands in mine. "You're never broken to me."

Give me your pain, baby. Let me take it all away.

"I'm safe now." She whispers and my heart falls apart. "I got out." Her skin is cold to the touch, and I pull down the blankets, helping her lay under them.

"I won't let him ever hurt you like that again." Tears fall down my face.

She looks at them with concern.

"Sorry," I wipe at them with the back of my hand.

"No, I'm just jealous."

"What?" I chuckle, sadly.

"I haven't been able to cry with actual tears in a really long time."

"Oh, well here, we can share. I've got plenty." I use my finger to wipe one of the tears on my face and press it onto her cheek.

Her whole body trembles with those dry sobs again. "Thank you. You don't have to share."

She leans into me, letting my tears cut a track across her cheek. "You didn't have to, but you have no idea how good it is to feel tears again. It's like a desert that's been waiting for rain finally getting a taste."

I smile. "Very poetic, baby." I bring a kiss to her forehead. "I can be your rain if you need it. Everything I have to give is yours."

Trish

It's been a week since I showed Zac my scars. I feel better. Something about opening up to Zac gave my heart more space to feel what I need to. The scars will always be a part of me. But maybe one day they won't hurt so badly anymore.

The last thing I want is to string him along. I've been honest about where I've been at with the whole thing. But I *do* want more with him. Especially now. It's time to make this a bit more formal, for both of us.

He's leaning against my kitchen counter wearing a tight white shirt. The fabric hugs all the ridges of his abs and arms. Even though we're both insanely busy, we're finding pockets of time to get together. Means a lot to me he drives all the way to Willardson just to see me for one night.

Tonight, he cooked me some out of this world alfredo. Says it's his dad's recipe. We just finished cleaning dishes and I've got some cheesecake I picked up from the local bakery. I take his hand and lead him over to the couch to eat it with me.

"So I'm ready to officially date you." I watch his smile, the expression warming my chest the longer I look at it. "So, are we doing this, then?"

"Fuck yes, we're doing this." He leans in and kisses me. "I want to."

"I want to, too." I straddle him, holding the cheesecake off to the side.

"You're what I need."

"I know I am, baby doll." He smirks, letting me know that he is using a name I like to call people. "You're absolutely what I need."

"I wanna be." I pull back, gazing into those perfect brown eyes of his under those long eyelashes that anyone would kill for. "Be my boyfriend?"

"I already am, baby doll."

"That's my nickname, thank you."

"You don't own it."

"I own you." I make sure to sound as absolutely sexually promiscuous as possible with my tone. I take a spoon of cheesecake and feed him.

"Mmmm, I love when you do that." His cock gets hard and makes me need some physical attention as soon as possible. I arc my hips, grinding against him. He gets even harder. "And fuck, I need to be owned right now."

"And I need to send you flying out of this world."

"Take me, then."

All my reservations melt away. All that we've worked for becomes ours. I can be his. He can be mine.

His lips peck my nose. On my cheek. On my chin. On the sensitive under skin leading down to my collar bone. Trails of kisses, lovely sweet. The feel of his lips like a tender rose against my skin. Tickling. Teasing. Tantalizing.

His hands pull apart the buttons of my shirt, exposing my tits for his every desire.

"I'm gonna take you. And it's gonna be different this time." I whisper against his ear. That hard johnnyboy in his trousers jumps up again like he needs to play.

"It already is, baby doll." He takes the cheesecake out of my hand and feeds me a bite.

"You're gonna stop using my nicknames." I take the cheesecake back, in a playful fight, and feed him another bite.

"Make me." He snickers.

"You're gonna wish you hadn't said that, Willey."

"You're gonna wish you didn't think about telling me what I can and cannot say." That rough tone has me soaking wet. He knows I like that intensity. His strong hands rip off my shirt. I hop off his lap. My pants hit my ankles in a swift motion that has me all kinds of hot and bothered.

"I need you." He pulls his tight shirt up to his neck, gorgeous muscles outlined with all his hard work. "It's only been you."

I bite my lip, enjoying the torture I see on his face. "It's only been you, too."

"Phew," he smiles, relaxing into a passionate kiss. "And I will be owned by you. But tonight, Trish? Tonight, we need to make love."

"You love me?"

"Truly." He kisses my lips. "Deeply." He kisses my neck. "Immersively." He nibbles on my earlobe. "Passionately." He kisses the spot between my eyebrows. He rubs his nose against mine. "I love you, Trish."

"I love you." I whisper the words. "And I've never loved anyone like this." I tilt my chin upward, meeting his lips with mine. The kiss holds infinitely.

"I've never loved anyone else like this either." His forehead rests on mine.

Time slows. There's a pounding in my ears that fills with desire. His lips claim mine. My soul melts into his. Fucking hell, how does he get me so naughty and dirty with his filthy mouth just to sink me into a puddle at his cleats?

"Worship me." I bite my lip, looking into the sea of longing in his irises.

"Oh, that's my plan."

Warmth spreads, starting at the tip of my toes and working all the way through my middle.

He lifts me up, heading toward the bedroom. Unlike the many times I've enjoyed him throwing me on this bed, this time is tender, deliberate. It melts my heart like a really good chick-flick.

His lips go to my ankles, kissing under my socks as he pulls them off my feet. His strong hands massage me, working away the tension of a lifetime.

"You've been working too hard, baby." He glances up at me with those brown eyes, taking me to another universe in their depths. His strong hands grip my hips and edge me to the end of the bed. With a tender expression, he brings his mouth for a kiss between my legs. His tongue flicks, dancing around my clit and sending tingles through me. It's like he's conducting energy with his mouth.

He goes slowly, massaging my hips. "One sec," he goes into my bathroom and brings back my favorite vanilla lotion. "Can I use this?"

"Um, yes please." I smile.

The smell of vanilla fills my nostrils. He's so talented with his hands. Those hands that catch baseballs and strum guitar strings. The skill and technique he uses to play baseball and guitar is working away every bit of tension in my thighs and hips. His touch is glorious.

He returns to the bathroom and washes the lotion off his hands. Then he goes to my top drawer for some of my sex toys.

"In the mood for either of these?" He holds out a couple vibrators and I pick my little pink one. With careful precision, he tucks it in just far enough that my opening receives it into the best spot. It begins to vibrate.

He kisses along my body, starting at my belly button and dipping lower and lower. The teasing mixes with my quivering insides, driving my pleasure. His tongue flicks against my clit. With his hand on my belly, he sucks my clit with just the right amount of pressure that I'm unraveling in mini-orgasms that flutter so much I can't tell where one ends and another begins.

The longer I melt into his touch, the more amazed it leaves me. How is it he can worship my body this way, just as I asked him to? I relax against the bed, allowing his hands and mouth and my vibrator to send me off into oblivion. That rush of heat burns like an eternal flame, taking all the harm of the past away, burning it off. His fire's strong enough to remove all trace of what was. Replacing it with what I want it to be.

Zac's warmth is all I need. I focus on his touch and the way he looks as he pleases me. I've never known anyone more giving.

"Thank you," I whisper. He pauses, and I worry that maybe I've pulled us away from this moment. But instead, he looks touched like this gratitude is new. He lifts his head, coming up to my face.

"Thank you," I raise my head to his, our faces aligned. "For giving me the most exquisite pleasure I've ever had." I rub my nose against his. "For being the one who wants to share this with me." I lick my lips and lock them against his, deepening the kiss as our bodies clench together. Our skin meets like a long lost friend, that warm and silky feeling making my dead heart live.

"Thank you," I whisper against his neck. "Thank you," against his tight nipple as I rub the muscles beneath. "Thank you," against his cock. I wet my hand and stroke in rhythm with my sucking.

A single tear finds its way out of his eye. He catches it in his thumb and rubs it on my eye lashes.

"Awwww, look, I found another one for us to share." His words bring with them the promise I need to believe in us.

Zac

She's my girlfriend.

I keep replaying our sweet and sexy night. The next morning, I get out of the shower and dry my hair with the towel as I step into her room for my clothes. She's on the bed checking her phone.

Then I hear the sound of my voice. On my professional Sprinkle account.

A sly smile takes her face as she sees me.

"Wait…why do I feel like I've seen your dick before?" She's teasing but the blood has entirely drained out of my face. I may pass out on her carpet.

"Because we've fucked tons of times?" I wrinkle my eyebrows, trying not to make this worse. Why haven't I told her?

Am I really *that* ashamed by my sex work?

"You remind me of this one guy I follow on Sprinkle."

My throat gets real hot. Memories of how horribly wrong it all went with Valerie rush to mind. My heart pounds in my chest, a sense of panic building. No, this isn't what I want.

Flying fish sticks. We just made this no-strings-attached arrangement into a relationship. I got one night as her boyfriend.

Now this.

"You're on Sprinkle, aren't you?" Her smile is coy as she shows me her phone.

The room spins around me and I force air into my lungs, bracing myself against the wall.

"I should've guessed. Ballboy97?" Her tone tells me that it's okay with her, and I breathe a sigh of relief.

"You mad I didn't tell you it's my account?" Heat rises to my cheeks. This could be it. Everything good we have can vanish.

I shoulda told her to begin with.

"Am I mad? Oh, hell no. I love your account. It's so good." She turns off her phone and sets it on the nightstand.

"You're not mad?" I blink back weird spots of vision that refuse to focus.

She walks over and puts her hands in mine. "No, baby. Why would I be mad?"

"It's okay with you...that I post sex videos?" I clear my throat, constricted from rising panic.

"Yeah." She gives me a face that says she's supportive. "Wait." She runs her hands through my wet hair, pulling it out of my face. "You were really worried about this, weren't you?"

"Yes." I choke out, my throat so fucking tight. *Anxiety, it's okay. We're okay.* I try to self-soothe.

"Honey, I don't mind at all. In fact, I'd love to help you. I keep thinking how I ought to pose you for some photos."

"What...Seriously?...You'd do that?" The adrenaline shifts from anxious to excited, the sister emotions only half a beat away from each other. "I've been wanting to grow my account."

"Are you kiddin'? I'd love to help. You've helped so much with my website stuff."

"That'd be amazing." I try to smile but it feels like there's a weight on my body keeping the corners of my mouth down.

"You need to sit down? You're looking a little pale." She eyes me, seeing past my sorry attempt at concealing the rapid breathing and the way my fingers are already on my wrist checking for a pulse.

"I'm sorry. Just, just gimme a sec." I sit on the bed and put my head between my knees, trying to regulate.

"Here, I'll be right back." She goes down the hall and comes back, sitting on the bed beside me and handing over a glass of water.

I sip slowly, taking long, slow breaths. After a few minutes, I feel my body starting to calm. Trish has been amazing with this. She doesn't judge me or sit back and stare like I'm a rabid dog that she doesn't know how to help. She's a safe place. I don't know how, but she's accepting this part of me that I have trouble accepting myself.

I set down the glass of water on my nightstand.

"Take as long as you need." She moves behind me and starts rubbing my shoulders. Her touch brings comfort like nothing else. I'm feeling so much better.

"Oh, I got this for you." She hands me a little wrapped box, an excited look on her face as she does a little shoulder shimmy. "Consider it your early Christmas present."

"What's this?" I open it. Inside is a fitness watch.

"I know you're always checking your pulse, worried about your heart and such. Thought this may help." She unfolds the instructions and helps me set it up. "Keeps track of all kinds of stuff. Heart rate. How well you sleep. It'll be good for baseball, too."

"Awwwwwwwww." I glance over the instructions and go ahead and plug it into charge. "Damn, this is so thoughtful." My lips raise in a smile. "I love it."

"Hoped you would." She looks delighted. "Maybe you'll get some relief."

I relish the thought. "Thank you."

Trish

That night with Zac ended way too quickly. I already miss him something fierce. Who knew an hour and a half drive could feel so far away?

While doing laundry, my phone buzzes in my pocket. It's Lex.

"Hey, Lexie Leigh," I balance my phone in the crook of my shoulder and ear, using both hands to put away laundry.

"Hey girl, hey." She sounds utterly delighted.

"Catch me up." I grab a hanger and hang up my yellow cardigan. "How've you been?"

"I've just had the most incredible weekend of my life." Her words come out fast.

"Oh, do explain." Finished with the laundry, I go to the couch. Snuggling into my pillows, I get comfy.

I've missed our chats.

As much as I'm around people for work, I get pretty lonely. Most of my friends are long gone. Don't know why I stay in Willardson.

Nana's face appears in my mind. She's the reason. I don't wanna miss time with her when I'm not sure how much she has. I know how fast you can lose someone and how much it hurts to wish for more days and hours together.

I can't leave Willardson yet. Just wish Zac wasn't making me wanna up and move. It's these kinds of crazy impulses I have to worry about. They'll turn into regrets.

"Trish, Bobby's incredible." She says.

"So I've been told." I shake my head. How is she still in awe of him? Doesn't she see through it?

I don't see through Zac. But that's *not* the same thing. Zac wants a relationship. Bobby is allergic to them.

"No, like even more than all that. Just the other night, after our first time, I was like '*oh so I've experienced an infamous Bobby hookup,*' and he was all like '*that wasn't a hookup to me*' and I was like Oh My God this actually means somethin' to him." If she was falling for him before, it's only gotten worse.

Yeesh, there's no stopping this train. They've already boarded and aren't gonna get off.

"Wait, you and he just hooked up for the first time?" I shoot up on the couch enough to make my abs sore from yesterday's core workout.

I anxiously await her response. All that comes is a long pause followed by a nervous laugh.

"Lexie?" My jaw is gonna be too sore to chew bubblegum with how far it's dropped–all the way down to the carpet.

"We didn't wanna rush it, okay?" She tries to sound confident, but I hear every little bit of insecurity in her tone.

"Oh, yeah, I get that."

"Bobby wasn't sure if it was okay to kiss me, much less go all the way. You remember when Cody clobbered him at prom after dancing with me? I bet that was part of the trauma he's been trying to work through. He's at therapy right now."

"I'm glad he's getting some professional help." I think that's huge. Good for Bobby.

"I swear we all need it." Lexie says.

"You're right about that." I hop up from the couch, getting my camera bag ready to go.

"Did I tell you what he said about having sex?"

"Um no, it's been radio silence now that you don't need me any more." I definitely shoulda hid some of the snark in my voice before it flittered from my lips to her ears.

Me and my big mouth.

"Girl, you know it's not like that." Lexie's quick to reply.

"It kinda is." I sigh. "But seriously. Tell me. I wanna hear this."

"Okay, just let me talk."

"I wanna know as much as you wanna tell me." I work to convey my sincerity. No matter the ups and downs we have, Lexie's my BFF.

"In my entire life, I've never had *this* much sex. I lost track of how many times I came." She goes on in a romantic tone.

A warm rush goes through the middle of my body, touching each rib as it eases through to my core.

"There's nothin' better than losing track of orgasms." I bite my lip. I really haven't had a partner that spoke to my body the way Zac does.

"I barely came at all with Cody. I mean I'd have these like mini orgasms I thought were the real thing. But no. That wasn't even close to what happened this weekend. I felt like my body was gonna explode with how much pleasure Bobby gave me. Like I worried if I could handle it because I felt so fucking much."

We're gonna keep going until your body can't take any more.

"Wait, hold up. You *never* had a big O with Codester? Ever?" I grab my throw blanket and drape it over my shoulders, settling onto the couch again.

"Kinda. Maybe. I don't know. Sex was so different with Cody. I told Bobby I felt more like a virgin especially with how much experience he has."

"Okay, okay, fine. But I have a lot to tell you, too." I run to my closet and grab Zac's hoodie and some fuzzy socks. It's so freaking cold. My God. Are we gonna have an actual winter this year?

"Oh? Like what? You got some news? Spill." Lexie says.

"Let me just say Zac Williams is capable of beautiful home runs on the field and in the sheets." I chew my Juicy Fruit thinking about the time he stole my gum out of my mouth.

"I already knew that." She chuckles. "When we went Christmas shoppin' I figured you and he were having a lot of quality time."

"Well, um, that's true...and...he's officially my boyfriend." It feels weird to say, like I'm just as allergic to relationships as Bobby. But then I remember all the sweet moments with Zac.

"Sweet Jesus." She gasps. I don't have to see Lexie to know that her eyes are wide and her fingers are strumming on her lips like she always does.

"So that night at Garrison's y'all hit it off?" She draws out the word and I melt into the couch, cuddling into Zac's hoodie, pretending it's his hug.

"And now I'm actually in a relationship." I'm so fucking twitterpated it's not even funny. Never in my life have I wanted to be with a guy so badly. I'm happy with him.

"No shit?" Lexie asks.

"He's my boyfriend, Lex." I swallow hard.

"Zac's a really good guy." She says.

"You know him pretty well?"

"Yeah, he always hung out with us his freshman year before the accident...." Lexie trails off and I feel that punch to the gut with the grief we share. It's one thing to talk about her past sex life. Another thing to send her down memory lane of hanging with the baseball team before Cody's last breath.

"I didn't mean to–"

"It's okay." Lexie's voice is choked up, and it makes my throat all tight.

"Why's it easier to talk about how Cody was in bed than when we all used to hang out, hm? Tell me. Because I don't understand this grief thing." There's fire in her tone, like she's angry at the grief.

"We can't. There's no way to understand." I rub my chest through Zac's hoodie. That pain in my heart grows with each tight breath. We know way too much about grief. It ain't right.

"There's really not." She sniffles, and I beg my eyes to shed the tears trapped for years. I want to cry with my friend. For the life she lost. For the friend we both cared about. The one who held us all together.

Now we're drifting. What's life without Cody here? What's time if we can't all spend it together?

"I'm sorry." She sniffles again.

"I'm the one who's sorry. Can't even cry with you. Pathetic." I cough.

"This is your way of crying." She tries to soothe me.

The yearning in my heart is so severe, if it was my choice, I'd let those tears out.

"One day you'll be able to." Lexie knows why. She knows the day I figured out why tears stopped coming from my face.

Dipshit broke something deep inside me.

"Do you see your Mama at all?" Her tone is cautious, and I appreciate the concern.

"Only when I have to for lunch. She and I visit Nana every week for lunch. But it's not quality Mama time. That's about all I can handle. Gotta stay far away from that house." My chest burns. "Why does it have to be this way? I love Mama. Wish I could spend more time with her." I sigh. Lexie gets it because her relationship with her mama is at least as complicated.

"Doesn't sound like you're mad at her. Just that you don't wanna hang around Dipshit." She uses my nickname for him and it makes me smile.

"I'm not so much mad as I am disappointed. I wish she woulda done something." A guilty knot forms in my throat. I'm sure she tried. Just wish she tried harder. I feel bad for wishing that. I know how hard Daddy's death hit me. It broke Mama.

Shouldn't she have figured that out and done something, though? I've never understood why she lost herself and didn't go to find it.

"I know she does the best she can." I shake my head.

"Neither of our Mama's have a clue." Lexie says.

Without realizing it, my hand is under my clothes, feeling that tender skin that never healed quite right. The past hits with a vengeance. Every part of my body seizes up as I navigate through the intense rush of memory.

"Muscles and bones remember." Cody told me on a camping trip. We were all up in the mountains. Everybody else had passed out in their sleeping bags. Cody and I stayed up late. Maybe it was because I'd drank a lot or maybe it was because we both kinda knew what the other person was going through, but we had a real deep conversation. He told me about his dad. I told him about Dipshit.

And there's that knot in my throat getting bigger. I feel burned, like when I drink coffee that's way too hot and it scalds every inch of muscle on the way down.

Cody got it. He knew what it was like.

Does his body still have those scars? Are they the last ones to decompose in a casket filled with worms eating away rotting flesh? Or do they exist forever, never to be healed?

I swallow hard, feeling that spiral taking hold of me. "Let's grab coffee when you get into town."

"Yeah," Lexie says. "I'm excited to see you."

"I'm leaving next week for the photo shoot in Hawaii. So let's go sooner rather than later."

It was sweet of Zac to offer for me to go to Kentucky with him. I love that state so much. I really should go with him sometime. Too bad the dates didn't line up.

"Oh, that's right. Well, text me what day you're free, and we'll go then."

"Love you, boo." I smile, trying to keep myself away from the hellish abyss calling me. I can't handle a relapse now. Need this pain to diminish.

"Love you, too." Lexie says.

After clicking off the phone, I get in a shower as hot as I can stand it, letting the water run over me until I'm numb.

Because feeling numb is better than feeling pain.

"Oh, I totally understand. Not a big deal at all." I hide the disappointment in my voice. Being a photographer, I have a lot of cancellations. But this hits harder than it should, because now I don't have plans for Christmas.

"Thank you so much." Mrs. H. is relieved that I'm not charging a cancellation fee. It's bad enough they had to cancel the wedding.

Plopping on the sofa, I take a minute to process my change of plans. There's no way I'm staying in Willardson. I'll go somewhere else.

Or I could….

I pull up Zac's number.

"Hey there, little miss. You have good timing. I just stopped at the 7 Eleven and was thinking about you." His sexy voice stops my shivers in this freezing December.

"Does the offer still stand?"

"Which one?"

"A Kentucky Christmas?"

"Hell yes, it does. Um, I'm already north of Willardson so I can circle back and I'll swing by your place in an hour."

"I'll go pack. Bye."

"Okay, bye."

Frantically, I pack up having just enough time to shove my last few things into my bag before he gets here.

He knocks.

"Glad I caught you in time." I welcome him in and close the door before all the heat rushes out. I take his hands and go up on my tippy toes to kiss him.

"You didn't." He pins me up against the wall. "But since we're already late…" A mischievous smile takes his face. Those dimples shine bright. "I'd love to make us even later." He bites his bottom lip and I trace the movement as his teeth edge upward. "Would you like that?"

"I'd love that." My body heaves. Literally heaves. I'm weak in the knees, about to come everywhere from his voice. "Pretty sure I'm gonna come just looking at you."

"You're not allowed to come." He playfully bites my lip, and I feel myself drenching my thong.

"I'm not sure I can help it, Willey." I thrust my hips against his, that massive cock hard against me. "Fuck, Zac. Do me right here."

He reaches under my leggings, edging his fingers into my panties, pulling my clothing down. He kneels in front of me. With careful attention, he rubs his tongue against my bundle of nerves. "I told you you're not allowed to come."

I'm writhing with each motion. Fire fills my core. Anticipation holds in my chest.

"Then you're not allowed to touch me like that." I raise one eyebrow, taunting his reaction. My body misses the feel of his fingers. I need them back under my thong.

"Oh, should I stop?" He playfully pulls away.

"Don't you dare." I flick my tongue as he proceeds to touch me, knowing I'm only teasing about him not being allowed to touch me. "Please, can I come yet?" I tease him with my eyes.

"You have to wait." His attitude sends a wave of pleasure through me.

"I don't think I can." Every muscle in my body tenses, trying to get closer to my peak that he's playfully forbidding.

"Don't come yet." He breathes against my body. Slow swirls of his tongue against my clit tests every bit of my will to hold back my full culmination.

"Don't come yet." That tone is so intense it makes me laugh. He's an alpha male cinnamon roll. Best of both worlds? Guess so.

"Please, you're torturing me. Let me come." I beg.

He slips two fingers inside my core. "You can come now." He winks.

I prop my back against the apartment wall while he eats me out.

"Fuckkkkk," the word emerges from my trembling body, already squirting into his mouth. I'm quaking from my orgasm, begging for more. He's sliding out of his tight jeans and into my opening. I wrap my ankles around his back. He holds me against the wall, pounding hard into me.

His kisses bring me to heaven and back. The angle couldn't be more perfect. His strong arms make me feel secure and safe. He's hitting that amazing part of me that's hard to get from any other position. How does he tap me just right?

My body adjusts to how enormous he is as he bounces me up and down. Faster and faster, we come together. He relaxes against my chest, both of us relying on the wall to hold us up until we sink to the carpet.

"Damn." I lick my lips, burning from those rough kisses I live for.

"I may have to call off the whole trip if you're gonna treat me like this."

"Who says we can't?" I hop up and take his hand. "That's just a taste."

"I hope so." He holds his dripping cock and hurries into my bathroom for a tissue. Watching him try not to spill is eleven kinds of adorable. I follow him into the bathroom and clean up. His smile is so satisfying. I pull on my leggings and wash off my hands.

Damn.

Hot fucking damn.

Zac

"Okay, so what questions do you have for me?" We've been driving for about five hours. We're getting close to my house and I wanna make sure we talk before we get there. I keep looking at her gorgeous eyes every chance I get.

"I didn't get you any presents. Is that okay?" She asks.

"You being here is the best gift." I send her a wink.

"You're so cliché, oh my god."

"You give me a reason to be." I peck her lips at the stoplight. "Can you text Ma real quick and let her know you're comin'." I pull my phone out of my pocket and watch as Trish's fingers fly across the keyboard.

"Is she gonna be okay with me just showing up? I can get a hotel. You can drop me off and pick me up when you wanna hang out. That way you'll get some time with your family. It's not a big deal." She messes with her phone, pulling up hotels in Elizabethtown.

I chuckle. "Baby doll, I'm not lettin' you outta my sight for a second. No need to stay at a hotel when I bring you home for Christmas."

Trish's glares at me, letting me know she's not buying it.

"What?" I ask.

"Ain't your Ma really Christian and stuff? I'm pretty sure people think I'm a slut when they first see me." She looks down at her outfit. "Guess I could be a little more presentable." She messes around in her bag and pulls a makeup wipe out to work off her bright red lipstick.

"Trish, stop." I gently set my hand on her thigh.

"I shoulda thought of this when we were cleaning up earlier."

I take her hand, halting the wipe before it gets to her face. "Trish, please stop. They'll accept you, alright?" I give her a sincere look. "We aren't the conservative Christians most people think of. I only go to church when I want to. Sadie's an out-of-the-closet lesbian. They won't judge you for how you look. They don't subscribe to all that."

"Are you for real?" She waits a while, like I'm supposed to correct it.

"I am, baby. They'll love you as you are. And even if they didn't, I wouldn't want you to change any bit of yourself to please them."

"Are you sure though? Because I can just take this off."

"If you want to for *you,* please do. But don't do it to impress my parents." I give her hand a squeeze, hoping she believes me. With the corner of her lip raising in a smile, she puts the wipe away.

I clear my throat. "Now, my house ain't nice, alright? We don't have much, and it's just a modest little place."

"I'm not worried about that." Hearing her say it brings the last bit of relief I need. Didn't figure she'd care, but it's good to hear.

"Are they gonna make us sleep in different rooms?"

"No." I say.

"You're joking."

"Little miss, you better listen." I give her a playful growl. "I told you. They aren't like that. It's not gonna be awkward. We'll just stay in my room, and they probably won't say anything."

"Okay then." She says.

"Okay then." I nod.

Car in the driveway, I run around and open her door. We grab the suitcases from the backseat of my truck and head to the porch. I put my key in the front door and open it up. "Ma, we're here!"

Sadie hug attacks me, "Zac!"

I set my backpack and our suitcases down to hug her properly. "You cut your hair again?" I step back and see that she's got more layers than I saw last time we video called.

"Yeah, you like it?"

"Looks great." I smile.

"Angela showed me a picture and told me I had to try it." Sadie adjusts how her hair sits on her shoulders. "I mean she was so right. Like it frames my face so well."

"Oh, yeah." I swallow, thinking it's a little strange Angela picked out her hair style. Sadie's never been one to get opinions. I guess it's okay though. "This is Trish." I smile at my girl, thrilled as pickles she's standing in the entry of the place I call home.

"Hey Trish." She gives her a hug, and I watch Trish's surprise.

It just takes a second for her surprise to melt into comfort and she wraps her arms around Sadie. "Zac talks about you so much I feel like I already know you."

"He talks about you all the time too." Sadie smiles. "It'll be so fun having you for the holidays."

"Zac? Honey? You're here?" Ma comes through the kitchen, wearing her old apron and holding a potato peeler.

"Ma, this is Trish." I nod.

"Hey sweetheart, welcome to our house." She gives Trish a hug, holding the peeler to the side. "You make yourself plenty at home now, Trish, ya hear?" Ma takes Trish's hand. "So good to meet you."

"Looks like you're in the middle of cooking. Can we help?" Trish asks.

"Oh, you two get settled in first. Zac, make sure to show her around." Ma heads toward the kitchen.

I lift the bags. "My room's this way." I tilt my head to the left where there's a long hall and my room next to Sadie's. "Can you grab that door? Thanks."

Trish opens up my room with a full sized bed and all my Lou Gehrig posters. My blue and white Yankee's bedding.

"This is cute." She picks up some of my old baseball trophies.

"I haven't really updated the decor since I was twelve, so yeah." I set the suitcases in the corner and step into the hallway. "There's the bathroom. We've got towels and stuff in here." I show her around. Our house is really small so there's not much to show, but I want her to feel at home here.

We go back into my room and she sits on the bed and gives my pillow a big hug. "I wanna see pictures of you when you were a kid."

"Oh, sure." I go over to the bookshelf and grab my photo box.

"Wow, look at you." She smiles, pulling out different pictures.

"That's when Mitch almost got us in huge trouble for letting Mrs. Smith's chickens out." I chuckle, remembering too well that rush of adrenaline. "He was always doing stupid shit. I was the idiot that followed him around."

"Do I get to meet Mitch?"

"Yeah, I'll text him. And you have some relatives? Did you wanna see when we can get together with them?"

"Oh, I'm not sure." She yawns. "Let's just see how it goes."

After a while of reminiscing over the old photos, I put the photo box back on the shelf. It feels good to show her things from my past.

"I'm so glad you wanted to come." My lips find hers, hungry for all the sweetness that is her kiss.

"Worth having to turn around and come get me?" She runs her fingers through my hair.

"I'd do it again a thousand times if it means getting to spend Christmas with you." I lick my lips and melt into hers. "Even if you called me right now, I'd drive all the way back to Willardson to pick you up." I rub her nose with mine, absorbing her gasp.

"You'd really?"

"In a heartbeat." I put my arms around her.

We enjoy dinner with Ma and Sadie. They ask Trish a handful of questions, but thankfully don't embarrass me too much. As usual, Pa's working.

After dinner, Ma heads to work. Trish, Sadie and I sit in the living room. Our cat, Snickers, is having a great time on Trish's lap. Usually when I come home for the holidays, I just play it by ear. Sadie and I have never had a problem finding plenty to do.

"You guys wanna go see a movie?" I ask.

"Oh, no, I have plans." Sadie points to her phone. "Angela told me she can talk. I've been waiting all day." Sadie jumps off the couch and runs down the hall before she shuts herself in her room.

"No Sadie, then." I rub my forehead. "She's not usually like this."

"Oh? What's different?" Trish pets Snickers' ears.

"We just normally hang out a lot."

Snickers flips onto her back and Trish scratches her belly. "Maybe she'll be free later."

"Did you wanna go to a movie?" I play with Snickers' tail.

"Yeah, that'd be fun. I'll pull up the showtimes." Trish types in the local theater to her phone browser.

"Lemme see if Mitch and Sarah wanna come." I type out a text.

"Yeah, that'd be fun."

We all catch the next showing of The Wolf of Wall Street. It's sweet to watch my favorite person with my friends, like she belongs. In my mind, she'll always belong with me.

Come morning, the house is quiet. Just as I remember, my folks are gone most of the time. Sadie was still on the phone when we got back from the movie and I heard her off and on until wee hours of the morning. Guess she's sleeping in.

Trish and I go to the kitchen and start up some coffee, making out while it brews.

"It's good to be here." Trish sips coffee from a mug, leaning against our cheap laminate countertop. "I needed this escape. Just some time not to do anything but relax."

"Relax? I didn't know you knew the meaning of the word." I tease her, taking a sip out of her mug. My face close to hers, I run my tongue along the rim of the mug.

"That's real funny." She rolls her eyes. I'm still pretty hard from spooning her all night and making out but that snark of hers makes my semi shoot straight up.

I covertly check to make sure no one can overhear. "Fuck, do you make me hot." I lean into her, letting her enjoy my firm cock. She gasps and I suck the air out of her mouth with my kiss. My hands find that soft part of her ass at the base of her butt, running my thumb up and down her cheek, the way she likes. Her nipples press firmly into my chest, no bra between us since she's in my pajama shirt. The clothing is still too much of a barrier. I start to reach my fingers under her shirt, dizzy from her kisses.

"This is your parent's kitchen?" She whispers. All at once, I realize we're at my parents' house and someone could walk in on us.

"You're cute when you blush." She tickles my cheeks with her fingertips.

"Way to take me to another planet. I forgot where we were."

"Magic." She smiles, setting her coffee mug next to the sink.

"Hey, Zac?" Sadie strums on the kitchen doorway, and I turn around. "You think we can all go to the lake? The cousins are driving up. Would that be something you'd like, Trish?" She turns to Trish to ask.

"The lake? Yeah, sure." Trish nods.

"I know it's early, but since it's been cold they're ready for ice fishing. Memaw texted me this morning." Sadie's happy, but not as excited as I'd expect her to be. Bet she's tired. Come to think of it, at dinner she didn't talk as much as she normally does. Is it because Trish is here? Is she feeling awkward about sharing my attention?

"Aren't you thrilled?" I ask Sadie.

"Yeah." She shrugs, but her face tells a different story. What's going on with her?

"Ice fishing?" Trish asks.

"Yeah, Memaw, our grandma on Ma's side likes to get us all together." Nostalgia fills me with the memory of all the winters we spent on the lake. Ice fishing is the best. Memaw's gear and Poppy's fresh bread when we got back into the harbor. Pa and Uncle Joe would grill up the fish. We'd go with all my cousins. I wasn't holding my breath to be able to take Trish. It's usually something the ice ain't ready for until January or February.

"That sounds like a good time." Trish says.

"Is Angela comin'?" I ask Sadie.

"No." Sadie says. I'm surprised we haven't been introduced.

"Y'all are dating?" I dare to ask, wondering if she'll care if Trish is standing next to me.

"Yeah. She told me I better not even look at anyone else." Sadie shrugs. This doesn't sit well with me. I mean, they're exclusive? And Angela's in college? And she's being possessive? Doesn't seem reasonable.

Sadie folds her arms and leans against the counter, an expression making it clear she doesn't wanna talk about it right now. We stand in awkward silence while I try to read Sadie's mind. It's stupid, but I feel like something is really off and I hate that Sadie's not telling me more.

"Let's go get ready." Trish gently takes my hand and leads me down the hall. "You gotta tell me about this ice fishing thing."

"Here, wear these." I get her some warmer clothes from my closet, the ones with the drawstring so she can fit into them, ruminating on how nice it is that Trish is so perceptive. "I'll find some boots for you to borrow. I'm pretty sure Ma's will fit."

"She won't need them?" Trish asks.

"Nah, she's working today."

"Your folks really do work all the time." Trish pulls on the thermals.

After getting all the gear together, we drive through the country roads leading to my grandparents' house in Louisville. The countryside is covered in snow.

We get to their beautiful southern home and I park the car on the long driveway. Sadie hasn't said a word the whole way. She keeps checking her phone constantly, like she can't miss a single text. When we get out of the car, it's like Sadie doesn't even notice and just stays put.

"Not sure what's going on with her." I say to Trish under my breath as we walk up the winding sidewalk.

"Yeah, seems like something's bothering her." Trish says.

"Zac?" Sadie runs up behind us.

"Yeah?" I stop on the sidewalk a few steps behind Trish.

"Can I take the truck?" Sadie reaches out for the keys in my hand.

"What?" I pull them out of her reach.

"Angela texted me. Her car broke down just west of Lexington. I need to go see her." Sadie gets closer to where I'm holding my key ring.

"Can't she call someone else?"

"Are you serious? Her car broke down. It's super cold. I need to help." Sadie's talking like this is a frantic emergency.

"She can call for a tow. You're more than an hour away. Someone else can get there faster." I think about how Sadie was glued to her phone the whole drive. If Angela was texting her that whole time, why is she suddenly having car trouble? It isn't adding up. "We just got here. You can't miss this. Text Angela the address and see if she wants to come out after she gets her car sorted out."

"Zac, please?" Sadie's looking at me real intense.

"Why would you miss this?" My stomach is doing somersaults.

"I'll take care of the truck, I promise. And I'll be back in time to pick you up." The look in her eyes says she needs this.

"Okay." I hand her the keys.

She wraps her arms around me and gives me a huge hug that lasts a long time. "You're the best." She hurries to the truck and drives away. Really hope it's just anxiety that tells me this is all wrong.

I catch up with Trish and we walk the rest of the way to the house. After I knock on the door, Memaw opens it wide. We hurry into the heat and wipe our boots on the welcome rug to keep from dragging in dirt or chunks of the salt lining the driveway.

I give Memaw a hug and then turn to introduce them. "Memaw, this is Trish."

"Oh, hey honey." Memaw wraps Trish in a greeting embrace. "Y'all drove up from South Carolina? You having fun with us Kentucky folk, Trish?" Meemaw sticks her hands in her overall pockets.

"Trish's got some Kentucky blood in her." I mention.

"Oh, does she now?" Memaw looks invested in the conversation.

"Yes, my daddy was from Louisville."

Memaw scratches her head. "What's your last name, dear?"

"Montgomery."

"Oh, I know a lot of Montgomerys. Are you kin to Harry or Tim? Wait… you're not related to Harvey Montgomery, are you?"

"That's my dad."

Memaw looks like she's seen a ghost. Her eyes hold Trish's then dart back to me like she's wondering if I knew.

Trish's face goes pale. "You knew him?"

Trish

The world around me blurs and all I can see is Zac's grandma telling me something unbelievable.

I think about Daddy. The times he'd smile so big talking about Kentucky. It was home to him. Hearing he knew Zac's family hits me like sunshine on a beach, warm and comforting.

My throat gets tight as I absorb the feelings circulating in my system.

Zac's grandma's face is kind and reminds me a lot of Nana.

"Knew him? Oh yes." Zac's grandma grasps her chest with her hand, gasps and blinks back eyes welling up with tears. "Oh yes, we definitely did. What a small world." She grips my hand in hers. "He was such a good man. We considered him family. Come here, child." She leads me into the house. I look at Zac, a bewildered expression written all over his face.

"My stars. I can't believe Harvey's flesh and blood is standing in my home. It's so wonderful to see him living on, in you." Zac's grandma looks at him. "Did you know, Zachy?"

"No." He lets out a surprised chuckle.

"Horace, Horace?" Zac's grandma calls into the house looking for someone. "You'll not believe who your grandson's brought into our home this lovely mornin'." She says as we get into the kitchen.

"What are the chances? Memaw, I swear you know everyone." Zac's eyes go wide.

Someone's sitting at the table, kneading some dough. "What'chu got here, Evelyn?" He stands from his chair and brushes some flour off his hands.

"Harvey Montgomery's daughter, Trish." There's a glimmer in Zac's grandma's eye, like she's tearing up. "That was just tragic to hear about his early call to heaven." She shakes her head. "That heart attack." She sniffles, wiping her eyes with the back of her hand. "I'm sorry, it's just…wow. I can't believe you're here all grown up, Trishy. You musta been young when he passed. How old were you?"

"Nine." I let out a shaky breath, working to keep my teeth from chattering.

"My, my. Hi Trish, I'm Zac's grandpa. Everyone here calls me Poppy." Poppy shakes his head. "Last time I saw you, you was knee high to a grasshopper. I'm guessing you don't remember." Poppy goes to the sink to wash up his hands and then wraps my hand in both of his.

"I'm sorry, I don't remember. You knew me when I was younger?" I swallow against the knot forming in my throat.

"Oh yes, Harvey may as well have been our adopted son. He worked for us for many, many years. Built that hutch, right there." Zac's grandma gestures to the beautiful piece of furniture in the corner of the living room.

My body freezes as I look at his furniture.

When we moved in with Dipshit, he took all of Daddy's pieces to the dump. He said Mama would never move on if Daddy's shadow lurked in the house.

I didn't know I'd ever get to see his work again. My teeth rattle against each other as I take slow steps toward the hutch. Heaven's whispers fill my soul and it's like Daddy's right here with me in this living room. I take a deep breath to soak in the peace living on in his memory. I reach out my shaking hand touching the polished wood. Strong and sturdy, like the man I knew Daddy to be.

"Zac?" My lips are trembling, crying in my own way.

He takes me in his arms and holds for several heartbeats. "I had no idea."

"Me, neither."

The piece is beautiful.

"Can I take a picture?" I ask Zac's grandma.

"Of course." She says.

I get my phone and adjust the lights in the room. His hutch. A piece of him I always longed to be reunited with. Zac's face is kind as he watches me capture the photos.

"Thank you." I wipe my sniffles with the back of my hand, returning to the kitchen with Zac's grandparents.

"I'm so shocked." I lean against their counter, weak at the knees from all the emotions riddling my system as I try to process the shock.

"Yes, ma'am. I'm shocked too. He worked for us for several years. Then you guys moved to South Carolina and well, I'm sure you know all the rest." Zac's grandma says.

"I'd love to know any stories you have. Anything you remember." My heart beats hard in my chest hoping for things I've never had before.

"Of course, pumpkin. After y'all get back, I'll pull out all the old photo albums and we'll have a grand time talking about those days." Zac's grandma smiles wide.

"Yes, please." My tone is somber. "What a treat to meet you." I bring her into a hug.

"Y'all comin' or what?" Someone I don't know stands at the door.

"Just a second." Zac's grandma blinks back more tears. "This is wonderful, Zac. Just wonderful. It's nice to see family come home. And just so you know Trishy, you're family, you hear?" She gives me another big hug. "Doesn't matter what happens between you two." She points a finger between me and Zac. "Zac, you treat her right. If she's got Harvey's blood in her, she's a keeper."

"Thanks Memaw." He smiles.

"I can't believe any of this."

"Wow, what a small world. I mean, sometimes I swear Memaw knows every person who's ever touched the bluegrass of Kentucky. But that's just crazy." Zac put his arm around me and guides me out the back door.

"Yeah, I had no idea. I just don't think much about all of Daddy's connections out here, I guess." I'm still taken aback.

"That's so surprising." He raises his eyebrows. "I mean, there's lots of small towns here. But what are the chances?"

"Good thing they're just claiming my daddy as an adopted son and we're not real family. Or then that'd make this," I gesture between us, "really goddamn awkward."

"I've been worried about the same thing." He chuckles.

"Our kids would've been blue or something. You know like the Fugate family? The ones that were blue? You've heard of them right?"

"Oh my goodness, yes." He grins. "I was fascinated with them when I was younger. I mean who would ever think that a recessive hemoglobin disorder could cause bright blue skin? And it was exasperated through inbreeding? It's almost like *The Twilight Zone*." He laughs.

"Hell no. I'm drawing the line. I may want some youngins someday, but definitely not blue ones." I laugh with him.

"Oh, come on. You couldn't love a blue little kid?" He teases. "I'm sure I could, but I'd feel awful for making them look like somethin' outta a UFO."

"Then I guess we can all be thankful there's not really a family line crossing in our genes." I wink.

Zac

"**B**out time y'all came out." My cousin Charlie hollars.

My cousins are already getting the gear loaded up in their truck.

"Glad you're coming." I smile at Trish, helping her into the cab. "I always love ice fishing and it'll be a million times better with you here."

After about forty-five minutes of gabbing with the cousins and laughing at their stupid jokes, we get to the lake. Snow falls on the truck windows.

The lake comes into view—masked in white with bluish swirls where the ice is more clear and the snow has been removed or blown away. Heavily frosted trees hug its border and splashes of color dot the calm surface from other fishers who have set up their holes already.

"Wait, I've been here." Trish grips my knee hard as we come to the dirt paved parking lot. "This lake. What's it called?"

"McNeely Lake." I wrinkle my nose.

She puts her hand on her chest, an overwhelmed expression on her face.

"What is it?" I lean close so only she can hear my whisper.

"This is the place I took my first photograph. The only one I ever took of Daddy." Her voice is quiet.

My throat tenses up realizing how much this particular lake means to her.

"First, your grandparents knew him. Now, this is the lake." Her lip trembles.

How can it be the same place? She told me about that picture. They'd gone to Kentucky, obviously, but it was taken here?

"This lake?" I put my cheek to hers, feeling her quaking body next to mine.

"This is the one. The pink cabin." She takes my hand and puts it on her racing heart. "If this isn't a sign, I don't know what is." She leans her head against my shoulder, melting against me. My chest adjusts to her weight, but something else is heavy in a good way.

I always knew there was something more to us.

If this is really where she came with her dad, is it God's way of telling me I'm heading the right way? That this is where we both should be? I snuggle her closer, giving her all the time she needs to soak in this moment.

"We've come here so many times. I wonder if I saw you that day." I clear my throat, realizing how tight it is.

She jumps up from my shoulder. "Are you serious?"

"You came here in the summer, right?"

"Yeah."

"We lived at this lake almost every day of summer vacation. If you were nine, I wouldn't have been playing ball that summer. I woulda been here. At this lake."

Her eyes gloss over. "It must be our sign."

Part Two
February

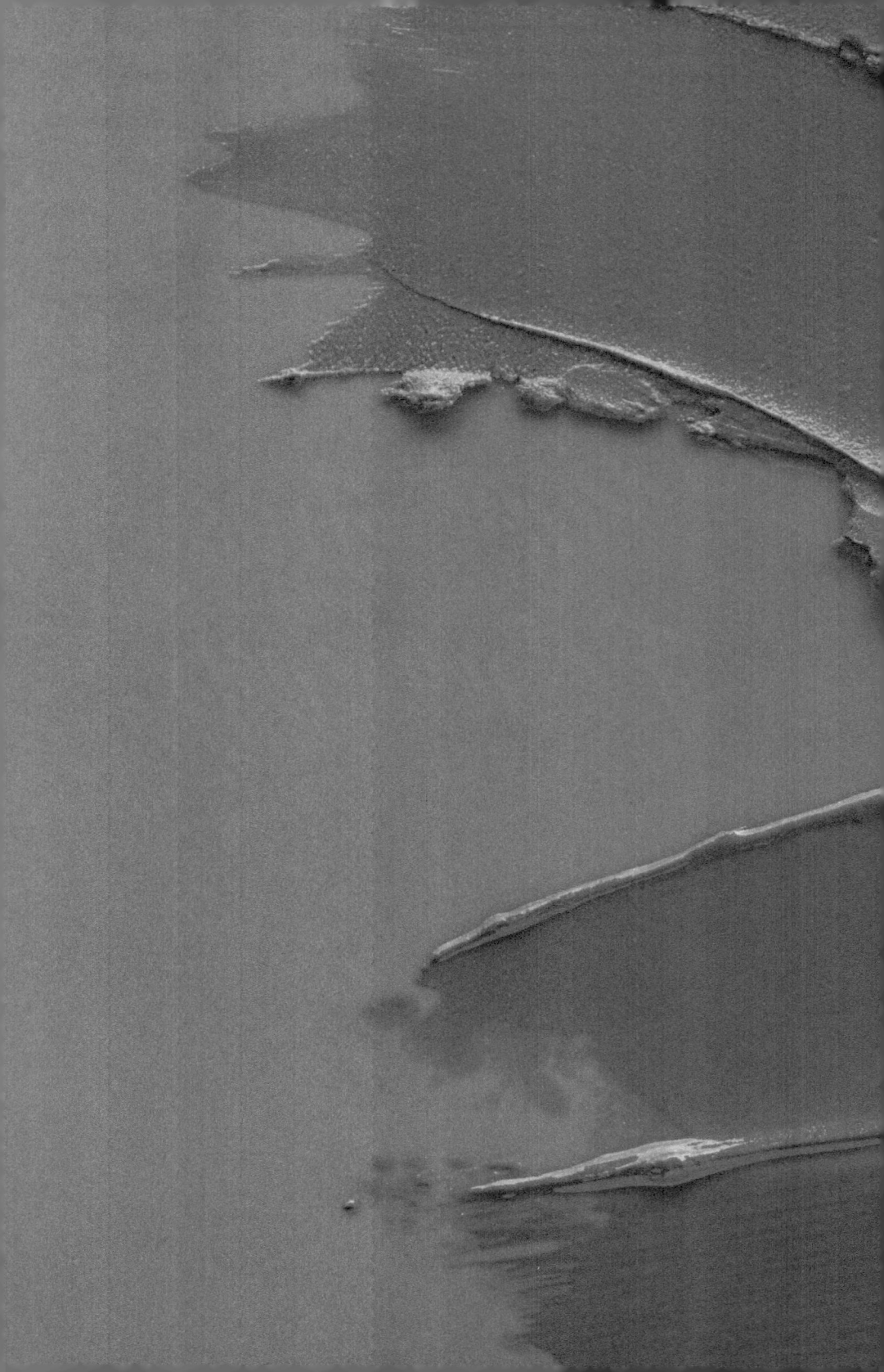

Trish

The last two months have flown by. Christmas in Kentucky was everything I didn't know I needed. I learned so much. Zac's grandma told me stories I'd never heard. Daddy was there with me, every moment.

Since then, it's been work, work, and more work.

Zac's getting ready to start baseball season. Our weekend trips are getting harder and harder to make. Even with the distance, it feels right to be with him. I have my signs. My answers.

It's a little after eleven and I'm finished with work for the night. I hop in a hot shower after removing my makeup.

"Love Story" by Taylor Swift keeps going off with my phone ringing. I figure it's a client I can call back, so I finish my shower. But it keeps going off.

Is it Zac?

Is he okay?

When I click the screen it lights up with *Lexie boo*. Lexie?

"Hey, what's up?" I ask.

"Can you come to my place? Now-ish?" She sounds as bad as she did the night Cody died. Worry grips my chest like I'm being squeezed by something strong and immovable.

"Yeah…" I don't have the nerve to ask why, but I can tell something is majorly wrong and I better get my ass over to her place quick.

"Hey girl, I'm here!" I open the Lexie's unlocked front door, cheap wine tucked under my arm as I ascend the stairs. Standing outside her bedroom door, I gasp. Looks like the tornado from *The Wizard of Oz* blew through here. Papers and boxes everywhere. The floor is covered in stuff.

Setting the wine on the nightstand, I ditch my purse. "What the hell is goin' on here?"

"I walked out on Bobby. We broke up, I think. I don't even know." She sobs into her hands, a quiet scream joining the ominous vibes of this room.

"Oh, honey." I pour the glasses as fast as I can, not sure what else to do.

"I don't know what I was thinkin'." Lexie's got that hopeless tone of voice I wish she never had to use.

"You were thinkin' you felt somethin' for him."

For the next several hours, I listen to Lexie as she tries to make sense of this sudden and horrible breakup. Bobby kept some secrets about his past. Really big ones.

I lay in Lexie's bed staring at the ceiling. I had to be strong for her. But my mask is dwindling.

My chest hurts as I try to process all that is coming into my mind and heart. It's too much.

Why is this hitting me so hard? I told her Bobby was all wrong for her. But then I saw so much happiness between them. He was good to her. I was warming up to the idea. My stomach wants to heave. My chest feels like it's stuck under a rock so big and heavy I can't remove it.

Bobby has a lot in his past.

So do I.

Bobby's too fucked up to be in a relationship.

So am I.

Bobby couldn't share his whole self.

Neither can I.

I look over at Lex, sleeping so restlessly. Damn, that fight with Bobby tuckered her out. I tuck the blanket around her shoulders and she settles.

Maybe I was reading the signs of being with Zac all wrong. Or maybe we needed to be together for a brief period but not any more. What has felt right the last few months now feels wrong.

My heart races in my chest. I've barely caught a wink of sleep. This has turned everything on its head. The longer I lay here, the more I stew with worry and regret. Bobby can't be with Lexie because of things in his past. I can't be with Zac because of things in mine.

Their breakup is a sign.

I won't lead Zac on for even one second now that I've been given a sign to counteract all the others. I have to talk to him as soon as I can. It's not right to feel this way and keep it from him.

If Bobby wouldn't have kept so much from Lexie, their fight wouldn't have hurt her so much. I won't do that to Zac. He deserves better.

I get up carefully to not wake Lexie and open my phone.

Me: Can you come over? I'm at Lexie's beach house.

Zac: You're in town?

Me: Just, please, come over?

Zac: Are you okay?

Me: Physically? Yeah. Emotionally? Not so much.

Zac: I'll be right there.

I go outside and wait for his truck.

As he pulls up, I want to take back everything. I want to rip this off like the wrapper on gum.

He stands, in his flannel pajama pants and oversized t-shirt, reminding me of the many times he's video called me at one am on a Tuesday to sing me to sleep.

"Hey baby." He wraps his arms around me, like he knows I'm going through hell, and I inhale his scent. His lips take mine and leave me breathless even when I don't want them to. It takes all I have to keep my heart in my chest, it's surging so hard.

"Didn't know you were comin' into town." He looks tired, and I realize I probably woke him.

"Lex and Bobby just broke up. She called beggin' me to drop everythin' to get here fast as I could." I shove my hands in my pocket to keep from getting too close. The look on his face tells me he noticed my physical distance.

"Bobby had some huge fuckin' secrets he waited until now to tell her."

"Damn." He raises his eyebrows. "Is she okay?" He sounds genuinely concerned.

"No. She's not." I take a breath, hoping for some resolve. "Let's go to the back porch." I take his hand, and we walk around the house. The water crashes against the beach, and I look out at the ocean.

"I know Lexie has you, but it seems like it's hitting you hard. It's a lot. Can I do something?" Zac looks at me for a while before I'm able to find his eyes.

"I'm not okay." It doesn't answer his question, but it's all I can say.

"It's okay to not be okay." He tries to take my hand, but I keep it far away. There's hurt in his eyes.

"I can't be with you anymore." The words sit in the air without reply or acknowledgement for a figurative eternity.

"Um, what?" He asks.

"I can't."

"You can't?" He sounds deflated. Neither of us speak for a long time. Too long. Eventually he leans against the railing of the porch. A gust of sea breeze blows my hair behind my face.

I hate watching him this way.

But I can't stay.

I won't stay.

Better to rip us apart now.

Less wounds to heal.

"Trish, I care about you."

"And I care about you enough to know that I can't do this. It's not what we need."

"What do we need? And excuse me, but how are you suddenly an expert?"

I swallow hard. "We all have secrets, Zac. Even me. Things you don't know. Things you can't know." I shudder. As much time as we've spent together, he doesn't know how bad my depression gets. I bury myself in work to hide from my own thoughts. I push everyone away.

The fantasy of a perfect future with Zac explodes, shattering piece by delicate piece. I reach for them in the void of darkness only able to grasp a single shard as they all flitter away.

"What?" Zac asks. "Seriously, Trish. What the actual fuck?"

I expect to hear anger, but it's genuine confusion. Am I really not making any sense?

"Didn't you hear me? They just broke up because Bobby has huge fuckin' secrets he just now told her."

"What's that got to do with us?" His tone is soft.

"Everyone has skeletons in their closet. I have so many dead bodies of pain and anguish living inside of my tormented soul built out of nights I tried to cry myself to sleep. Bobby should've told Lexie. I should be able to tell you. But that's just it. I'm fucked up. Bobby's fucked up. We can't be in a relationship."

"Well, Bobby's secrets are a shock, of course." He turns and leans against the railing. "But it doesn't mean we all have skeletons in the closet. Trish, this is about *them,* not *us.* That's the truth. Not everyone is gonna lie to you." He shakes his head. "I'm being honest." He leans closer. "And whatever it is you have in your past, I don't care if you tell me or not. You do what you need. And I'll be here, supporting you."

I feel like I'm falling. The world swirls around me and I'm as lost as that little girl inside me looking for love.

Breaking up isn't really what I want, and looking at his eyes I know that. He's offering me so much. Understanding, friendship, support, and privacy.

But for how long?

When will it be too much?

He deserves better. The thought keeps going through my head.

"Tell me," he says.

"Hm?"

"What those thoughts are saying."

"That you deserve better." I rub my eyebrows.

"Do I get to pick that or you?" He's got that sweet seriousness in his tone.

"Why would you get to pick?"

"Because I choose loving you over this ethereal concept of what I may or may not deserve." He does air quotes for the word deserve, like we don't have the same definition.

"Fair, but…there's so much Zac." I hug my body tight.

"I'm far from perfect, I swear. You've seen my panic attacks."

"And even your far from perfect is way closer on the scale of perfection than I am."

"Hard no."

"Hard no?"

"On *my* scale of perfection, you come pretty fucking close. In fact, to me you *are* perfect. Your worth has never been dependent on your scars."

It's like the first flowers in spring are popping up through a frozen winter. His words breathe new life into me. Renewal. Strength. Truth.

Could this be?

Is there worth to me besides all the shit I can't seem to work through?

"We've been dating a couple months. Can we give us a little bit longer before you decide if we're forever or not?" His words find the only path of clear thoughts into my head. "I don't want to pressure you to stay with me. But if the reason we're breaking up is because you have secrets, which I've given you permission to keep from me, and because you don't feel like you're good enough…" he sighs, "I think maybe we need to make some changes and I also think we can stay together. Just my two cents. You can think about it. Make a pros and cons list in your planner. Maybe?" He's being cute.

"I don't know how to do this." I sink onto the deck floor, feeling a horrible headache from all that has been the last several hours.

"I know you don't." He sits a few feet away, like he knows I need space.

See, Trish, he's so different from what you've experienced. I know you're worried. But what if you don't let him go?

For a while I look up at the stars. *What would you say, Daddy?* I take a deep breath watching the clear moon. Daddy would tell me it's going to be okay. He'd tell me no matter what happens, I'll figure this life thing out.

Dipshit would tell me I'm stupid to even think someone could love the bitch I am. Sobs riddle my system as I beg for tears.

Why won't they come out of my face? I'm miserable. Lost. I want to cry.

"I know I can't change the past. But sometimes, I wish I could." I swallow thick saliva, not sure if I will ever be in a place to tell him all my darkness. I wish I could just heal.

"Hey, emotions are high right now. You need time to clear your head. And you likely need a lot of rest. I bet you haven't slept at all yet, have you?"

"Not hardly." I rub my eyes.

"Look, like I was saying, I'm not going to force you to stay with me but

I'm not going to go storming off when you need me either." He waits for a bit while I navigate his words. I feel the fog lifting. His eyes perk up like he's having an epiphany. "You know what you need right now?"

"Hm?"

"Twizzlers." He gives me a big old smile, and I burst out laughing. How does he do this? How? One minute I'm sinking into dark despair and the next I'm laughing up a storm.

"Come on, little miss." He clicks his tongue, offering me a hand after he steps up. "Let me take care of you."

My body relaxes for the first time since arriving at Lexie's. He's easing my soul. I'm torn between logic and what I've come to accept as his love.

I want to run. But part of me knows that's not really what I want. It's the impulse. Maybe he's right. Emotions are too high.

I sigh heavily, trying to shake off some of this tension going wild in my body.

"This is what I need." I nod. Something to chew. A way to release this energy.

"I know it is."

I get close to him, letting him know I'm okay with being touched. God, he is so understanding of all I'm still working through.

My hand finds the hip pocket of his flannel jammies and he pulls his arm around my shoulder so the sides of our bodies hold close while we walk to his truck. He gets my door and helps me into the seat.

"How do you always know what I need?"

"Because I love you." He winks.

"No, that ain't it. Tons of people love each other and never have any clue what the other person needs."

"Eh, maybe I'm just observant then?" He shrugs, turning his key and pulling onto the street.

I take a moment to regulate my emotions, realizing I wasn't being fair to him. "I'm sorry, Zac."

"Sorry for...?" He sets his hand on the gear shift. It's sitting there if I want to hold it, but he's not pushing me.

"You're right. Bobby and Lexie's breakup isn't about us. I think it's my past trauma talking." I grind my teeth hard together. "And I'm sorry for taking this out on you in the middle of the night." I watch his face and see a tiny bit of hurt that's there. "I know it isn't okay for me to treat you like this."

"Thanks for apologizing." He raises the corner of his mouth and I see the exhaustion I've caused.

We sit in the quiet for several minutes.

Zac looks at me when he's stopped at the redlight. "Have you thought about talking to someone? I mean, a professional? About the trauma?"

"I probably should." I sigh, slowly bringing my hand to hold his. The connection feels right. It's oftly hard to interpret signs when my meter is so off. Time to give some more attention to my needs.

"I know it's hard." He squeezes my fingers. "And I'm here." His lips turn up in a sympathetic smile.

"Thank you." I lean over and rest my head on his shoulder, a big yawn coming out of my lips.

We get to the nearest store but he keeps driving. "Oh, I think they'll have some here."

"Nope, we're going to 7-Eleven." He winks.

"Baby doll?" I look at him a long while. "You don't need to drive me across town."

"It's your favorite and your comfort. You need your comfort. We can get slurpees or ice cream or whatever. Lexie'll be okay for a while, right?"

"Yeah, she's sleeping."

"Then what're you in a hurry for?"

"You need to sleep. You've got class tomorrow. And practice. A game in two days–"

"And I've got you in my front seat. All we have is right now." He turns his lips in a sweet expression and I want to capture this moment forever. I pull out my phone and snap a picture, the shadows framing his features with only the lights coming off the streetlamps and the sliver of moon.

"Here, be sure to get my good side." He angles his jaw just so, and I take a dozen more pictures of the two of us. Even after I tried to screw things up, he's somehow still here for me.

How did I go from being certain I couldn't be with him to being certain I can't be without him? I'm going to give myself whiplash. Yet, somehow, he's not even phased.

He loves me anyway. Like the mirror, he sees the bigger picture.

Your worth has never been dependent upon your scars.

Zac

Good thing I have therapy this week. When Trish wanted to breakup two nights ago, I almost lost it. Need to clear my head before the baseball game tonight.

To make matters worse, Sadie hasn't replied to any text I've sent her in the last week. I thought by the time we left our Christmas vacation, she and I were doing good. But now I'm confused. I'm even more concerned.

Sometimes silence means it's too hard to talk.

Pulling into my spot outside Doc Roger's office, I notice Bobby's truck. Huh. Haven't seen that before. I head toward the clinic doors.

"Oh, hey." I see Bobby come out of the doors.

"Hey, man." He gives me a knuckle bump. Looks like hell warmed over.

"Sup?"

Bobby looks at the ground for a long minute. "Didn't know I'd run into anyone I knew here. I mean, I guess it makes sense since he's the team psychologist." He sounds upset…or maybe embarrassed?

"No shame in therapy…" I say, hoping to diffuse some of whatever he's feeling.

"Tell that to my inner critic." He chuckles, grabbing the back of his neck with both hands.

"Were you seeing Doc Rogers? That's who I see."

"Yep. You do too, huh?" He sounds so insecure, it surprises me. Weird coming from him. "How are things with Trish?" He sounds eager to change the subject.

"Honestly? We almost broke up." I feel that pain in my chest and rub my sternum.

"Yeesh." He sighs. "Sounds like hell."

"I think we got through it." I try to smile. "I mean, she's great. Amazing. I love her."

"You love her?"

"I think so." I swallow hard. "At the same time, she just scared the shit outta me."

"Trish is pretty unexpected." He laughs. "I'm glad y'all are mostly happy. Good for you." There's a sadness in his tone, and then I realize I probably shouldn't be bringing up a relationship when he just got out of one.

"You and Lexie just taking a break, or?" I fumble with my pockets.

"Dunno," he shrugs. "Did Trish talk to you about that at all?"

"She says Lex was pretty upset."

"Yeah, but did she tell you why?"

"Not really." I don't want to lie to Bobby and I also don't want to make him feel worse. "Trish didn't go into many details. I guess something about secrets? Didn't say what."

Visible relief washes over his face, and I wonder what that was about.

"And just so you know, I'm still rooting for you guys if that's what you both want."

"Thanks."

"I gotta get to my appointment. See you at the field."

"Yep." He nods. "And um, maybe don't mention you saw me here? Trying to keep it on the down low." He tugs the bill of his Yankees cap so it's hiding his eyes.

"Yeah, of course."

"Thanks, man." He pats my shoulder. "Appreciate it."

Therapy went well. I was able to sort through some things. Doc Rogers encouraged me to keep reaching out to Sadie like I normally would. I've kept replaying Christmas break in my head a hundred times. She was distant and wanting to spend all her time with Angela. The day we went ice fishing was tense for a second but she hugged me so tight I know she's not mad about that. There's nothing I can think of to explain her silence, unless she is spending so much time with Angela she doesn't have any left.

Doc Rogers also helped me process some of why Trish trying to break up with me rattled me so hard. I didn't show that side of me to Trish, because I needed to support her. But Doc Rogers did a good job of reminding me my needs matter and we need to make sure to balance that in our relationship. Trish has trouble letting me love her and I have trouble giving all of myself to her until there's nothing left of me for...well...me.

After winning our three home games, it's on the road again.

I'm excited for the game tonight. We're in Wolf Country. Our rivals. Most important game until the playoffs.

Their fans line every chair, so much navy blue, their team color.

In our corner of the stands, there are a handful of our devoted fans who come with us to away games. Most of them are parents or siblings of the players.

Wish my family coulda come.

Even if I offered to fly them to a game, they couldn't come. They're always too busy.

I see Trish on the front row. So glad *she's* here for me.

Bottom of the ninth.

Bases loaded.

Two to one, in our favor. If the Wolves get another run, we're gonna go into overtime. It's already late. Long game. I'm fucking exhausted.

Bottom of the ninth.

Bases loaded.

If I can catch this ball and throw it home…

I'm on high alert. Too much at stake. Coach Conners is pacing near the dugout, biting his finger nail, cussing at Coach Blakeslee. Coach Densen is staring at his clipboard.

Bottom of the ninth.

Bases loaded.

No room for error.

Dexter winds up and throws. Fast ball.

"Strike one!"

Nervous energy pulses through me leaving me hungry for the finish. We can strike them out. I know we can. It's not even about can. We *have* to. Everything about this game will determine our standings. Our ranks. Everything. All of it.

The fucking Major League Draft.

Man alive, I am on edge.

Father in Heaven, help me play my best. I force hot air in and out of my lungs. Sweat drips from my brow, onto my arm. I swipe my sleeve against my face. Adjust my hat. Eyes on the ball. Always on the ball. Just like Pa taught me. Just like everyone who plays knows better than they know their own language.

Dexter winds up and throws.

It's a hit.

Player comes for me. I'm reaching for the ball. Come on, Bobby. He throws it to me. My glove is out to catch it.

The hitter runs straight at me. I try to move out of the way enough to avoid his hit, but my cleat is planted good. It's like I'm watching it happen from outside of my body and I can't do anything to stop it. The hitter slams into my shin, torquing my knee. I hear a snap.

I wince, trying to stay up, but he falls on top of me. We both go down. Pain erupts through my leg. Vision goes white for a second while I endure the most heinous pain. I look down, surprised my leg isn't laying on the ground in two separate pieces. My tendons are firehot rubber bands, pulled tight enough to make my entire body rigid and afraid to move.

"You alright, man?" The hitter asks.

I'm gripping my knee for dear life. Fuck, it hurts. My heart rate skyrockets as I see every dream I have fade into the horizon like the setting sun.

No, Zac, it's not that bad. Wait for the doctor to tell you. Maybe it's just a sprain.

The pain hits harder and my eyes start watering. I don't need a doctor to tell me it's bad. This is gonna ruin the season. Maybe I'll never play again.

This isn't happening.

The hitter dusts off his pants and holds his hand out for me. When I try to stand, my knee gives out. Fire needles surge through my entire leg like lightning bolts made of molten steel.

Oh fuck.

"Ho, easy there," the hitter steadies me.

This is it. My career ending injury. I can feel it.

Bottom of the ninth.

Bases loaded.

I'm out.

Zac

Mindy kneels in front of me in the dugout.

Coach Conners looks me over then turns to the other players and gestures to the field. "Chase, go in for him."

I squint my eyes tight, everything Mindy's doing is sending shooting pain through my leg. She does a physical examination, gingerly trying to see what's wrong without hurting me worse.

"Fuck, I feel like I'm gonna pass out." I wince through my teeth.

Mindy looks to the side where someone from the wolves team is standing. "We're gonna need an MRI."

"Yep. Daxton Sports Medicine Clinic is the closest." The Wolves' Athletic Trainer says.

"I'm thinking you tore your MCL, Zac." She takes an ice bag from Lexie and wraps my knee tight. "Prop it up." She brings over one of the ball crates and turns it so I can lean my leg up.

"What does that mean?" I'm sitting up on my elbows, practically shouting.

Mindy's holding up a phone describing a bunch of medical stuff to whoever's on the line. She turns the mic away from her face and whispers to me, "We'll get an MRI, and maybe an X-ray to see how bad it is."

MRI? X-ray?

No. This isn't happening. This can't be happening. Things were going really good. Why now?

Anger runs through my veins. If my cleat wouldn't have been planted. If the hitter hadn't run into me. If I coulda moved out of the way.

I don't even feel the pain through my anger, boiling through me like some weird sort of adrenaline rush.

"Here, Zac." Jae hands me a water bottle and some pain pills. They burn going down because my throat is so tight with worry.

"Let's get you to the clinic." Mindy goes to talk about details with the other athletic trainer.

I'm alone on the bench. Not really, people are everywhere. But I feel alone. Alone in the darkness that is me throwing away my season. Players are never the same after injuries like this. At least not for a long time after. And the draft is coming up. I won't be better by then. What if I miss my chance? Years of breaking myself to play better. Years of missing out in high school in order to fit in one more hour of strength training or batting practice. Years proving myself on the field. It's all gone. This injury? It's throwing away my career.

I swallow down emotion that has me on the verge of fucking tears. This is it. The moment. The one that I don't get to turn back from. I can't handle this. My body is shaking.

"Can I see him?" Trish's voice comes through the fence like the sound of an angel. Lexie opens up the fence and lets her through.

"Oh my god, Zac." She kneels beside me, holding my hands. Everyone is watching the game. I should be watching the game. But all I see is her.

"Baby." She brings her lips to mine, making a hot tear fall out of my face. "It's gonna be okay. I promise." And her consoling words are all I feel. For a moment, I'm transported away from the screaming pain, from the screaming demons in my mind. It's me and her. That's all there is.

And somehow, it's all I need it to be.

Trish

After hours of waiting at the clinic and them telling us he's got a bad MCL tear, getting him bundled up and on crutches, we're finally back in the hotel where the rest of the team is staying. The team offered to help, but I put him in my room so I could take care of him. His knee looks like a huge bruised cantaloupe. Swelling and discoloration makes the skin hot and tight.

I got us in the room and helped him with a sponge bath since he can't get the wraps wet and he's not supposed to put weight on his leg.

He pulls his shirt over his head while I carefully ease the shorts up his knee, propped on enough pillows to make a pregnant mother in her last trimester jealous. I know because I've done so many pregnancy shoots and those mamas always want as many pillows as they can get.

A groan comes out of his clenched teeth.

"So sorry, baby doll." I try to be even more careful, but man is it hard to get him dressed without moving his knee. Both exhausted, we try to get comfortable enough to relax.

I hold him in the hotel bed. He's so worried about losing his baseball career. It's been a bunch of scattered thoughts coming out of his mouth ever since I found him in the dugout. Now he's either too tired or too loopy from the meds they gave him to talk about it more.

Or maybe he's just so devastated there's nothing left to say.

My head rests against his heart, my legs far away from his to keep from bumping his injured knee. There's a heaviness weighing on both of us. From today on, everything is different. This is one of those life altering moments.

I want to give him some hope. To help comfort him while he's going through so much. But I don't know how. It's like I can't find any more of myself to give.

I'm here, with him. Holding his broken heart as it rests beneath my cheek like something that needs to be put back together. But it won't be able to heal today. It's gonna need rehabilitation, just like his knee. In fact, for whatever reason, hearts seem to break worse than tendons and ligaments.

"Can I get you anything?" I whisper against his skin.

"I can't even think." He closes his eyes. "And at the same time, a million thoughts run through my mind like a broken record."

"I can ask Mindy if we can do anything–"

"No." He tenses his fist. "Trish, nothing I could take will fix this."

His words break my heart to match his. "I'm sorry, now's not the time to try and fix it."

"Nothing's gonna fix it." His voice is raised. "It's not gonna fucking fix."

I open my mouth to say something, but no words come. So instead, I hold him, hoping that is enough. If we can't fix it, we can sit with the broken.

Several moments pass as we lay in the excruciating silence of the hotel room. I feel close to him, despite how hard this is.

"I wish I could take the pain away." I lift up carefully and place a kiss on his chest, lingering on the skin made hot from my cheek.

"It wasn't supposed to go like this." His throat sounds strained.

A million things dance through my brain, maybe I'm absorbing all those scattered thoughts he's always talking about. Somehow I doubt he could let them go, even if I did telepathically remove them from his brain to mine. If only.

The helplessness makes me antsy. I remember how helpless I felt when Cody died. As much as I wanted to, I couldn't help Lexie. Her world ended that day. Zac feels like his world just ended, too.

I'm a doer. I find solutions. When there isn't one I work hard enough that one appears. But right now, I'm useless. No amount of hard work will reverse the clock and stop this from happening.

His arm goes around my shoulders tighter. "I'm never gonna play again."

"Don't say that."

"But I know the truth. I'm not a child. I've watched this happen to other players. It won't be the same."

"Does it have to be the same?" My question hangs in the air like a Polaroid Picture waiting to develop. What will it look like when the picture settles in? Will we love the people in the picture any less if they were blinking when the camera clicked? No. Even with something not quite right about it, it remains perfect in its imperfection.

"I wanted it to be the same."

If I could sink lower, his words just made me. There has to be a silver lining somewhere and I'm more than ever determined to help him find it.

The team won after all that, but it's hard to celebrate right now.

"Has Mindy texted me yet?" he's sounding really groggy with all the meds they've got him on.

"I'll check." I gently get off the bed and rummage through his bag full of baseball gear.

"Side pocket," he says after I've been fishing for a million and three eternities.

"Holy wow, baby you have ten thousand notifications."

"Say what now?" he perks up. There it is. The silver lining.

"Well of course you do. Look." I pull up the video that's trending. "Looks like Ethan put together a video and tagged you."

I hand him the phone, and he stares in disbelief. "This was only posted an hour ago."

"It's blowing up, baby doll."

"This is insane." He looks at the number of likes. It's cruising up over a hundred thousand. Tons of comments are bubbling over his phone screen. "Feel better, Zac. We love you. Can we send you flowers? Look at all this." He reads them off with disbelief.

"Looks like you're about to be internet famous." I smile. Everything feels a million times better now that I see all the good attention he's getting. "Oh, look at your other videos, they are blowing up too." I click out of the current video and see that his views are way up from their normal. "Zac, this one has a million views." My heart pounds in my chest. It's the cover he did of "Sometimes" by Britney Spears.

"You're kidding." His cheeks flush and he starts breathing real fast.

"It's happening. Baby doll, you wanted this. You wanted your personal account to get famous so you could make a little extra money. Today is your day." I bring my lips to his, sealing a huge kiss that lingers for several heartbeats.

"They always say, it's the darkest before the dawn." I look at his knee. "We do need to get you some fresh ice though."

I call up Mindy.

"Hey Mindy, it's Zac's girlfriend. Can you come show me how to wrap his knee? We're in room 322." I stuff his clothes back in his bag and get him a fresh bottle of water.

"Yep, I'll be right there." Mindy hangs up.

My phone buzzes in my pocket.

Lexie: You guys want me to bring some dinner?

Me: Please.

A knock sounds at the door. I open it to Mindy with a bucket of ice and an arm full of Ace wraps.

"Mindy, look." Zac shows her his phone. "A million views. Ethan's gone and made me famous over this injury." He looks like a proud little boy, the way his eyes light up.

"A million? Damn. You sure you counted those zeroes right?" Mindy smiles.

"I guess it's one good thing about all this." I shake my head.

"Guess it is! So I talked to Dr. Brown and he's got the MRI and X-rays. When we get back to Suncastle, he'll do an evaluation but at the moment he's leaning toward not doing surgery." Mindy sets the bucket of ice on Zac's nightstand.

"That's a relief." Zac props up on his elbows. It's like the life has returned to his face. His color is better.

Mindy sucks air out of a plastic bag, making it tight against the ice inside. "The swelling looks worse than it did earlier." She pushes against his knee. "I want you to stay off it as much as you can. No weight at all."

Zac nods.

"You can stay here during the games tomorrow, and then I'll make sure they plan on an extra seat on the ride back home so you can prop your foot up." She looks at him.

"No, I can't miss the games." He clears his throat, and just like that the moment is all heavy again. I try to grasp that bit of peace he just had. But I can't. This *is* heavy, even with the amazing outcome on his internet following. I just wish I could do more to help him. A lump fills my throat thinking about how I raced from the stands to the dugout and how it was so hard to convince security to let me past the gate.

"You're not going to sit on a bench for hours in the heat with a brand new MCL tear. Besides, if you're getting a million views we probably need to keep you out of the public eye until you're off the crutches. I don't want a huge fan club rushing you outside the field. I'll talk to the athletic department about what we can do to keep you safe once we are back in Suncastle." Mindy's attitude makes it clear this isn't up for negotiation. "It'll be hard enough to get you back home without aggravating that knee. Someone with googly eyes can bump into you and set you weeks back in recovery." She packs the ice against his knee. Zac winces while she positions it right over the swollen areas. "It's Trish, right?" She motions for me to come over.

"Yeah, it's Trish." I hurry to her side.

"Now we want the swelling to move up toward his core, so we are gonna start the wrap on his shin, okay?" She winds the Ace wrap over his iced knee.

"Makes sense." I watch closely, memorizing her motions so that I'll be able to help out.

"Here, try on this knee." She hands me an Ace wrap and gestures to his not injured leg. I start wrapping just like she showed me.

"Yeah, that looks great." She smiles. "We're gonna keep ice and compression on it for the first three days. Will you be able to stay at his place and help him?"

"Yeah, of course." I notice Zac shiver and run to get him an extra blanket from the closet. He smiles while I tuck it over his arms to keep him from getting too cold. "And he can have more pain meds–"

Mindy grabs the prescription meds off the table. "This one is every four hours." She looks at her watch. "He can have it again at seven. If he can't sleep, give him this one." She hands me the bottle.

"They won't mix with my anxiety meds?" He's tapping his finger and thumb frantically.

"No, you can take them all together." Mindy gives him a sympathetic smile.

"Thanks, Mindy." Zac relaxes into the pillows like he's got the life sucked out of him. It's hard to see him so miserable and fighting anxiety on top of it. I'm sure we'll get through it, but I have a feeling it's gonna be a really long few weeks.

"If you need anythin', call me." Mindy talks more to me than to Zac, who may just drift off into sleep. "I'll check in again later tonight, around eleven."

"I'll make sure he stays off it." I walk her to the door. I'm not halfway back to Zac before someone's knocking.

A bunch of players stand outside the door.

"Can we come in?" Briar asks.

"Yeah, of course." I open the door wide and several guys huddle around the bed. They're talking and laughing.

There's another knock on the door. It's the coaches. Everybody crams in the room, checking up on him. I snap some pictures. This is too precious of a moment not to capture.

"Well get some rest." Coach Conners puts his hand on Zac's shoulder. "Everybody, let's let him get feeling better."

The coaches and players take turns saying goodbye and offering well wishes. I've just shut the hotel room door when there's more knocking.

I open it up to Lexie. "Oh, hey."

"Here ya go." Lexie hands me a bag from Panda Express.

"Thanks, girl. You wanna come in?" I open the door wider so she can see Zac propped up in bed. I'm going crazy without something in my mouth. Where's my gum? Oh, yeah...I finished my last piece. I search for a fortune cookie and put it in my pocket before setting down the food.

"Jesus." Lexie shakes her head, heading over to Zac. "It's terrible you got hurt like this."

"I know." Zac closes his eyes and then stares at the ceiling like all his prayers haven't been answered and never will be.

"This ain't medical advice, I'd get in trouble for that." Lexie steps closer. "Depending on how the sports med team looks through the MRI and X-rays, it may just be intense rehab."

"I sure hope I don't have to go the surgery route." He stares at his knee and gives his head the smallest of shakes. Pain fills his eyes that has nothing to do with the injury. The high from his million video views has worn off all at once and reality is landing again. That fleeting happiness was just a bandage, like the Ace wrap on his leg. We gotta heal what's underneath first, or it won't do any good.

Lexie brings me in for a big hug. "You doin' alright?" She whispers.

"Yeah," I run my tongue along my teeth, hating the lie but knowing Zac's got way too much on him to hear me say I'm barely hanging on.

Why don't I have emergency gum? I clench my teeth. Dammit. Been frantically chewing piece after piece all afternoon. I shoulda asked Lexie to bring me a pack.

"I'll be right back, baby." I kiss Zac's forehead, then lead Lexie out to the hallway for a much needed chat. "He's devastated." I swallow hard. Pulling the fortune cookie out of my pocket, I pop open the wrapper and chomp on half of it, relishing the feel of my jaw moving up and down.

"It's devastating." Lexie's tone holds compassion. I read the fortune cookie *Someone you love is about to change.*

A little late for that, fortune cookie.

I'm too exhausted to figure out what this sign means.

"I don't know what to do. Don't know anythin' about what he needs or how to support him through this. I'm worried about canceling all my photo shoots, and then I feel sick that I'm being selfish right now. I mean fuck, Lex. People lose their shot at the big leagues over smaller injuries. Knees don't tend to get all the way better."

"Stop." She gives me a firm smile and fusses with her purse until she finds a pack of Ice Breakers.

"Oh my god. You're my hero!" I swallow the fortune cookie and pop the gum in my mouth.

"I'll grab you some Juicy Fruit if they have it at the giftshop."

"Thanks, boo." I lean my head against her shoulder.

"You're stressing too much. Stress isn't gonna help him. He's already got tons he's dealing with. You're both in shock. Just let it be for a minute, and go into problem solving mode later on."

Her words sink in, and I appreciate that I have a friend who will tell me what she thinks, even if it's a shit ton of advice dropped in my lap. "You always know what I need to hear."

"'Course I do."

"God knows I need some support." I straighten my back. "My *boyfriend* just fucked up his body on the field. He's only supposed to do that tangled in the sheets with me."

Lexie grins. But then her face falls.

"I'm sorry...I know you're going through hardcore Bobby withdrawl." I scrunch my lips together. "I shouldn't be bringing up stuff like that." I look at the wall for a minute. "How you feelin' about all that with Bobby?"

"It's hell." She lets out a depressing breath. "I didn't even get a day to process our breakup before I had to be with the team for practice." She sits on the carpet and hugs her knees to her chest.

"Ain't right." I join her on the floor.

"I try to act normal. But everyone's noticing." She shakes her head. "You didn't tell Zac about," she drops her voice lower, "about why we broke up."

I let out a scoff. "No, I didn't think tellin' Bobby's secret to his teammate was a good idea."

"You're right." She brings her hands in front of her face. "Bobby doesn't know I told you." Several moments pass. Wish we weren't so fucking sad.

"Pretty sure he still wants to be with you. Do you think you'll give Bobby another shot?"

"I wish I knew." Lexie looks at me. "Stop making this about me. It's about Zac right now."

"Yeah, I wish I could take his pain away. Or turn back the clock. Somethin' to change what happened."

"I'm sure he's just glad you're here." She gives me that look that I've given her many times, that says *you're overthinking all this.* "If it's just a tear, he can make a full recovery. You gotta have hope that he'll get back to where he was before."

"That's what I'm worried about." We sit on the carpet in the hallway. "I wasn't planning on a relationship in the first place." I stare at the horrible lights overhead. "Now I'm here, and he's hurt. I promised the athletic trainer that I'd stay with him the next few days. Wish I could take his pain away."

Lexie leans her head on my shoulder. "I know, boo." We both let out a long sigh, in sync. She chuckles and I laugh with her. It's cleansing to let out this tension.

"Hopefully it seems worse than it is. He's in good hands." Lexie gives my arm a squeeze.

"Of course, he is. You're gonna be there in the training room while he's doing the physical therapy stuff won't ya?" I remember her talking about helping the athletes rehab an injury.

"I won't let him suffer any longer than he has to." She wraps her arm around me in a half hug.

I hear someone coming down the hall and glance up to find Bobby heading our way. He's carrying a bag of takeout from some burger place.

"Thought you may need some food." He holds up the bag. I chuckle because they're two peas in a pod. Don't know that I woulda thought to bring dinner. Here they both are trying to take care of us while Zac is laid up. It's cute.

Lexie sits up straighter and follows his body with her eyes. He stops in front of the hotel room and looks silently at Lexie for a long moment. Their eyes are intense. Bobby grabs the back of his neck, like he's still not sure what to do.

I fish the key out of my pocket.

"Here, you'll need this." I reach across Lexie to hand it to him. She jumps back, like she can't risk Bobby's hand brushing against her.

"Thanks." Bobby spins the room key between his finger and thumb, a frown on his face. Lexie looks like a little girl staring at a puppy in a window. Wants what she absolutely cannot have–even though *she* technically broke things off with him.

"You played good out there today." I stand up, pulling Lexie beside me before she melts into the floor like a puddle.

"Yeah, you did." She croaks like her throat is giving out.

I feel a funny need to help them patch things up. "Have y'all talked much since the other night?"

"No." They say in unison.

"No, it's–"

"Yeah, it's–" They both stammer like neither of them have a reason not to hash it out.

"I thought you and Zac probably needed dinner." Bobby hands me the food, leans against the hallway wall, and stuffs his hands in his pocket.

"I already brought them takeout." Lexie pulls me in for a quick hug. "I'm gonna run."

"You don't have to go," Bobby says.

We stand here awkwardly, for what feels like forever, until Bobby opens and closes his mouth a few times. He must be calculating what to say. "There's a party in Tate's room if you wanna–"

"Think I'm gonna get some sleep." Lexie pushes past him, a skip-walk down the hallway like she can't get away gracefully or fast enough. I watch her go, wondering if I need to follow after. Bobby has a look on his face that says he's wondering if he should be doing the same thing.

"Just give her some time." I raise my lip in a half smile, feeling in such a funny spot.

"I fucked up, and I don't think I'll get another chance."

"Lexie is a lot more understanding than I am. You never know." I hold his eyes, hoping that in some small way, I can let him know that I accept him. That no matter his sexuality, he is who he is and I'll never judge him.

A lump forms in my throat because this hits too close to home. I really care about Zac's sister. He's been concerned about her. I think most of it boils down to how cruel people have been to her since they found out she's not straight.

Sadie needs acceptance. Bobby needs acceptance. Because we live in a world where many people perpetuate an idea that being straight is the only way to be.

Bobby opens up the hotel room and hands me back the key.

"Had to see how you're doin'." Bobby pulls up a chair next to the bed.

"Feel like shit." Zac sighs.

"Fuck, of course you do. I think I heard that snap all the way from third."

I watch them, glad to see Zac in a little better spirits since his buddies have been here to check in on him. Bobby is a good guy. Seeing Lexie in the hallway made me guess she wants to fix it with him.

"You need more ice or anythin'?" Bobby looks at his super wrapped knee.

"Nah, I'm good for a while." Zac says.

"Of course, he's good. I'm here." I nod, feeling protective.

Zac presses his hands over his face. "I may have to go in for surgery. I'll be out the whole fuckin' season. Or worse—"

"You kiddin'? Quit talkin' like that, man." Bobby rests his hand on Zac's shoulder.

"I don't know what else to say." Zac stares at the ceiling.

"Who was there when my elbow blew out? You. Tellin' me that I'd be right back in to play. Well, now it's my turn to tell you that. This knee hurts like hell today, but you'll be out one season at the most."

"I hope you're right." Zac sounds hopeless.

"I am right." Bobby stands up. "And if you're out, you'll bounce right back, a'right man?" Bobby pats his shoulder. "You look exhausted. I'll get out of your hair. Holler if you need anythin'."

"Thanks for comin'." Zac tries to smile, but it barely turns up one corner of his lips.

I walk Bobby to the hallway. "When you blew your elbow out, what helped?"

"Lots of ice and pain meds. Hopefully they won't have to put him under the knife. If they do, he's gonna need someone for at least the first week. Surgery is no joke. His folks aren't around, and I doubt they could help."

"I know." I swallow hard. I could fly his mom down here, but she couldn't afford to miss much work.

"The real hit comes here." Bobby points to his head. "It's so much mentally. He needs as much support there as he does on his knee. Maybe even more."

"Thanks, Bobby."

He gives me a hug and heads down the hall. I click the hotel room door shut.

"It was nice of them to come by." I grab the bag of takeout and help Zac sit up enough to eat.

"I'm really not hungry." He's barely touched the food.

"Probably all those pain meds. You just wanna rest?"

"Yeah."

I eat a few more bites, then put the food away.

Zac

"What do you mean eight weeks before I can play again?" I grind my teeth, ready to throw something. "I thought that if we didn't do surgery, I'd be back faster. Eight weeks is half the season!"

Everyone in the training room stops what they're doing to watch me cause a scene.

"If you have surgery, you'll be out the whole season." Mindy keeps a level tone. "You can miss six to eight weeks while we do an intense rehab on your knee, or we can get you a hardship waiver and you'll get another season of play. Up to you."

"We could operate, but you're just below the degree of tearing that would absolutely indicate surgery. This is a gray area. We've seen tears like this bounce back. But we've also seen complications down the road if the athlete doesn't get it surgically repaired. You can take some time to think about it." Doc says. "If anyone can get you rehabbed back to play sooner rather than later, it's Mindy."

"Thank you." Mindy says.

"But if I have the surgery, will my knee be better? Am I gonna deal with long term stuff if I opt out?" I stare at the triple Ace wrap keeping tight compression on my knee. Anxiety runs through my head. What if it's worse than it looks? What if one day I can't play or even walk anymore?

Anxiety, get back under control. They'll figure something out.

"With the results from the X-ray and MRI, I believe you can make a full recovery without surgery." Doc Brown holds his notes. "We were concerned about an avulsion of the femoral attachment, but thankfully that doesn't seem to be the case. There's no fracture present. Just the tear."

"So if we go no surgery, we'll rehab it and I'll still play the end of the season?" I make sure I've got it straight. It's Briar and Bobby's last year at Suncastle. I still wanna play with them.

"If you're healed and back to full strength." Mindy makes sure I understand this caveat.

"Okay, yeah."

"Sleep on it, and we can talk about it when you come into the office tomorrow." Doc Brown pats my non-injured knee before he heads for the door.

"Eight weeks is so long, Mindy." I lean on the exam table, eyeing the tile ceiling. "If you were me, would you have the surgery?" I turn my head to look while she sets up the electric muscle therapy unit on my knee. "Honestly?"

"I can't tell you what to do. But I think it's likely we can get you better without the surgery."

I hate having to stay off my knee. More than that, I hate relying on others. Trish came home with me and stayed the first few days, but she had to go back to Willardson. Ethan is driving me to and from campus and recording tons of content for Sprinkle. Mindy's making sure I get lots of ice and showing me some really gentle exercises.

Some days I don't even show up to class because I'm so fucking swollen and in a shit ton of pain, even with the meds. My professors have been good about letting me keep up without being in class.

Sprinkle is the silver lining. My videos are blowing up. Paid ads are allowing me to have enough extra money to put into savings and investments. It's been the boost of visibility I needed to reach my financial goals.

Sadie is still radio silence. I never knew we could go this long without talking. I send her a text every few days. With my injury, I hoped she'd reach out. Something is so off and I don't know what to do. The extra stress isn't helping my recovery.

I show up every day to the training room, and ask for Mindy's help to make sure we're on track.

"I'm worried about losing my stamina. It's like I get outta breath just going around on these." I eye the crutches.

"You need to let the tissues heal." Mindy sips some coffee. "We're doing the exercises you're ready for at this point."

"What else can I do?" There's a fire in me wanting to explode because I won't passively lay here while all my buddies are in season. I can't handle how much I've already missed. Chase is thrilled he's getting a lot of game time while I'm out, I can tell. But I need to get back.

"Make sure you're resting. Once we get the swelling down, we can get you into some more strengthening exercises.

"Thank's Mindy."

"You'll get there." She smiles as I crutch out the door.

It takes so much goddamn energy to use my crutches. I used to workout with the team and run five miles every morning. Now, I'm limited to whatever activity I can do without adding to the swelling. It fucking sucks. My chest is on fire. I've already lost so much ground. It's like my heart can't handle it.

Because you're dying....

Shut the fuck up, Anxiety.

I have no power over my spiraling thoughts. Panic takes hold, and I sit on the couch trying to calm the fuck down. This is worry. It's fear of all I'm losing.

My phone rings. I scoot over to it, careful to stay off my knee. It's Trish.

"Hey, baby." I try to sound normal, but it is so fucking hard to do.

"You doing alright?" She asks.

"Not really."

"I'm heading up tonight."

"No, you've got your photo shoots." I clear my throat, opening up my water bottle.

"I rescheduled. It'll be okay. I want to take care of you." There's a desperation in her tone that meshes with mine.

I want to argue more, but I need her. "Okay."

Just like that, she's calmed my racing heart.

"See you soon." She clicks the phone off, and I sit here dumbfounded. I go from being in the middle of a fucking panic attack to feeling at peace.

How does she do that?

How does she calm the storm I've fought for years?

My phone rings, again. It's Bobby.

"Can I come over?"

"Yeah, um, Trish is gonna be here soon."

"I'll be quick."

Not five minutes later, he shows up. I hobble over to the couch while he sets two boxes on my coffee table.

"What's this?"

"The first couple weeks are the hardest." Bobby rummages through the box and hands me some t-shirts that say *Suncastle Mama's want Zac to feel better.*

"You didn't have to do this." I chuckle.

"Ya know, I did. Ethan wanted it to say Suncastle MILFS, but Coach vetoed that one."

"That's too funny." I chuckle.

"Ethan's setting up an online store to sell these." He opens the second box. It's got a bunch of goodies in it. New reusable ice packs. Ace wraps. There's a card everyone on the team signed. "Briar baked these. He remembered you like chocolate." He hands me a tupperware container full of cookies. "I can't promise they're edible. But, Briar can normally cook so hopefully they're okay. And you can't live on sugar so here's this." He hands me a big container of healthy snacks. Fruit leather, trail mix, protein bars.

"Oh my gosh. You *really* didn't need to do all this." I swallow hard, feeling how much they care.

"Most people don't get what it's like to be at the top and get thrown to the bottom. I just want you to know you're not alone in all this. We're here for you, and you'll get back." Bobby stands. "I know Trish is comin', so I'll get."

"Thanks, man." I smile. "Hey, do you talk to Lexie anymore?" Rumors have been all over the training room. Carter keeps saying he's gonna ask her out. Briar threatened hell and a half so that hasn't happened.

"Nah, I fucked that up." Bobby shakes his head.

"Maybe she'll come around." I give him a sad smile.

"It's been several weeks since we broke up. I wouldn't blame her if she never talked to me again." Bobby sighs and shakes his head like he'd rather not think about it. "Feel better, okay?" Bobby heads out, and I see my angel standing behind him in the doorway. They say hey to each other for a sec and then she comes in, carrying a milkshake. A teasing smile is on her lips. She shimmies over to me and carefully comes on my lap.

"Look what Bobby and the team did." I show her the stuff on the table.

"That's super thoughtful of them." She smiles, setting the milkshake down. "I brought you some stuff too." She sets her bag on the table and pulls out a bunch of comfy clothes for me including new flannel pajamas. "Figured you need some easy stuff to wear."

"Thanks, little miss." I hold her close. "How was your week?"

"I got everything done back in Willardson, so I'll stay here for a couple weeks."

"You're kidding," I gasp. "It's gonna be awesome having you here. You sure you can be away that long?"

"I did a lot of the photo shoots. There's tons for me to edit still, and I can do that here, while you're in class. I know you need someone." She kisses me tenderly. "And I want you to have everything you need."

"Thank you."

"Missed you." She straddles me on the couch, soothing me into a life bringing kiss.

"Needed this." I bring her hips closer. Her mouth frames mine, rubbing, sucking. She pops her lips, tingles exploding through me. I'm instantly hard for her, the longing of our days apart filling this moment.

She rocks her body into me. I'm gasping for air as I weave my fingers through her curls. Her tongue glides against the roof of my mouth, tingling, playing. Pulling back, she shows me the most teasing face.

"In a few minutes, I'm gonna make us some dinner. But first..." She reaches behind her and grabs a chocolate milkshake off the table. "I wanna give you lots of dessert." She bites her lip. It gets me hot so fast.

For the next several minutes, we feed each other the milkshake. Each bite slides off the spoon onto my tongue. She kisses me between spoonfuls. I put the cherry stem in my mouth and she bites off the cherry. Each bite is scrumptious.

"Now, for an extra special treat." She slips her hand under my workout shorts, warm fingers in the most arousing touch. Precum drips onto her fingers as she works me with her magic.

Taking her time, she stimulates every part of me. Her fist holds my cock, fucking the shit out of it. Waves of pleasure rip through my system. My pain melts away. Her touch heals me.

"Fuck, Trish, I'm gonna come." I slip my shorts down.

"Of course you are," her hand pumps while she repositions to kneel on the floor.

"Mmmmm," I moan as her mouth descends upon my cock. She rocks back and forth, her hands and lips exciting every part of me. Drawing back, she gives me a sexy smile.

"Come in my mouth." She whispers against my tip. "Let me taste you."

"Oh, fuck. Ohhhh, fuck." My head falls back, my peak approaching fast.

"Don't hold back, baby. Gimme that cum." She winks, catching my eyes with hers for the most exotic heartbeats. "It's all mine, and you're gonna give me what I came for."

My abs go tight. Shutting my eyes, I see white. All at once, I burst. Hot spurts of my release shoot into her mouth, body trembling in pleasure. I reach for a tissue from my side table and hand it to her. She cleans up and slides out of her leggings to give us that incredible skin-to-skin sensation. My body hums against hers, as she presses her skin into mine. I wrap my arms around her and hold, embracing eternity here and now.

She is my forever.

The next couple weeks go quickly. Trish is being so kind. I can't believe she rescheduled all her photo shoots to be in Suncastle. It's been a sweet time for us. She helps me with my Sprinkle content and I do my best to rest and recover and keep up with school.

It's the day I've been dreading: the day we have to say goodbye.

"I really appreciate you being here for me." I hold Trish on the couch. Her suitcases are by the door.

"You're doing so well with rehab and everything. Lexie told me you're twice as dedicated as most of the athletes."

"I wanna get back to where I was before the injury."

"You will." She kisses me slowly. "I'm gonna do my in-person photo shoots and then plan on being back here as much as I can."

"You need to go see Nana, too."

"I know, she misses me. Will you plan on coming to her big eightieth birthday party with me?" This is the first time Trish has mentioned having me at anything for her family.

"Yeah, of course. I'd love that." I squeeze her tight, wanting to remember what it feels like to hold her on the lonely days ahead.

"I'll be back to you as soon as I can." She kisses my lips.

"Text me when you get home?"

"Always."

March

Zac

Ma: You need to talk to Sadie. She's shutting us out. I'm worried.

I'm sitting in class when the text comes through. I gather up my notebook and pull my backpack over my shoulder, discreetly leaving class early.

I call Ma. The rings go on forever until it gets to her voicemail. I call again.

On autopilot, I head toward the practice fields. I'm barely off crutches and my knee still hurts like fuck.

I dial her number again, and luckily she answers this time.

"Ma, you gotta tell me what's going on." I clear my throat. "Sadie's barely talked to me at all since Christmas." I've been trying to get in touch with her. We've missed our usual video calls. I've been in hell and she's been ignoring me. Now Ma texts me all worried?

"I shouldn't have said anything."

"Ma, I worry every hour of the day. Can you please tell me what's going on?"

"She's not doing so good." The words coming through the line paralyze me. Ma's optimistic. But she's not having any hope now. "She's tired and she's not herself. The bullying keeps happening. I know it's worse than she'll admit."

I hold my shaking fist tight in a ball. "Can't they do anything? Switch her classes. Get her away from those girls? Transfer to virtual school?" Emotion fills my throat. "Can she come stay with me for a few days?"

"We need her to finish high school or it'll jeopardize her scholarship. She just has to get through this."

"Let her transfer. Suncastle High isn't far from my apartment."

"Zac, I appreciate your offer, but it's not what she needs."

"You don't know that." Weak in my knees, I carefully slide down to sit against the wall of the field. My knee screams in pain as I remember I'm far from recovered. Every part of me screams. This is all too much.

The static of our connection burns a hole through my ears. Silence speaks so loud.

"Look, just keep texting her. Okay? If there's anyone she'll talk to, it's you or Angela."

"Do you know about Angela? She's in college?" I work to keep my tone in check. It was one thing when I was an anxious mess of a kid and Pa refused to take me to the doctor for mental health care. But Sadie's being bullied and shunned by people who used to be her best friends. They need to show up for her.

"I've met Angela." Ma says.

"Well, is she helping? Or is she making this worse?"

"Sadie needs support. I think Angela is trying to do that. I don't know why she's shutting us out, but she talks to you the most anyway."

I think about all the days Ma and Pa were working late and it was me and Sadie at home. I'd make us PB&J sandwiches and we'd watch PBS on the antenna TV.

"My break is over. I'll call you later. Love you." Ma clicks off the phone, leaving me here, helpless all these miles away.

"You okay?" Briar stands above me, his voice making me startle backward into the concrete wall, hitting my head.

"Man, you scared the crap outta me." I rub the back of my head where it bonked. "How long you been standing here?"

"Long enough you didn't notice." He offers me a hand up, and I take it, putting all my weight on my good knee.

"Thanks." Wow, I was out of it if he's been standing there a while.

"Grabbing dinner at the caf'. Wanna come? Mama always says that the best way to change a mood is with some good ol' southern mashed potatoes in your tummy." He rubs his belly, then mine.

I'm not that surprised because it's Briar, and he's like that.

Briar looks at his hand on my belly. "And you're in luck, because our lovely little ladies at Suncastle College go all out for Saint Patty's Day and there will be all sorts of potatoes to cheer up your mood. And they don't seem the least bit Irish, so you can bet that it's still gonna just be good ol' southern mashed potatoes."

"Yeah," I slip my backpack over one shoulder. "Bobby's right, ya know."

"About?"

"You're the team's mother hen."

"That's Captain Mother Hen, to you." He chuckles. We go to the caf' and swipe our meal cards on the register.

"You weren't kidding about Saint Patrick's Day." What appears to be leprechaun vomit overtakes every inch of the caf' with green and rainbows. The staff are dressed up in leprechaun costumes too. "Did Pinterest explode in here?"

"More like the mundane turned into the magnificent." Briar stretches out his hand like it's the horizon. "How've you never been here on Saint Patty's Day before?"

"Not sure. But I've never seen this."

We stand in line for the corn beef and sure enough, mashed potatoes. Comfort food. Carbs. Something I can convince myself to eat while I'm stressed out of my mind.

"Long day?" Briar brings my attention back to the conversation he overheard a few minutes ago.

"Just some bad news I'm not sure what to do with." I sit at the table across from him looking over the meal in front of me, realizing even mash potatoes aren't going to sit well tonight.

"You can talk about it if you want." Briar takes a bite of his corned beef.

"My sister's dealing with some real shit back home." I let out a long sigh.

"That sucks. What kind of shit?"

"They're bullying her because she's lesbian."

"What is wrong with people?" Briar's face is angry.

"I don't know. But my folks aren't doing enough. She isn't handling any of this."

"How could she?" Briar asks. "And yeah your folks need to do something. I mean, my brother got beat up. One time I kicked those bullies' butts and ended up planting some cow patties in their lunch." He chuckles.

"Ewwww. Did it work?"

"It did. They mostly left him alone after that. Maybe your sis can find a cow pasture."

"Maybe she can." Pulling up my phone, I text Sadie.

Me: Hey. How you doing?

I watch the phone for a long time, wishing and waiting. But our conversations have been completely one sided for months and I have the text history to prove it.

"Briar!" A couple guys come over and he bumps knuckles with them, starting up a conversation.

I zone out and choke down a few bites, but they feel like rocks on a trampoline, trying to vault back up. Sadie's not okay and my parents aren't doing a damn thing.

Please, Heavenly Father, tell me how I can help.

My phone buzzes and I hold my breath.

Trish: Can't stop thinking about you.

I stare at the words, a smile forming on my heart. While everything else makes the world feel like it's crashing in on me, she's the one holding a roof over my head to shelter me through the storm.

I type out a few different responses, and finally send a simple reply.

"What's her name?" Briar's friends have left, and he's already eaten half his food by the time I look up from my phone.

Has he not seen me with Trish?

"Oh, um, you know Trish, right?" I shove my phone in my pocket.

"Trish. The one with the camera all the time." He gives me a knowing nod. "Wait. Weren't you dating that one girl? The one that had really big hair. She lived with you, didn't she?"

"Valerie?" I take a bite.

"Yeah, that's it. Not dating her anymore? Or hey, maybe both of them? Gettin' some poly action?" He raises his hands in the air. "For the record, I am a no-judgment kinda guy so if you've got a side hustle with several women, or maybe a little modern day harem going on, I wouldn't fault you one little bit."

"Oh, no. Valerie moved out last summer."

"She moved out? You've gotta tell me these things, bro." Briar's gaze shifts from me to someone standing behind us. He focuses for a second and then leaps off his chair and goes over to whoever he was looking at.

"Twenty bucks for your sweater. I gotta have it." He pulls out his wallet and gets the cash. I turn around in my chair to see what made him jump up. It's a hideous green sweater with a huge rainbow on the front.

"Please, twenty bucks." Briar pushes the cash into the guy's hand.

"It's not for sale. Not for twenty."

"Okay, fine, thirty." Briar fishes through his wallet. "Zac, you got ten bucks?"

I chuckle, holding out the cash.

"Um, I don't have anything under this." Sweater Guy says.

"Oh, I don't mind. Here." Briar takes his shirt off and a few people *oooo and awwww.*

"Shirt required in the cafeteria!" One of the lunch ladies shouts.

"Come on, hurry, before we get kicked out. I got corn beef to finish." Briar tells Sweater Guy.

"Okay, fine." Sweater Guy gives Briar the sweater and takes the proffered shirt.

"Happy now?" Briar asks the lunch lady, and she shakes her head as if exchanges like this are all too common for her liking.

"You do this a lot?" I gesture to his sweater.

"Nah, just every few weeks. See, I think of campus cafeteria as a living second hand store. That guy probably didn't care about this sweater nearly as much as I will." He looks down at the rainbow with a pleased smile. "I'll go to the ATM later and give you cash."

"More like refill your wallet. Never know when you're gonna need to ask another guy for the sweater off his back." I chuckle at this random distraction, thankful for a break from all this worry.

I call Trish on my way back to the apartment. "What're you doin' tonight? Can I see you? Please?" I'm begging her, all reasonable acting thrown out the window.

There's a million reasons why I don't have time to meet her, the top of the list being my game tomorrow night. But she's what I need. It's like I won't survive to do all the other stuff if I don't get some time with her first.

"I'm gonna be in Suncastle for the game." If nothing else has melted my entire being, *this* does. She comes to my games as much as she can. Never seems to be an imposition. She makes it a priority to watch me play.

"I can't wait that long." It's desperate coming from my lips. "Please say I can see you?"

"Meet me in between? In Harbrooke?" Trish's voice ignites my need.

"I'm walking home. I'll be there in about an hour and a half. Meet me for drinks at the Marriott on Main?"

"Okay." She clicks off the phone, and I pick up my pace, hopping in the shower, calling up the Marriott for a reservation. I put on my nice button down and the jeans she likes. Brush my teeth. Wear the cologne Trish loves.

I head to Harbrooke. She beats me there, in a red sleeveless dress and a big flower clipping up her dark brown curls.

"You changed your hair." I bring her close for a long hug, the kind you give your best friend or someone you haven't seen in too long a time. "I love it."

I twist a curl around my fingers, bringing my lips to hers. I play with her gum, shoving it to the side of her mouth as I deepen the kiss and take her breath away, standing in the lobby of this fancy hotel.

"You seem heavy." She wrinkles her brow. "What's wrong?"

"It's been a long day."

"Let me take some of that pain away." She winks.

"Believe me, you already have." I kiss her again, this time sweetly, just lips to lips. My hands grip her hips, beautifully filling my palms with her curves.

"I'm glad you asked me to come tonight." She looks lovingly in my eyes.

"I wish I was with you every night." I take her hand as we walk to the bar.

We order and sip for hours while she drowns out all my anxiousness with the sound of her voice. For a long time, I just listen. She spends half an hour telling me about this adorable toddler she had a photo shoot with earlier.

"You were so heavy when you walked in. What's up?" Her question brings me out of the blissful distraction. That tense feeling overtakes my gut again.

"It's Sadie." I clear my throat, forcing another sip of my whisky as my throat tightens with emotion.

"Oh, no. What's going on with her?" Trish leans closer to me, and it's like I can feel her support transfer from her heart to mine. Like I've been floating down a rapid filled river, barely clinging on for dear life, and now that she's here the water is smooth and calm.

"Sadie's shut down mentally. She won't talk to me. She won't talk to them. Bullying is as bad as ever. They keep tryin' different meds for anxiety, depression, PTSD. None of it's helping. I mean I get it. This stuff doesn't just magically get better. I wish it could."

"But what about her volleyball career? How's she gonna keep playin' when she's not coping with everything?"

"I don't know." I swallow a tight ball of muscle down my throat.

"Well, what about your old man? Is he giving her shit for it?"

"I doubt he's giving her shit, but he's not good at being supportive of this kind of thing." I would know. That pain in my gut intensifies, wishing Pa wasn't so stuck in his own ass sometimes.

"That's a lot to deal with." She rubs her knuckles with her finger tips. Our eyes lock and I see in hers this sea of longing. This closeness I've craved filling the space between us.

"I hate being so far away." I ball my fist tighter. "Far away from Sadie when she needs me. I wish I was closer." The cold air of the bar comes in my lungs and I swallow the rest of my whisky to keep me warm. "Closer to you." I hang my head, the weight of the world on my shoulders, despite the relief she gives me.

"Let's get you a break from all this." She stands, pulling me toward the room.

The elevator is ours, and she holds me tight. Her kisses make me dizzy, mixing with the buzz of the alcohol.

She's tender with me. Taking the lead as we get in the bedroom. Our kisses turn faster. Needing to be inside of her, I shed my shoes, these jeans, my shirt. She plays music on her phone. Our playlist.

"It's going to be okay." She whispers against my ear.

I take her body in mine, dancing to the music. She sheds her dress. We dance skin to skin. Every part of our bodies align, her head on my shoulder as we rock back and forth.

She walks us over to the bed and lays me down on the sheets. With her hands, she strokes, getting harder the longer she touches me.

"Let go of all this stress. Give it all to me, baby." She places her mouth on my cock, coaxing the sweetest pleasure with each motion. "Just like that." She licks precum off my tip, flicking her tongue. With her hands and mouth, she brings me to heaven.

I'm lost in her grasp, this incredible connection that makes me sure she's it for me. She's the one that I've wanted. The one that I've craved. The best part of this fucked up life. The part that makes it worth all the heartache.

It's her. My girl. Who can love me hard and wild, but knows when to be tender. She's taking care of me tonight and knows I'll give that same care right back to her. We need *this*. This gentle touch, this sweet embrace.

She finds my eyes, rubbing my cock between her boobs, rocking her body against my legs.

"I love it when you do that."

"I know." She smiles, putting my cock back in her mouth, switching from boobs to lips. I flow through a million levels of pleasure.

"Want me to come in?" I lock my eyes on hers.

"Yeah. Please?"

She slides my hard cock into her slick, beautiful opening, slowly rocking up to a fast pace. Each ridge of her hugs me. Every bit of what I need washes over us. I adjust our hips to drive deeper inside of her. She holds her breath, feeling all the sensations I'm giving her.

"Mmmmm," she purrs. We relish the motions until we're both so needy we're gonna pop. I speed up, grabbing her hips and thrusting against her hard until she screams in ecstasy.

Her body falls against mine, and we tremble in synchronized aftershocks.

"How do you do that?" she whispers against my chest. "How do you make me feel so much?"

"Because I love you."

"I'm so glad you love me."

"I'm so glad you let me." I rub the small of her back, the tender skin between each vertebrae.

She sounds thoughtful, heading toward the bathroom. I put my legs over the edge and rest my elbows into my knees, catching my breath.

After a minute, she's back in her jammies. She brings over a washcloth, leaving the hall light on.

"Oh, thanks." I get cleaned up.

"It's my turn to take care of you. I want us to get some sleep." She yawns.

"Since when have we ever slept?" I put the washcloth away and turn out the light.

"I didn't say I was gonna sleep for long." She turns down the sheets for me.

"Thank you." I kiss her forehead.

"For?"

"For tonight." I cuddle her close, feeling peaceful for the first time in a long time. The worries are still there, but somehow more bearable when she's beside me. She's keeping me from falling apart completely.

Please, Trish, let me keep on loving you.

Trish

I step out of my car, looking at the long driveway to Mama's house. It's Nana's eightieth birthday party and a bunch of my relatives are here to celebrate. "If anyone asks, you're older than me."

"Older than you, got it." Zac nods. "Why would they ask?"

"I don't know. But if they do, you're older."

Jesus, all I have to do is survive the next hour. "Let's just get this over with, shall we?" I apply fresh red lipstick.

Lipstick, make me brave. I'm counting on you, girl. Make me stronger than the lions we're about to face. I'm safe now. Dipshit can't take that away from me.

I pop the trunk of my car and Zac gets the cake I ordered from Publix. Carrot Cake. Nana's favorite.

Knock, knock, knock.

We can still turn around. We can still leave. We don't have to do this.

The same old porch swing stands next to the steps, the same overgrown rose bush guards the porch, and the same cracked sidewalk leads to the door. It's a part of who I am, but it was never home.

The hinges squeak as the door opens.

Welp, too late now.

"Trish!" Mama wraps her arms around me, her considerable boobs smashing against mine. I've always loved her hugs and the way she's shaped. Wish Dipshit could see her beauty. I know he only sees her as being too big. Her and Nana are the only reasons I'm here. The only ones worth saying hello to.

An hour. We will stay for an hour.

"Hey Mom, this is Zac." I smile at my gorgeous man. Didn't think I'd be bringing anyone home. But here we are.

He puts out his hand to shake hers, but instead she pulls him in for a big hug like he already belongs.

"Welcome, Zac. Lovely to meet you. Make yourself right at home, ya hear?"

Knew she'd like him. Wasn't worried. I'll never understand how someone who is so good at loving ended up with an asshole that couldn't love anyone besides himself.

Speaking of assholes, there he is.

Dipshit sits on the couch with his feet on the coffee table. Doesn't move when we get here. Won't be bothered with introductions. Hasn't lifted a finger in all the time he's lived here, why start now?

A bunch of my cousins are running around in the backyard. Relatives I could care less about gather in the corner of the back porch. It's loud and hectic and everything I hate about family gatherings. I only like my cousin Rick and Nana. Of course Rick isn't here. Wish he was. Zac still wants to meet him.

"Need help in the kitchen?" I ask Mama, to keep from looking at that jerk loitering in what used to be a home. Dipshit will likely drink away the afternoon while we get the food ready. He'll stay in that same spot only moving to yell Mama's name and ask her to bring him another beer. He's a cancer, feeding off everything good in the home and leaking nothing but poison back out.

"That would be great." Mama leads the way through her modest house into the kitchen. Steam bubbles from pots. Smoke drifts in from the grill on the back porch. I watch out the window. Sure enough, none of my relatives are tending to it. Leaving all the work to Mama.

"How long has the meat been on?" I go for the tongs.

"Oh about long enough. It's ready to flip." Mama says.

"Got an apron?" Zac asks.

"Yep, here." Mama hands him the pink pineapple patterned apron.

We go out on the back porch for a blessed moment of quiet. My relatives have dispersed to play some football.

"Calm before the storm." I open the top where a bunch of ribs are on the grill. As always, Mom has outdone herself. Spending money on this big party that I know Dipshit will give her shit about. Not that it's his money. Prick can't hold a job. He can't hold anything besides his liquor.

Zac's staring at Dipshit through the sliding glass door. His jaw is tense and his hands balled into fists at his side.

"You look any harder, those daggers are gonna come outta your eyes and shoot Dipshit in the head." I say.

"That's what I'm hoping for." He purses his lips and lets out a slow shaky breath.

"I told you. He didn't get the nickname for nothing."

"Trish, I..." he stammers, "I hate seeing this." His hands come to my hips. "Do you need to go? We can say hey to Nana and I'll make up some lie about having to leave. We don't have to do this." His eyes are kind.

"I think I need to stay. Just for a little bit, ya know? We're here for Nana. She'll be here any minute. That's who I'm excited for you to meet."

"I'm excited to meet her, too." He brushes a stray lock of hair out of my eyes. "And if at any point, this gets too much. You tell me. We'll go. Okay?"

"Okay." I nod. "Let's get this meat checked." I lick my lips, hoping to distract from the feelings begging to come alive. I need all those bad memories to stay buried.

"Your mom seems nice." Zac takes the basting brush and jumps into action coating the ribs after I flip them. Don't have to tell this man what to do. It's so fucking refreshing. A lot of the boys stand there like a lost puppy wanting me to tell them how to breathe. Zac knows. He's got that intuitive sense about him—especially in the bedroom. My body heats up thinking about last night and how it keeps getting better every time I'm with him.

"Have I told you how much I love that you are so helpful?" I whisper into the shell of his ear.

"About a hundred times, but I'd *love* to hear it again," he says against my mouth, "little miss."

My body turns as hot as the coals on the grill. This is not the place I want to be. Daydreaming with Zac is a welcome escape to the unhappy memories attached to this house.

I clear my throat. "Yeah, Mom's great. It's Dipshit that isn't."

"Yeah, I saw him." Zac's tone shows that he hasn't forgotten that Dipshit is the monster in my closet. But he's restraining himself, for me. He's observant, I didn't have to say anything. I know he won't tolerate any bullshit either. I love that about him. As much as I hate being at this house, I feel safer when he's here.

"I'm just hopin' we can get in and out of here without an incident." I flop into the lawn chair sitting by the grill, clasping my arms across my waist. The kiddie chair is tiny and half my ass sticks off over the side. But I need to sit. I'm exhausted. It's like all the energy is sucked out of me by having to be in this house with *him*.

Zac kneels in front of me, rubbing my knee. "Whatever happens, I'm here," he kisses my hands, and sweet prickles creep up my leg. His tongue circles the smooth surface while his eyes take a path right into my sweet spot. A hungry expression works on his face. "And when we get back home, little lady, I'm gonna take all this unpleasantness off your mind." His thumb sneaks under the hem of my shorts, reaching toward my center.

"Mmmm," I purr.

"It'll be like we were never here at all." He stands up, spanking my dangling asscheek with a grin on his face. "And that's a promise. You'll be more juicy than these ribs."

"Damn, boy." I look over my shoulder. "You better watch out before my mama comes through that door and hears those dirty lips of yours. She'd put your head over the sink and wash your mouth out with soap."

"She'll have to catch me first. I'm still in pretty good shape, even with this bum knee." He gathers up the bottle of sauce and goes into the kitchen, returning with Mom's aluminum leaf serving tray.

I kiss him. "You're the only reason I can handle being at this house."

"You sure I can't beat up your stepdad? I mean, I'm sure I can take him." Zac raises one eyebrow, looking toward the couch where Dipshit guzzles another beer.

"I'm sure. We're here for Nana's birthday. Just gonna keep the peace and peace out."

"Fine. I'll restrain myself this time." Zac rolls his eyes. "If I *have* to."

"You promised me you'd be on your best behavior." I tickle under his ribs.

"I'm the one who tickles, little miss." He flicks my hands away and gets my most ticklish spot under my bra.

"Hey," I shriek backward. "Keep the peace, remember."

"I'll be as peaceful as a rose garden." He winks.

"Let's get this over with, shall we?"

"Is that my favorite granddaughter slaving away?" Nana's voice fills my ears and I turn to greet her.

"I'm your only granddaughter." I chuckle. "Hey, Nana." I wrap my arms around her.

"And this must be that charming fella you keep mentioning at lunch." Nana smiles at Zac.

"Great to meet you, Nana. I've heard nothing but good things." Zac shakes her hand. "Happy Birthday."

"I'm gettin' too old for these." She teases. "Better go make my rounds." Nana taps Zac's shoulder and heads down the stairs to the field.

"So now you've met everyone I care about in the family besides Rick. We still need to make that happen." With the ribs loaded up on the tray, I open the doors.

"That is completely true." Zac follows me into the sunroom. Mama's set up the long table and two folding tables at the end to make room for everyone to sit. The family gathers without needing to be called. Two of my uncles and aunts sit with their sons. Nana sits up by Mama and Dipshit.

"You sit here, Trishy Lou." Nana motions to the chair across from her. I'd hoped to be on the far side of the table. Out of range if Dipshit pulls one of his stunts.

Zac gives me a concerned expression, like he senses my apprehension. I nod and we sit where Nana wanted us.

My aunts and uncles and cousins make small talk I couldn't care less about. They've never been supportive of me. Relationships are a two way street.

"So Zac, you play baseball?" Mama asks Zac a get-to-know-you sorta question.

"Yes, ma'am." Zac wipes his mouth with a napkin.

"Yeah, right. He's been out all season. Figures Trish could only get a wanna be player." Dipshit mumbles.

"Zac's started for Suncastle every year until he got an injury. He's one of the best players." I correct.

"Is that so?" Uncle Chuck asks.

"Yes. And he's about to start playing again." I smile at Zac.

"Oh there she goes. Making shit up again." Dipshit says.

Just ignore it. We're almost through the party....

"So besides baseball, what do you like?" Mama's trying to get to know Zac and I wish I woulda had him come to lunch to avoid this conversation here. Everything gives ammo to Dipshit's rude behavior.

"I'm hoping to graduate next year in computer science."

"Oh, maybe he could look at your computer." Aunt Chessie elbows Uncle Chuck.

"Oh yeah, that's just what I need. Someone to get it to turn on again." Uncle Chuck says.

"About time Trish contributed something to this family." Dipshit tries to cheer his beer bottle against uncle Chuck's but he can't reach. He stands to shorten the distance, but he's a wobbly mess and beer spills on Chuck's plate.

"Fuck you. Wasting perfectly bread." Chuck pulls up his roll, dripping with beer.

"Get me another, Mama." Dipshit claps his hands.

Mama leaps to the cooler and pops the cap on his bottle. Dipshit nurses his beer like it's the only thing keeping him alive.

"You want me to say something?" Zac whispers against my ear.

"No, let's not rock the boat. It's not worth it." I focus on my plate, trying not to hear the conversations around the table.

"Okay." Zac holds my hand under the table.

My plate's almost empty. A few more minutes and we can do cake and get out of here.

I've had about all I can handle when Dipshit gropes Mama in front of all of us. She squirms away, and he twists her wrist so that he's holding her where she clearly doesn't wanna be.

"Get over here, woman. Sit on me." He jerks Mama, smushing her in the tight space between the table and his lap. "If you was skinny enough to fit. No cake for you." He pinches her belly. The conversation at the table goes hushed, everyone watching. If only this was an unusual occasion. He's always body shaming her and I hate it.

For a moment, I dare to hope Mama will stand up to him. We're here. She'd be able to take her hand away, and he couldn't do much against all of us.

But instead, she smiles and gives him a kiss. "Whatever you want."

My heart breaks for the woman my mother once was and the woman she's become. No one deserves this.

There's not enough red lipstick in this world to save me from the harm this man can cause.

Is he even a man? I cannot find a being less worthy of the term. Of all the days and weeks and months I've spent under his power. Of all the nights I've cried myself to sleep–never to shed a single tear. Of all the nights I hoped to

God that I could break free.

And here I am. Still in his chains.

I had one goal: keep the peace long enough to get through dinner and be here for Nana. The house is suffocating. Even though Mama's cooking hits just the right chord of nostalgia, I can't handle being here.

"Maybe it's time to head out?" Zac whispers. "I mean we can stay as long as you want, but I don't see this going uphill." He raises one eyebrow in Dipshit's direction. There's four empty bottles of beer next to his place setting and six more by his easy chair.

"I think we're gonna go." I search my purse for my keys, dropping it on the floor and gripping my Kentucky kitty keychain tight. "I've got some work to finish up tonight."

"Maybe if you got a real job you could afford to spend more time with your mama and the rest of your family. But no, your little hobby is more important than family. What Trish wants is more important than anything or anything else. Ain't that right, Sport?" Dipshit tips his beer to Zac and takes another long pull.

"Don't talk to her like that." Zac's face tells me he's reached his limit. One can stay on the boat and try not to rock it only so long before it capsizes. We're stuck swimming. He's got the life raft and he's getting me to shore, out of the treacherous waters.

My face heats up as I feel the eyes of everyone on me. My heart is pounding, and as much as I love that Zac stood up for me, I have to defend myself. He doesn't need to push the raft. It's time for me to swim.

"I do have a real job, thank you." My voice comes out quieter than I mean it to, like I can't speak up to him. That hurt fills me as much as it did when I was a little girl.

"Bullshit." Dipshit slams his fist on the table and I jump. "You've never worked a day in your life. All you do is take advantage of people. It's been years and you've never paid me a penny. I'd say a real woman would pay off her debts instead of being the town slut." He flings a rib bone onto his plate and licks his fingers.

A sick feeling settles deep in my gut like all the food has turned to poison, and I'm gonna toss my cookies if I stand here much longer.

"Don't you dare call her that." Zac says. But I can barely hear him. I'm in a tunnel with the man who only abuses.

The light of his fury closes on me like the headlamp of a train on a collision course. There's no way out of this tunnel. Zac's hand finds mine and squeezes, bringing me back to the present day.

No. Not this time, Dipshit.

I'm not a frail, lost little girl anymore. I don't have to put up with his shit. I'm proud of who I am.

"Payback? How much you want?" I spit the words, trying to find some strength. No more timid Trish. No more beaten stepdaughter. This ends here. I'm beyond embarrassed that he's doing this in front of Zac and Nana.

"You were under my care for eight years. Basic living expenses for that time–"

"What was I? Your tenant?" I stand, summoning all the resolve I can. Out of the corner of my eye I glance at Mama. Her head's down, mouth shut. Typical. I beg for any bit of a rebuke from her lips. I pray for her to care more about me than this asshole. I cry inside for that little girl that put up with years of her silence.

"Well, you certainly weren't a grateful member of this household. You never pulled your weight around here. You're nothing more than a stupid, selfish bitch." Dipshit's voice is like the growl of a rabid dog.

"Russell, you shouldn't say such things." Nana looks at Dipshit. Everyone at the table looks at him. This was too far, even with the shit he usually pulls.

"It's not my fault she has a sorry excuse for a life." Dipshit slams his beer against the table.

"It's more of a life than you'll ever have." I'm surprised by my own volume. I'm yelling. "Let's go." I grab Zac's hand.

"You'll always be a disappointment!" Dipshit sweeps his arm across the empty beer bottles, knocking them all over the sunroom. Glass clanks and shatters against the floor. I flinch. My bones shake. Too many memories.

Muscles and bones remember.

"Baby, come here." Zac's arms are around me, keeping me safe. "It's just noise, okay. I won't let him hurt you." He kisses my forehead and time stands still, like he's broken the trauma spell I was just trapped under.

I force a shaking breath in and out of my lungs. We shouldn't have come. This is too much.

"Come on, let's go to the car." Zac moves the hair out of my face, tucking it delicately behind my ear. "He's too drunk to reason with. This is just gonna get worse."

"Don't go before the cake." Mama's voice finds its way through the noise.

Is she kidding? How can she think of cake right now? "The cake?" I seethe. "Can't you see what's going on right in front of you? Do you really think I want to stay for cake after all this?" My heart burns in my chest, the hurt boiling over into physical pain.

Mama averts her eyes. Nothing. Not an apology. Not an acknowledgement. Not a damn thing.

Forcing my body to move through the shakiness taking over my system, I go next to Nana. "I'm sorry." I kiss her cheek. "Happy birthday, you need us to drive you home?"

"Thank you, dear. But no, I'll get a ride." She kisses my cheek, and I swallow, not wanting to leave her here with all of them. I wish we coulda gotten through the evening without that charade. Nana glances at Mama with a sad expression. "I need to talk to my daughter. Apparently it's been needed for a while."

Adrenaline sizzling in my veins, I hurry to the car.

"Trish, wait." Zac chases after me. I hadn't realized how fast I'm going. He puts his hand in mine. "Hey." He pulls me to a stop, slowing my body while my heart still races ahead. Like it wants to run away even though my steps have stopped.

"I told you." I swallow the wave of tearless bawling that rips through me. "I told you he's no good." My chest heaves with the pain that's been locked inside for so long. Pain Zac just saw. If only I could turn back the clock and stop this day from happening.

My lip trembles, and my throat constricts, remembering how Mama just stood there while Dipshit tore me down, once again. "And she won't see it. She won't ever do a damn thing." My pain morphes to anguish, just wishing for the mama I remember from my early years. I lost both parents that day. When I was nine years old and on my Daddy's lap when he had a heart attack. Mama didn't survive the heartache. Not really.

Why'd it have to be you, Daddy? If you were the one still here, I never woulda gone through so much pain. I wouldn't be so broken.

Zac's arms come around me. My body shakes, my eyes burning so hard with the tears I wanna cry. I need the release of letting the tears drip. The cleansing of being able to let go of all this. But I can't. I can't set it free because I'm always gonna be imprisoned in this hell. The hell Dipshit burned into my skin and mind.

"Hey," Zac's calm voice brings a bit of soothing into my anguish. The balm to my wound. The light to my darkness. "Let's get home." He picks me up and carries me to the car.

I have to get numb. It's too much pain. I need a way to get some space away from it all, mentally. I can't stay this close to it or I'll never find a way out.

He sets me in the passenger seat, and runs around to the other side of the car. For a second he looks at the house we just left. "I'll be right back."

Before I can stop him, he's gone.

I sit in the car trying to catch my shaking breath. It's one thing to go through it alone. But to bring the person I love? I never shoulda let him come. I can't handle him seeing it.

Zac's too tender of a soul. He's too precious to be caught up in the drama of Dipshit.

I take a tissue from the glove box and blot my red lipstick. Very little has survived on my lips after eating the ribs but I find myself disgusted with the bits that remain. Lipstick is supposed to mean power. Instead I only felt weak. It didn't help.

I did stand up to him. I replay that moment with fondness. But then I remember we ran away. Dipshit still wins.

Zac comes back with my purse.

"Oh My God. I forgot it." I gasp. "Thank you."

"I got you." He brings a tender kiss to my hand and drives us to my place in an uncomfortable quiet. Every few minutes, he looks at me like he wishes he knew what to say.

I feel like I've been run over by a reindeer. I don't know how it got so late, but it's dark as hell, and I shiver against the cold. I thought I was doing better. Thought I was taking care of the past. Thought I was finding my way into a better future. Thought what Dipshit says wouldn't ever affect me again.

I was wrong. I'm just as fucked up as I've always been.

Always will be.

No, this isn't how I was–not if I go back farther into the past. There's that little girl inside of me that *was* happy and loved. All I want is to go back to those days. To go back to the place where I was taken care of.

Hell, I didn't even need much, it wasn't like we were rich. I just needed to be safe. Was that really so much to ask?

Muscles and bones remember. Cody was right. There's no healing from this. No amount of therapy or meds or making love with Zac will make me better.

There isn't a "better."

I'm damaged.

Ruined.

Burned.

Zac's not talking. But there's nothing to say after that.

I hate that it's so hard for me to be reached. Even if he said wonderful things, I wouldn't be able to talk. He's gotta know. Maybe that's why he's not trying.

He's too pure to be with me.

"I don't know if I can keep doing this." Comes out of my mouth and hangs in the air like the fog we're driving through.

"You don't have to. There's no reason to put yourself thought that. You don't have to see them again."

"I can't get Dipshit out of my head."

"We'll figure something out," he says.

"What if we can't?" My throat burns like I've been swallowing acid.

"We will." His confidence in us doesn't waiver. Sometimes I wish it would. It's not healthy that he's so sure about being with me. I haven't earned that.

"I can't." My voice feels weak like I'm gonna be forced to silence by Dipshit and his rage. So many nights after he'd lose his temper on me I'd stay perfectly silent. Try to listen for his footsteps. Avoid anything that would draw his attention or tip his anger.

"Then I can, enough for both of us." Zac's eyes are wet when I find a way to look at him. A single tear traces its way down his cheek. "Here," he wipes the tear with his thumb and puts it on my face. He's sharing his tears with me. Again.

"You don't have to give me your tears."

"I'll give them all to you, if it helps." He sniffles, and it comes out with a touch of a laugh.

"That's sweet." I hold his hand to my cheek, the ghost of his shared tear tickling my skin.

"You're sweet." He smiles, but it's like he has to try really hard to get the corners of his mouth to rise halfway. There's only the barest hint of his deep dimples, proving the smile is forced.

He unlocks the car and gets me out, carrying me all the way into the apartment.

Tonight feels like a gigantic failure I'm in no place to process. The sliver of hope living inside me was dependent on working through the past so that our future wasn't dragged down by all the things I've been through.

I was hoping time would help. I've been living on my own for years. Cody and I used to talk about this all the time. His father was shit. So was my stepdad. Talking to Cody helped. Fuck, I miss him so much.

Maybe if I really could talk to someone.

To Zac?

It's so hard for me to process on my own.

Yet tonight, I'm speechless. It's like that ordeal sucked all the words out of me. Dipshit made the tears stop coming out of my eyes and the words stop coming out of my mouth.

It's hopeless. I'm hopeless. This realization sends me on a freefall into a dark abyss.

Because if I can't get better, then I won't let him stay.

It's not fair to him.

I think about telling Zac to leave once we get to the apartment. Being alone is better. Let me face my darkness without turning out his lights.

I'm too tired to say anything. He's never seen this side of me.

He doesn't know the secrets I keep.

That night haunts me.

No, no, anything but that.

Zac

My heart throbs in my chest. She's gone here before. This dark place. I hate that she has it. What I hate most is that I'm not allowed to follow her there. She runs away. To her little spot inside of herself that takes her just out of my reach.

Come back, baby. Please. I'm begging her to hear my words and know I mean them. She's never been able to trust a guy since her dad died. That's no small thing for us to overcome. I hope one day she knows she can trust me. I need her to trust me. *Please baby, just let me help. Let me ease this pain. Heal these wounds.*

I think some part of her has broken. But *she's* not broken. I know she's not. She's the strongest person I know, despite all that she's gone through.

I can't relate. What I've been through is so different from the things she's told me about her past. But I do empathize. I know she feels there's no way to get through this.

And I know what *that* feels like.

Her breathing slows as she relaxes into my chest. I scoop my arms under her and pick her up, carrying her to bed. "It's been a long day." I whisper into her ear, grateful my knee is strong enough to hold her. "It's just been a long day."

I help her out of her heels and under the sheets. My body is shaking, anxiety taking control as the fear of losing her carves out a place in my mind. She's told me about the hell she's been through. Seeing the state of her childhood home made it clearer.

I don't care if she never changes. I love her as she is. But I want her to feel happy and safe. I hope she can see she has those things with me. I worry my voice won't be strong enough to silence the fears put there by her dipshit stepdad.

The time she called me in the middle of the night and tried to break up with me plays through my mind.

Will she eventually shut me out forever? Could she retreat so far into herself that I won't be able to reach her anymore? When? How much time do I have? Will this keep getting worse?

Whoa. Anxiety, are you listening to me? Because it's time to shut the fuck up.

I put her purse on her entry table where she normally keeps it. Grabbing her almost dead phone, I take it to the charger by her nightstand.

She's staring at the ceiling like she can't believe the night we're having.

In my heart, I know.

It doesn't matter if she can trust me right now. It doesn't matter if she can trust me tomorrow. Or next week. Next month, or next year. It doesn't matter if she can trust me ever.

I'll prove it to her again and again if she needs me to. I'll be there for her when she feels fragile and vulnerable. I love her enough to stand with her and fight those demons one by one.

Even if she never heals. Even if we do this retreat-inward emotionally thing until the end of time. Even if I only get to be as close to her as she will let me.

Even then, I want this. I want us.

She has a hard time with trust. It's okay. I can trust enough for both of us.

"Toothbrush?" She looks so utterly exhausted that she may fall asleep right now. This little request makes me smile. Everything is harder to process when we are tired. How could we not be tired? It's just exhaustion that's bringing out both of our demons.

"I'll get it." I lean down with one more kiss.

Toothpaste on each brush, I return to my little miss, her eyes closed and chest rising and falling in slumber. I sit on the edge of the bed, careful not to disrupt her, leaving her toothbrush on the end table.

We can get through this, baby. I climb in bed beside her and hold her close, hoping my presence can keep her nightmares away.

Trish

From the second I open my eyes, I can't stop thinking about last night. About how he tried to find me but there was no way to break through when I was so lost inside of myself.

Staring at the ceiling, I wish I knew what happened. It was like everything came crashing down on me, and I didn't know how to function. My body shut down. My mind spiraled into overload. My sense of self drifted into the atmosphere.

I couldn't cope with it. Couldn't cope with any damn bit of it.

I risk a glance. Zac's cuddling the pillow, his back to me, deep in restful slumber. I roll over and drop my feet off the side of the bed. Before I'm standing, he's wrapping his arms around me, holding me stuck to the sheets.

"Where you going?" His voice is groggy.

"I'm sorry, baby." I move his hand enough that I can get up. Slowly, I walk to the kitchen and start a pot of coffee.

He walks in, rubbing his eyes. "Sorry for what?"

"Last night. I was such a disaster." I can't believe Zac was there for all that. And he only had a whiff of what I went through growing up. Worse than seeing that, he saw me lose control. Not the way Dipshit does. But the way I do. I disappeared and my dark thoughts nearly consumed me. That familiar monster of embarrassment rests on my chest. Air won't enter my lungs. I grip the countertop and lean forward, trying to relax. I thought I was past this.

I haven't healed.

I think it's time I get some professional help.

"I didn't think you were a disaster." He sits on the barstool, stretching out his back.

"You didn't?" I let out a sad laugh.

"I think your stepdad is the disaster, not you." He says it like it's a fact.

A snort is all I can manage.

We sit at the bar eating out of the yogurt container with two spoons while the coffee brews.

"I wanna know more about your past, about your family." He sets down his spoon, moving a lock of hair behind my ear. "Whatever it is, you can tell me." His face is kind and so full of concern. He could be selfish right now. Could be telling me it's not worth it. *I'm* not worth it. That this is too much drama to navigate. Instead, he wants to talk about what I need. That big heart of his keeps reeling me in, closer and closer. Do I want to be caught?

Hell no, not happening.

What if I can trust him?

"There's no pressure. But if it'd help to talk, I'm here." He bends the corner of his mouth into a smile.

I want to trust him, want to tell him. It'd feel so good to get it off my chest, especially after how bad last night went.

He licks yogurt off his spoon. "I hate how he treats you like that, and that the others aren't there for you. You deserve better." His words are genuine.

What he wants is to be there for me. I want to let him. Maybe I'm ready. If I'm going to have a different reality, I need to work toward that with different choices. Like actually opening up to someone, for once. But am I up for it? The pain in my chest agrees that I'm far from ready.

I swallow hard. "It's not a good story, Willey."

"But it's your story." His tone is almost cautious.

The coffee machine beeps, and I pour us both a cup. Mine in my navy mug that says *But First, Caffeine,* his in my white mug with a snuggled up in bed kitty cat that says *Five More Minutes.* He pours us some creamer and I pop the big container of yogurt back in the fridge. We go to the couch with hot coffee in hand.

Nana always says, 'If you don't try, you've already failed'. I have to try this. See if it helps. Give it a chance. I take a big breath and stare into the steaming cup in my hand. "You already know Daddy died when I was nine." I guess this is the best place to start. "After that, Mama just wasn't herself. She slipped deep into depression and deeper into the bottle." As if I've hit a wasp nest with a baseball bat, all those long nights come rushing back. "She'd spiral so bad. Nine-year-old-me didn't know if she'd wake up after long nights of drinking. I slept by the phone most nights so I would be that much faster, in case I had to call 911. I didn't know how to get myself food while she stayed in bed and our pantry was totally empty besides her booze. We went hungry so many times. Sometimes, when I was extra hungry, I'd wonder if it was all just a test to see if I could handle it. I imagined Daddy walking through the door and saving us. Daddy wouldn't have let me starve."

I bring a trembling hand to my face, a wave of grief crashing hard against me. Zac takes the mug out of my hand and sets both of ours on the table. He scoops me up into a tender hug while I cry those dry sobs–like dry heaves when you have nothing left to vomit. His comfort gives me strength to keep going.

"It wasn't long before Mama was looking for anyone to marry. She didn't know how to be alone. She got desperate. Married someone she met while out on a drinking binge. And just like that, Dipshit entered the picture." I gather myself with a tight breath and retrieve our coffees, all done with whatever version of crying I do.

"And he started hurtin' you and your mom?" Zac asks.

"So much." I look at the wall behind him. "You're the first guy I've ever really told about this."

I feel a bit of calm in him knowing. He's like a breeze blowing away some of the dirt covering me. I have someone who'll listen. I have a boyfriend. A supporter.

Gratitude blooms in my chest, a welcome feeling. Like I didn't know how much I needed to have this.

There's so much hurt in his eyes. Guilt takes over my body, wondering if this is too much for him to bear.

He's already a pillar of strength for his sister. And I've added to the pain he's feeling. Because it's written all over his face. Shock and devastation.

I shouldn't have told him. Too bad I can't take it back.

Me and my big mouth.

Zac

There is no end to the anger running through me. As thrilled as I am she's opening up to me, it's overshadowed by pure fury I may never overcome toward the asshole that raised her. Anger toward both of her parents. No nine year old should have to wonder if her mom's gonna wake up.

"And your mom did nothing while all this was happening?" If what I saw at the party yesterday was any indication of how her childhood was, I already have my answer. No family is perfect, but this cuts really deep. Not only *was* her stepdad a mean guy, but he's *still* abusing her mom every chance he gets. My neck gets hot. Grinding my teeth, I feel my tight jaw. I'm holding back a growl that wants to climb up the back of my throat. "Did your mom know what your stepdad was doing to you?"

"I think so. I mean, how could she not have any idea? We were all living in the same house. I'm sure she heard me scream at least some of the time." Trish's lips are turned down and her jaw trembles. I get off the couch so that I can find her some gum.

Coffee isn't gonna be enough for these nerves. My shirt is warm from when she was crying into my shoulder, hot breaths vibrating through me as each sob overtook her.

There's some gum on her nightstand. Just like I'm always fidgeting with my hands, making paper stars and stuff out of straw wrappers, she's always chewing. It's how we cope with the extra energy floating around in our system. Mine from my overactive anxious mind. Hers from the trauma she carries so deep.

I wanna give her anything that'll help.

"If your mom knew, then why didn't she do anything?" I unwrap the pack of gum and hand her a piece.

"That's the question I've asked myself a million times. Mama was broken. I mean, Daddy died so suddenly. He was her whole world." Trish chews the gum, and I can tell it's helping by the way she's able to take much calmer breaths. The nervous energy has somewhere to go. "Mama used to care. When all her energy didn't go into feeding a narcissist asshole, she used to have some attention to give me."

I lean into the couch, ready to hold her. Maybe in some small way, I can steady the storm within her. I'll be her anchor.

"But losing your dad messed with you, too."

"It really did."

"Trish, it's not right she kept someone who wasn't safe with you in your home. And if she knew you were being abused, it was her responsibility to do something."

Something *could* have been done by her mom.

The scars on her back are burned in my mind like they are burned on her skin. The scars on her heart are even worse.

I put my hands in hers, watching her chew the gum faster and faster like she's not able to handle this. She needs to get this out of her system.

"It's okay." I hold her hand and she collapses into my chest again. There's a knot in my throat that gets bigger the longer we sit here. "None of this was okay, Trish. But it's better now. You never have to see him again. And you never have to forgive your mom, either. It's not okay that she didn't give you a reasonable childhood. It's not okay that she put you in a dangerous situation when you were so young."

"I always wanted to believe Mama couldn't have done anything about it.

But that's not true." Trish trembles against my chest and I hold her tighter.

"No, it's not true." My eyes sting, and I blink back the tears that are forming. I can't stop picturing her as a little girl, all alone, going through that hell. She's been through so much. She had a great life until her dad died, and then it drove in a crazy direction.

"I'm here now, okay?"

"I wish someone woulda been there before." She chokes out the words and they go straight to my soul.

"Did your nana know?"

"I shoulda told her." Trish shakes her head.

"I'm sure it was hard to know if you could talk about it."

"Yeah." She lets out a sad sound.

That flame of all I feel for her burns brighter. She's letting me in. She was able to tell me something so personal. Something so important to her. Something so close to her heart.

This means so much.

We're going to be okay. And if she goes back behind her emotional walls, I'm gonna hold onto this moment. I'll remember no matter how hard things get, we can always come back to this. The place where we share the deepest, hardest parts of us and support each other through them.

It's all I've ever wanted with someone. To be ourselves, ugly parts and all.

Trish is all I'll ever need.

April

Zac

Tonight, I get to play again.

"Good luck, baby." Trish gives me a kiss as I head to the field.

"Thanks." I nod, for once not hating the rush of adrenaline in my system. This is the good kind of stress. I finished all the rehab stuff. We did a followup MRI and everything looks good.

Coach gives us a pep talk while the stands fill up with fans. So glad Trish is here.

"Make it count," Bobby says as we walk out.

"Man, it feels good to hear that again." We say it at every game. Ever since my freshman year. "Make it count." I echo.

It feels right to be on the field again. The butterflies in my stomach as I keep my eye on the ball. I play my best.

All that worry I felt about never playing again drips off of me like the sweat off my brow.

But as the game goes on, a different stress overtakes my system. There's a girl on the front row who looks a lot like Sadie. Ma's phone call keeps replaying in my mind. Horrible mental images flash in my head. Sadie getting beat up. Being in trouble and not having anyone there to help.

I don't want to think about this. It's all anxiety.

Sadie will be okay. I hope.

I do my best to focus on the game. We win, five to four. Close game. Glad I didn't fuck it up with how distracted I am.

I got through it. I'm playing again. Things are looking up. And my girlfriend is here to share it with me.

"I'm excited you got to play again." Trish sets her phone on the nightstand as we get back to my apartment.

"It felt really good." I try to breathe through the tightness in my chest. It was a big day. My teeth start chattering even though I'm wearing sweats.

Trish yawns, pulling off my jersey and getting into some of my pajamas. She climbs under the covers.

I go to get ready for bed. Before I realize, dark and troubling thoughts are running rampant through my mind. I keep picturing Sadie in a bad situation. Keep worrying about those girls on the team backing her into a corner. If Ma's worried, it's way past the point of when I'd start worrying.

I'm sweating. The blood flowing through my body feels different. Something is wrong. I'm going to die.

No, no, no, come back Zac, don't go down there. Not now. We don't need to go down that dark road right now.

But I can't help it. Fuck, I've done it now. I've ignored my needs too long. I've spent hours feeling guilty and helpless. I've pushed too hard trying to get back to playing baseball. I've run myself dry with making videos and keeping up with fans. There's nothing left of me to pull myself up out of this hole.

Looking around the room, I reach for something tangible to keep me here. Trish. Her beautiful body is already sleeping.

Seeing Trish helps me center. I remember the calming things she's said when I'm anxious. Her support has pulled me out of multiple anxious moments.

But right now? She's out of reach. I can't wake her up.

I'm on my own.

Sadie's just finding her own way. I try to convince myself that's all this is. But these moments building up one after another shake me. Waves of a panic attack spin inside, building to a tsunami. Teeth pounding against each other, body shaking, hard to breathe.

Freefalling. Plummeting. Departing.

I want to return to the moment, but I can't. It's too late.

I'm all by myself.

My body isn't under my control. Ache spreads through my chest. Pain radiates through my arms. Skin crawling like those fucking ants on an anthill. Cold sweat morphing into something sticky.

I'm dying.

No, it's just panic. I'm okay. It's just panic. I'm okay.

It's not working. My heart races. My chest tightens up. My arms go numb. I'm trying to calm down, but I can't. I'm too far gone.

I stumble into the bathroom, grabbing my toothbrush for a distraction. *Just ride the wave. Just ride the wave.* The shakes come bigger, stronger. My quaking hands drop my toothbrush on the side of the sink. I slip down the cabinet to the cold tile floor, hugging my knees to my chest, rocking back and forth.

I'm dying.

No one will find me for hours.

When someone finds me, it'll be Trish. That will destroy her.

It's just panic, Zac. It's just panic, It'll shift soon. It'll shift.

Terrifying thoughts spiral through my mind. My heart shutting off entirely. My body motionless on the floor. Trish crying, trying to wake me up. Sadie hurting herself because she's too low. Ma telling me she can't find Sadie. It's like playing pingpong against myself, upside down, in *The Twilight Zone.*

I want to get help. I want to call Sadie. Sadie can't help. She's not talking to me. Trish is asleep. I can wake her up, but my body won't speak. I cough, trying to clear my throat. "Trish?" She can't hear me. The room spins. I'm too dizzy to walk to her.

I don't have anyone.

Pain in my chest intensifies. Is it a heart attack? My arm hurts. Oh fuck, it's real this time. Something's wrong with my heart. I *am* gonna die.

No.

I try to reign in the thoughts but I'm lost in a fog. All the logic in the world isn't strong enough. I'm drifting into an endless sea. Sinking under the crashing waves of the panic attack.

I'm already gone.

Keep trying. Logic. Find some logic to combat the panic.

I just had a checkup. My heart is okay. They know my heart is okay. Doc Brown said my heart is okay.

Sweat runs down my brow. I'm burning up. Maybe I have an infection. Maybe I have a fever. Oh, fuck. Oh, fuck. Oh, fuck.

God, please, take this away.

Just panic. Please, just be panic. Please, don't be real. It only has to be real once. These things *do* happen.

Don't be real this time. Please. Please. Please. Please.

I close my eyes. Try to breathe. Can't breathe. It's gonna shift. It always shifts.

What if it's real? It could be real. If it is, I'm killing myself right now by not listening. No. Not real.

We're gonna figure things out. We're gonna figure things out. We have got to figure things out.

The tension releases just enough for me to take a breath. Then another. One more.

Breath…one…two…three.

There's pain in my heart when I breathe. What if I'm not okay?

No. Stop. *Please, God, help me stop.*

I need Sadie. This is a new kind of emptiness I've never felt before. We've always had each other.

"Trish?" It's barely a croak.

I stumble to stand, gripping the counter and breathing through another dizzy spell.

"Zac?" Trish eases up in bed and rubs her eyes. She blinks a few times, then comes over to me. "What happened? You alright?"

"N...n...no." I hang my head, and my body starts shaking again. She wraps her arms around me.

"Oh, baby."

"I'm sorry. I'm just–" my teeth chatter, making it hard to speak, "just anxious."

"Breathe with me, baby." She counts off breaths, holding me tight. Tears spill out of my eyes, trying to find her peace. She calms me. I can be calm now.

Taking my hand, she brings me to the bed. We stay here a long time, with her cuddling into my chest.

"What if it's my heart?" I'm still shaking, bad.

"It's not." She sounds sure.

I try to believe her.

"What if I need to go to a hospital?" My throat burns from trying so hard to get air.

"If you do, I'll drive you." She puts her nose against mine. "What would help right now?"

"Music?"

"Yep." She gets her phone and finds an acoustic playlist. I focus on the music, aware of the way my body feels like it just got beat up.

"It's a bad one." I swallow, embarrassed that she has to see me in one of the lower places mental illness takes me.

"It's gonna be okay." She pulls down the covers and helps me get tucked in.

I roll over, pulling away from her, feeling awful for having so much panic when she's staying over. I'm sure it's hard to watch.

She reaches around me to hold my hand.

marissa j. gramoll

"Zac, I know your heart is okay. I've seen someone have a heart attack before. It's different."

"You have?" I choke out.

"Yeah, when Daddy had one and I was sitting on his lap." She spoons me, like every part of her is hoping to comfort me. I imagine a little Trish sitting on her father's lap, him clutching to his chest and slumping over, her screaming for help and crying because she doesn't know what to do.

"It's different. Like way different. If I am even worried about that happening to you, I'll go get help, okay?" She holds me tighter. "I know you're scared, baby. I'm here. I'll be the light in the tunnel until you get through it." Her words seep deep inside me, the proof I'm okay. If it was a heart attack, I'd be getting worse instead of better.

For several moments, I focus on her touch and the music playing. It helps me regulate enough to turn and face her.

"I'm sorry you had to be there with your dad." I pull a lock of hair away from her face.

"I'm sorry you have to fight your brain telling you you're having one." She makes that sobbing sound and I know she's crying with me in that special way she does. I blink out a tear and take my thumb and wipe it on her cheek.

"Thanks for being here." I say.

"You're not alone."

I don't know how, but she knows exactly what I need.

Thank you Father in Heaven, for giving me my angel when I need her most. Please, send someone to look out for Sadie too.

First thing in the morning, Trish heads back to Willardson.

During class, my hands start shaking really badly making my pencil scribble in my notebook. It's like there's a huge rock on my chest. I can't get a real breath. Looking at the fitness watch Trish gave me, I see my heart rate is too high for my normal.

I go to the training room before my next class.

Strumming my knuckles on the office door frame, I wait for Mindy to look up. "You have a minute?"

She's got a bunch of windows open on her computer.

"It's okay, I can come back." I turn to go.

"No, come on in." She motions to the chair next to her desk. "What's up? How's your knee?"

"Knee is okay. I actually came to talk about something else." I plop in the chair. "I had a bad panic attack last night. They've been happening more lately."

She's looking at me with her listening face. A kind smile, gathering information. I love that about Mindy. She's here for me, but she's not in my face.

"Kinda caught me off guard." I lean back in the chair, looking at the ceiling tiles. "I'm thinking maybe my meds aren't working right and I should try new ones or somethin'. What do you think?"

"Yeah we can at least have you look into it. You're still taking Zoloft?"

"Every day." I let out a long breath. "Doc Rogers can do the med switch, yeah?"

"Yes, or you can go to Dr. Brown and talk about med management."

"Okay, yeah." I look at her again, thankful she's so encouraging. "I've had a lot on my mind, too." I clench my hands in my lap, heart racing from being here and trying to get help. It's like anxiety doesn't want me to get help.

I shake my hands out, dangling them over the edge of the chair. My arm starts convulsing something awful. "What if I get a panic attack on the field, Mindy? What then? I have to keep playin'. It's been such a rough season." My throat gets all hot, and I hate that I'm sitting here telling her all this. "Yesterday scared the fuck out of me. I felt like I was gonna die. What if I miss a catch because that surging in my chest flares up?"

"Then we'll figure it out." She waits until I meet her eyes. "I don't want you to worry about still playin', alright? That's gonna add to the stress. Have you ever had a panic attack on the field?"

"No, not yet."

"Well, if for some reason you do, Chase can sub for you until we get it under control." She puts her hand on my shoulder. "Are you done with classes for today?"

"Yeah," I say.

"Maybe you can have some self-care. Do something that helps you feel better. Something that brings peace. Take a walk, spend some time outside, read a good book, eat your favorite meal. Take a break from homework and anything that's stressful. Give yourself as long as you need."

"How do I know what will work for me?" I swallow hard, wondering if I can let my mind take a break from life.

"Try different things? It's definitely a process to figure out what helps the most. So be kind to yourself. It's okay to be hard on yourself on the field. Good, even. But after practice, you need to focus on Zac."

"I'll try."

"I know you will." She smiles.

"Thanks."

Zac

Self-care. Self-care. I can figure out freaking self-care.

Flying fish sticks! I've been trying for an hour to read a book. It's not working. The words get fuzzy the longer I look at the page. I'm only on page two. Jumping Jolly Ranchers, why is this so hard?

My eyelids are heavy because it's almost midnight.

Trish and I have been texting back and forth, but it's hard to talk when she's so busy. I wish I could drive to her place. That would make me feel better. *Self*-care isn't go-hookup-with-your-girlfriend-care. But fuck, I wish it was.

My phone goes off and I see a video call from Sadie coming through. Oh good. This'll help me breathe easier.

The screen is really dark and I wonder if she butt dialed me from a movie or something.

"Hey!" I sit up, an excited smile on my face, hoping she meant to call and is taking a sec to see if I answer before going to a lighter room. Only her breathing comes through the line. I can barely see her.

Why aren't you turning the light on?

"Zac?" Her voice trembles.

"Sadie, what's wrong?" I lean closer to the phone trying to make out more than the shadow.

"Something...happened."

"What is it?" Before I could make it feel small. I could hope that I was overreacting. But this is reality. She's in trouble, and we both know it. "What happened?" My heart rate increases like it's gonna leap right out of my chest and run all the bases before it comes back into my body.

She's not talking. I hear her shift, like she's looking over her shoulder for someone.

"Where you at?" I keep my voice down, not sure if she's safe. Fuck, what if she's not? I couldn't get to her if I wanted to. I'm so fucking far away.

"I can't go home...not like this." She's crying. I can tell the way her voice comes through like a little whiny squeak. "I can't go home, and I can't stay here." Her teeth chatter so loud I can hear it on the line.

"Why can't you go home?" I keep my voice quiet. "Where are you?"

"I'm downtown."

"What part of downtown?"

"Behind Nichols...It wasn't supposed to go this way. It wasn't supposed to–"

"Hey now, you can always go home." I try to coax her into it, but I don't know how she got there or if she has a ride. I'm not sure what's going on. A million graphically terrible scenarios spiral through my brain.

I click out of the video call and text Pa, stat.

Me: You need to help Sadie. She's behind Nichols, downtown.

"Sadie, are you alone?" I get back onto the call screen.

"I think so. I don't think they followed me, but...I don't know."

"Who'd you run away from?" I ask.

She just shakes her head like she can't tell me.

"I told Pa where you are. He'll come get you."

"No," she gasps and a wave of nausea rolls through me, wondering if I've done the wrong thing. No. Ma and Pa need to help her. She's only seventeen.

"They can't see me like this. I don't think I can ever go home. Look." Her shadow turns and I catch a glimpse of her beat up face under the streetlight.

My brow starts sweating, my heart sinking deeper into my gut wondering what the fuck I can do. I'm too far away. Of all the moments I wished I could evaporate the distance between South Carolina and Kentucky, it screams at me now. I did this. I left her. I knew it wasn't okay. I knew she wasn't okay.

I let this happen.

"Sadie, listen to me, Pa is not going to be mad at *you* for this. You need to get somewhere safe. Should I call the cops instead?"

"No! No cops. I–I can't do that right now."

I bite back an argument and try to just be there for her. "Can you get somewhere safe? Are any of the shops open?" My throat dries up on the last word, and it comes out as a croak. My sister is downtown, alone, at midnight with a beat up face.

"Nothin's open."

The phone stays quiet for a long time.

"Sadie, who did this to you?" My voice is a pleading whisper. "Was it the girls from school?"

"No." She sniffles.

"Was it Angela?"

She nods, bringing her fist to her quivering lips. "A bunch of her college friends got together. They started acting rough with me. I tried to get them to stop." She keeps talking while I hang on every word. "Angela told me I had to strip for the camera."

"And…?" I'm delicate, but I need to know in case Ma and Pa need to call an ambulance. I can barely see her. How bad did they beat her up?

"I told them I wouldn't strip. One guy said I don't like cock cause I've never had cock and I didn't know what I was missing. And I told them that was bullshit. Then they said they'd beat me up if I didn't suck them off. I didn't think they would. Then they did it anyway, Zac. They took swings at me and Angela just stood there and watched. I fell over and they kept throwing punches while I was on the ground." It comes out between sobs.

My heart drops to the pit of my stomach. Vomit sneaks up the back of my throat.

"They weren't gonna let me go. I agreed to suck them off so they'd leave me alone. But then they just made me strip and Angela stood there and filmed all the guys—"

Oh fuck.

I can't breathe.

I don't want to ask, but I have to. "Sadie, oh, no. Sadie…how could they?"

She starts crying harder, and I don't need her to say the words to know she got raped and beat up. Guys raped her while her *friend* recorded it. My veins turn to fire and rage, wanting to hurt every last one of them. Wanting to destroy everyone who hurt her.

"Sadie, honey, you need to go to the police."

"I can't."

A text comes through telling me Pa's heading there and my lungs relax enough to get a half decent breath, "Pa is on the way. He needs to take you to the police."

"They won't do a fuckin' thing." She's sobbing into the phone. "Don't you see? Nothin' can be done. They're just gonna get away with it. They've gotten away with so much—" She puts on a mocking tone, "They just wanna fuck the fag straight."

Angry, hot tears fall down my cheek. "Fuck, Sadie. I'm so sorry." My voice goes out, and I swallow hard. I wish I could teleport through this phone and go take care of her. "Pa is coming. He'll know what to do."

"No, he won't." She says words I wish weren't true. As great a man Pa is, he isn't good at helping. But, he'll at least get her home. That's a start.

"I want to help, okay? I'll get on a plane right now." I go for my laptop.

"It won't help. Nothing will help." Her words stop me.

I can't leave her to fend for herself. I need to help my sister.

"I never shoulda–" she stops, weeping into her hands like they are over absorbed tissues. "Why did I call you? I'm just making this worse. This isn't your problem."

I squint my eyes tight, worried she will just hang up on me and run. "Sades, you listen to me. You needed to call. I'm so fuckin' glad you called. This is not your fault. No one deserves this. No matter what. No one deserves this. And your problems are always my problems."

"But what if I do deserve it?" She presses her palm into her eye, and then winces from the pain it must cause to put pressure where she's been hit.

I thought my stomach dropped before. But I can't handle this.

She thinks she deserved it? Their bullying is worse than I realized, and I knew it was bad.

"You don't." I swallow, rubbing my throat with how tight it is, worried that my airway will constrict and never open back up again. There's that pain in my chest again. No, not now. I cannot have a panic attack now. "I promise you don't. Even if you were the worst monster on this planet, you wouldn't deserve what happened tonight."

"I am a monster." Her voice is low, like her eyes, gazing far off the screen, taking her to another time and space far away from reality.

"Sades? Sades!"

She doesn't meet my gaze. I grind my teeth hard enough to make my jaw ache.

"You don't deserve it. You're not a monster. They are." I go into the texting menu and tell Pa to call the police. As fast as I can, I return to the video screen.

"I wish I could believe you." She's drifting, her head rests against the wall behind her.

The image on the phone shifts, like she dropped it.

"Sades!" I jolt upright, like it will help me get from where I am to where she needs me to be. "Sadie!" I'm staring at a streetlamp.

"Darlin'?" It's Pa. Thank fuck. "Darlin', let's get in the truck."

"Pa, you gotta take her to the hospital." My voice is loud, urgent, trying to get his attention from a video call.

"I've got you. Sadie? Can you hear me?" Pa says.

Oh, fuck, she's really passed out.

"Ma, she's breathin', but she doesn't look good. Help me get her into the truck." Pa says.

For seconds that last way longer than normal seconds I wait, just hearing shuffling around.

"Zac?" Ma holds the phone up to her ear like she doesn't notice it's a video call.

"Ma, you gotta get her to the hospital."

"He's got her. She's in the truck. Did she tell you what happened?"

I tell Ma everything. She needs to know, for Sadie's sake. My adrenaline runs through me worse with each second I relive this hell. "I'm coming. Let me get on a flight."

"I'm not sure if coming is a good idea." Ma's reaction is hard to gauge. "I'll call you when we get her to the hospital, okay?"

Ma, don't hang up... I want to scream the words but they're stuck in my throat. I can't find a way to say anything. My phone returns to the menu. Call ended. They're gone.

Father in Heaven, you've gotta help her.

I replay everything again and again, the shock building the more I think about it. Why did she pass out? Was she that out of it? I know trauma can do a lot to a person. Was her head injury worse than it looked?

They raped and attacked her.

Her *friend* let them.

I collapse onto my carpet, at the foot of my bed hugging my knees into my chest so tight it hurts.

Ma and Pa are too busy. They don't get it. They better get it now. They better open their fucking eyes.

My phone rings, and I startle, reaching for it, hoping it's Ma.

"Trish?" I clear my throat because it sounds all wonky when I talk. A bunch of coughs emerge, burning my tight chest.

"Zac, what's wrong? Are you gettin' sick? Is your knee actin' up?"

My body shakes, and I can't tell her. I can't say all that out loud again.

"Hello? Zac?" She snaps her fingers like she's trying to get the attention of a three year old to look at her camera during a photo shoot. "Baby, are you okay?"

"No," I rub my throat, vocal chords taken over with emotion.

"What happened?"

I want to bring myself to say something, but I can't. Anxiety keeps a hold of me. The monster in my brain wrapping tendrils around every part of my body to the point I'm not me, Zac Williams, anymore. I'm a mess of misfiring neurons.

"Talk to me, baby. Let me in." She says the words I have so often said to her.

"Sadie got beat up. Some guys forced themselves–" A wave of nausea mixes with the shock. I can't go on, but I don't have to.

"Fuck, Zac." Trish's tone tells me that she understands, and I don't need to say anymore. "When? When did it happen?"

"Tonight." I slam my forehead into my knees. I can't imagine how much this hurt her. How much this night must've destroyed her. She's already been through hell.

"Is she getting help?" Trish's tone is considerate.

"Yeah. I hope so. I made Pa take her to the hospital. I didn't know what else to do." I rasp through my dry mouth.

Just wish I believed it would be enough.

It's not enough. I'm getting on a plane.

I flew to Kentucky, the first flight I could get. We're in the hospital room.

Pa's working with the cops to fill out a police report. The hospital did CT scans. When those assholes beat Sadie up, they gave her a gnarly concussion and that's why she passed out.

It's around noon and Sadie's sleeping in the hospital bed. I look at Ma sitting beside me.

"Thanks for texting us." Ma holds my hand.

"I'll stay here with her. Or she can come back with me. Have you called a lawyer?"

"We can't afford that. I don't know how we're gonna afford this." She gestures to the hospital room.

"I'll pay for it."

"Don't be silly." Ma says.

"It's silly to think she doesn't need a lawyer after last night." I grind my teeth together. Ma doesn't fight. It's like she's too tired.

For the next few hours, I call several lawyers until we find one that's gonna help.

When Sadie is discharged from the hospital, I help her get settled at home.

"You wanna come to Suncastle with me?"

"I can't." She says.

"Why not?"

"I'll just be a burden."

I sit next to her on the bed. "You're never a burden. Not to me." I wait until she finds my eyes. "Just come for a week or two. The next games are at home. Come watch me play. Get a break from all this. Wouldn't that be nice?

She gives me a slow nod.

I go to her closet for a suitcase. "Tell me what to pack."

Trish

I'm standing outside of Anna Mae's house. I'm not sure how we convinced Mama Jones, but she's coming to Suncastle with me for the weekend.

Zac flew back from to Kentucky with Sadie. I figure she and Anna Mae are about the same age and may like hanging out. Plus I heard back from the admissions office, and they wanna meet with Anna Mae in person to talk about her options for college.

Suncastle has three home baseball games, too. I'm gonna help Anna Mae capture the games to add some sports flair to her portfolio. Pretty sure this photography scholarship is in the bag.

"All set?" I ask as she gets to my car.

"Yep. I'm ready." She puts her suitcase in the back and we get buckled. "Thanks, Trish. This is seriously gonna be the best weekend of my life."

"I'm counting on it."

We grab food on the way and rock out to my long distance playlist.

"This is Zac's apartment." I park outside. Anna Mae and I grab our suitcases. "You been to Suncastle before?"

"No." Anna Mae looks at the complex.

"He's apartment 107." I lead the way. We knock.

"Hey, baby." Zac opens it wide. Inside, he's got the couch bed pulled out.

Sadie walks over to us as Anna Mae and I kick the dirt off our shoes on the welcome mat. Her face is bruised up real bad. I can tell she tried to cover it up with concealer, but it's still peaking through. Maybe I can give her some of the strong stuff I use.

"Sadie, meet Anna Mae. Anna Mae, meet Sadie." I walk my suitcase into the kitchen. "Y'all both have brothers addicted to baseball and you're both seniors in high school, so I figure the common ground starts there."

"Anna Mae, make yourself at home." Zac smiles. "I remember playing with Cody. It's good to meet you in person." He shakes her hand.

"Thanks for letting me come over." She says.

"You can put your stuff over here." Sadie walks into the living room and Anna Mae follows.

"You've got class in half an hour?" I kiss Zac.

"Yeah."

"I'm gonna take the girls to the mall. We'll be back in time for the game." I snuggle into his shoulder. "I'm glad you brought Sadie back."

"She needs this." He rubs my back.

"I think Anna Mae does too." I look at them from the corner of my eye. Seems they're chatting already. Good. I hoped it wouldn't be awkward.

If there's anything I'm really good at, it's makeovers. Lexie meets us outside the foodcourt.

"Now you girls get whatever the heck you want. It's girls weekend, my treat." I walk them toward Sephora.

"You hanging in there?" I hug Lex while the girls start picking out makeup.

"Yeah." She sighs. "This is a good distraction."

"I figured it would be."

We spend the afternoon trailing through every good store at Suncastle

Mall. I spoil Sadie and Anna Mae rotten with everything they desire. It reminds me of shopping trips with Nana.

We all pick out adorable Suncastle outfits to wear to the games this weekend. After checking out, we get mani/pedis.

"Is there anything you don't like to eat, Sadie?" I pull out my phone to text Zac a place to meet us for an early dinner before baseball.

"Sardines." Sadie says.

"Me neither." Anna Mae chuckles.

"Okay, let's go to The Splat, then."

"Thanks for taking care of Sadie while I was at class." Zac puts his arm around me as we wait in line at The Splat. "Y'all look cute." He admires my purple lacy top.

"She's so fun to hang out with. We had a blast." I look at the girls. "They've really hit it off."

"Sadie needs a good friend." Zac looks at the ground and I can tell it's all still hitting him really hard. "I wish I coulda been there for her more."

"Hey, you're here. I love that she's spending some time away from it all."

"Her lawyer called me. She needs to go back to Kentucky to appear in court." He leans his head on my shoulder.

"Then she can come back." I kiss his head over his baseball cap. "Anna Mae is a sweetheart. I think they've both been through way too much shit for seventeen year olds." I shake my head.

"That's the truth."

When we get our food, I can't stop thinking about Zac and my first night here. So much has happened since then. I'm so glad we're together now.

"Um, this pizza is even better than Pa's." Sadie says.

"It's the best pizza." Anna Mae agrees.

"How can you eat a salad?" Sadie teases Zac.

"They're salads are way good, too." He gives her a bite.

"Okay, I guess you're right. That ranch is incredible." Sadie says.

We finish the pizza.

"Good luck baby doll." I give Zac a kiss in the parking lot. "We'll see you out there."

"Love you." He whispers against my lips.

"So much." I give him a hug. "See you soon."

We get settled at the apartment until it's time for the game to start. I take Sadie and Anna Mae to my usual spot on the front row.

"Are you kidding me?" Sadie gasps.

"What?" I ask.

"Zac has his own cheering section?" Sadie looks at a dozen girls wearing his number.

"Oh, yeah. He does." I chuckle.

"And that doesn't bother you?" Anna Mae asks.

"No. I think it's fun he has so many fans."

"Damn, you really are perfect for him, aren't you?" Sadie smiles.

"I sure hope so."

Zac

Sadie went back to Kentucky a couple weeks ago, but we're talking a lot and I feel better about all that. I'm standing outside of the campus chapel with Ethan. He's got his phone out showing me my profile.

"We have four million followers?" I stare at my phone wondering if someone's played a trick. If someone's hacked the system. We've been doing awesome. But even this is a huge jump. I'm floored.

"You're fuckin' famous, man. They can't get enough of you." Ethan smiles so big. I'm sure he's been jizzing himself happy after this rise in popularity. We were doing just fine before. But now? This is nuts.

"It's you as much as it's me."

If he hadn't filmed the day I got my injury and uploaded it at just the right time with just the right music and text, none of this would be happening. He hit the sweet spot. The fans are crazy about both of us. I was worried about being famous on my personal account, but Coach didn't care. He says it's good for the college publicity.

A thought comes into my mind. I can use this. What good is having a big audience if you don't use it? I can make this into something good for Sadie. For everyone who feels out of place for being gay. We can help them know they aren't alone.

"Hey, let's do something big for Pride." I look at the watch Trish gave me. We have enough time to think of something good.

"Pride?" Ethan raises his eyebrows.

"Yeah," I go to Pride every year. But the only other Suncastle baseball player I've ever seen there is Briar.

"You can. I have no clue about that stuff." Ethan raises his hands up. "Wait, are you...."

I tense my jaw, catching a breeze of homophobia coming from his lips.

"Am I what?" I lean in closer, one eyebrow cocked, my tone intense.

"You know?"

"Gay?" I say the word and he looks at his shoes like I've said something worse than telling him to drown a cat.

"And if I was?" I look at him for a long time until he finds my eyes.

"Then no big deal." He takes a step back, his hands still up at his sides.

"You sure? Because it seemed like a big deal just a second ago." I force a breath.

"No, it's just that..." Ethan's stumbling for words.

"Just that what?" I wanna listen sincerely, but it's a huge trigger for me when someone is mean, insensitive, or set in old ways. Our culture is filled with people who don't think love is love and confuse being queer with being a predator.

It's so far from the truth. It's so far from my worldview. It's so far from what I tolerate in my friends.

I really hope Ethan isn't one of those people.

"You know my girlfriend?" Ethan's question feels out of nowhere but I go with it.

"Dalilah?" Obviously.

"Yeah." Ethan looks like he's having a war in his head. Like maybe he needs to say something about her but doesn't know how. After a while, he speaks. "Dalilah just came out to me as 'not super straight'," he puts up air quotation marks like it's something she said. "She likes me but she likes girls too sometimes, and I guess she's barely figured this out about herself and…I don't know. It just happened. I have no idea what any of this means. I didn't know you're in the community. Am I getting that right? Community is the term?" He scrubs his hands over his face, frazzled. "It's all so new. I don't know. B, L, T…"

"LGBT Community?" I correct, eyebrows raised high in surprise. I've seen a lot of sides to Ethan over the years, but never a side like this. He's acting real embarrassed and maybe worried? I don't know. He's not homophobic. It's more like he's confused.

Thank you, Father in Heaven.

I didn't need to deal with that today. Especially not when things are going so well. That would've been a monkey wrench in every bit of everything.

"Yeah, all those letters. It's overwhelming." He kicks his sneakers against the curb. "I sound pathetic."

"Well, I'm not gay, but I'm sure as fuck an ally. And if Dalilah felt comfortable enough to tell you about discovering her sexuality, it means she trusts you." I look at the campus chapel, feeling a little self-conscious. A lot of *Christian* folk have a long way to go toward actual acceptance. I'm not always sure how people will react if they see my Rainbow Crocs or overhear me talking about pride stuff.

"You really care about her, don't you?" I smile, thinking about Trish. It means a lot when you can share everything with a person.

"More than anything." Ethan's voice holds conviction.

"And does this news change how you feel about her?" Even if he loves her, he needs to be able to love every part of her. The real her.

"Not even a little bit." His tone is sincere.

"Come to Pride Club with me this weekend. See if she wants to come."

"You can go to Pride Club? Even though you're not LGBT?"

"Yeah, Suncastle's got an awesome group. Briar comes, too. We all hang out."

"You're serious?" Ethan's eyes go wide.

"Why wouldn't I be?"

"I don't know. I mean," his tone is soft, his eyes glancing behind us to see if anyone's listening. "Don't you worry what people will think if they see you there? That they might think you're gay or something?"

"So what if they did? You've been taught it matters. But I swear it's not true. Doesn't matter to me. If you're ashamed of being seen with queer people, then you're ashamed of being seen with your girlfriend because she is queer. I love my queer buddies and my straight buddies. And if people make assumptions, that's their choice."

"That's cool."

"It's a journey, Ethan. I didn't understand everything the first day. There's years of unlearning and deconditioning. You have to break down the beliefs that a toxic society has fed you your entire life." I put my hand on his shoulder. "Spend time listening. Learn their stories. Find out why they feel the way they feel. A lot of people aren't straight and a lot of people spend a lot of their lives not even knowing it. We live in a heteronormative society."

"Thanks." He walks toward the chapel. "Guess we better not be late for service."

"I think God would appreciate the conversation we're having." I chuckle.

"You figure?" His brows furrow, and I know it's a lot to take in. "You're about to step into a whole community of love in a way you've never embraced before. There's something really beautiful about it, really. That's what religion is to me. God is love, right?"

"Right." His eyes look hopeful.

Zac

We just won our second game in the double header.

My eyes glazed over the blurry word *accident* and *get here as soon as you can*.

Ma texted me while I was playing and I just read the words.

I rush behind the field. Skidding down the wall, I collapse into the ground. Parking lot is emptying up.

Just. Can't. Breathe.

My chest is so tight. Am I about to pass out? Stuck in some weird space time continuum.

Every part of me shakes. Tremors getting bigger the longer I sit here without adequate air. Thoughts are spinning. Dark, horrible thoughts.

Sadie's not okay. She's not. I know she's not. And I'm six-hundred and fifty miles away. They were getting her help. She was supposed to be okay.

"Zac?"

I'm dizzy. Can't quite make out the voice talking to me.

"Zac?"

It's Mindy, I catch her face out of the corner of my eyes. She kneels in front of me, "Hey, I'm here, okay?"

I grip my chest tight. "Can't breathe. Everything's spinning. Can't stop shaking."

She grips my shoulder. "Let's try together. Can you breathe with me?" She counts off a breath like a meditation video, telling me to breathe in, one, two, three, breath out, one, two, three.

Every breath hurts my chest as I force the air in and out. Nausea runs acid up the back of my throat. I hope I don't throw up in front of Mindy.

I wish Trish was here.

"It's my sister." My voice is a wheeze. How long can I go without a good breath? How long before my brain shuts down? My body?

Mindy's here. She can help.

"There's meds in my backpack." I choke out. The emergency pills I'm always afraid to take but sometimes need.

"Lexie!" Mindy yells across her shoulder. Lexie runs over here.

"Zac's backpack, can you get it?"

"Yeah." Lexie rushes off.

"Let's sip some water, alright?" She hands me a water bottle. I hold a mouthful, trying to focus on the liquid in my mouth more than the fear in my mind.

"Lexie's getting your medication. Then we can help you get back home, alright?"

"I can't go home." I know I sound crazed. "Have to get to Kentucky."

"Okay, let's take this one step at a time." She holds the water bottle while I hang my head between my knees.

"Here," Lexie sets my backpack next to me.

I rummage through until I get the medication.

I take the pills and hang my head between my knees again. It's a heart attack. I'm scared it's a heart attack.

"You're safe." Mindy keeps her hand on my shoulder. "You can breathe. It's gonna be okay. Just one step at a time. We're here for you."

A half an hour later, I'm still coming down from the adrenaline rush that always follows my intense attacks. Mindy helped make sure I got back to the apartment. I'm eating a banana and drinking some Gatorade to try to regulate my blood sugar.

"Ma, how is she?" I hold the phone up to my ear.

"Not good, Zac."

Not the words I need to hear. Not Ma's typical faith filled optimism.

No. No. *Please, Father in Heaven, no.*

"I think you better get over here. I have to go." Her voice lingers in my ear long after she clicks to end the connection.

I call Coach Conners while I drive. "I have a family emergency. I'll try to be back for the game, but I don't know if I will be. I'll let you know when I know more."

"Alright, Son. Take care. Hope everything works out." He doesn't give me shit for missing the game like I thought he might.

I speed all the way to Trish's place. I don't even know if she's home. I just have to get to Willardson. Willardson is closer to a major airport.

I'll tell Trish goodbye on my way there. I don't even have a plane ticket. I can't do this. I can't just leave. I need to just leave. Sadie is in the hospital without me. She can't be there without me. I have to get there. But what if the plane crashes? Or is hijacked? Or. Or. Or. Or. What if she leaves this world before I can get there?

I tap my fingers on the steering wheel, trying to come out of the anxiety. I'll get there. I'll get to her. I'll help.

I pull into Trish's driveway. I was right. She's home.

Thank you, Father in Heaven.

In less than two seconds I'm standing inside, trying to compose my thoughts.

"What are you doing here?" Trish's got a sloppy bun on her head and a Twizzler sticking out of her mouth.

"Sadie's hurt again. I'm going to see her."

"Oh fuck. What's wrong?" Trish pulls the Twizzler out of her mouth.

"I don't know. Ma said they took her to the hospital." I'm pacing outside of Trish's apartment. "Can you give me a ride to the airport? Can I leave my truck here? Maybe I should just drive to Kentucky so I don't have to wait for an available flight. I don't know."

"Zac, breathe, baby. Breathe." She grips my shoulders, stopping me from pacing.

I take a breath, the inhalation burning every centimeter while my lungs expand. I hold it tight like if I let it out I'll never breathe again.

"Come in for a second. Let's figure this out." She takes my shaking hand and pulls me inside the door. It's like the room is spinning. Like there's no air left in the world. And the longer I'm here, the more danger Sadie is in.

As if I could do anything.

But I definitely can't from a ten hour drive away.

"Sit for a sec. You're all worked up."

I flop into her plush couch and tap my heels against the fuzzy rug.

She goes to the kitchen and brings back a cup of ice water.

The ice water goes down my throat. I'm trying to ground myself. Trying to let this moment bring me some comfort.

It's too much. I'm so worried.

Trish sits beside me on the couch. "They got her to the hospital, okay? They're helping her."

"What if they can't help?"

"They're doing what they can for her."

Trish offers me a twizzler. I chew. The sugar will help bring me into the moment. Need to be in the moment to think straight. Need to think straight to get to Sadie.

"I'm gonna grab my computer. Don't go anywhere." Trish leaves but it barely registers.

I look at the door. It's all too tempting to drive all the way to Kentucky. I just want to be moving in the right direction, not sitting here. And in Willardson, I'm almost two hours closer than I was. Only an eight hour drive left. Can be there by morning if I leave now.

Trish plops beside me and searches for flights.

"What's the airport we're going to? Which one's close to Elizabethtown?"

"Louisville."

"Okay. There's a direct flight out of Columbia at eleven. Fly back early Monday for class. You got someone there that can give us a ride? Or should I rent a car?"

"No, you can't come. You've got stuff this weekend. What about that wedding?"

"I'll cancel." She nods her head, like she's telling me it's gonna be okay.

"You can't miss it. Not for me."

"Zac, I'm not letting you go there alone. Just last week you told me that your anxiety is amped up way more than normal." She clicks through the menu to get our tickets ready. "You don't have to do this by yourself." She points at my pocket. "Now call Pa or a buddy or someone to pick us up."

I text my buddy Mitch, knowing he'll come pick us up when we get to Louisville.

Trish grabs her purse and starts entering in payment information for the six hundred dollar tickets.

"No, here." I pull out my wallet.

"Stop," she clicks all the buttons and then puts her laptop away, hurrying into her room to get some things.

It takes all my emotional energy to walk down the hall and find her in her room. She's half way out of her top and all the way out of her jeans, lacy panties on those perfect hips of hers.

"Thank you." I reach around her middle, my hands sinking under her elastic ribbony band. The touch of her skin is heaven to my fingers, my only comfort in an unsure time. I rest my head on her shoulder, bringing a tender kiss to her neck. "For taking care of the details."

"Honey, you're a mess right now. Of course, I'm gonna take care of everything." She flips around to face me, my hands gliding from her belly to the small of her back in the smooth motion of her spin.

Her lips envelop me in warmth and acceptance. It's moments like this, when we hold, when we kiss, that I know I need her. I need to be with her for more than just a little while.

"I'm gonna grab my toothbrush, then I'm all set." She pecks my lips. Once. Twice. Three times. "Okay, okay, we have to go." She pulls back when all I want to do is hold on tighter.

"This isn't how I wanted you to spend the weekend." I grind my teeth, looking out the window as she drives us to the airport.

"This isn't how I wanted you to spend yours either. I wish none of this was happening, but I'm happy to be with you, baby doll." She puts her hand on my leg and I rest my hand on top of it.

The closer we get to the airline, the more anxiety escalates. I don't handle quick changes of plans. My mind keeps going to the dark thoughts of worry.

"It'll be fine." She squeezes my hand. "Breathe, baby, you're about to turn blue." She taps her hand on mine, since she knows that helps calm me down.

"I can't believe Sadie's in the hospital. I don't even know what happened, or how she's actually doing. Ma won't tell me a damn thing." I rub my forehead.

"We'll get there, okay. We'll get there." She leans her half smile toward me as we wait at a light.

The whole flight I couldn't calm down. It's like one big, long, anxiety attack. Everything feels like a threat. It's just a short flight. Direct. No reason for problems. One lift off. One landing. An hour and a half in the air.

My teeth start chattering, heels bouncing on the floor, banging my knees into the crowded tray tables attached to the row in front of us. "I hate flying."

"Don't you fly a lot with the team?" Trish snuggles into my shoulder, offering another Twizzler, since she packed her stash before we left her apartment.

"Yeah." I can't decide if it would help or hurt to eat this Twizzler. Trish has downed half the bag herself. "But I'm terrified of flying. It's the worst part of baseball." I take the Twizzler from her and try to calm my nerves by chewing. She's always doing it. Maybe it can soothe me too.

"We're almost there." She says. "I'm so scared." I blink hard.

Trish rests her head on my shoulder. I draw from her comfort, hoping that I can find some calm, again.

When we land, I text Mitch. By the time we've collected our bags he's already there waiting for us.

He brings me in for a huge hug. "Sorry to hear about Sadie, man. Is she doing alright yet?"

"Ma hasn't said." I turn to Trish, "This is Mitch."

She goes to shake his hand while I open up the door to the backseat for us to climb in. Kentucky fills my nose with all the scents of home. The humid air.

I call Ma as soon as I'm in the car. "We just landed. Are you still at the hospital?"

"Yes. I'm with Sadie. Pa's at home." Ma says.

I lick my teeth, still tasting the remnants of those Twizzlers. Sadie's in the hospital and Ma's there with her alone.

"Will they let us come visit?" I sigh into the phone.

"I don't think they allow visitors this late. She's stabilized since we got here. Best for you to get some sleep and come in the morning."

"Don't you need rest?" I'm fighting the boulder resting on my chest that we rushed so fast to get here and it doesn't mean a thing.

"I'm fine. I'm already set up here. They let me sleep in the recliner. You go get some rest, it won't do any good to argue. Good night. I'll see you tomorrow." Ma clicks the phone off before I can protest again. I keep it in my hand for a long time, wishing she'd call back.

"Can we crash at your place?" I ask Mitch.

"You know it." Mitch looks back at me. "Y'all can sleep on the pullout sofa."

He parks outside the apartment and Trish and I go inside, flipping the light switch on as we enter.

"Thanks again." I set my backpack on one of the kitchen bar stools.

Trish

The hospital is sterile. I hate these places. I swear there's a certain smell in every hospital. Makes it feel ominous.

I hate seeing Zac like this. I wish I could do more for him. But what do I have to offer? Especially when he doesn't seem to want much.

Zac gets us both a name tag and we head down the long halls to the right room. He knocks and his mom opens the door.

"Hey, Ma." Zac smiles, but it doesn't reach his eyes. Everything about this moment is too heavy.

"Hi." I wave.

"Zac?" There's a strained voice coming from within the room.

"Hey, Sadie." He leans down and wraps her in a good, long hug.

He's worried he almost lost her. This scene of the two of them hugging is so precious to observe. I almost wish I had my camera out, but some moments can't be duplicated on film.

After they let go, he pulls the chair up so it's real close to her hospital bed.

"We brought you one of those McDonalds' breakfast biscuit things." I hand the paper sack to Mrs. Williams' and go over to sit by Zac.

"Hey, Trish." Sadie looks weak, with the oxygen line going into her nose and an IV drip running from her arms. Zac holds her hand.

"She passed out at school." Mrs. Williams says.

"She passed out at school?" Zac looks over to his Ma sitting in the corner. "What caused that?" The touch of anger in his voice makes me tense, his angry tone bringing back memories.

"That's not really what happened." Sadie whispers.

"You were gonna lie to me?" Zac looks over his shoulder at his mom and his voice raises more than I've ever heard it. My vision blurs. I'm in a dizzy haze. Yelling. All the yelling I grew up with rings in my ears like I never left that abusive home.

"It's not a lie." Mrs. Williams sets down the McDonalds sac and comes closer.

"I did pass out at school...but it's because–" Sadie's voice cuts off.

Zac's eyes are pleading with her to go on. "What happened?" He turns his cold tone to his Ma. I jump in my seat. Everyone has a dark side. But I've never seen Zac's before.

I struggle to breathe. He's mad, with good reason. Dipshit never had good reasons. This is different.

It is.

But I can't convince myself. I feel nauseous. I need to rush to a bathroom.

"I'll give y'all a minute." Next thing I know, I'm running down the halls.

You always run away, don't you? Dipshit's voice echoes in my ears and I try to shove it back.

I'm here for Zac. It's okay that he's angry about this. Looks like Ma isn't helping his sister enough. She's in denial, which doesn't help anyone. I'd be angry too. Anger's okay for people to experience. Zac won't hit anyone. Zac won't hit me.

It hurts that I have to fight these voices in my head, these memories. I don't want to feel this pain. Not now. Not ever.

Zac

I'm in an alternate reality. Floating. There's nothing for me to hold onto. The words buzz against my ears.

"I just thought that if I did it at school, it'd be easier." Sadie's explaining. But I can't quite hear it. Life's happening all around me like I'm in a glass room watching it.

"Zac, please, say something?" Tears run down her face and I realize I'm crying too.

"I didn't mean to hurt you." She gasps.

I clench her hand for dear life.

"You have to stay. You have to fucking stay." My voice cracks as the magnitude of everything hits me like a giant wave. It breaks the glass room where I want to hide. A place to be safe from this heartache. A place to be that is far, far away from here.

Suicide.

She tried to kill herself.

Because of all the people bullying her. Hurting her. Making her feel worthless.

"What are you going to do?" I stare at Ma who has no answers. "Don't you see it yet? The Lord won't provide, Ma. This isn't gonna get better no matter how much faith you have. Sometimes you gotta do more than just pray." The words spit like venom. I'm so done with all of this. All the times that Sadie's been screaming for help. They've done nothing.

Ma doesn't say a word.

"She's coming back with me." I say.

"There's just a little bit of time left in school." Ma says.

"Then she'll transfer." I look at the IV running down her arm. Maybe Ma's too tired but she doesn't fight.

Time goes slowly. I stay by Sadie's side as doctors and nurses check in with her. Ma goes to work. Pa goes to work. I stay, Trish and I sitting in the same chairs all hours of the day and night. I missed the game to be here. If I could miss a game, then Ma and Pa should've been able to miss a shift of work. Close the restaurant for a few days. Leave someone else in charge for a while. Something.

"Do you want to stay here?" I clear my throat, still raw from all the emotion I've been carrying since the moment I heard.

"No." Sadie's eyes are red, and her eyelids are heavy.

"I'm gone a lot with class and baseball. But you can live at my place. Just get you somewhere that isn't here." I squeeze Trish's hand.

"You can live with me, Sadie." Trish offers. "Willardson High is great. My friend is the volleyball coach there. Maybe she can help."

I turn to look at my girlfriend. Can't believe what she's offering.

"My place is bigger than Zac's. You'd have your own room. Whatever you need." Trish's smile touches me real deep.

Sadie looks at the ceiling. "Things haven't been good for a long time." Darkness replaces all the light in her eyes.

"Come with us. Let's get you out of this place."

"I think I need to stay, Zac." Her voice is weak. "I know you're my big brother and you wanna protect me–"

"If I woulda been here, I would have." I cut in, trying to keep her from turning down our offer.

"I need to fight my own battles. I shouldn't have done what I did. I'm glad they found me. I won't do it again. I want to live. I promise." Tears rush down her cheeks. "But if I leave, I'm running away. I can't do that."

"It's not running away. It's getting you out of a tough situation." I bounce my heels against the tile floor.

"I'll stay here, Zac. And I promise I won't get this low again." Sadie raises her eyebrows.

"It's not about not getting low, Sades. It's about asking for help when you do." I lean my elbows against the side of her bed.

"I'll ask for help next time." She promises.

"We're here for you." I hold her hand. "And I'm gonna look at some mental health hospitals here."

"Thanks, Zac." She yawns.

After a while, Sadie settles to sleep.

"You didn't have to do that." I hold Trish's hand.

"Do what?" She pulls a Twizzler from her never ending Mary Poppins bag and pops it in her mouth.

"Offer to let Sadie live with you." I rest my head on top of hers.

"I wanna help if we can." She runs her fingers through my hair.

"I think I've got an idea about how we can help her from here." I get out my phone and text Ethan.

Me: You free tomorrow night?

Ethan: After practice, yah. Why?

I fill him in on everything. Maybe, just maybe, my plan will work.

May

Zac

S adie is at a mental health hospital. I refused to leave Kentucky until I knew she was getting the help she needed. I also made sure she knew she's welcome to come live with me at any time.

My heart is heavy as I adjust my phone camera to start filming.

"Hey everyone." I clear my throat, watching the live messages flow into the screen. This is the time for helping Sadie. I glance at the picture of us years ago that's framed on my desk. "I've got something big to ask. And it's only possible if you all pitch in."

My hands are shaking, and I rub my fingers, reaching for my ball to squeeze so that I have something to do to take these nerves down.

"I don't usually talk about my personal life, but tonight I'm gonna. Please share this, so we can get as many in the live feed as possible." I force a breath, knowing that I can still turn back. I'm worried about how this is gonna go. The internet is so unpredictable. I may be throwing myself to the wolves.

"My sister is lesbian. I asked her if it was okay for me to talk about."

I watch the number of viewers trickle down a few thousand. Thought so. Another deep breath. Doesn't matter how many are left. I'll be me. Say what I need to say. Be here for however many are left.

"Sexual identity is just that. Identity. I know there's still a long way to go. So many people don't understand. Don't accept. But I'm asking for your help." My throat gets tight, and I force some cold water down in attempts to talk more clearly.

"You see, some pretty mean people started bullying my sister, because she's lesbian." I swallow hard, the need to protect her and worry that I've failed is resting heavy on my chest. My eyes wander to the chat screen, worried about what may be on there. Anyone could be trolling tonight.

It's not just trolling though. A lot of it is genuine concern. Comment makes my eyes wet. Things like:

Oh no.

Is she okay?

What can we do to help?

Love is love.

Tons of rainbow emojis take over the screen.

"Y'all are making me emotional." I blink back some forming tears, and the chat goes crazy with more love and kind messages. That heaviness in my chest starts to lift. Perhaps the best part of social media is knowing that there are others in the world who can truly relate to me.

"Here's what you can do to help. She needs money for lawyers and to cover costs from her hospital stay. Enough to get her on her feet until she figures out her next steps. I set up a donation page for her. If you are able, maybe you can help. " I plug in the link so that my viewers can click it. I'm doing this for her. I've already started up an account for the money to go in. She needs a place of her own, far away from these nasty people. She needs a fresh start.

My eyes burn as I watch the many fans showing support in the chat and making donations. For the next half hour, I bring awareness to how many LGBT youth are bullied. I talk about how many take their own lives. How many are disowned and left homeless.

It feels incredible knowing I have an audience and I can use this platform for good.

"I'll hop on here again next week. Goodnight everybody." I blow them kisses, like I always do. They reply in real time with kissy faces and all kinds of stuff.

"Thank you for helping her out. She needs it." I swallow hard again. I can't go back to that night when she got beat up. But I can do this. I can get her enough donations so that she can go far away.

"I saw your live." Trish says into the phone.

"I need to hold you." It comes out like a desperate groan, expressing exactly how I feel. "It was a lot to be that vulnerable. A lot to ask for help. Didn't know it would be this hard to do." I flop backward in my bed, wishing it still smelled like her. "Please tell me you're on the way?"

A knock comes from my door.

"Hold on a sec." I stand, fixing my hair from the anything but smooth flop on the mattress. Not expecting any company.

"I'm on my way." Trish clicks her phone off and tucks it in her pocket, smiling as I blink in disbelief. "Knew it was a big day." She wraps her arms around me while I stand completely dumbfounded.

"You're here?"

"I'm here." She steps into my apartment and closes the door. "You did amazing, baby. I told all my friends to watch."

"You did?" My insides heat up, truly touched that she's here and she supported my video.

"Of course I did." She brings her lips to mine. "And did you see those numbers climbing up and up and up some more?"

"It's the most viewers I've ever had at once." I take her hand and bring her to straddle me on the couch.

"You're such a good brother." Her lips are my ecstasy, all that I need here and now, waiting.

"How long you staying?" I'm out of breath from making out with her, my cock begging to sneak beneath those panties of hers.

"'Til Monday."

"Monday?" I wanna cry, that sounds so good. "You been planning this a while?"

"I drove over early and watched from Lexie's place. Thought about coming before you hopped on, but didn't wanna distract you."

"I was a nervous wreck. Probably a good call." I slip my hands under her top, that smooth skin welcoming me without a bra strap to stand in my way. I was so shocked she got here that I haven't registered what she's wearing. My jersey and leggings and absolutely no bra.

She grinds into my cock and I can tell there are no panties. "Fuck," I moan against these incredible lips, ready and waiting for all that I'm gonna give her. "Get your clothes off."

"You're reading my mind." She stands in front of me. In an adorable striptease, she slips off my jersey and kicks out of her leggings.

My face near her waist, I wrap my hands around the smooth skin of her ass. I bring my mouth to her clit, licking in the way she loves.

She leans into my mouth, purring as I get her all kinds of turned on. I slip in two fingers, hitting her g-spot.

She runs her hands through my hair, bringing my head closer to her so I have even more access as I lick away. I swirl my tongue round and round, wiggling my fingers to hit her just right. "You taste fucking amazing."

"You feel fucking amazing." She bounces against my mouth, fucking my tongue while her orgasm reverberates around my fingers. Juices rush into my mouth.

"Mmmmm," I rub all those liquids up and down her folds while her body buckles against me.

"Take me to the bed."

"You got it." I cradle her body in my arms, walking to the mattress and letting her down easy on my unmade bed.

"I need you." She spreads those toned legs of hers, fingering the spaces between, an open invitation on her face. "Now, Zac." Her tone is desperate and it pushes me closer to that ledge. The fact that she's telling me what she wants. It's driving me wild.

I'm delirious from her touch, her motions, the way she feels against my skin. The sound of our bodies coming together, pulling apart, then racing back together again, is music to my ears. I let out a loud moan as she wraps her ankles around my hips, driving me in and out with so much more power. Our forces are collaborating in the breathtaking goal we share.

"Flip me over," she says through clenched teeth, and I know she's already been to orgasm and back a few times. I grab her hips with that roughness she enjoys and flips her body with enthusiasm.

We stand on my carpet, feet close together as she braces her elbows against the mattress. With her ass in my direction, I massage her muscles. Those cheeks of hers tighten up with anticipation as some juices slide between her legs, drizzling onto my shoes.

"You do me so right." She welcomes my cock as I dive inside of her. "Oh yes, that's a good angle." She thrusts against my hips and we carry the rhythm until I'm lost for breath or words or even thoughts. My balls tighten up hard as I ride a glorious orgasmic wave. I'm so buzzed from this explosion.

With a sheen of sweat, I take her hand and we climb into bed. "That was a good way to kick off our weekend together." She presses her lips against mine.

"So glad we're just getting started."

Saturday, we go on the boat with Harvey and the gang. It's like deja vu in the best way. Perfect weather out on the boat, eating with his parents, and Trish and I cuddling in the beanbag for an outdoor movie.

All day long, my stomach has been plagued by swarms of butterflies as different moments conjure up memories from our first real date. This time though, it's different. She's different. We're different. Nostalgia mixes with the homemade ice cream, calling up a sweet memory I know I'll never forget. A memory of kisses I worried would be our last. Of kitty cat keychains and no pickles on a sandwich.

"So glad you're here." I plant a kiss on top of her beautiful mess of curls held in place by a big ol' hair flower.

"Where else would I be?" She shimmies a little closer, and I'm dying to get her home.

I tug on her arm. "Why don't we get out of here?"

She nods, covering a big yawn with her hand. "Sounds great. I'm beat."

We make the rounds saying a hasty goodbye to our friends before hopping in my truck.

We get back to the apartment and spend some time getting ready for bed.

"I wanna go to church with you." She looks up from brushing her teeth. "I even brought a dress." She winks. "Can I?"

"You can. I mean, if you want to?" I'm a little tongue tied, not sure where the fuck this is coming from. She knows I love Jesus, but we've talked about how it doesn't matter to me what she believes in. I've never been *that* kind of Christian that is on a self-righteous quest to bring salvation to everyone. Salvation is personal. I find it through my faith and also through myself. I don't care how Trish finds it. She knows that.

"Yeah, you don't think I'll get struck by lightning do you?" She snickers, giving me shit.

"You know I don't believe in all that." I chuckle while she swishes out her toothpaste. Something about seeing her in my bathroom feels so natural. I always wanna see her here, getting ready for bed with me.

"Come on," she rubs the sheet next to her. We snuggle to another movie, making out so much she puts it on pause while we get it on. I don't even care about the movie. All I want is her.

Sure enough, after a long sweet, sexy morning, we go to the campus chapel.

"You know I don't care if you like church or not." I wanna make sure she's not worried about that. I promised myself a long time ago that my relationship with God is only about me and Him.

"I know. But you like to go, so why not go with you?" She brings her silky lips to mine. "Op, hold up a sec." She fishes through her purse and gets a tissue. "Got a bunch of red lipstick on you." She chuckles, wiping the smeared makeup off my lips.

"Is it my color, though?" I ask.

She laughs and I keep the sound on replay, storing it for the long days ahead without that sound filling my ears. "It's not your color. I'd def go more neutral with your features." She licks her finger and works at the corner of my mouth where I'm guessing the stubborn color ain't coming clean.

"Well darn it, looks like we'll have to go back home and wash this off." I whisper deep against her ear. "We may not make it back in time."

"Zac Williams, you're not allowed to make me come in a church parking lot. I'm sure as sin gonna be struck by lightning now."

"Is that a challenge?" I raise my eyebrows. "Judging by those gorgeous dilated pupils and the way your heart is beating so fast," I run my hand along her shoulder, "and all this gooseflesh…seems to me, I already have made you come baby doll."

I take her to a campus bonfire with the Suncastle Pride Club on Sunday night where we roast marshmallows and listen to everyone. I love the community. Though I identify as straight, I love being an ally. They make me feel so welcome here. I'm always learning how to be more respectful. How to be more educated and help other people understand.

I realize maybe Ethan would like this, too.

Me: Hey, meet me on the south lawn. I'm at a Suncastle Pride bonfire. Think you oughta be here. Bring Dalilah.

Ethan: Oh, okay. Thanks. I'll ask her if she wants to come.

A few minutes later he and his girlfriend come over and sit with me and Trish.

It really has been everything I needed to be with her. Like a recharge. So much has been draining me lately. She breathes me back to life, in every way.

We walk home in the moonlight, her arm wrapped around my waist, our bodies in step.

"I'm so glad I came."

"I'm not ready for you to go." I sound like a sad little puppy dog, begging her to stay.

"I can look forward to our Tuesday night video call." She sounds like she's trying to be excited, but it's hard to ignore the sadness in her tone.

"I just need about ten minutes to get this turned in." We get back to my apartment and I start going over some of my homework at my laptop on the coffee table.

"Take your time. I'm gonna shower off this campfire smell." Trish heads down the hall while I get to work.

A little while later, the bedroom door squeaks open and Trish stands there in my pajamas. An old Suncastle shirt I got back at freshman orientation. My boxer briefs on her hips. Long baseball socks up to her knees.

So fucking cute.

"Ready?" She leans against the door.

"Yep." I shut my laptop.

"You coming or what?"

"Oh, I'm *coming*." I sneak through the small space between her and my room, our bodies so close I'm living off the connection.

"Well, good." She takes my hand with a little giggle on her lips that makes my cock strain even harder against my jeans.

"Strip," she commands.

I pull the corner of my lip up. "You don't get to tell me what to do."

Teasing desire flickers in her eyes, and that's my cue to keep going. I love that she loves it rough. She loves it different every time. Sometimes I worship her body slowly and other times it's wild.

"What are you gonna do about my dirty mouth?" She spits the words my way with all the sass that exists in this universe.

"Get the box and you'll find out." I look under my bed.

"Yes." She bends down in a mix of a sexy strip tease sort of dance and a mix of *I dare you to smack my ass* as she leans under the bed to my box of toys.

My boxer briefs slide down the silky skin of her legs.

My old shirt becomes a heap on the floor like a puddle after a rainstorm.

She is the storm.

I'll never ask for an umbrella.

"Now, what am I gonna do with you?"

"I don't know." She shakes her head, playing along with her body language and her tone. Acting like she's in big trouble.

I'm the one in trouble.

I never knew someone *could* be this cute.

And here I am, with her, playing any game we want. I pull out a handful of pleasure toys. The good lube that makes her all tingly. I know she likes this one.

She lays in the bed while I shed my clothes. When I look up from undressing, she's hiding under the blanket. She's hiding. So fucking cute. Oh. My. Gosh. I think I just died of adorableness overload.

"You're not allowed to hide from me." I pounce beside her, bringing the covers down to her little grin. Her cheeks are all red while she holds back a chuckle.

"How are you so fuckin' adorable? Huh?" I tickle her under the sheets, her laugh becoming my lifeblood as it enters my ears.

"You better do something," she teases, tickling me back.

"Oh, I intend to." I grab the vibrater and take my time warming her body with tingly lube. Then I pull out her favorite toy. The metal dildo that she goes nuts for.

"Fuck, Zac, I don't know how you do it." She's writhing against my sheets, grabbing handfuls of the fabric while her legs kick around. Giving her this much pleasure makes me lose my mind. I *love* when she comes this hard.

My sheets get soaked with all her pleasure. Every part of her body is heaving with my touch. Trembling. Tightening.

"Get in here." She demands. It makes me laugh that she likes to be told what to do and then she'll turn this on its head. I love whatever this turns into.

"You want me to come inside of you?" I act like it's the most ridiculous suggestion I've ever heard.

"Please." She's begging me. "I need you for this relief."

"You don't get relief until you've come so much you can't come any more. I wanna push this body of yours to its limits. You better give me all you've got. Right here. Right now." I rev up the motions, using several fingers both inside and outside of her core. When she's come again all over my hand, I give her this pleasure she's dying for.

I squirt a bunch of the sensation lube on my finger and stroke my cock a few times. She pulls her legs up high, and I slide right into her body where she's made the perfect spot for me.

"Hot damn." I grunt against her forehead as I slide all the way back. I'm in so deep. It's like there's new parts of her I've never felt before we tried this angle.

"I don't know how you keep doing this to me." I hold her close, all the pleasure and passion feeling so perfect with her.

"You're the one who's magic."

"No, you." I kiss her slowly. With each motion, pleasure surrounds us. I come undone.

Zac

I t's the last home game of the season. If we win today, we're going to
Regionals. I'm confident we can. This season's been so much better than
last year's. I'm filled with nervous energy as we head out for the fifth inning.

Ever since I got back from this injury, the season has flown by. Trish is in
Vancouver all week for a wedding shoot. I cannot wait until she gets back and
we can celebrate the win today.

Wilson University is at bat. I'm on first. Ethan's on second. Bobby's on
third. Lourie's shortstop. Briar's got right field. Carter's catching. Roger's got
left field. These are my boys. We've got this win. I can feel it.

It's hotter than Hades out here.

Dexter pitches to Wilson's hitter. Line drive right to Bobby. Perfect.

Only he doesn't catch it. Ball slams into his chest.

What?

He shoulda caught that. I coulda caught it with the sun shining in my face.

He's down.

After the play, I run over to Bobby. Ethan's right in front of me.

"Bobby? Bobby? Come on, Bobby?" I shake his shoulder frantically. He's
not moving. He's not breathing right. He's...unconscious?

Briar is on his other side, "Fuck."

"Mindy!" I'm yelling for help. Looking at his chest, it's rising, but doesn't look right. His breaths are quick and shallow. Looks painful too. Like he's working hard to get any air.

Mindy and her students rush onto the field. Lexie's looking pale. Of course, she is. If I saw Trish passed out like this, I don't know what the fuck I'd do.

"Jae, call 911." Mindy's at Bobby's side, checking for a pulse. "Rapid, thready, and weak."

911?

Oh, God, help him. Please, help him.

Do I need to get out of the way, or help somehow? How can I help?

Please, God, I'm beggin' you, help my buddy.

"We need to cool him down." Mindy says. "Let's get him off the field."

I can help with that. Several of us work with Coach Conners to get him on a stretcher. Thought he'd wake up by now, but he hasn't. Cool him off, Mindy said? Did he get overheated or what? I thought the ball hit his chest. Why the fuck is he unconscious? I know it's hot, but....

I try to stop getting distracted, but it's like I'm in shock and disassociating.

Mindy strips off his jersey and starts checking out his chest. I've been hit by a line drive before. It hurts like hell if it hits you just right. But man, in all my time playin' it's never knocked anybody out cold.

My heart is racing faster and faster, wondering what to do.

"Get the towels wet." Mindy tilts her head. "Get me the hose. We've gotta cool him down, now."

I kinda remember learning about heat stroke in one of those mandatory first aid classes they make the team go to. Is that what's going on?

I glance around at the stunned team.

"Let's dump the ice water from the coolers, then go to concessions and get more ice," Mindy instructs, and some of the players run off to get it.

The crowd watches, the game forgotten for now.

"Lexie! The towels," Mindy yells.

"We can help." I kneel near them, taking one of the towels from Lexie.

"Yeah, we can help." Briar is on her other side.

Mindy's preparing the tarp and the hose. "Get him over here."

We move him where she says and Tate pours the ice water from the cooler over him. I rub the ice over his hot skin. He's definitely overheated.

Mindy's holding Bobby's head up, cold towels all over him. Lexie looks like she's seen a ghost. Flashbacks of Cody's funeral come to mind. How broken she was. How Bobby took care of her that day outside of Shakey's.

"Temp is 105.7. Mickey, did he get drunk last night?" Mindy looks at Mickey, but he isn't saying a word.

"Lexie, do you know anythin'?"

"N-n-no." She can't hardly talk.

Fuck, it makes all of this hit that much harder. He'll be okay, right? He has to be. Just got too hot out there. That's all.

"Mickey, you *live with him.* Did he do anythin' last night? Does anybody know? Zac? Ethan? Briar? Who knows? Anyone know?" Mindy needs this info, but we're all at a loss.

We shake our heads. I wish I knew.

"He went home after practice, I think." I say. It's hard to focus on last night. Bobby's been in his own world the last several weeks. Hardly even seen him. When I have, he's been distant. Now, I'm worried there was something going on that I shoulda known about.

Like Sadie. Why am I so bad at paying attention to the silence in others?

"No, he went somewhere after. Saw his truck parkin' at the apartment a little later than I got back." Briar's using the towel to help cool him off. "Looked fine, though."

I look at Bobby's face. He's not waking up. There's a horrible feeling in the pit of my stomach. A siren rings in my ears, competing with the pounding in my head.

An ambulance came for Sadie, too. The mental images of her laying on the school floor motionless and alone flood my mind.

That guilt I always feel for not being there for her gets bigger and bigger until it's like I'm not on the field anymore. I'm not at this game. I'm not in Suncastle, South Carolina.

I don't know where I am. Lost. Broken. Floating away from reality and worried I won't be able to find my way back into it.

This isn't about me.

Fuck, I need to help. Need to do something.

What can I do?

We all step away to give the medical team space to work.

My jaw starts rattling. Bobby's got some serious medical shit going on and didn't tell anyone on the team.

Oh, fuck. If Trish kept something like this from me…

She keeps everything from you.

Now is not the time, Anxiety. It is not the time!

I overhear bits and pieces of what the EMTs are saying.

"Veins are collapsed, likely from dehydration." The paramedic is trying hard to get it to stick. "After we get some cold saline in him, we're gonna stay here till he cools down."

Dehydration.

"Are his parents here, Lexie?" Mindy asks Lexie.

She looks around, "Don't think so."

"Did you know Bobby's got this medical stuff going on?" Briar asks me.

"No, did you?" I shove my hands into my pockets.

"No." Briar holds the back of his neck.

I look over at the players, every one of us in shock. My heart pounds in my chest.

What if he doesn't wake up?

"Is he supposed to be out this long?" I ask Dexter, because he's pre-med.

"My mind is going straight to a collapsed lung based on where he got hit. But he's got symptoms that don't add up. I mean, this doesn't look like a textbook injury." He shrugs.

My pulse pounds harder in my head, signaling that familiar wave of panic starting to build. Fuck, not now. I can't handle it right now. I need to find a calm, dark place, to steady my breathing.

They take Bobby away in an ambulance. Everything moves in slow motion. We get ready to play again.

"I'm sure you're all shook up." Coach Conners stands in the dugout with his back to the field, like when he gives us a pep talk before a game. "But Bobby's getting help. He's in good hands. There's only so much we can do from here. You can pray or send vibes or whatever it is you believe in." Coach takes his hat off his head and puts it over his chest. We all do the same. Coach looks over each of us, like he's assessing where we are at. "Let's give Bobby a moment."

Please God, help my friend. He doesn't need anything else hard in his life. My eyes drift to Lexie. She's pale and shaking. Jae's next to her. They both look as shook up as I feel.

"The game is about to resume. Zac? You good to play? Briar? Everybody good?"

We nod. We have to. The game must go on. Maybe it'll distract me long enough to stop worrying so much.

"Todd, you're goin' in for third." Coach Conners looks him over.

"Oh, okay." Todd sounds like he's gonna piss himself. He's only a freshman. Don't know that he's ever played a minute of actual college ball. Bobby doesn't ever need someone to go in for him.

"You got this, alright?" I put my arm around him as we walk to the field. "Make it–" I stop myself. I won't say *Make it count* like I always tell Bobby. "Do your best." I pat his shoulder.

Trish

My phone rings again. It's Zac. Four missed calls.

"Alright let's take five!" I clap my hands, sneaking away with my water bottle to a place where I can call him back.

"Trish? Thank God. I've been trying to call. Bobby's in the hospital." He's talking so fast it's hard to keep up with him.

"What do you mean he's in the hospital?"

"Bobby got fucking heatstroke in the middle of the game." Zac's sounding nervous and flustered.

"Wait, what?" The words register, my body feeling them before my mind has a chance to make any sense of it.

"Heatstroke? What the hell?" Nausea bubbles in my throat, wanting to make my granola bar come back up. Fuck, this isn't good. People die from that. "What about Lex? Is she okay?"

"No, of course she's not okay. Looks like she's seen a fuckin' ghost." Zac's voice is shaking.

"She's still there? Why isn't she at the hospital?"

"Our athletic trainer went with Bobby and left Lexie here. Trish, an ambulance came. It was that bad. They couldn't even get an IV in his arm. Fuckin' hell, Trish," he pauses. "Lexie ran to her car the second the game ended.

I shoulda known. Shoulda helped him." Every word sounds like a croak, like he can't bear to talk about this.

"This is not your fault." I swallow, knowing how much that guilt hurts.

Whenever anything goes wrong, we both blame ourselves. Zac and I have always had this in common.

"Hang in there, alright. I'll be back home as soon as I can."

"I need to go see him." He's gotta be having some intense flashbacks of all he's been through with Sadie. This has unsettled him to his core and there's no question about it by the depth of his voice.

"Where you at right now?" I ask.

"Sitting outside the field." He's breathing really fast like he doesn't know how to stay in control of his body. I've been with him during some of his panic attacks. Fuck, this is pushing him to his limits, I can feel it.

I close my eyes. I'm worried about him.

I force a shaky breath and try to return to this moment. He needs me.

"Are you safe?"

"Yeah." His voice is more shaky than before.

"Can I help? Need me to talk you through it?" I'm trying to remember all the things I read about anxiety. Struggling to shift from being work focused to getting this call. God, I hope Bobby's okay.

I need to help Zac. "You can talk to me, baby. I'm here." It's always hard to ask for help, especially when we really need it. "What's under all this panic? Huh?"

"I don't know if I can go to the hospital, Trish." His honest admission hits like a bullet to the chest.

"I know, baby, I know." I close my eyes tight, trying to think of something to say.

"But I need to be there for him. What if–"

"No, don't go there." I interrupt. "You're feeling anxious. This is anxiety, okay? This is anxiety talkin'. It's trying to take over, but we aren't gonna let it, okay?" My mind scans through everything I've learned about how to help him when he's in the middle of an attack. I need to help him focus on something that isn't the anxiety. "Bobby's getting help, baby. He will be alright, okay? Let's say a prayer." I know how much faith means to him. "Can you pray?"

"I've been praying this whole time."

"Right."

Of course, he has. That won't help. As much as prayer and God can help with some things, this isn't just a matter of faith.

"I'm with you. Can you feel me?" I drop my words to a whisper, hoping that him having to focus to hear will help him snap out of this trance of worry. "I've got my arms around you, my lips on yours. Your head is resting on my shoulder. I'm here. Can you feel me?"

"I want to."

Wish I could wrap my arms around him and remind him that he's going to get through this.

I try to get a breath in but my chest is so tight the longer the reality of what is happening sinks in. I'm worried about Bobby. Worried about those same *what ifs* that are making my baby suffer right now. Worried about how fucking terrified Lex must be. Worried about what we are gonna do if this is another tragedy.

Fuck, Cody… don't let Bobby join you in the sky. Not yet.

Zac's breath comes through the line. He's still not breathing well.

"Is Briar goin'? You don't have to go to the hospital. But if you decide to, see if you can tag along with someone else." If he can find a solution, even temporary, it will help him shift through some of this.

"I'll see if I can." He's trying, that's clear.

"Baby, it's gonna be okay, I promise." I swallow hard. "Let me call Lexie. I'm sure she needs support."

"Yeah."

"Go find Briar, okay? Can I stay on the line until you get to him?" I need to know that he will be with someone else. Sometimes his hyperventilating gets so bad, just like that one time when I thought he was gonna pass out. I can't handle something happening to him.

"I see Briar. I'm walking over there. Love you."

"Love you, too." I wait for him to click off the line and stare at my phone, too stunned to remember what I am supposed to do next.

Lex. Of course. Lex.

My insides twist as I imagine what she must be going through. This is bringing up all kinds of pain for me too. Pain from losing Daddy and pain of losing Cody.

I think about Bobby, how much he means to her, to all of us. I can't add another friend to the list of people lost too soon. We can't handle the devastation of what that would look like.

Please, whoever is out there listening, help Bobby pull through.

I dial Lexie's number and put it to my ear. "Zac just told me. Bobby had a heatstroke?"

"Yeah. He's in the ICU." Lex's voice is a mix of fire and pain. The words enter my ear like an echo, adding to how stunned I am.

"He hasn't woke up yet." Her voice comes in thready gasps, like she's trying hard not to cry into the phone. "I'm in the waiting room with Mindy. They're tryin' to get him stable. Supposed to be able to see him soon."

I say the only thing I can think to say. "You have to be strong right now, doll baby."

"I know that." The emotion in her words forces my eyes to burn. I'll finish up the shoot and get back home to everyone as soon as I can. Until then, this is all I can do. "Keep going," I recite our mantra.

"Keep moving." She needs it now more than ever.

"Get through this." We say together.

I finish the photo shoot as fast as I can, speeding all the way to Suncastle from the airport.

My knuckles rattle on the doorframe as I wait for Zac.

The door swings open, revealing his broken face, weighed down by so much anxiety. I fall into his arms, soaking in his embrace.

"Are you okay? Are you hurt?" I plaster kisses on his lips between words, his need hungry on my lips, our bodies gripping tighter to each other.

"You're here." He kisses me deeper. "You're here." Not an answer to my question, only the affirmation that he needs to hear.

"I'm here." I search his eyes. "Lexie told me Bobby's doing okay?"

"Yeah, and thanks for talking me down earlier. I hung out with Briar for a while and then we went and visited Bobby in the hospital. He looked way better than he did on the field." Zac pinches his eyes shut like memory is bringing up anxiety. "I need you." He grips me tighter, squeezing his body against mine. I feel his chest, the expanding of each breath as he grips us tightly together. His scent fills my nose, the sound of his voice is heaven to my ears.

"I need you too." I walk him over to the couch. "You went to the hospital? How was it?"

"So hard." He puts his elbows on his knees.

"Reminding you about Sadie?"

His face is red as he glances at me. So much pain in those eyes. "It's too soon."

"I know, love." I lean back on the couch and hold his head in my lap, playing with his hair, massaging his scalp, wishing he didn't have so many neurons misfiring making his life so hard to navigate. "You can relax now."

"Now that you're here."

"I'm here." I lean down and kiss his forehead.

"How'd the photo shoot go?"

"It was too long without you."

"Got that right." He sits up and brings me into the sweetest kiss he's ever given me. We kiss longer, sweeter, every moment of the outside world blurring into us. The focus shifts from life and heartache to this. To us. To the way we feel for each other.

I press my head into his, licking his teeth, deepening each kiss. Stronger and more connected with every passing moment. This is for us. This moment. This time together.

I wiggle his shirt up his abs, and he pulls one arm through and then another, separating the kiss just long enough to get his head out of the collar. He traces his thumbs under the hem of my tank, lifting away my braless top. His lips move to my chest, smoothing his tongue over my areola, flicking tingles of ever sweetness through my body with each tantalizing touch. He lingers, hovering breath over my aching nipples as they perk, wanting to be closer to him. I reach for his belt and unbuckle, unbutton, unzip. He eases me out of these clothes, until we're both naked.

I come back to the moment. Come back to his kisses.

I lower my lips to his cock, hard in my mouth, the tip soft against my lips. His taste is one of which I will never tire of. Little precum slipping onto my tongue as I loop his ridges with my saliva and his seeping liquid.

A groan comes out of his mouth as I work him with my hands and mouth. It's different with him. Everything is different with him.

"Let me love you, baby. Please just let me love you."

"I need your love. I need every part of your love. Give it to me. Give it all to me."

"You have it. You have all of it. All of me." I suck him deep, bringing his tip to the back of my throat and pumping him hard with my hands.

"Mmmmm," he hums, feeling all the pleasure I'm giving him. When he's close to orgasm, I feel him edge away from my lips, his way of letting me know he doesn't want to finish yet. He steps off the couch and puts his hand on my folds, softening me with his fingers, working me into so many sensations.

"Thank you," I let out my breath, watching him kneel before me to get closer. His tongue works my clit, his fingers applying pressure to my opening. My body forms around his hand as he moves in and out, in and out.

After I get home, I'm overwhelmed by the past. Nana's birthday dinner plays on repeat, haunting me each night. I wake up in a cold sweat.

Dipshit's voice screams in my head telling me I'm not good enough to love.

I was afraid of this. As much as we've loved our time together, I don't know if I can stay.

The last several days I've kept to myself. I need some space to sort out my feelings. I know I love Zac. I've admitted that.

I'm only happy when he's around. Like my entire existence is on pause until we're together again. And I don't like that. I don't like depending on him to make me feel. . . like me. He's messaged me here and there, and I've sent back short replies, but I've kinda shut down emotionally.

Baseball season is crazy busy. He's finally playing again. He doesn't need my drama and I don't need him to carry my burdens.

This goes against all the independence I've worked so hard to get. I have my own place, run my own business, make my own schedule. I like it that way.

I had enough of that control crap with Dipshit, and I promised myself I'd never let someone take over my life like that again. It's suffocating. Yet, I feel like I can't breathe when I think of not being with Zac. The "With or Without You" song by U2 echoes in my head as I consider what's been rolling through my mind.

"Something's not quite right, is it?" Lexie asks and I realize how long I've been silent on our shopping trip. We've been hanging out since she came to Willardson to chat with her dad.

She gathers up the swimsuits.

"Lex, I'm not good at this."

"You mean, actually being in a relationship?"

"Yeah." I sigh. "Zac's great. It's not him. It's me."

"What would help?" Lexie zips up her jeans as I organize the empty hangers in the changing room.

"I wish I knew." I take the swimsuits from Lexie, and we head to the checkout. Sure enough, Zac texted me several cute little notes between practice and his summer classes.

What used to feel right, just keeps feeling wrong. There's all these signs he's a good guy. All these signs we're good together. But I can't bring myself to need him.

It feels like I'm losing myself if I give in. I worked too hard to find myself to give that up now.

"You're gonna figure it out. You always do." Lexie offers me an encouraging smile as we wait in the checkout line.

"And you and Bobby?" I ask.

"Things are looking up for us."

I want to take it as a good sign. But either my meter is off, or the universe is trying to tell me something. Because as much as I'm happy for my best friend, I can't shake this anguish in the pit of my stomach telling me my life's not on the right course.

Back at my apartment, there's a text on my phone.

Zac: You trying to ignore me or just busy?

I pick up the phone and call him.

"I'm sorry baby. I know I'm being distant right now." I sigh into the phone.

"That's okay. I just wanna know where you're at." He says.

"I'm looking forward to seeing you this weekend." I look at my planner. It's our last get together we have scheduled.

"Me too."

"I'll see you then. Bye." I click off the phone and stare at my ceiling. If I can't get my shit together, I don't know what I'm going to do.

June

Zac

We're about to go to regionals. This is my only weekend home before it gets crazy, so Trish cleared her schedule to come. She's been really emotionally distant. I'm trying not to feel shutout, but it's hard.

It's a really nice day. Love being outside with my arm around my girl. The relaxation I've been needing. We're sitting on our favorite park bench near the ducks. They've gobbled up half a bag of frozen corn from the dollar store right off campus.

"I have to tell you somethin'." Trish spits her gum into a tissue and pops in a fresh piece.

"Yeah?" If she's already chewing fresh gum, this can't be good. Everything that was chill about this moment turns upside down. My chest starts aching, and I rub at my pecs, wishing I could make it go away.

Fuck, I wish I wasn't dealing with this. I've been keeping my bucket full, like Doc Rogers says to do. Been keeping up with the trifecta. Sleeping, eating, taking my meds.

Zac, it's okay. We don't know what this is about; could be nothing.

"I've had the best time with you." She licks her lips, and I can smell the Juicy Fruit flavor.

"But?" I ask. Most of the time, I'm here for anything she wants to talk about. But I get the feeling she's gonna try to break up with me. Again. Are we always gonna do this?

"But." She sits on the bench while the ducks huddle close to us for the corn. "But I don't think I can do this." She tosses some corn out and there's an instant flurry of feathers at her feet. A bunch of baby ducks following their mama waddle up from the bank. It's adorable. This is one of those moments I expect Trish to take out her camera and lose track of time taking pictures. But she's not thinking about photographs.

"Are you trying to break up with me, again?" I look into her eyes, remembering the last time she was talking this way. It's the rollercoaster ride I knew I was signing up for. And I told myself I could handle it. But all the up and down has me motion sick.

I dig my elbows into my knees. My chin rests hard against my palms while the ducks peck at my feet, yapping for more corn.

Something feels different.

"But," she sighs, "I need to be independent. Since Daddy died, I've had to do everything on my own. As nice as it is to be with you, I can't. I'm not a person who can need someone. You deserve to be needed, Zac."

I swallow back some of the annoyance building. Most of the time I'm fine with her push and pull. Most of the time I want to do whatever she wants. Most of the time it makes sense.

But here? She's wrong about this. We belong together. I keep trying to be patient. Give her the time she needs to see it too. But I don't wanna be patient. I want her to get it. Want her to be so caught up in the miracle of us that she can't let those thoughts scare her anymore.

"You and I both know that there are so many strings attached to us right now that we could be a yarn store." I find her eyes, putting my arm around her on the bench.

"Cute." She focuses on the ducks like she wants to take a picture of them.

See, I knew this was a perfect Trish photo op. I wish that's all she wanted. To stay with me and take photos.

But I feel the distance. All those walls she rebuilds seconds after I've torn them down. The walls I keep hoping I can permanently tear down.

I don't know how anymore. Hell, I don't even know if there is a *how*. What if this is all there is? She and I and the walls between us stretching higher than the Empire State Building.

Do I really wanna be here? Fighting this hard? All the time?

I know the answer before the questions fully form.

Yes.

"I can't keep stringing you along. We need some scissors to cut the strings." She leans her head against my shoulder, tossing the corn near the ducks.

"Is this what you really want?"

"Maybe. I don't know." She moves her head from my shoulder to my lap.

What happens here? Do I indulge her need to break up? Sometimes I wonder if she needs us to go down this path just to see if it's the right one or not.

My hand runs through her hair, the smooth feel of her scalp under my fingers.

"Mmmm," she hums.

"I'll do whatever you need. A break? Let's do that." I lean enough to kiss her head, feeling that stretch in every vertebrae as I reach for her. "I really love you, Trish." I watch her eyes close, hoping my words reach her. Hoping she knows this is what I want: her happiness. Even if it costs mine.

The wounds she's healing may need a break. I understand how hard it is to juggle all these emotions. So I'll do what she needs. Give her the time and space.

"I'll still be here. When you're ready." I bring my face close to hers, resisting kissing her.

"I don't know if I'll ever be ready." She whispers against my lips, melting into the kiss that could be our last. I focus on every sensation, memorizing the slight nuances that make these kisses so different.

When she pulls back and rests against me, the words she said fully sink in.

I appreciate her honestly more than she knows.

Thank you, Lord, for giving me patience. Thank you for giving me the chance to love this angel, even for a little while.

Before long, her breathing slows. She's taking a nap on my shoulder, on this park bench. It's so fucking sweet to just hold her. I know how tired she must be to fall asleep in the middle of the day with that hot as hell South Carolina Sun burning into our flesh. She's barely been texting me this week. Summer is a crazy time for her. And with this on her mind, I bet she hasn't slept in days.

I'm calm with her. My demons are gone. Even though she needs some time for herself, I'm at peace. She's brought a peace into my life I didn't know existed. Now that I know it's there, maybe I can hold on to it.

How can she be breaking things off, yet I'm feeling okay? Everything about this is paradoxical. I have that much faith in us. She believes in signs. There are so many signs for us. It may not be perfect timing, but I hope one day it will be. That tiny fragment of hope keeps me going. It's enough.

While still respecting her wishes, I'm going to help her as much as I can.

"How long did I sleep?" She lifts up from my shoulder, and I miss the feel of her body on mine. It's instant, the moment there's space between us.

I look at my watch. "About an hour."

"Oh, Jesus. Sorry, Zac." She smoothes out my shirt and messes with her hair.

"How about you come back to my place, rest a while?" I hold her eyes, watching to see how she takes it. "If you're this tired, I don't think you should be driving."

"I can't do that. I just broke up with you. Don't you feel like I'm using you if I come over?" She rubs at her temples.

"I'd rather you be able to drive safely, even if we're not together. I still care about your safety. You're not feeling good, are you?"

"I've got a bad headache."

"Come on, we'll figure something out." I reach for her hand, and we walk to my truck.

"Did your arm fall asleep while I was laying on you?" She twirls her hair, trying to get that curl to fix after being squished.

"No, but my legs did from sitting still so long." I chuckle but it only hurts the pressure building on my chest. Am I just in denial? Am I too stressed from the end of baseball season? Am I so in love with her that it's not sinking in that she's trying to take our love away? I should be raging or crying or something.

"Sorry." Her cheeks turn pink.

"I'm glad you got some rest." I put my arm around her shoulder. "Even if you did break up with me." I pinch her arm.

"You butthead." She smacks my hand away. "I don't know why I'm so tired."

"Because you never stop working." I smirk, "...or maybe you're getting sick?"

"Fair enough." She goes to open her door, but I put my hand on hers.

"Uh, uh."

Her cheeks flush pinker.

"Even if I'm not your boyfriend right this second, I'm still gonna get your car door." I open up the door and give her a hand into the seat. It takes all my willpower not to go in and give her a kiss. It takes all my willpower not to fall apart, realizing I can't.

"I'll just sleep for a bit and then head home." Trish rubs at her eyes, a yawn coming out of her lips.

"Whatever you need." I take her purse from her and carry it.

Trish

We walk into his apartment, and I'm filled with that lovely scent of his that I can never get enough of. I told him I wanted to break up, and he's being sweet.

I'm just tired. This headache is awful, too. There's so much pressure I'm gonna blow up.

"I've got some bath salts. We can get your muscles warmed up before your nap." He sets my purse on the coffee table and heads down the hall to draw up a bath. "I'll make you some hot chocolate."

He had me at bath salts. I take a few steps toward him in the bathroom, just watching as he feels the water temperature to make sure it's warm.

Why is he taking care of me? To show me what I'll miss?

My head hurts so bad I can't think. Need to take a break from this stress. I'm sure it's not helping. Hell, it may be the reason I don't feel so good.

He's a perfect gentleman, waiting with the door shut while I undress and get settled under the bubbles. Epsom salt sticks to the bottom of the bath, coating me in the relaxing friction like sand on a beach.

Why can't I let myself have him?

Wish I deserved the love he gives.

A while after I've been soaking in his tub, he strums his fingers on the door.

"I won't look." He opens it just a crack and turns his head to the wall away from me while he sets down a mug of hot chocolate and some Milano cookies.

"Thank you." I say as he steps out of the bathroom.

What the fuck is happening right now? This is more TLC than I've had in a very long time. Talk about eleven kinds of selfcare.

I'm so confused.

When my skin is all pruny and my hot chocolate all in my belly, I grab Zac's towel and dry off. His scent fills my nose, and I miss the feel of his body against mine.

Achoo! I sneeze into the towel. But the sneeze turns into a cough. Before too long I'm hacking out a lung.

"You alright?" He's outside the door, I can tell by the way his voice sounds close.

"Yep." I rasp, clearing my throat from the coughing. The room spins. I'm suddenly lightheaded and dizzy. Must've gotten overheated in the bath.

Wearing only his towel, I stumble to his room.

"Here." He tosses me some clean boxers and a t-shirt.

"Thanks." I ditch the towel for his soft clothes.

I slip into his sheets, curling into a little ball. My body shivers, going too quick from overheated to chilled. Goosebumps cover my arms as I rub them.

"You can look. Hell, come help me get warm." I was half teasing, but he climbs beside me.

His hands rub out the knots in my shoulder and back, careful not to go too low.

I wish I knew what I wanted. He feels so good he's taking the pain away.

"Let me know if I get too close. I wanna give you the space you need." He warms my heart as much as my body. Before I know it, I'm fast asleep.

A while later, I open my eyes to his dark room. Zac's sound asleep beside me. It's so comfortable. So perfect.

Maybe I don't want to take a break from this?

Dipshit's face while he guzzled beer and insulted both me and Zac comes to my mind. That horrible birthday party proving I can never bring Zac home again. He didn't deserve that. As hard as it is, I'm doing Zac a favor. He'll get over me one day, even if I never hope to find love again.

I reach for my phone, but it's not on the nightstand. When I go to get up, I feel super weak. Jeez, something is going on with my body.

I find my purse on the coffee table and see that it's after midnight. Debating waking him up, I decide to leave. I'm too weak to fight him if he asks me to stay.

It's now or never.

There's still a key to his apartment on my key ring. I lock up on my way out the door.

Pulling a notebook out of my purse, I jot a little note and set it with the key under his mat.

Zac

"**T**rish?" I hop up, rubbing the sleep out of my eyes and search the apartment. No response. "Trish?" I call louder, wishing there was more of my place to search. She's not in the bedroom or the closet or the bathroom or the kitchen. Nowhere.

She's gone.

I flop onto my bed.

She fucking left?

Even when we were casual, she never left before I woke up. We always grab a bite to eat and then have a lengthy goodbye.

But leaving?

That isn't what we do.

When I brought her breakfast for the first time, I told her all those guys who skipped out on her without even saying goodbye were rude. Not just rude. Assholes. Now she's done the same thing. My stomach twists into a knot so tight I don't think I'll ever eat breakfast again, or any other meal.

After all we've been through. After how well I handled her breaking things off. After all the love we've made.

She did this.

I open up my phone and there's no text or anything. I type out a quick message.

Me: You left?

A long time passes and nothing appears on the screen. Maybe she hasn't read it yet? Or she's ignoring me.

I can't fucking move. Hours go by while I do nothing but wallow in bed.

How could she do this?

As much as I felt at peace yesterday, I feel nothing but a boulder on my chest weighing me down. I'm pinned to this mattress.

I don't wanna leave the last place we were together.

I don't understand her. But I don't have to understand her to love her, right? Isn't our love enough?

I yank a bunch of my hair, wishing I was more confident.

I've never fallen asleep with her and woken without her.

Until now.

It's fucking slap in the face.

I cover my face with the pillow, sunlight burning my tired eyelids. Maybe she'll come through the door with bagels and coffee? I look at the clock. No, it's been too long. I've been awake for two hours. No coffee line is that long. She didn't leave for a surprise. She left to get away from me.

My fingers find her number and call.

"Hey," she sneezes and then starts coughing.

My fingers go limp from the shock of her answering and I nearly drop the phone. "You left."

"Yeah."

"Why didn't you tell me you were leaving?"

The only answer is her coughing.

"You sick?" Every bit of anger I've been feeling melts away, concern taking its place.

"Probably." She sounds awful.

"Then why'd you go and leave? Let me take care of you, ba–" Baby is on the tip of my tongue, but I stop myself. No. None of that. She wants space bad enough she fucking left in the middle of the night.

"I'm fine." Her throat wheezes like it's scratchy while she's trying to talk. "I left a note under the mat."

"Note?"

"Yeah, go check."

I start walking to the front door. "For the record, you don't sound fine."

"I think I'm just gonna sleep." She clicks the phone without a goodbye. I need to drive to her place and bring her some soup. No. She doesn't want that.

She doesn't want me.

Valerie didn't want you, either. Anxiety taunts.

This is different. What Trish and I have is different.

All Anxiety does is kick me when I'm down.

Rubbing my sternum brings no relief. The demons that shut up when she's here get loud.

I knew I couldn't rely on her to keep them at bay. Knew it wasn't healthy. But it felt so amazing just to get a taste of relief.

The pressure gets bigger, and I try to stretch my arms, do anything to get some relief.

It's just anxiety, Zac. Sometimes reminding my worried mind can calm it down. Not today.

I get her note from under the mat. It's attached to my apartment key.

My eyes water as I read the words: *Sorry, Zac. In another life, I coulda been yours.*

It takes all my willpower to stay in Suncastle. Hell, she's probably working today, when she feels shitty. I need to go over there.

No, I don't.

I've texted back and forth with her a bit, responding whenever she says something so I know I'm not waking her up. But as the weekend goes on, the span between texts gets longer and longer. I worry.

But she's probably fine. Just like Doc Rogers tells me—unless I've got a real reason to believe something is wrong, it's anxiety.

But that level of anxiety riddles my system like a bad drug. I'm shaky all over while I try to focus on my workout. When I get home from the gym my chest hurts.

Heart attack.

No, not now. Please, not now.

Everything feels scary. I sit on the floor, hugging my knees, rocking back and forth, begging the panic to subside.

I'm in a dense haze where it's hard to see straight.

Fuck, I can't take this anymore. I stumble to my backpack, to the bottle of pills I keep in there, praying they can take the edge off.

Please, Father in Heaven, just take the pain away. Just take the edge off.

Wish it was a matter of faith. I have enough of that to be healed. This is a matter of health and not a matter of faith.

I pull my phone out of my pocket and dial Sadie while I force the emergency medicine down my throat.

"Trish left me." I manage to get out. "Wants a break. I can't handle it." I hate that I'm begging for help, but so thankful I have Sadie to call.

"Hey, it's gonna be okay," Sadie says.

"What if it's not?"

"Zac?" Sadie's talking loud, and I'm sure I just zoned out, hard. "Put on a movie."

On autopilot, I listen to her and go inside my apartment. Turn on the TV. Play whatever's still in the DVD player.

"Get a drink of water." She says.

I go to the fridge, her instructions a lifeline between me and the spiraling abyss.

"Focus on the movie. What is it?"

"Encino Man."

"Oh, that's a good one." She stays on the line talking to me, working with the movie to distract me. "There ya go. Feeling better yet?"

"Yeah," I choke out. "Thanks."

"Always."

"I'm sorry I call you in a crisis."

"Why are you sorry?"

"I wish it didn't happen at all."

"You don't choose this, Zac." Her tone is kind, and I know she gets it.

"You can always call me, too."

"I know." I hear her moving around in the background. "Hey, I gotta run, but tell me if you need help again. Always here."

"Thanks, Sades. Love you."

"Love you, too. Take it easy. Trish'll be okay. You guys will be okay. I bet she'll talk to you after she has some time to think." Her words bring a little bit of hope. I want to believe it'll all be alright.

Trish

Zac's with the Suncastle Baseball Team on the road to regionals and I've stopped texting him. That horrible cold I came down with has tapered off enough I'm back to working my normal hours.

My eyes wander to the closet where I've got the swimsuit Zac bought me our first weekend hanging out. Swallowing thick saliva burns my throat on the way down. That was such a great weekend. We had so many great weekends.

He's all I've ever wanted.

I sink into the carpet, hugging my knees to my chest. I need to feel his warmth. But I can't have it. I don't deserve it anymore, not when I keep hurting him.

I want to make it right.

So why did breaking up feel like what I needed?

Now, all it feels is wrong.

I torture myself by pulling up his videos. Thousands worship his every post. Dozens wear his number. Hundreds ask for his autograph.

But he chose me.

There was never anything to worry about. He didn't cheat.

He's so pure. And I'm so damaged.

I can't bear to tarnish him by the filth that is my broken soul.

An image I captured comes to mind. The man in a white suit and the woman covered in mud. It's always been one of my favorite collections, even though I've never truly understood it.

Rushing to my closet, I finger through the many plastic protected prints until I find the one that I'm thinking of. It's a whole set titled, Redemption."

In the first, it's only the woman sitting on the floor, covered in the forest of her agony. Her white dress is stained in mud.

The next is of a man wearing a white cloak, with a concerned expression. *Don't come near me*, her face seems to say. *Don't let my dirt stain your perfection.*

But I'm not perfect, he seems to reply.

In the next print, he removes the cloak of white to a red shredded suit.

I used to be covered in dirt, he says. *But now I'm wearing these scars. These scars bring power, once I heal them.*

The next print, he takes her hand and lifts her from the forest floor.

The final print, he clothes her in his cloak. *You can have this power if you heal* is the message. Redemption. Not only of the woman, but of the man.

Your worth has never been dependent on your scars.

Zac doesn't want me trapped in my pain. Dipshit did. Dammit, even Jimmy Hendricks did. They didn't care if I stayed in hell. They didn't want me to grow. They wanted me stuck.

I reach my fingers under my top to touch the scar tissue.

I cannot keep back the emotion I'm drowning in. I want to have Zac back. But I can't.

Not until I know how to be me.

The prints stand against my closet door. One after another. The man is changed to Zac, in my mind. The woman in the mud is me. I see us, in them.

I think of the times when he fell apart in my arms. The times I fell apart in his.

Broken together.

Maybe that's what love is. This isn't about perfection. It's about more.

It's about being flawed, and allowing the other person to be there with you in your damaged places.

Zac wanted to be.

I just wasn't ready.

My phone rings. I leap off the floor and run, that patter in my chest hoping it's him, not knowing why I can't be the one to call. Oh, God, I wish that I could change what I said. I shoulda thought about it more. I shouldn't have destroyed him this way.

The phone keeps ringing.

It's him.

I know it's him.

I sink into my mattress, wishing I could answer.

Maybe I'm the reason I'm stuck in hell.

One foot in front of another, I step into Nana's care center lobby for our lunch date.

It's hard to be here, for so many reasons. I love Nana. I've missed her. But knowing we're meeting Mama for lunch today when I haven't talked to her since Nana's birthday party is wearing on my last nerve.

I *want* to have a better relationship with the woman who birthed me, but ever since I opened up to Zac that morning after the party, I see how much she hurt me.

The last several weeks, I've brought Nana a latte to avoid Mama. But I know Nana really enjoys seeing both of us. She lives for these lunches.

I never told Nana anything. I guess I was protecting Mama. I didn't want to get her in trouble and I knew Nana would've been upset.

Nana didn't know what all was happening, or I'm sure she woulda stepped in. We always went shopping at the mall for my birthday and Christmas. That added up to eighteen. Eighteen days I got taken care of and shown any amount of love out of nine years.

Took years of Mama's neglect for anything to change. And then, it wasn't Mama that changed, it was me.

I walk into the sliding double doors of the care center. The teal walls and gray counter try to look inviting. It's an eyesore. I'd rearrange every bit of this place if I was in charge of the decor, like I did with Nana's room.

"Hey, is my Mama here yet?" My fingernails tap the countertop.

"Not yet." The lady at the desk says. "But you can go on back."

The beep lets me know the lock is ready for me to open the door. I walk to the end of the hallway, to Nana's room. If Mama didn't live with Dipshit, then Nana could stay with her. But instead, all that money she saved up her whole life is spent at an overpriced old folks home with horrible color choices and desperate need of better air freshener. I begged her to live with me, but she didn't wanna impose.

I knock on the door.

"Trishy, is that you?"

"Yes, Nana, it's me." I walk in, enjoying a minute just for us, I inhale her loving hug. She has a good old person smell, like love and wisdom mixed with her lotion. In contrast to the hallway, her room smells like vanilla. The candle I gave her flickers on the table out of the corner of my eye. Her room is proof that she's out of place in this care center. If she still felt comfortable living alone, she'd have kept her own place. But when she fell a few years ago, she decided it was time to live where someone could help quickly if she needed it again.

"I'm craving salad." I glance at the worn books on her shelves wondering if she wants me to get her a few new ones.

"Salad is always a winner." She sits on her bed and pats the spot next to her for me to sit. "Now come over here and get comfy while we wait for that mother of yours. Tell me how your day's been?"

I take a moment to relish how good it feels to be asked this. That little girl inside me only gets fed on the rare moments I come to visit Nana.

"It's going real good, Nana. I've got so much work that I'm not wantin' for anything." Mentioning work makes my to do list yell a little louder in my head. Always feels like I need to be working even when I'm not. Finding that work life balance is a forever struggle.

Zac understood that so well. He was never rude about me needing to put work first, even though Dipshit holds that against me.

"And now you got a nice beau to share it with." She winks. "When's the wedding? You know I've still got that dress I wore back in the day. We can get it altered like you always talked about when you were a little girl. I could get it ready for you–"

"Oh Nana, Zac and I broke up. Would you quit planning my weddin' already?"

"You broke up?" She gasps.

"Yeah." That ache in my heart gets bigger.

"But he was so lovely, Trishy."

"I know he was."

"Didn't you love him?" She asks.

"So much." I swallow a lump in my throat.

"Well at my birthday party he told the whole family off and I just thought, damn that boy is the one!"

"Nana?" I chuckle thinking I haven't heard her swear before. "Wait. When did he tell the family off?"

"Oh, you were already gone. But he waltzed right to that table and he picked up one of Russell's beer bottles and used it to get everyone's attention. Was a beautiful speech, really. He told the family they didn't know how wonderful you were and they didn't even deserve to know you. I got a little teary eyed watching it. Russell has always been rude and Zac, well he put him in his place. After he left everyone was quiet for a long while."

"He didn't?" I rub my temples, wondering why he never told me. Must've been when he went back for my purse.

"I wouldn't make this up, sugar." She pats my knee.

My mind goes to Zac and wondering what it would be like to have that wedding Nana keeps trying to plan for me. The idea brings a smile to my face.

He'd be so sweet to share a lifetime with.

Maybe we could try again?

A shiver runs down my spine. Why has his impact on my life burrowed so deep within me? Why do I feel so drawn to him? It wasn't until Jimmy and I had been sweethearts for more than a year that I even *thought* about bringing him to meet the family. Nana is special. I haven't brought any flavor-of-the-weeks to the care center.

But Zac is so much more than that. He wants to be mine.

Don't count your chickens before they hatch. Hell, there's not even any eggs. Quit counting non-existent eggs that will never be chickens.

"Hey," Mama slips open the door and comes inside. That burning in my throat gets real hot. I've put a lot of distance between us, not able to make a lick of sense out of the feelings Zac got me to admit out loud.

But then the guilt hits. She looks tired. Not well. Not like herself. Almost like she's not gonna live much longer if she doesn't take care of herself. I swear she's aged a decade since that party.

"Trishy Lou wants a salad." Nana grabs her keys. She doesn't seem to notice how bad Mama looks. "I'll drive."

"No, you won't." Mama takes the keys from her hand and they start bickering like old times.

After Nana convinces Mama she's driving no matter what, we pile in her car and head across town. I follow them inside our favorite salad place.

We follow the waitress to our table. I spot Bobby's mom and some lady at the corner booth.

"Oh hey, Trish." Bobby's mom says as we walk past their table. "How've you been honey?"

"Never better." I smile.

"Well, hello," she tells Mama. "This is my girlfriend Nira. I told her she had to have the best salad in town."

"This is the right place to be, then." Mama smiles at Bobby's mom and Nira and then heads toward our table mumbling under her breath. "I cannot believe she'd bring her lesbian lover out in public, acting like it's a freaking pride parade. What's she even doing? It's embarrassing." Mama's eyes of scorn trail back to the table with Bobby's mom and her girlfriend.

"Why do you care? At least she has love in her life. That's more than I can say about you." I'm furious at Mama's blatant homophobia. Would she say this if I did end up with Zac and Sadie brought a date to our wedding? There's a knot in my chest at the thought.

Could he forgive me for walking out on him?

Mama points a finger at me. "I oughta grab a bar of soap from the bathroom and wash that tongue of yours off, Patricia Louise."

Me and my big mouth. If only she knew how much more I needed to say.

Just you wait, Mama...by the end of this luncheon we'll need more than soap to put the Humpty Dumpty that is our dysfunctional family back together again.

Resolve builds in my soul. I've had enough of pretending all is well when it's not. Mama's gonna have to apologize and if it doesn't happen at this lunch, I'm not sure I'll ever want to give her another chance.

Our salads make it to the table in record time. Mama and Nana start chatting, that's more bickering than communicating, while I enjoy my sugared walnut and strawberry spinach salad.

As much as I want to confront Mama, the longer I sit here, the less I wanna go through with it.

Irony washes over me. It's always me and my big mouth. I say things I shouldn't, and I've been so conscious of it. It's what I've been told about myself. But me and my big mouth have yet to stand up to Mama.

It's time. Past time. There's no room in my life for this negativity and pent up hurt feelings.

"Mama," I clear my throat, eyes darting to Nana and back. "It's not okay what you did. It's never been right that you let him treat me or you this way."

"Whatever are you talking about?" Mama's playing dumb like the many times she has before.

I glance at Bobby's mom and her girlfriend, and it's like they give me silent strength to be who I am. Everything about the two of them sitting on that bench is the epitome of going against the grain of our southern small town. If they can, I can.

Enough is enough.

"This." I stand from the chair, the bottoms of the legs screeching on the tile floor. Time to show my scars.

I rip up my shirt so it's high off my back. "I'm talking about when your husband Russell did this to me and you did *nothing*," I run my hand along the raised skin in the shape of a target, then tap each of the old cigarette burns.

Every eye in this salad place turns to watch the scene.

I force a breath into my lungs to keep from passing out as my whole body tingles with adrenaline. I did it. Finally.

So many feelings wash over me that it's hard to pin them down.

Vulnerable. Naked. Alive. Seen.

Free.

There's no shame in who I am and what I've been through.

Slowly, I lower my shirt. "You can pretend all you want that it didn't happen, Mama. But I have the scars to prove it." I soak in the look of horror and shock playing on her face. Public humiliation may be the most hurtful thing I could've done.

But I need her to see. I need it to be in a place where any excuse she tries to make will be paper thin. And there's too many witnesses for her to pretend it never happened.

"For years your husband abused me. When I brought Zac home, your husband still verbally abused me and was rough with you in front of us. But I don't have to put up with it anymore. I'm never going back to that place." A knot builds in my throat. "Zac was good to me, Mama. He treated me like an angel. A goddess. So did Harvey. They were good men. You coulda been with someone like that. But you chose to put us both through hell and pretended it was heaven." I let out a long shaky breath. "It's time for you to open your eyes and see the harm that's come from years of silence and inaction. Russell's not gonna get better. He's already stolen so many years from us both. Can't you see that?" A hand comes over my fingers, and I have to look down to see who it belongs to. Nana's fingers clasp mine. Her soft vanilla smelling hands. When I look up at her face, there's tears running down her cheeks.

Mama's vacant eyes are fixated on the salt shaker. She doesn't move.

"When you're ready to apologize for years of damage, let me know." I say.

We sit in awkward silence for a while before anyone picks at the salads.

Bobby's mom and Nira come to the table.

"Love you, sweetheart." Bobby's mom leans down and gives me a hug. "Nira, Trish is one of Bobby's best friends. I told you about how their group all got together so much. Well, now Trish has her own photography business. In fact," Bobby's mom turns to me, "I'd love to schedule you soon." She pulls out her business card. "Can you send me a text?"

"Absolutely. I'd love to." I smile, thankful for this break from the intense lunch.

"Strong work." Nira gives me a knuckle bump. "You show those scars, baby. No one deserves that. We'll never shame you for where you come from. Only love you for where you are and where you're going."

"I'm proud of you, sweetie." Bobby's mom gives me another hug.

"Good to see ya." I wave as they head out.

"Let's go, honey." Nana puts her purse on her shoulder.

"Of course." I set a tip on the table.

We walk to the car, Mama alone in the backseat while I ride shotgun. We drive in an eerie quiet until I get to the parking lot of the care center.

Mama gets out of the car and closes the door gently.

"Trishy?" Nana reaches for me so I don't get out of the car.

"Yes, Ma'am?" I turn to her.

"I didn't know." She puts both hands on mine. "I'm so sorry I didn't know. Russell was always rude but I had no idea he was abusive. We coulda got you out of that house." She tugs on my arms until I'm hugging her over the console.

"It's not your fault. I never told you."

"I woulda loved to have you at my house. I wish I could turn back the clock."

Nana's words are like the damn breaking inside of me. I had to build that damn to keep me safe from Dipshit. But this wall can come down.

I was wanted.

My soul absorbs the words, telling me love can exist.

I can be with Zac, who loves and cares about me. It's like something snaps into place. I didn't ever need to break up with him. Didn't ever need to push him away. I'm so sad about what I've done.

Nana always woulda been there if she woulda been aware. Zac was still there after I showed him my scars.

The child inside me feels like she's coming home. She can be herself again. It's what she's always wanted.

To be loved.

Water rushes to my eyes. My tear ducts actually fill. Instead of burning with dry sobs, I'm all wet. Tears come out of my eyes.

Real tears.

The ones I've been waiting for. The ones I've been wanting. The ones that have been stuck for so long. They run down my face and onto Nana's shoulder. When I pull back, she's crying too.

"I just wish Mama would get it." I grab tissues out of my purse for Nana and me.

"I think she will. Give her some time." Nana's smile is kind, and I dare to hope for a minute.

"Even if she never does, I feel better for saying what I needed to."

"I'm glad you told me. And I'm glad Zac's good to you. Maybe the two of you can work things out. All wedding teasing aside, I'm glad you're not following in your Mama's footsteps." Nana's scowl makes me laugh.

"I call that lovely stepdad of mine, Dipshit."

Nana chuckles. "It's a fitting name." She grabs the door handle and pushes, letting the smell of fresh air enter the car. "Thank you for a lovely lunch."

"Sorry if I ruined it."

"Nonsense. You needed to do that. Even if it caused a scene. Probably the only way that stubborn mother of yours would listen. Maybe now she'll think about it. I hope so. And if not, well, you always have me."

"I do." I smile as I hop out to help her into the care center. "That's part of why I stick around here in Willardson. To see you."

Nana stops midway to her room. "You don't want to live here?" She gives me a pointed look.

"No, I mean, I've always wanted to move back to Kentucky or at least go somewhere new."

"Then do it, sugar." Nana takes both of my hands in hers. "I've lived my life. I've loved every moment I've spent with you. But please don't stay here for me. You've got to spread your wings and fly to wherever life takes you." Until the words leave her mouth, I didn't know how much I needed them.

"Thanks, Nana."

Zac

We got into the College World Series and I'm hanging out on the Suncastle practice fields, anxiously awaiting our trip to Omaha. This season has been amazing. The fact we did so well at regionals and super regionals is still surreal. It's a dream come true.

I'm laying on the field, stretching and flexing my knees. I'm so glad I didn't have that knee surgery. It barely bothers me at all *and* I can play with my best friends while we win the college baseball lottery.

This should be the happiest time of my life. I've worked my ass off for this kind of a season since I first picked up a bat in little league.

Yet, here I am, so distracted by a broken heart I can't actually enjoy it to the full degree. I need some kind of resolution.

"Do I give her space? Do I go after her? Do I give her space? Do I go after her? Do I give her space? Do I go after her?" It feels like those *she loves me, she loves me not*, verses people say while they pick apart flower petals. I don't have any flowers, I'm just throwing my baseball up and down in the air.

"You go after her." Briar startles me.

"Fuck, man. Thought I was alone." I hold the ball tight in my hand and jump to my feet. "What the hell are you doin' here?" My chest hurts from pounding so hard. Didn't even hear his cleats approaching.

"I hadn't heard this was a closed practice." He takes the ball from my hands, pacing back a ways to start a game of catch. "And, you probably need to go after her."

"You think?" I toss the ball his way, landing it in his glove.

"Can't say I've ever seen you this cozy with somebody before." He tosses it back.

"She broke up with me, though." I stretch my neck, and send back the ball.

"What is with all the players of this team gettin' broken up with?" Briar shakes his head.

"Says you. Who, last time I checked, hasn't ever been in a relationship."

Briar chews on his nail. "That's what I want you to think."

"Oh, I see."

"Yeah, it's just like Frank William Abignale from 'Catch Me If You Can.' I give you the information I want you to have and you create the picture you wanna see."

"You and your movie references."

"Well, they do come in handy while I'm on the many dates I go on that are none of your goddamn business, thank you very much."

"Touché"

"So Trish broke up with you. Have you slept with anyone else?"

I swallow and cough, nearly choking on the personal question.

"Didn't think so." He throws. "Have you thought about it? Anyone in your sights?"

I shake my head. Never even considered it.

"That's how you know."

"It's how I know, huh?"

"If you're ready to move on, then it probably wasn't it. But if you haven't gone cock divin' since your pretty little miss done broke your heart, then you ain't gonna get over her anytime soon. That's the real shit, right there."

"What movie did you get that one from?" I toss the ball, catching the way he said *little miss*. God, I miss her.

"That one's no movie. It's just all my wisdom." He gives me a smug smile.

"Wisdom? Hm. Well, it ain't half bad, I guess." No other girl has even tempted me. Trish is the only one I want. Has been since the night we danced at Garrison's.

"I'm goin' to the caf'." I toss back the ball, and grab my bag.

Briar runs to catch up with me. "I'll join you."

"You gonna ask some dude to take off his shirt again?" I ask.

"If I want it."

I shake my head.

"I'm right about your girl, though. You watch. I'm a movie expert, particularly in the category of romance. And this thing you and her had going, I don't think that was just some fling. So, you either figure out how to get her back, or she's gonna be the one that got away."

I dare to hope he's right.

"Good practice today." Coach Conners pats Briar's shoulders as he walks past.

Bench Coach Blakeslee raises his voice to get our attention. "Alright, men. You've got four hours. Get some rest. Get some food. We want you back here for warmups by 5pm." He claps his hands, dismissing us.

I gather my gear and head toward the parking lot. Doing a double take, I realize Sadie is standing right outside the field exit.

"Sades." I wrap my arms around her in a big long hug.

"Pa let me take the car. Figure I can stay with you until I get a place of my own?"

She looks good. Really good. Almost like her old self again. *Thank you, Father in Heaven, for helping her so much.*

"Of course you can. I'm glad you came." I deposited all the donations from Sprinkle to her personal bank account after the payments went through. She's all set to have what she needs for college, with or without the volleyball scholarship she's hoping for.

"You mad I didn't tell you I was comin'?" She looks at the ground.

"Nah, I'm just glad you're here." I pull her in for another big hug. "The offer didn't expire. I'll be in Omaha next week for the College World Series, so you'll have the place to yourself for a bit. Make yourself at home. Oh, and I need you to feed the fish."

"You have a fish?"

"No, but let's go get one."

"Or I'll just go with you to Omaha." She suggests.

My heart warms at the thought. "I'd love that."

"Maybe we can convince Ma and Pa to come." Sadie offers.

"They wouldn't miss work."

"Zac, this is a huge deal. I'm sure they wanna be there."

"I don't know." I let out a deep sigh.

"They've changed a lot." Sadie gives me a sad smile that reflects all of our shared hurt from our childhood. "Even parents are forced to grow up sometimes. I mean, I guess they needed to with all the drama I've caused."

"Hey, now, it's not like that." I find her eyes. "What happened to you isn't your fault. Please stop thinking it is." I wait until she softens her expression. "There's healing and I'm here for you every step of the way."

"You always have been." Her eyes get a little wet and I bring her in for another hug.

"Now, let's go get that fish."

I open the door and wave my hand dramatically. "Welcome home, sis."

She glances around the apartment. I set our bag of takeout on the counter.

"Where's Trish? I need to show her the photos I took. She was right about the camera angles. It helped so much for my school project."

A sour feeling spreads through my stomach. Sadie's face lit up while she was talking about the camera stuff.

"We aren't together." I swallow hard. "Remember, I told you that." The horrible anxiety attack rushes to mind when I called Sadie like a lifeline.

"What?" Sadie's face drops.

"Yes, I told you." I sigh.

"Yeah, but that was like two weeks ago. I was sure you'd have fixed things by now. She doesn't seem like the type to really let you go. I mean you guys were basically the perfect couple. What happened?"

"I'm not sure." I try to make sense of things, to put my confusion into words, but I can't. I don't know what her final straw was. I thought all the little signs pointing to us were enough.

What changed?

I put the food out on the table and Sadie comes over to eat with me.

"You looked good out there. I watched all the games from regionals." She pokes her fork into her cobb salad.

"You look good right now. Like way better than a few months ago." I let the words sit here. "I'm so fucking glad you're here."

I feel like I have to keep telling her. But I don't wanna make her uncomfortable either. It's a funny thing, not knowing what to say. So much has changed since I lived at home.

"You need to forgive yourself, Zac."

"What?"

"You keep saying it wasn't my fault. But really, it wasn't your fault I–" she doesn't finish the sentence, but she doesn't have to.

"I'll keep on saying it. What happened wasn't your fault."

"Sure it was." She sets the fork on a napkin like she hasn't got an appetite anymore. "I never should've trusted that bitch. And I shouldn't have stopped talking to you when I needed you most. Angela kept giving me red flags. I just ignored them."

"Was she ever good to you?" I take a drink of ice water.

"No. She wasn't." Sadie looks at the table. "Not for most of it, anyway. I wish I would've seen earlier."

"Sometimes we see in people what we wanna see instead of what's really there." I think about Trish. No, I saw her. Really saw her.

She couldn't see herself.

"You look like a lost puppy dog." Sadie chuckles, and it feels good to hear her laugh. "You miss Trish, I can see it in your eyes." Sadie takes a bite, and I'm glad to see her eating.

"I really, truly do." I swallow the lump in my throat wondering if I'll ever stop missing her.

"And back to the subject. It's not your fault. I shut you out. I fell into my own pile of shit. I'm just thankful you cared enough to help me get back up." Her eyes are wet as she looks at me.

"I love you, Sadie. You didn't deserve any of it. Angela and those girls at school beat you down. You were a victim."

"And thanks to you, and the lawyer you hired, justice is coming."

I swallow the glob of emotion in my throat. "I'm really glad to hear that."

Me: Hey, Trish. Can we talk?

I sent the message several hours ago. I haven't heard back. I keep checking my phone.

I reach over, grab my phone off my nightstand, and check again.

Nothing.

We've never gone this long between talking.

I call her and it goes to voicemail.

"Hey," I start to say *baby* but stop myself. Don't know what she's dealing with and definitely don't wanna make it worse. "Haven't heard from you in a while, just wondering how you're doing. Thought maybe we could get together? Maybe, I don't know, talk? K, bye."

I toss my phone onto the bed and sink into the mattress. It still smells like her. Or maybe that's my imagination.

I try to think if I've got any reason to worry about her. I don't. But at the same time, worries are spiraling all around and I'm in a web of anxiety.

What if she's physically hurt?

What if she never calls back?

We had such a beautiful run. I don't know how anything could be wrong enough to really shatter all the good. Maybe she's just busy.

Too busy for me? Yeah, right. That's never stopped her before. Anxiety is grasping at any reason for the silence, but none of them fit.

I've never felt so vulnerable and alone.

I light up my phone looking for a call or text. Nothing.

Again.

Again.

One more time.

Log into Sprinkle. Trish is online.

What the fuck? That means she's literally ignoring me.

Oh you did not. I clench my jaw, the betrayal cutting deep, and let out an exasperated sigh through my nose.

I text Ethan to go for a run. I need to get out of this apartment.

We run twice around the lake. With every step I try to get out this nervous energy. It's not working. "Another lap?"

"The fuck are you running from?" Ethan slurps water from his bottle.

I shake my head. "She won't call me back."

"What'd you do?"

"Nothin'."

"Is that the problem?" He nudges me in the shoulder.

"Not since she wanted space." I let out a low growl, so fucking upset Trish *still* hasn't texted or called back, yet she obviously has free time to browse Sprinkle.

"Six miles, Zac. That's all I'm good for. Let's go get cleaned up and hit Garrison's or something."

"I do *not* wanna go there." I think of the many times we spent the evening beneath those lights. I want her to come tonight. Missing her like crazy. Worried out of my mind.

Why is she doing this? It's bad enough she broke up with me. But I'd really like to talk about it. I deserve at least that, don't I? My heart won't give up until I find some closure.

Trish

I wish I could bring myself to call him back. But I can't. All I can do is mindlessly scroll social media that I couldn't care less about. It's numbing. Because I need to be numb.

Too much is going through my system to find a way out. I can't unravel the tangled mess.

Zac says he feels trapped in a web when anxiety hits. I'm there. Being cocooned by a spider. Can't get out. Too far gone. I have to do something more than eat away the hours online.

I dial Lexie.

"Hey girl," she answers.

"Hey," I sigh.

"What's wrong?"

"I can't talk to Zac," I admit.

"Why not? What happened?" She sounds so troubled at the news.

"It's just too much."

"Do you want to work it out with him?" Her question is the raw honesty I'm used to getting from her.

"Part of me does." A bigger part than I'm willing to admit out loud. I'm not sure I'll ever figure out the other parts.

It's been five weeks since I walked out on Zac. I saw the papers saying our boys won the College World Series. I didn't go. It feels so wrong. I could've at least been there for Bobby and Lexie. They've gotten back together and it feels funny Zac and I have switched places with them.

Nana gave me hope that day. I wanna tell Zac I can cry with tears. I'm waiting until I'm confident I can really stay with him. I don't want to return to his arms to leave again. To prevent that, I'm working through my shit.

I'm seeing a therapist. It helps.

Several sessions later, I find myself still talking about the same things.

"He's a good guy. You know, one of the good ones. I'm pretty sure he is. I just can't shake this feeling that something bad is gonna happen. Or that he's gonna take over my life somehow." I slurp the last sip of my iced vanilla latte sitting on the couch of my therapist's office.

"Has Zac done anything to make you feel this way?" She asks.

"No. That's the whole problem." I lean against the chair. "I don't think it's him. I really don't." I think about his soft skin against mine. The way he'd do everything I wanted even when he didn't have to. He made our long distance relationship work.

"Sometimes when you've experienced trauma, it becomes difficult to know what is reality and what is a trauma response." My therapist finds my eyes. "Search your heart when you're with him. If he treats you with love and respect, and doesn't do anything to harm you, then you may be having a trauma response."

"That's just it. I'm not talking to Zac right now." I set my empty latte cup on the coaster. "I only know how to be with people who treat me like shit."

"I don't think that's true. I think that you've been in many difficult situations and had to cope with them. But I also think you seek out positive relationships as much as you can." She looks at her notes. "Think about your friends from high school. You keep in touch with them, don't you?"

"Pretty sure Lexie and I will always be tight. The rest of our group has sorta fizzled out since Cody died."

"Cody? I don't think you've mentioned him." My therapist adjusts her big framed black glasses with lots of glittery diamond bling on the side so they're riding higher on her nose. I'd have to angle them down if I was taking a photo from this angle.

"Cody and I were tight." I feel an unexpected pain in my body as I talk about this. Why haven't I mentioned him in our earlier sessions? "He was such a good friend to all of us. And he got it. Ya know? Like he really got it. The shit people go through and how you can't stay in that shitty place. In a lot of ways he helped me see that I don't deserve it."

"He was there for you."

"Of course, he was. He was there for all of us. He's the only one I trusted with my scars, until Zac."

There's a pain in my heart that comes whenever I think about how good a friend Cody was. The pain gets bigger as I think about how I lost the ability to talk to Cody when he died. Zac's here and I still ruined everything.

"Maybe you should try talking with Zac." My therapist's eyes are hopeful, peering at me through those lenses. "Because you deserve to feel love in the way that you experience it."

"Thank you." I stand from the chair, knowing my fifty minute session is up.

I walk out to my car, lost in thought.

Could she be right?

Zac

When she still didn't call me back, it took a lot of sleepless nights to come up with something. I know I need her. I know she needs me. Whatever the fuck changed that needs to be reverted.

If I can show her how much she means to me, maybe it'll help. So of course, I came up with this grand plan that is probably entirely stupid.

Please, Father in Heaven. Let her see past whatever it is pulling us apart.

This could go horribly wrong. This could go horribly wrong. This. Could. Go. Horribly. Wrong.

Deep breaths, Zac. Deep breaths.

We're at a coffee shop in Harbrooke. The owner, Natalie, is a huge fan of my band, so I called in an unusual favor.

I scan the crowd. Sadie and Anna Mae are here with some other friends they met at Suncastle Orientation. Briar and Bobby and Lexie are at a table together. I keep looking at the door. Every second she's late tears me apart more than I'm ready for.

What if she doesn't come?

She will come. She thinks it's for work. She never misses anything for work.

Except that one time when she dropped everything to hop on a plane to Kentucky for Sadie. For me. My thoughts drift to the memories I want to relive. The way I felt when we were together. I've ached for her with every part of my being.

Fuck. We aren't done.

The band who opens for us finishes their third song. I eye the crowd, hands super sweaty as I shove them into my pockets for the tenth time. Am I just missing her? Is she behind somebody? I lean my head around the corner, catching Natalie with a confused expression. Trish isn't in the hallway. She's not at the tables lining the stage. She's not here. She didn't show.

"Welcome to the stage, Suncastle Armorists!" Natalie announces from the standing mic. Delilah gives me two thumbs up as she holds her phone out to record it from the front row–next to the empty chair that I asked her to save for Trish.

I want to throw up. Haven't had stage jitters like this in a long time.

We play our first set. I stop for a drink of water. I want to go talk to Natalie and make sure she told Trish the right night.

It's like my fingers don't remember how to play.

No, not now. My heart rate picks up like it always does when I'm not okay. I'm not okay. Oh, hell I am not okay.

Fuck, what am I gonna do if she doesn't show? My stomach cramps tighter as I get this euphoric otherworldly dissociation spell. It's like I'm floating. Like no matter how hard I focus my eyes, they won't see clearly.

What am I going to do?

Keep it together. I'm going to keep it together.

Every song gets closer to the end of the night.

We finish the concert. She doesn't show.

There's a lump in my throat the size of Texas. I smile. Keep smiling for the cameras. For the fans.

I'm not ready for this. I knew it may not work out. I knew it may go to shit. I knew she may not accept what I have to say.

But I thought I'd at least get to see her again.

The crowd goes wild for an encore. We play another song. They keep going wild. Ethan has Delilah filming the whole thing. I already have several ladies asking for a personal note after the show attached with a guitar pick.

The clapping revs up as I take the microphone.

"We wanna thank you all for–" I blink away the fog over my eyes that hasn't quite cleared. These damn misfiring neurons make every light in the joint feel blurry and put me in a haze.

I hold my breath and count to three. Too much adrenaline courses through me. Keep it together.

Karma, my bitch, did you forget all those good things I've done to deserve a free and clear moment now? All those good times we've had? Remember?

Trish

Fuck traffic. Fuck this rainstorm. Fuck almost hitting a goddamn deer. I need this gig. I've been wanting to branch out on my coffee shop vibes for a long time. I've got a collection going that I want to submit to be curated at the museum in Columbia.

I texted Natalie an apology and promised I would be there as soon as I could.

When I arrive, there is no parking. Of course. It's just one of those days.

As the rain falls on my shoulders, I remember the day Zac gave me his hoodie in the Shakey's parking lot. Wish I could melt into his arms right now. Fuck me and my stubborn heart.

After I get through this work thing, I'm calling him so we can meet up and talk this out.

I walk almost a block, pepper spray firmly in hand as I meander through cars and people out smoking on the sidewalk. This place is packed.

I pull out my camera and snap through the window. Natalie was supposed to get release forms signed for me to be able to use the prints with people in them. There's music playing from inside. It makes me miss Zac, something fierce. I hope he's doing well. I think about calling him, but I'm running late.

I clench my Kentucky kitty keychain as I gaze through the rain covered windows.

It's Zac's band. He's here, playing.

What the fuck?

As I walk through the door, I connect the dots enough to know I'm not here for a photoshoot. I'm not here for Natalie. I'm here because he wanted another chance.

The heart knows what it wants.

I can't speak, but I don't have to. The look in his eyes says he knows. That connection we've always shared gets stronger.

I'm forever his.

He's forever mine.

Nothing else matters anymore.

Maybe, it never really did.

Zac

Everyone is waiting quietly. So quietly I hear the ding of the bell as the door creeps open.

There she is.

My girl.

I breathe, as if it's the first breath I've ever taken. Our eyes meet as I bring a smile to my lips.

She gives me a look, and it's like we're telepathically communicating because I can tell she's thinking *you did this didn't you?* And I'm answering back, *of course I did, it was the only way I could see you.*

All at once, I realize I'm standing here silent with the microphone.

"It's not every night we get to play for the people we really care about. We haven't played much for our families. But sometimes, we get to." I look at Trish. "I want all of you to know I didn't think I was gonna get to play for her tonight. But my little miss," I pause for emphasis, that smirk on her face sending warmth through my entire body, "just walked through the doors."

The crowd erupts in applause.

"Trish, I met you a long time ago. And from our first night together, I was forever changed. The truth is—" I unhook the mic from the stand and walk with it–thank fuck it's cordless–toward my baby. "The truth is, I've loved you since

I first saw you. And since that night we spent together, I haven't been able to think about anyone else." I turn the mic away from me so it won't pick up this next bit. "Join me on stage?" I whisper.

"You're fuckin' crazy." She laughs. It sets fire to my being. My heart's surging.

The moment it takes her to make up her mind feels like an eternity.

She offers her hand to mine. We go up the steps, and I help her to my stool. Standing with my guitar, I start the song my band has been waiting for.

I reconnect the mic and clear my throat, relieved to feel the lump dissolving. I pluck out the first few notes to "Sometimes" by Britney Spears. Our song. Though the entire room is filled with people, my eyes are only for her.

Each lyric goes from my lips to her soul, I hope. By the end of the music, there are tears on her cheeks.

Actual, real tears. The happy kind.

She's here. She hasn't run. She's here.

Oh fuck, did this actually work?

My heart pounds in my chest.

"You comin'?" Harvey puts his hand on my shoulder. We finished the concert. He's packed up most of the stuff.

"Just a sec." I take Trish's hands in mine, taking her away from the chaos of the crowd. We sneak into the bathroom. It's still loud, but now I can hear her.

"You planned this." There's not a lick of a question in her tone.

"Had to do somethin'. Had to try." I clear my throat and lick my lips, dry from being on stage. My throat is all scratchy. "I had to see you again."

Trish looks amazing. Of course she does. Even with her rain drenched hair and slightly smudged makeup. I wanna ask her about us, but I'm afraid. I am ecstatic she showed up and came inside even when she saw it was me. The last thing I want is to drive her away. She needs to tell me on her own terms what she's thinking.

"How you been?" She looks into my eyes.

"Lost." I grind my teeth together wondering if this is too much too soon. But it's God's honest truth.

"Same." Her lip comes up in the corner, hinting at a rye smile.

Just being with her is everything. I don't care what we're doing. I don't care if she has to go later. This moment is perfect. Even in a bathroom reeking of cheap air freshener.

"You don't have to leave, do you?" She licks her lips, and I dare to hope that was an invitation in her words.

"I don't have to do anythin'." I step closer, coming from the sink to where she stands. My arms wrap around her. It feels like home and happiness and everything I've been dying without.

"Get your stuff and let's get in my car."

"Done." I clear my throat. Flying fish sticks, I need a cough drop to soothe me after singing for so long. My muscles are raw.

She smiles and just like that I dare to hope that we may just be getting back together. Or maybe that we never really were apart. Because this feels fucking right. I can't make sense of anything else. I don't care what the future holds. I don't care where we live. Or what we do.

All I care about is being with her and her feeling safe.

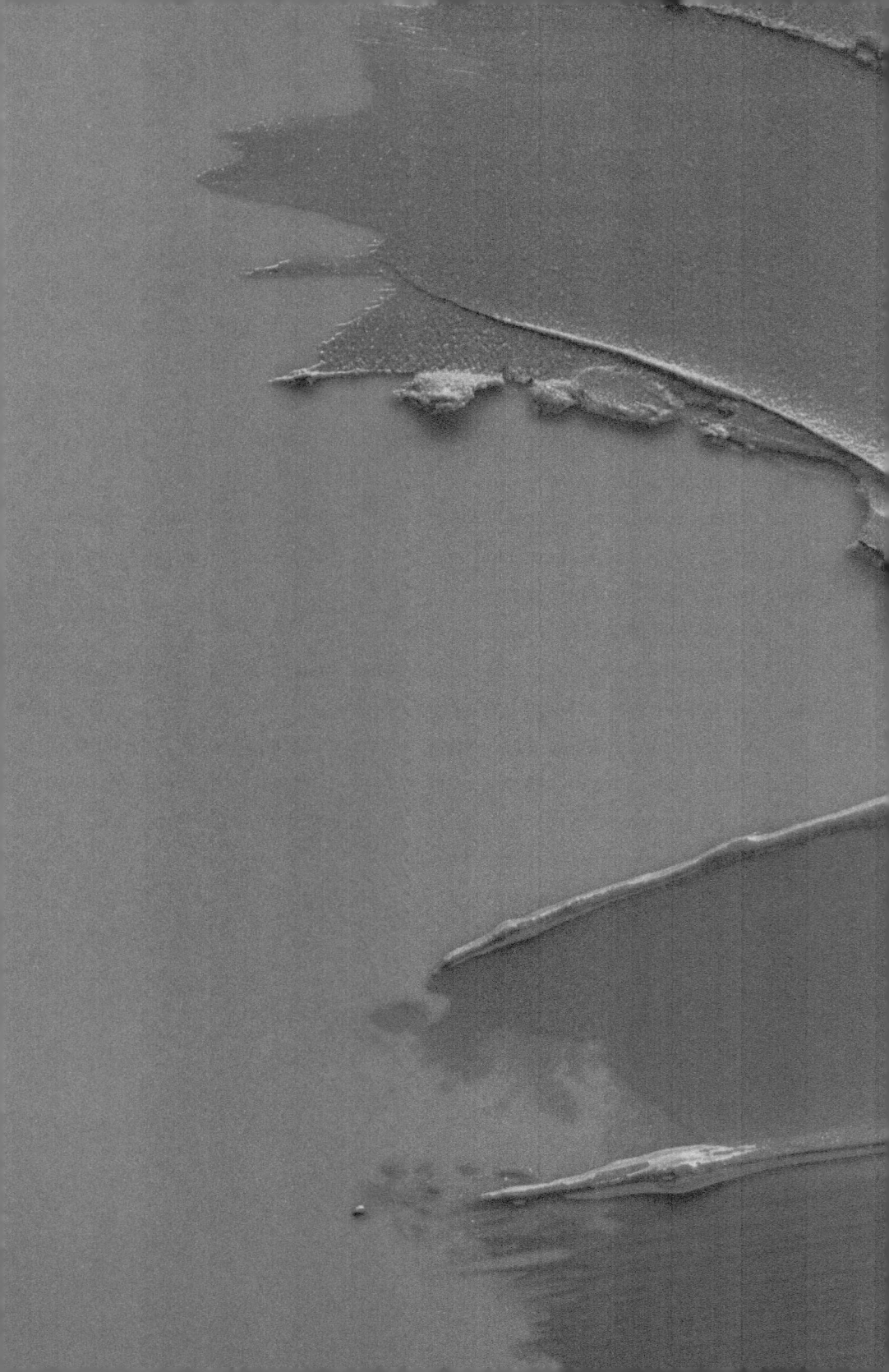

Trish

I don't know how this worked. After the concert, we got in my car and drove until we made it to a hotel in the northern part of South Carolina. It's a little bed and breakfast I stayed at once.

We unload his stuff into the corner of the room. I need to be close to him. I trace his body with my fingers like I'm outlining a god. Tight muscles clench as I move through the fabric of his shirt.

"Little miss," he purrs.

My lips meet his, all the caution I've felt evaporating. I'm better now. I want this. I coulda just gone home. Coulda told him that it was a nice gesture, but there was no way I could get back together with him.

But there is a way. And it's happening.

"If we do this, I don't ever wanna break up again."

"Done." He breathes against my ear, the heat flowing from my skin into my soul.

I lick my lips, watching the happiness in his eyes as he cautiously wraps his arms around my waist.

"And I want it to be whatever we need. Not just those societal norms for long term relationships. I want to keep my independence. Needing you scares the fuck out of me."

"I want you to be independent. And I want to help calm those fears about needing someone. Needing someone can be beautiful." He waits, letting me take the lead. Like he knows it's what I need. He always seems to know what I need

"I never stopped." I pop my lips.

"Hm?" He looks at me for a while, and I take a mental photograph to remember this moment. The way his deep eyes glimmer, giving me his full attention. The way his razor missed just a touch of scruff on his chin. The way his lips are chapped, and perfectly shaped.

"I never stopped wanting you." I take a step closer, taking my time to feel each inch of my body against his.

"I never stopped being yours." His raspy voice comes out sexy as fuck.

"We're doin' this, then?"

"Please?" There's so much longing in his tone. Like he can't handle what would happen if I didn't come to him. Like he can't live without this thing that we have.

"I'm sorry." I take a deep breath. "At some point between how amazing we were together and how much I couldn't handle being in a relationship, I got freaked out, and I put you through a lot of hell. It wasn't right of me. I'm sure it gave you so much anxiety. I'm sure it caused you so much pain." My eyes get wet and he holds me close. "Zac, I'm so, so sorry."

"I think I could've been better at giving you space. I'm sure it didn't help..."

"Zac, it's okay. Most of this was my shit coming up. You encouraged me to get some help. I've been seeing a therapist. And I think I need to move out of Willardson. Nana will be okay if I still come visit. But I can't be there anymore. Can you forgive me?" I look into his eyes and he shows me that vulnerability he's been encouraging me to embrace within myself.

"I'd be lying if I said it wasn't hell. These have been some of the worst days of my whole life." He bites his lip. "But yes, of course I can forgive you.

I love you Trish. Like I said before, your worth has never been dependent on your scars. I know you have things you're working through. I just wanna be here to help if you need that."

"I do. I'm learning I can need *you* and still be *me*."

"I'd be sad if you lost yourself needing me." He brings a sweet kiss to my forehead. "I've never wanted that. I fell in love with you, as you are."

His words enter my soul like the final thing I needed him to say in order for me to come back to this relationship.

"Thank you." I slowly edge toward his lips, hovering there until he closes the space between us. The kiss seals all the longing we both feel.

"You're here. I'm here. I don't care what the fuck it takes to keep it that way." He means it.

That part of me that has been resisting. The one that wasn't sure if I could really trust him melts away. I want to be his. He wants to be mine.

"I'm not perfect." I choke out.

"That's a fuckin' relief." He plays with his eyes.

"Sometimes," I smirk, "was a very nice touch, Willey. I've always loved our song."

"Sometimes, you need me to remind you we both want this." He chuckles.

"Sometimes, you're absolutely right."

"Wanna know what else I'm absolutely right about?" He leans closer.

"What?"

"You need to fuck the living shit outta me." He bites his bottom lip. "Little miss."

"You're sure about this?" I breathe against his neck.

"Would you quit askin' already?" He lifts me up and I yelp, my butt against his hands and my core against his six pack. "I am absolutely, completely, one hundred million, infinity times infinity, *sure* about this. Now are you gonna believe me so we can get on with this earth shaking release or what?" His words are so sexy that my body hums in orgasmic pleasure.

"Absolutely."

"That's what I thought." He puts me on the bed, gently. For what stretches on forever, he shows love to each part of me. My chest, my hips, my sexy places.

"Fuck, I missed the way you taste." His tongue flicks around, the cullulingus of a god happening in my body.

Two of his fingers enter my opening, rubbing them into sweet ecstasy.

"Oh, yep, right there."

"I know that," he teases. My heart heaves with complete happiness.

Tears come out of my eyes, taking me by surprise. "Zach, come here. Hold me."

He looks up, concern in his face. "You alright?"

"I'm better than alright."

I pull his body over mine, his hard cock slipping into the place where he belongs. "I'm just so glad you did this."

"I'm just glad you let me," he kisses the tears off my cheek, sweet thrusts taking me slow and deep. "You can cry with tears now?"

"Yeah, maybe I'm not broken anymore."

"You never were, baby."

"You've always seen me better than I see myself." I rock against him, that perfect rhythm we always seem to find. Naturally mine. Unforgettably exquisite.

"And I always will."

I blink in the sunshine coming from the windows. Must've slept in with how bright it is.

"Oh, hey baby. Didn't know you were up." He returns from his seat by the window, and gives me a good morning kiss. His voice is raw, like he's lost it from last night.

"You couldn't sleep?" I say through a yawn.

"Nah, I was just gettin' some coffee and room service. Didn't wanna wake you."

"You need some tea with honey and lemon, not coffee."

There's a knock on the door.

He coughs into his shoulder, gets up to answer it. "Looks like I have good timing." He opens the door to room service.

I sit beside him. "How'd you know?"

"Know what?"

"That I wanted to see you again."

"At the coffee shop?"

"Yeah."

"I guess I didn't." He looks into my eyes, brushing some of my hair out of the way. "I knew it may not work. I mean, talk about a risky play. I knew you could be mad or run away. I was worried I'd never see you again. But I knew losing you was worse than all that."

"I guess it's good we both won, then."

Trish

I'm still wondering if this is a dream. Still wondering if there's gonna be a moment that brings me back to reality. Because I swear this is all too good to be true.

He is what I want more than anything.

"I'm so glad you're here." He wraps his arms around me.

"I'm so glad you're mine." I bring my lips to his, needing that taste, that presence to fill me.

Things are better with Mama. I'm able to think about her as a flawed person and accept that. I don't have to see who I wish she was anymore. It wasn't helping me. I can see that though she's made mistakes, she is who she is. I don't have to let her into every part of my life, but I get to decide where she can be.

Nana was so happy when I told her Zac and I are back together. She's been the voice of support I need to get through the dark days.

I still have dark times. I wish that I didn't, but I do.

I'm always going to have the remnants of what Dipshit caused. It changed me on a cellular level.

That's what abuse does. It takes kids who are still developing and shifts what would've grown naturally healthy into a traumatic response.

I'm so glad I'll never have to save our kids from Zac. He's a good man. If we have children in our future, it'll be so much different. They'll have the safety I longed for.

"You're not here anymore." Zac notices.

"How do you always know?"

"I can feel it, baby. Tell me what's on your heart."

"I was just thinking about how I won't have to save our kids from you."

His face turns somber.

"Sorry." I shake my head.

"No, don't be sorry baby." His arms wrap around my back, holding with the depth I need. "I'm sad that you've been through so much that it makes you worry about that." He strokes my back up and down. "And no, if we have children, they won't be hurt the way you were. Ever. I promise."

"You don't have to promise. I know you won't." My throat is thick.

"Give me your worry. Let me carry this one for you. You've already been carrying it for too long."

My breath shakes as a sob breaks free. I'll always be thankful to him for helping me set free so many feelings trapped inside. When my body needs this release, I can have it. The tears can fall again. I can let them.

Because I'm safe in his arms. The safety little Trish needed I get to experience now. The longing of my inner child is realized as I hold him close. I'm not scared about how long I'll stay here. He is the place where I belong.

"Thank you."

"For?"

"For wanting to be with me. For coming back when I broke it off so many times. For letting me have space. For knowing that it's not what I needed forever."

"You are my forever, baby." His lips find mine, so soft and warm. I relax into his taste knowing I'm going to be just fine.

I'm not worried anymore. I'm at peace.

Thank you, Daddy, for being my guardian angel and for giving me a real one while you're gone.

We got back together. He forgave me. I'm still in awe.

After moving my stuff to his apartment, we've been driving around town.

"Where are we?"

"Where does it look like?" He turns off the engine and runs around to get my door.

I step cautiously toward the little strip mall. He parked right in front of a tattoo parlor.

"I got an idea that you could get some tattoos over your scars. Something that represents overcoming. Like a phoenix. Thought it was time to make it happen."

I can't really move so I just stand here. "That's incredibly thoughtful."

"Come on. Put your jaw back together, you're gonna need it later." He winks. Fuck, that wink sends shivers through my middle. "Celebritory sex is a specialty of mine."

"All sex is a speciality of yours." I chuckle.

"You're not wrong." He flashes that smug smile with those super white and straight teeth looking back at me from perfectly pink lips. Then he draws me in close.

"I made a reservation, but you don't have to do this unless you want to." He looks at the tattoo parlor.

I shiver and take a moment to swallow, hoping that it won't send me spiraling into days I wish I could forget.

I give a nod. His head leans down and he brings a tender kiss onto the scar tissue. The part of delicate skin that's never really healed.

"You can remember something else when you see this part of you." He whispers against my skin, so tenderly. "But if you don't want to today, you don't have to. And if you want me here, I'm here baby. And if you need to go alone, I'll respect that. This is about what's right for my girl."

"Zac," I pull up on his chin until he's standing again, admiring that little dimple that's a bit scruffy from not shaving the last couple days. "Oh, Zac." I bring my lips to his, breath leaving his mouth and coming into mine. He is healing me. One step at a time.

He's told me these scars aren't what I deserve, so many times I finally believe it.

"So here's my idea. And if you hate it, it's okay. I just want you to be free from the past. I can't take it away. But I can take you here." He points to the tiny parlor, where neon lights shout its name across the parking lot of Dramatic Ink. "And they can put ink over your scars and make it into something that will remind you of something other than pain. Something like strength. I don't want anyone, or *anything* to ever hurt you again, including this reminder of your past. I don't want you to feel this destroyed anymore."

Zac's lips wrap around mine. The warmth brings me from the past into the present. I know that I need him. I need this.

It's okay to need him.

My heart is opening up. Like a flower, slowly revealing petals, hoping it doesn't get destroyed by an unexpected frost before it can fully bloom and feel the warmth of the sun for the first time. I want to open up to all that he is, and all that I can see I've been missing.

"Do you want this? Does it feel right for you?" He steps away from me, leaning casually on the side of his truck like we have all the time in the world. "No pressure, I promise," he reminds me.

I yank his white v-neck shirt and kiss the skin under his collarbone. "I want this. It feels right." I run my tongue along the bone in a circular motion. He lets out a groan and slides his hips into mine.

"I want you. You feel right."

"You feel right, too." He rests his cheek against the top of my head, cradling me. This comfort is amazing.

"I can't wait to take you home."

"Can I fuck after I get a tattoo? I'll have to call and ask Lexie. She'd know."

He chuckles. "Yes, I think you can still fuck after you get a tat. But we'll make sure." He winks and that surge of fire runs so deep that I clench his ass with both of my hands, bringing his hips against me.

He sits beside me as my scars are reformed into a phoenix.

As the days pass, I fall more deeply in love. The tattoo is amazing. I love looking at it. For the first time in my life I can wear short shorts with a bright strappy bikini top, showing off my belly, and I can't wait.

"I love this so much." He runs a hand along my ink.

"And I love you." I wrap my arms around him. He's my forever. So glad he was patient enough to wait until I figured that out.

THE END

Epilogue
The Next Fall

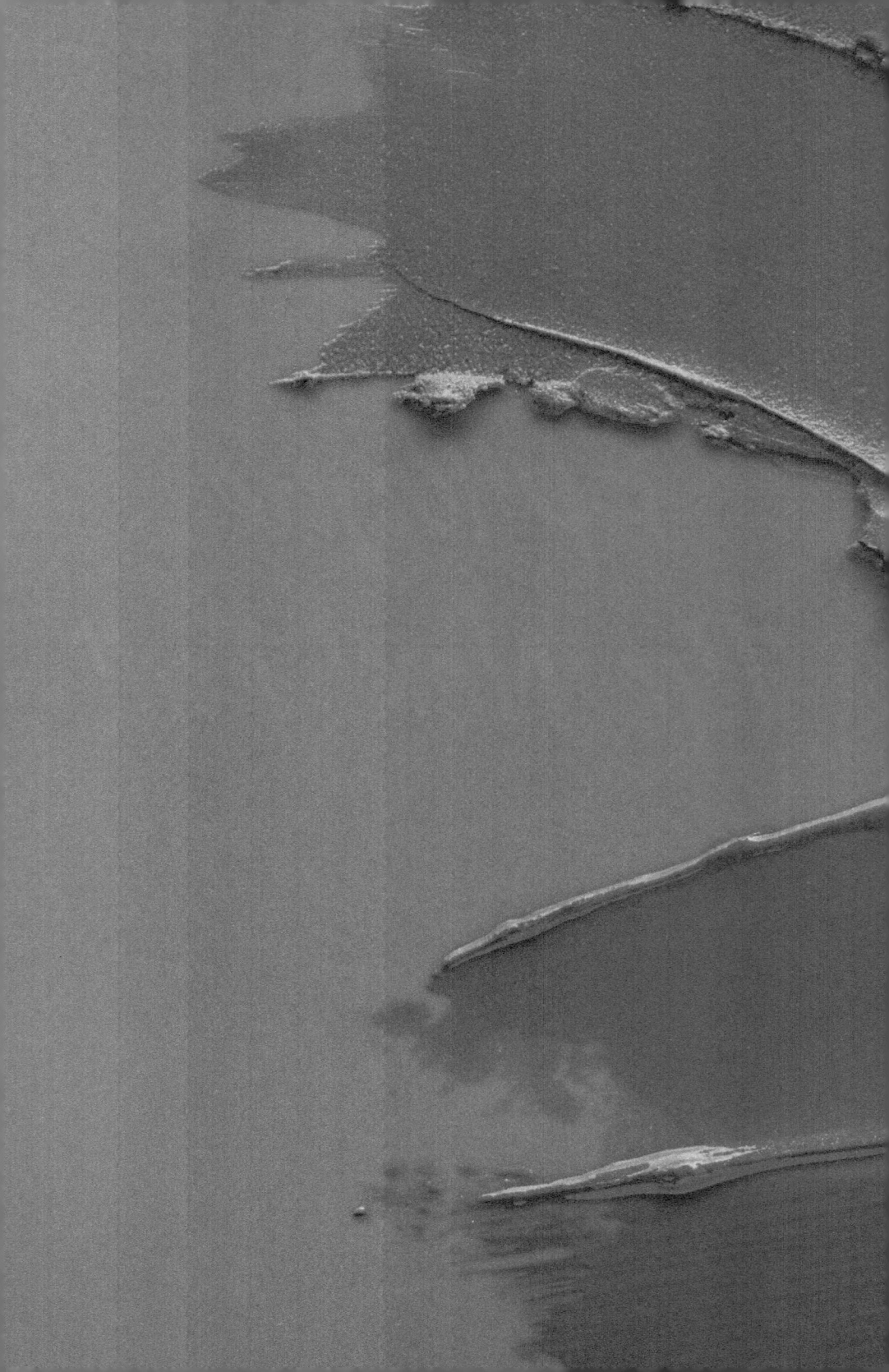

Trish

Zac finished a good, strong senior year at Suncastle. He graduated and was offered to play AAA ball. While I know he'll be gone a lot, we decided to establish a homefront in Kentucky. Sadie and Anna Mae are living in Zac's apartment in Suncastle and they've given us an open invitation to visit any time.

"That's the last box." Zac sets the cardboard on our new dining table. All done unpacking. Settled in, finally. We got an adorable little rental just out of town in Louisville. White picket fence. Gorgeous mature trees. So much potential for decorating. Zac somehow convinced his Memaw to part with the hutch Daddy made, and now it's in our living room.

I'm healing so much. I needed to move back here.

Home.

Every day keeps getting better. Just me and Zac. I've built my business up again and have enough clients to keep me plenty busy, the way I like it.

"You don't have any clients today, right?" Zac scoots the bottle of creamer close enough I can pour a delicious amount in my coffee.

"No, it's a pretty quiet day, actually."

"Okay, good. I have plans." He pulls our little cooler out and starts filling it with all kinds of picnic food. "Go put on something comfy. We're gonna be in the car for a while." He brings his lips to mine.

Once we're ready, we get in his truck. "You gonna tell me what these plans are?" I eye him suspiciously.

"Um, kinda…Where's your daddy buried again?" Zac starts the ignition.

"Oakdale Cemetery."

He fiddles around with his phone and types it into the maps app and starts driving. "I was thinking it was Oakdale, but wanted to make sure."

"You're not the least bit subtle, you know that?" I tease.

"Okay, okay, so you've figured me out…but you don't know *why* we're going there."

"I suppose not." I pop in some gum that he keeps under the dash for when we're driving together.

After hours driving through the gorgeous Kentucky country, we arrive in Oakdale. The scenery is beautiful. I'll never get tired of living in such a gorgeous place.

It's sweet Zac thought to come here. I've wanted us to go, but it's been busy getting settled and I didn't know when we'd have a day to make the trip.

He runs around to get my door and holds my hand as I get out of the truck.

"Will you introduce us?" His cheeks are a little rosy, like he's not sure about this. Even after all our time together, his insecurities are something I find absolutely adorable. At the same time, I hope one day he finds more of that confidence I know he has inside.

"I'd love the two of you to meet." I look around the cemetery, the old headstones and the newer ones. "It's been a long, long time since I've been here." I work to get oriented until I find where I think he is. Even though I begged her, Mama's never brought me back here and I felt funny coming alone. It's hard to remember the funeral from when I was nine.

No, it's not there. We keep walking around.

No luck.

My heart starts beating harder the longer I look. It feels wrong not to know where he is, like that nine year old girl should've kept better track.

"Trish," Zac's arms are around me. He knows I'm going down that dark road. Somehow, he always knows.

"We'll find him."

"I just should know–"

"Nuh uh. There's no 'shoulds' here." He runs his hand up and down my back. "Tell me his birth date again, please."

"September 9, 1949."

"Okay, we'll find him." He holds me for a while, neither of us moving in this cemetery. I look across the green. It dawns on me that I may be turned around. From the other corner, we can walk the way I thought he was. Then we'll find him.

"This way, maybe?" I take Zac's hand, and we weave between the headstones and plots.

The bench with the trumpeting angels carved into the back sparks my memory. I sat there the day of his funeral. "Over here."

Kneeling down, I see Daddy's modest headstone that was still more money than we could afford. "Hey, Daddy." My throat gets tight. "There's someone I want you to meet." Eyes burning, I look at Zac, kneeling beside me.

"Mr. Montgomery, it's an honor." The sincerity in his tone makes me feel a million times better. I relax my body against his. Daddy's headstone could use some cleaning up, and I make a mental note to put it on my calendar so we can make the trip more often.

Zac pulls away from me and ruffles around with his backpack.

"I know you don't know me, Mr. Montgomery, but the fact of the matter is I am totally and completely in love with your daughter." He holds a little velvet box in his hands.

"Zac," I gasp.

"So if it'd be alright with you, I'd like to ask your permission to have her hand in marriage."

A wave of emotion simmers from my heels, up my spine. He wants to marry me? And he came and asked Daddy?

He turns to me, "I know it's a little old fashioned, and it's not like you need anyone's permission to do anything, but I thought it just felt like the right way to do it, ya know?" His cheeks are rosy like earlier.

"Yes." I wrap my arms around his neck. "It's so very sweet and perfect and all the things that you are."

"Yes?"

"Yes. Please marry me." I bring my lips to his, tasting the salty skin as his tears mix with mine. "I'm so completely happy being with you. I can't even begin to hope for a better life than one where I'm with you every day."

Acknowledgements

Thank you for reading this book. I love to pour my heart and soul into writing. It's wonderful to hear when my book is able to touch someone's heart.

Thank you, Josh. My partner. My first cheerleader. My support. All the times I wanted to quit, you kept reminding me I can keep going.

My angel on the other side, Jeff. You got me out of the hell I grew up in. You saved me.

Deanna, always. I'm lucky to have you. Your support, your friendship, and your amazing editing super powers.

Thank you Sarah Scentz for the amazing cover art.

Thank you to my team of alpha and beta readers, particularly:

Melissa Rivett

L. M. Archer

Nichole Pierce

Miriam Cumming

Rachel Ruggiero

Cherie Burger

Kaitlyn Kenley

Somer El Jishi

Sabrina M

Thank you to my amazing sprinting buddies: Brianna Peterson, Michaela Cole and M. K. Deppner.

I so appreciate all the posts, reviews and love from my bookstagrammers and booktokkers.

Also by Marissa J. Gramoll

A Game Like Ours, Book One Of the Suncastle College Baseball Series
He's the player with a past. She's the surviving fiancée of his best friend.
When he tells her his secrets, will it be too late?
A Game Like Ours

The One She Needs, Prequel to A Game Like Ours
Bobby wants what he can't have. Cody's got what he doesn't deserve. Lexie's
not sure what to do with either one of them.
The One She Needs

Broken Piece, part of This Kind Of Ruin Enemies to Lovers Charity
Anthology for Cancer Research.
She holds the key to his heart. He wishes she'd tell him why they can't be
together.
This Kind of Ruin

About The Author

Lover of stories since before she could walk, Marissa has always had a passion for creating characters and worlds. Learning to read was a challenge, so she learned words by writing them–taking her notebook everywhere and asking total strangers how to spell. Since then, a laptop has replaced her trusty notebook and her stories have evolved into novels.

Marissa lives with her husband, two children and an endless collection of David Bowie hats. She enjoys reading in the sunshine, with a big bottle of chocolate milk and music playing in the background.

www.ingramcontent.com/pod-product-compliance
Lightning Source LLC
Chambersburg PA
CBHW031335070726
47496CB00017B/899